Also by Ellis Sharp

I0692897

Novels

Unbelievable Things
Walthamstow Central
Lamees Najim

Short Fiction

The Aleppo Button
Lenin's Trousers
(with Mac Daly) *Engels on Video*
To Wanstonia
Driving My Baby Back Home
Aria Fritta
Quin Again and other stories
Dead Iraqis: Selected Short Stories

Non-Fiction

Sharply Critical

ELLIS SHARP

THREE NOVELLAS

TO WETUMPKA
INTOLERABLE TONGUES
THE DUMP

Zoilus Press

A Zoilus Press paperback
First published in Great Britain by Zoilus Press in 2019

© Ellis Sharp 2015, 2011, 1998

A CIP catalogue record for this book is available from the British
Library.

ISBN 9781999735951

Cover design by The Ever-Shifting Subject

Typeset by Electrograd

ZOILUS PRESS
York, England

CONTENTS

TO WETUMPKA

for Anna and Andrew

Part One

1

THE END never is.

Tollinger woke up to it. All this. The pressing need for something to happen. A different future.

He lay for a while in a fold of white sheets. There was a smell of dust and vellum and old furniture. Experimentally, Tollinger moved his limbs. He squirmed and twisted and scowled, wrinkly as a newborn.

His face seemed to cloud over. There were times when he truly believed he didn't stand the ghost of a chance. He'd been running on empty for as long as he could remember. Night after night he had weird dreams. Bad dreams. In this latest one, in the dark corner by the door, there was either a small animal or a huge insect. For a long time it didn't move, and then, just once, its pale spine seemed to ripple like water. It was about the size of a paperback novella. Its body was covered in fur like a bumble bee but it had the horns of a giant beetle. The creature made no move to attack. In the end Tollinger decided to leave. He walked quickly past it and out through the door. Beyond lay a tunnel lit by a dim, reddish light.

Maybe it was time to go see the gypsy, who was staying in that big hotel on the other side of town. Maybe not. Tollinger woke up. He made himself coffee. He wanted a different kind of dream. A frenzy he'd come out of, say, like Popeye Doyle in *French Connection II*.

Tollinger quit the great city, heading first the other way, then north by north-east. Perhaps, he thought, he was imagining hayfields and barrens. Maybe he wanted the pattern of his nights broken, so that one day he'd wake up in a New York apartment where a telephone rang out from the bedroom, stinging him like some nasty metallic kind of gnat. He wondered if he'd read somewhere about a fractured assemblage of trivialities caught in the advance light of a great event. He conceived of a possible resemblance to that poet whose mind worked with astonishing rapidity in the final illness. It was not delirium. The greater part of those waking hours were passed in rapid soliloquies on a variety of subjects, the chain of which, from his imperfect utterance, those who attended to them were quite unable to follow. Yet in no instance – except in a final lapse of memory – was discovered the least irrationality.

At length, decisively, Tollinger holed up on the coast, in Lowestoft. There was no risk of him running into anyone he knew in that town. It was at the edge of nothing much, leaning out into the grey North Sea. Metal signs placed around the town warned that you could go no further east in the kingdom than this.

Lowestoft was the kind of place that dreamed of being somewhere else. Vancouver, maybe. No one he knew would ever be seen dead in Lowestoft. It just wasn't their kind of place. He knew he could start again here. Begin a whole new story, against a grey background. Here he was freed as far as was possible from the end of love, the cold presence of death, the thinning of friendship. He could begin at last to efface, expunge, erase, delete and hopefully move towards a different last page to the one previously planned. Along the way he might hope for the stimulus of fresh adventures and some awesome pictorial detail. *Hope.* A four-letter word derived from the Late Old English *hopa*, corresponding to the Old Low German *tōhopa* and the Dutch *hoop*. One who is hoping might be found *soaring* and *starry-eyed*. Such a character might be *would-be*.

Tollinger was confident no one among the population would recognise him in Lowestoft even though, once, briefly, he'd been keyboard player and trumpeter in The Mal Kontents. The band had had one hit – "The Hole in Me". Later, following five flops in a row, the group fell apart. After they disintegrated, they vanished into their individual obscurities and became old and shadowy. This was true of Tollinger too. He no longer looked like a once-upon-a-time MalK. Now his scalp was entirely different. His face – it was undeniable – was beginning to melt. Limpness and waste had somehow managed to stick to his days. In the mirror, below his armpits, he saw the rippled skin of a lizard.

Tollinger liked Lowestoft. It was at the end of something. The factories were derelict. There were numerous vacant plots. Beside rotting warehouses weeds spurted from fissures in plateaus of concrete desolation. The grey everywhere incubated tropical adjectives. The old harbour was a desolation of empty quays and shuttered buildings. Windowless structures and gates and high fencing shut you out.

A wind was always blowing. Always a low remote roar, which might have been traffic along a faraway freeway, or an ocean fringed with quiet furies. Metaphors clanked in the night, shadowing rolling Coke cans. Soon after Tollinger arrived there was a bad storm. The sea came over the harbour wall. It washed around Station Square and flooded shops in the High Street.

Some days, when the sky was paper white, clouds of corvids moved around in the space above the town like whirled specks of ash from a big industrial fire.

Once, a big crater appeared without warning in the road which passed by the station. It was filled in, but later others appeared randomly around the town.

If he had to, Tollinger knew he could wait out the time quite happily in this place. The sound of a harmonium reached his ears. It was someone like himself, playing a Nico album with the window wide open. Quite possibly, like himself, they felt a special affinity with certain words. Silk, perfume, pallid, marble, relinquish, for example. Temporal, nocturnal, central, wept, index.

Tollinger didn't know how long it would take to begin all over again. For a long time he'd felt flat and used-up. Almost as though he was due to die. Depleted was the word. It was his heart, you see. What's the bloody use of developing the cardiograms? Like an old gag-man, intolerable tongues tormented him, but few listened, few heard. Still, he was fortunate. He'd enough to get by on for at least one more year. Plus there was a trickle of royalties from the old hit. They still played it on the radio. Hungry new generations bought the last album, which defrauded purchasers with a GREATEST HITS label.

Twelve months were probably adequate. Long enough for sweet Lady Luck to take him on elsewhere – to a new heart, a new home, a fresh beginning in another landscape. A different, better narrative. Multitudes, multitudes: soldiers, doctors, nurses, taxis, drivers of jeeps, in a heat the hue of a yellow dream. The sky an inverted bowl of fleckless pale blue broken only about twelve degrees above one horizon by a light so glaring that it was difficult to look at. Plus the soothing accompaniment of slow gentle piano music and muted strings. And adjectives, many adjectives.

It was good to move on, good to discover a new dimension. You are always nearer by not keeping still. He was sickened by his trudge, which had become mechanical as he passed through the evening streets. He turned things over in his mind but they returned like rinsed socks, requiring heat before they became usable again.

Before he left the big city Tollinger had given away most of his possessions. He took them to charity shops. Tollinger felt better without objects. He needed to lose the weight of anchors. Naturally, realistically, he needed strong verbs and a certain quantity of nouns, but he could do without stuff like that pinewood chest of drawers or the television. They chained you to a particular room. As for all the books and DVDs, he could always them buy again, if he ever felt like revisiting them. Besides, the technology was archaic. Everything was out there in a cloud, if he ever wanted to reconnect.

The fridge he'd donated to the Red Cross. It was another monstrous possession. Bloated and heavy. It made intermittent odd little scratchy gargling sounds which rubbed like sandpaper against his mind during the silence of the long afternoons and the solitude of his nights. He was glad to be free of that vexatious structure. It was like giving away a copy of a much acclaimed novel, in the certain knowledge he'd never want to read it again. Also, defrosting it was a tedious chore, which he always resented and left too late.

Free of the heavy furniture of a thinning first-draft relationship, he was free to move on. But he wasn't sure how far or fast he could go before some flashbacks caught up with him. He felt they might be waiting to appear when he least expected it. A flashback can be useful in explaining obscurities of motivation or identity, he thought, suddenly remembering being alone on the sofa, staring at a large flatscreen, watching *Lost*. But he also remembered that memories can be false. He knew that from the time skinny Emily had persuaded him to watch *Blade Runner* and *Total Recall*.

The corner of a curtain was restless. The sky sagged with drifts of grey. It was trying to snow. It soon gave up.

Tollinger watched a movie released in the final quarter of the last century. It was bright with stars but curiously lacklustre. Jack Nicholson did his sly manic Jack Nicholson grin. Other famous faces looked sombre. In one scene a young Robert de Niro was sat in a car at with an actress Tollinger didn't recognise.

"Listen."

"What?"

"Nothing."

It was the best moment in a film that never caught fire.

That first morning in Lowestoft, when he went out, Tollinger had to step over a dead seagull. The gull was lying on its side in the alley. Up close, it seemed enormous. There was nothing to indicate what had killed it. The only movement was around its thick throat, where its pure white plumage was disturbed by the wind. Later, in random places around the town, he came across more dead birds. A robin on a soot-black verge, its head resting on a leaf. A blackbird on its back beside a kerb. A starling which had lost its sparkle. The origin of their termination was obscure.

The wind was blowing like mad. It felt icy and hard. It came in from the east, across the German Ocean. The Ocean had been deleted in the 1914 text but Tollinger decided to reinstate it. Knowing nothing of where he really was, he felt free.

A day after the interpolation the wind was still blowing like mad. It swept past the mute Bird's Eye factory and funnelled up the alley. Scraps of silver litter danced at its passing. It tugged at the dead gull, trying to shake it back to life.

As if propelled by some invisible force Tollinger walked around, exploring. He could still feel that wind. It came whirling down the side streets and rummaged under his shirt. It was as inescapable as a symbol in a set text.

The town was shabby and impoverished. The people looked poor. The shopping centre had cancer. The bus station was cramped and dismal. Cars trailing fumes flowed everywhere like slow-moving sewage. Handcuffed to the steering wheels were deformed lobsters.

There was a shop which sold second-hand goods. A radio, labelled "DOES NOT WORK BUT NOT BROKEN". A set of carousel wheels for projecting holiday slides. A pair of old, wrinkled boots once worn by a Dutchman, size 10. A second-hand light bulb, for the especially stricken.

The harbour pier was a banal slab of concrete jutting out alongside a grey dreary industrial lagoon. A solitary fisherman stood by a pair of rods, staring morosely at the oily water. He was there most days. Tollinger never saw him catch anything.

One day Tollinger discovered fencing blocking the pier entrance. The fisherman was no longer there. A notice attached to the mesh explained that the pier had been closed for reasons of safety.

Tollinger's monochrome low-rent apartment occupied half the top floor of a decayed old house imagined beside one of the Scores, as they were called. The Scores were narrow alleys which dropped steeply from the town's main street to the harbour below. In their cramped, walled-in desolation you could score. Lowestoft had a drugs problem, it was said. Not true. Lowestoft had a drugs solution. You could even get LSD.

Forget about E's and wizz. Oh boy! Onwards into the interior! La vuelta al día en ochenta mundos! In more senses than one, *senõr*!

Tollinger fell out of bed, repeatedly. He dragged a comb across his head, repeatedly. The frames were quivering slightly. The light was uncertain. Fever perhaps? Quite possibly. While over there, do you see? Down there. A gigantic wind turbine sprouts from the midst of the drab harbour buildings. It resembles a strange metal parasite, thriving amidst industrial waste.

Lowestoft bore no resemblance at all to the scenes in the heritage photographs which hung on the walls of The Joseph Conrad.

Yes, Lowestoft was the place for Tollinger. When the North Sea gales blew in, the blades of the slowly turning turbine swished and went faster and faster. At full speed they sent a low drilling whine through the long nights. The turbine was named Gulliver. Alcohol and nightly fistfuls of barbiturates numbed Gulliver's presence. By midnight everything was as black as the ninth plague of Egypt.

In the afternoons, in this part of town, there was the sound of throbbing music and raucous drinking. Girls sat on kerbs, queasy. Many had fat thighs and laddered stockings. Sometimes they vomited, while their friends laughed.

Half a mile to the south, across the street from The Joseph Conrad, stood the dark station. The trains went only in two directions, to places where Tollinger had no desire to go. He'd lost the will to visit cities.

Time passed.

How delightful it would be to spend a whole day on the beach, lost in dreams! But the charms of inertia and slow decay were starting to lose some of their lustre. Better would be to drive along the shore road four times, becoming a different person on each trip. It was on his tongue to ask what this meant. There were moments when he was tempted to take the shore road back to where he'd started from and await developments. But for that he'd need an auto.

It was undeniable. Cabin fever was beginning to make him restless and wild. *Where to now?* thought the central character at the beginning of Chapter Four in the translated novella which lay on the table in the kitchenette. The jacket of the paperback was illustrated by a detail from Gustav Klimt's *The Bride*. The introduction, by a once popular commercial novelist who was nowadays little read, asserted that at the centre of the novella author's art and life lay a *solemn playfulness*. The translated text had been transformed into a screenplay and the screenplay had been translated into a movie, which Tollinger recalled he had not particularly liked. It had gone on too long, the dialogue was lacklustre, and the stars had not shone all that brightly.

He finished the novella and turned to a second-hand five shillings Mayflower-Dell paperback he'd bought for a couple of coins in a gloomy little bric-a-brac-stuffed shop at the decayed end of the High Street. The pages were baked brown by sunlight and the cover was as wrinkled as Samuel Beckett.

The title and author's name were superimposed at a slant upon the voluptuous rump of a naked black woman. The book promised an account of a famous American novelist's red-blooded true-life adventures, involving card-playing, ferocious argument, swearing, fist-fights and memorable encounters with *men "gone bamboo"*.

Intrigued (for Tollinger had never before come across this last expression) he glanced at the book's preface. The famous American novelist – whom Tollinger had heard of but never read – abused other famous contemporaries "whose harsh artistry has flattened into smooth profundity". But in a world of tepid conformity there were still those prepared to take risks.

Rap the novelist's disorderly lair – "You in there! What are you up to now? *What's next?"*

You-In-There doesn't know what he's up to at midnight, 0230 hours, nor upon the gong of noon. He drives a collision course, lights out, along an untraveled way.

Tollinger decided it was time to consult an Ordnance Survey map.

Two days later he stood at the bus stop by the diseased bus station. He boarded a 61 bus that arrived seventeen minutes later than the advertised time. Its side panels were the colour of soot-speckled vomit. Tollinger was the only passenger. The tropically hot bus travelled across central Lowestoft in a sequence of erratic spasms – a sudden, jolting halt, then a throbbing, drawn-out pause, then a quick desperate gasp from the wheels as they rushed forwards with a dream of perpetual motion. And then the next abrupt, lurching stop. It was like being inside a machine designed to illustrate the processes involved in a heart seizure. Terminal cardiac arrest could not be far off.

This last illusion was reinforced by the sight of the sluggish river of vehicles ahead coming to a standstill as the wings of the Bascule Bridge unfolded in the distance. A section of carriageway rose vertically and became immobile. Red lights flashed urgently along a barrier.

There was a long wait. It was like arriving too early for a cremation at Stonefall. You sit in silence, waiting for the hearse. Nothing moves. Ranks of gravestones stretch away on all sides. You are left with your thoughts. That great triptych painted on oak slides, as though on castors, into your mind. Two wings enclose a panel teeming with energetic nudes. Zoom in and observe extraordinary spectacles. The densely populated landscapes darken and vanish as the wings are folded. Once the wings have closed the backsides display a grisaille sphere of uncertain significance.

On the outskirts of the town was a grey circular water tower, a magic mushroom twinned with a roundabout coated in dead vegetation. Further down the road, in the distance, could be seen the forlorn huts of a Holiday Camp. Arranged in stark lines and surrounded by a high mesh fence, they bore a distinct resemblance to the accommodation supplied at a concentration camp.

A rickety structure erected in a field displayed the bridge and flaking eyewires of a giant pair of glasses. One painted disc had dropped away, leaving only a single yellowish-grey retina to cast a jaundiced gaze at passers-by. A large section of the board concealing the scaffold had fallen away, leaving behind an amputated message: GET YOU.

As it receded behind the bus, which had now achieved a dizzying 40 mph, the eye seemed to close up and briefly wink at Tollinger. But this was plainly some kind of illusion, to be filed alongside sightings of a wild lion in Essex and a mysterious big cat outside Arlecdon. Unless, of course, the cat and the lion were inter-dimensional travellers, in which case the impact of the paranormal might well extend into the drearier parts of Suffolk. But Tollinger did not believe in that lion or the enlarged cat.

Tollinger went as far as Kessingland, just down the coast. The bus, diverted by roadworks, halted briefly by a parked car to wait for an oncoming lorry.

"I can hear lions," Tollinger said to the driver.

The driver explained there was a safari park behind the trees. *Africa Alive!* The lions were roaring in their enclosure.

The driver dropped him at the end of Rider Haggard Lane. From there it's a short walk to the beach.

Tollinger followed the road through an estate of modern brick bungalows. Beside a grass verge he saw a badger. It lay on its side, perfectly still. He had never seen a badger before, except in photographs and wildlife documentaries. But it wasn't asleep, it was dead. There was no obvious injury but some flies had gathered in an excited cloud around the badger's neck.

He came to a caravan park. The symmetry of the lined-up trailers reminded Tollinger of the Holiday Camp. This reiterated pattern squeezed out a trio of flashbacks. "K-Z" it said on the single decker bus parked outside the little rail station long ago. It was there for the tourists. What was most memorable of all from that day was what had preceded it. The soft announcement as the train pulled out of the terminus in Munich. A list of suburban destinations, including the softly articulated "Dachau". To those stolid regular commuters its resonance was blunted. There was no difference to the tone of the guard speaking into the PA system on Tollinger's old regular train from Waterloo. "This train will be stopping at Woking, Guildford, Haslemere, Petersfield, Havant, Fratton, Portsmouth and Southsea, and Portsmouth Harbour."

Beyond the caravans the settlement's dog walkers began to fade along the shingle.

2

SOON TOLLINGER had the beach to himself. It is hard work, walking across shingle. He crunched southward. The sky was manganese blue. The sea was grey. It did not look wet. It resembled paper which has dried out and become wrinkled after being soaked.

Ahead of him was a wood, rising behind a small cliff. Coastal erosion had caused some of the trees to fall over the edge. The trunks and stumps of dead trees littered the shingle. They were smooth and plausible, these salt-scoured wooden shapes.

Something dark bobbed up in the water.

At first Tollinger assumed it was a lump of wood or possibly a dog. It was just a few yards from the shore, at the fringe of his vision. Then the head vanished.

He expected it to surface again but it didn't.

Puzzled, he walked on. Across the blank sky a contrail began to stretch out behind a silent moving scrap of punctuation.

Far out on the horizon half a dozen tankers were anchored. He'd heard they were waiting for the price of oil to rise on the world's markets.

Three or four minutes later a dark, glistening shape briefly broke surface just a few yards offshore. It resembled a hump.

It happened again, twice, then disappeared.

Tollinger realised what he'd seen was a seal. This was obviously a stray from one of the colonies of seals that he'd read lived at certain points along the Norfolk coast.

He walked on.

The headland seemed oddly sinister. Most of the trees were dying. Their wrinkled bark had a bleached pallor. Many were leaning at a sharp angle, reminiscent of the aftermath of the great explosion at Tunguska. They stirred a distant memory of paragraphs by H.P. Lovecraft.

One tree, perfectly vertical, protruded incongruously from the waves. Lovers had carved their initials in the bark.

At the rear of the beach, at the edge of his perception, a small object broke into a run. It was the size of a rat. It ran on, paused as if for breath, then accelerated again. Finally it stopped, like a narrative.

There was no tail and the object was a little fuzzy. It wasn't a rat. Tollinger went over to see what it was. As he drew nearer he saw that it was a sort of green-brown seaweed. He picked it up. It wasn't slimy at all but dry and fluffy, like a clump of hair. On the underside was a shimmer of pink. It was sea fern, delicate and light. The way it moved resembled tumbleweed in an American movie. But it was much smaller than tumbleweed.

There were more clumps of the material in the vicinity. They had evidently been deposited there at high tide. From time to time some of the other clumps were lifted by the wind and went scampering across the shingle. The momentary resemblance to the rodents Tollinger had often seen in the great city was striking.

Beyond the headland's bulge Tollinger came to a small lagoon. It was separated from the ocean by a bank of shingle. As he crunched his way along this pebbly crest he came upon the remains of buildings and structures. There were slices of brick smoothed as flat as sole. Broken fragments of tiles. Bits of light brown sewer pipe. These turd-coloured fragments made Tollinger think of Beppo the circus clown. Before he took up clowning the man in the gigantic slippers had been a professional diver. Once he descended from a yacht in Loch Ness. The water was very dark. Suddenly he came up against some slime. It was pale grey and stretched out like a ribbon.

Beppo dived to avoid it. I got a very strange, cold feeling on me, he said afterwards. It was a very eerie feeling all the time I was going down. I had the impression I was being watched, by what or who I can't say. This strange feeling became an obsession with me. I found it very difficult to get away from this slime.

After returning to the surface he decided it would be better to become a circus clown. He changed his name to Beppo. As a clown you are part of a crowd. People laugh at you but they like you. It's a good feeling, falling flat on your face in sawdust while people hoot and cheer.

Tollinger went on.

On this stretch of beach, apart from shards and sections of pipe, there were big ragged chunks of concrete. Some had pebbles sunk in them. Some were embedded with rusty mesh patterned like a crossword puzzle. These were all evidently remnants of structures undermined by the sea.

And then what happened, happened.

Something moved in the water to his right. It started wriggling in the shallows.

Tollinger wondered if it was an eel. The lagoon had been formed by a flood tide, and he guessed that the creature had been trapped there when the tide had receded.

Tollinger had never liked eels. There was something brutish and bellicose about their appearance. He'd tried eating one once and it tasted vile.

He threw a stone in the general direction of the ripples on the surface. At once the disturbance died away and the surface became calm. He wondered if he'd hit the creature on the head and stunned it, or even killed it. But probably not, most probably he'd simply scared it.

He stood a yard or so from the edge, waiting and watching.

The wind sent fresh ripples across the surface, making it impossible to see whatever was in this shallow trough of water. It was all dappled and jerky.

After a minute, there was another swirl of water. This time Tollinger was more ambitious. He found a lump of ragged concrete the size and weight of a couple of bricks. He raised it up, level with his brow, and hurled it into the water. It landed with a terrific splash.

Tollinger was enjoying himself. This was the kind of fun he'd had as a child, when his parents took him to the seaside. The simple pleasure of throwing stones into the sea – sometimes at a bobbing bottle, sometimes simply for the sheer excitement of seeing how far he could throw a stone. He recalled that sensuous *plop!* as the pebble hit the surface and sank from view. One rare occasions he'd hit the neck of a bobbing bottle and feel a great sense of triumph as it cracked open and sank.

The ripples subsided.

Behind him the waves grated against the shingle, an ancient frottage.

It began to cloud over.

This little game was starting to bore him.

He decided to send one more missile into the miniature lake before going on his way. He selected a pair of broken house bricks.

They were ruddy-coloured, as if freshly baked. Cemented together, they resembled pieces from a giant's jigsaw puzzle.

Balanced in the palm of his hand, the twinned bricks swayed a moment beside his shoulder and then shot off along their brief trajectory. Their passage would have looked good in slow-mo, he reflected. And the arrival at the intended destination.

A new thought flashed across his mind: that this was like a miniature Hiroshima – a huge cataclysm in a tiny world. A spout of water rose up satisfyingly high, sending a big surging wave out to the shores of this inland sea. The spout collapsed and spattered the surface, adding to the turbulence.

That will teach you, eel, he thought.

The surface settled down again. The wind had dropped and the surface was flat calm, like a mirror. He stared into the depths, looking for the eel. But now the sun had come out again and the surface was as impenetrable as the blue-grey sky it reflected. He could see a few large submerged dark pebbles around the rim, nothing more.

It was time to go. The atmosphere had become close, as if a

storm was imminent. The air felt treacly and sticky and oppressive. Out at sea the sky had turned yellowish, and cumulonimbus was starting to billow up. The line of oil tankers looked like a row of tombs.

And then it happened.

There was a stirring in the shallows, as if the sediment at the bottom had been disturbed. A sandy swirl.

The surface of the water broke into an ever-expanding line.

Something was swimming fast towards the spot where he stood.

Tollinger was too surprised to do anything but stare. He might have been at Foyers, stupefied and helpless.

The line cutting across the surface moved towards the precise spot where he was standing. He glimpsed a slender shape, of no particular colour.

A small head broke the surface. It was the head of a snake, smooth, rounded, hard, with a pattern of sandy-coloured scales which seemed to shimmer with movement, as if each scale was a muscle. If you press the fingers and thumbs of one hand together to make an arrow head – well, that was about the size of the head of this creature.

Embedded in this snake-like head were two dark slits, which framed two slashes of faint, fiery yellow.

Tollinger had the distinct sensation that this strange creature was looking up at him.

He stumbled back a pace or so, unnerved. Tollinger had never heard of such a creature like this in a place as mild and domesticated as Suffolk. But somewhere deep in his mind a perception formed that this was a creature of the deep, of some faraway exotic location, which had somehow found its way to an English coast.

He recalled that on the news lately there had been items about how ocean currents were in flux around the globe, with huge expanses of algae appearing in the Mediterranean, and exotic fish following new currents of warmth to beaches which were previously cold and inhospitable.

This was a foreign fish, no doubt.

It had been tossed into this little patch of water by a high tide, and been trapped here. It was waiting to be reunited with the sea.

That theory collapsed the next instant as the snake flicked its back and came out of the water completely. It was *an amphibian.*

Tollinger retreated another couple of paces, then stopped. He felt a slight paralysis of shock, thickened by a growing sense of disgust, even fear. Throwing stones into a pool of water had seemed a harmless and safe occupation. Now that the water-snake was exposed to view, and on land, it presented itself as a much easier target. But he felt strangely vulnerable.

Are water snakes venomous? Tollinger had no idea but he didn't feel like throwing anything more, just in case it somehow managed to bite him.

To his horror, the creature began to slither towards him. This was worse than a movie. When its tail was out of the water he saw that it was, in all, at least a yard long. Its torso was considerably thinner than its head and was of a pale blue. Along the edges were silvery fringes of membrane, which he assumed were for propelling itself underwater.

The movements of the sea-snake were slow and languorous. It was a dream creature. It moved towards Tollinger, quite unafraid. But, weirdly, unlike a crawling snake, it held its head up, perhaps twelve inches or so.

The posture gave it an unmistakeably threatening appearance.

He decided to retreat. It was perhaps shameful, even a little cowardly, to be running away from what was, after all, some simple organism of very limited intelligence. Yet in the watches of the night Hemingway himself had heard retreat beaten.

Tollinger decided to put a safe distance between himself and the creature, then pelt it with stones. He'd scare it back into its watery home, then go on his way.

A low rise of shingle separated the lagoon from the main beach, and he ran to the crest of this ridge and stopped. When Tollinger looked back he expected to have put at least ten yards between himself and the exotic intruder. To his amazement it was only about two yards away. It had moved almost as fast as he had.

That settled the matter. He decided to run. Tollinger turned and sprinted along the ridge, heading south, to the nearest civilisation.

He ran some twenty yards as fast as he could, then, without stopping, glanced back.

This was when the affair became quite simply terrifying. The sea-snake had increased its speed and was moving across the shingle in a sequence of rapid flicks of its body. It remained just a couple of yards behind him, its head still raised high. Its eye slits regarded him with an unmistakeably malevolent intensity.

Tollinger felt indignant and a little angry, as well as fearful. It is a ridiculous thing for a fully grown man – a representative, after all, of a species which built Stonehenge without cranes, not to mention the Pyramids, and which has put men on the moon – to be humiliatingly chased by a much smaller, flimsy *thing* of very limited intellect.

Tollinger also felt a strong sense that the media had let him down. Surely creatures which spend their whole lives in the depths of the ocean cannot possibly see in the way that *Homo sapiens* can? He had read articles, watched documentaries, and listened to zoologists on the breakfast show. He had watched David Attenborough's programmes. The name Darwin was not entirely alien to him. He'd even once read his Penguin Classic, though he remembered almost nothing of its contents. Once, in a flush of enthusiasm, he had even visited Glen Roy.

The fact remained that Tollinger was being chased along a beach in Suffolk by a creature which seemed determined to defy accepted scientific knowledge. And he felt completely certain that those narrow burning reptilian eyes were watching him.

Or was he deluding himself? Perhaps it was responding not to sight but to sound. He was, after all, on a shingle beach. Every step he took created a loud muddy scrunching noise. A blind man could have chased him without difficulty.

Tollinger wondered how he could outwit the beast, and then realised.

Run down to the rushing water's edge!

He scrambled down the far side of the ridge and reached the sea's edge. The waves quietly slapped the beach, indifferent to the drama being played out there.

He ran into the shallows and paused. The snake stopped and seemed to be watching. Had he outwitted it? Tollinger walked slowly along in the surf, parallel to the beach. If the creature responded to sound, his presence would be lost amid the general crash and rolling of the waves.

Bad idea.

The snake simply kept pace with Tollinger, moving sideways along the beach, just a couple of metres offshore. Worse, it had now caught up with him and put itself between him and the beach. It seemed to have no obvious ill intent but its appearance and behaviour made him uneasy. It seemed to want to keep him company. But to what end?

Tollinger frowned. There was one shred of comfort. He couldn't work out why the creature didn't simply enter the water. Once back in its natural element it would be able to move much faster than him.

A possible reason for its tactic soon became clear.

To Tollinger's horror, his options were rapidly narrowing. Ahead of him a stream cut across the beach between two embankments of sand, emptying into the sea. As he drew near he saw that the volume of water, and the depth, made crossing it impossible. He could have gone deeper into the sea and tried swimming past this obstacle but that did not seem viable. For a start, to attempt swimming while fully clothed, wearing shoes, would have been foolish. Tollinger knew that the currents off this beach were strong. To plunge in fully clothed would be inviting death by drowning.

The alternative of stripping off his coat, shirt, trousers and shoes, was altogether too drastic. Even assuming he could get round to the other side while holding a bundle of sodden clothing, he would simply end up very wet and very cold. And even if he managed it, Tollinger had a horrible feeling the snake would be waiting for him on the far side. Or, worse – much worse, and much more probable – it would simply slide into the sea after him. It would finish him off before he was anywhere near to getting past the stream.

The situation, like the late stage of his relationship with Emily, was hopeless. His spirits were now at a very low ebb. He cursed himself for ever disturbing this vexatious creature in the first place. He was now almost at the stream and it was as if the snake was enjoying his predicament. It had sidled along to just below the first of the sandy embankments and was resting there, half curled, head upright, swaying and watching intently. Tollinger shivered. It reminded him very much of how a cat waits patiently for a nearby bird on a lawn. The cat crouches, motionless, eyes burning, its muscles tight with anticipation.

Tollinger realised, sick at heart, that there was only one real option. He would have to go up the beach and deal with this thing. He'd arm himself with as many large stones as he could find. Then he'd go towards it, get close, and pelt it with them. He would smash the brute's head open and break its back. And if he missed and it came up to him he'd stamp on it with his shoe. He'd stamp on it and stamp on it until it was broken and oozing beneath him. And then he would walk away and leave the tide to dispose of its strands of glistening filth.

That is what he would do.

So, decided, he came out of the water and began picking up the biggest stones he could find.

The snake, which was now a few yards away, watched Tollinger impassively. It was a thing with a very tiny, narrow brain. It could not hope to outwit a brain which had the benefit of inheriting the evolutionary advantages of thousands of years of human life on a planet full of danger. Man had tamed the dog, the horse and now the solar system. A snake was no match for a man on a beach in Suffolk.

By now Tollinger had assembled an arsenal consisting of six large stones balanced in the palm of his left hand. He had a

27

seventh, a bigger one, in his right fist.

He stepped forward to do battle.

3

A VOICE spared him the ordeal.

A woman's voice, shouting something. A name, Tollinger thought.

Something appeared on the sand embankment to his left. A black head, moving. A dog, a black and white dog. It saw Tollinger and began barking.

He heard the sound of someone scrunching along the shingle and a moment later a woman came into view. She was middle-aged, with short grey hair. She walked holding a thick stick with a decorated handle. Her khaki boots crushed pebbles in a way that suggested someone who voted Conservative.

"Middleton! Come, boy!"

The dog, an Irish red setter, ran along the edge of the embankment and sprang down on to the beach.

In the very brief space of time that Tollinger was distracted by this interruption the water-snake vanished.

He stared round anxiously, looking for it. The waste of pebbles was empty, devoid of life.

Tollinger wondered if it had slipped into the sea. He hurriedly stepped out of the water. The foam had slopped over his ankles, drenching his socks. His shoes squelched as he stepped on to dry land. Water fell out through the lace holes.

The woman saw him and waved her stick in greeting.

Tollinger dropped his collection of pebbles and hurried towards him.

"They say there's a storm coming," the woman said, in a gruff, friendly, one-beach-walker-to-another tone. She seemed vaguely familiar. Perhaps she was a minor actress of the type who regularly appeared in bit parts on TV or the movies.

"Yes, very likely," Tollinger replied, his voice a little shaky. He nodded at the sky over beyond the anchored tankers. There, the clouds had boiled up, blotting out the last expanses of blue. The colour of a bruise, they were moving closer. The atmosphere was cloying and heavy.

The woman walked on. Her dog ran past and went along the beach, barking frantically. Tollinger wondered if it had sensed the presence of the water-snake. The dog ran in zig-zags up and down the shoreline, as if in pursuit of an invisible adversary.

Tollinger was not a dog-lover but on this occasion he felt a keen sense of gratitude. This woman and her rust-coloured quadruped had spared him from the snake's unwanted attentions. Once she was past him and had her back turned – the woman was going on north, from where he'd come, in the direction of Kessingland – Tollinger made his way up the beach. He went around the back of the sand embankment, keeping a sharp eye out for the snake. Mercifully, there was no sign of it.

Here, a bridge formed of parallel railway sleepers, crossed the stream, allowing beach walkers to continue. To the west the stream was a narrow ditch which ended below the bridge as a deep, curdled, muddy mass of water. It emerged from a dense plain of sallow reeds which expanded back from the beach for half a mile or so, ending by some woodland. A path had been trodden down and led away into the shoulder-high reed bed, but it was an uninviting prospect. Besides, for all Tollinger knew, the sinister snake had vanished into it. On the beach side the stream, some two metres wide, had cut a gorge. The water was bluish, purified by its passage through shingle.

He crossed the bridge, went round a small headland, and to his delight saw, far away in the distance, the spectral outline of a pier. It meant he now wasn't too far from Southwold. The pier was a dark line to the left of a clutter of houses from which protruded the pale stump of a lighthouse.

Here, the line of cliffs started again, at first only two or three yards high, then slowly rising up, higher and higher, the further south one went.

The beach ahead was deserted.

By now it was mid-afternoon, and it looked like rain. Tollinger felt a new-found sense of freedom. The bizarre encounter with the snake was over and he was on his way. The miniature lake had dropped out of sight, along with the gloomy headland of fallen trees and the woman with her dog. He heard the animal yap once or twice, then heard it no more as the animal and its mistress continued into the distance, out of his sight and hearing.

He walked on for a couple of minutes, breathing deeply, his nerves beginning to settle.

This tranquil mood did not last.

A quick dark triangular shadow flickered along the beach, so quickly that Tollinger at first wondered if it was a spot in his bloodshot eye, abruptly rolling across his vision.

The next instant a massive roaring exploded above him, making him jump.

It was, he realised, the shadow of an RAF jet, screaming down the coast. It was moving so fast the sound of it wrenching apart the atmosphere occurred where the jet no longer was. Tollinger stared up at the reverberating sky. A little speck of silver was vanishing to the south.

As his nerves settled down again, he heard another noise. A kind of scratching noise.

No, not scratching. The sound of something moving very lightly on shingle.

He turned round.

This was much, much worse than the unexpected howling of a jet screaming past low overhead.

The water-snake was back. It was sidling along behind him, its head once more raised high. It was like being attended by a faithful pet.

But those eye slits did not strike Tollinger as being affectionate. Or was he being snakist? After all, a snake cannot help how it looks. Perhaps it was unfair of him to impute hostile intent. His prejudice had been shaped by movies.

It was then that something opened in the snake's blank face – something as small and wrinkled as an anus. What came out of the darkness of this grotesque, widening mouth was not venom but sound. It seemed to spit bolts of sound – little needles of excruciatingly high-pitched squealing which pierced Tollinger's ears and penetrated deep into his brain. His head started singing with pain, vibrating with it. Whole choruses of delicate agony howled inside his eardrums. He winced and clapped his hands to his ears.

The rubbery lips seemed to close and then fold away inside the yellowish scales of the hard, unyielding face. In its toughness the snake's physique appeared to be constructed not out of bone or flesh but something more like plastic.

Tollinger knew that this was a perfunctory demonstration of the creature's *power*. It was letting him know it was a bit more than a mere snake. It was monstrous. It was *a beast*. Probably its DNA went back to the time of the dinosaurs, although somewhere along the line it had been tampered with by Satan.

Tollinger cloudily sensed he was having a panic attack. His brain was getting a little starved of oxygen. His face showed a distinctly blue pallor. He felt like he was drowning. He was gulping and gasping for air, even though he was surrounded by the stuff. Lovely fresh air, the seaside, it was dripping with health-giving ozone.

He turned and ran. He decided to run all the way to Southwold. It was probably only a mile or so. He just needed another dog walker and he'd be safe as houses. The *thing* didn't like dogs, that was obvious.

But he was growing tired. Walking on shingle is hard work, running on it even harder. The pebbles sucked at his sodden shoes, reluctant to let him go.

A band of pain had developed in his chest. Sweat was pouring down his face and trickling into the neck of his shirt.

The horror grew worse.

Tollinger's accelerated speed made no difference to the creature. Far from disappearing far behind him, his exertions seemed to act as an inspiration. Its torso moved like a windscreen wiper on the fastest setting. It swished past him on the beach like a blurred, demented boomerang. Then it jerked sideways and caught him around the shin. It tugged like a wayward muscle. It dragged at him, anchoring him.

Tollinger lost his balance. He stumbled and fell.

He went face down into a mass of small yielding pebbles. They smelled of weed and dampness. They were cold and wet as ice. They stung his cheeks.

The creature was wrapping itself around one of his legs. He lashed out and kicked it off.

Tollinger staggered to his feet.

And then the worst horror of all occurred.

The creature returned to the attack. It slid over his shoe and corkscrewed up his leg, moving very fast.

Before he had even quite registered what was happening it had slid on, over his stomach. It wrapped itself around his chest like a restraint placed upon a mad person. Then, as if pausing for breath, it halted and then, a moment later, moved on.

Suddenly it was resting on Tollinger's shoulder.

Tollinger was close to fainting. The sense of horror and disgust and blind terror was almost overwhelming. His flesh shuddered. His heart thundered. He felt weak and feverish and sick.

The snake's face was just inches from his own. The eyes at close quarters were devilish things, little slender trenches of yellow fire, flecked with bits of gold and shards of dark emerald. The golden dots were restless and animated as maggots thriving in a blackbird's chest cavity.

It was an emperor of abomination. And it stank. This thin, wire-like creature stank of something rancid and decaying. It had fermented in filth, drank on dirt. It had feasted on faeces. It was the living embodiment of vileness. Tollinger sensed it was very old, a hundred years old, older, a thing brewed in darkness. It swayed and seemed to brush its cheek against his. It felt colder than marble – marble coated in slime. Even that slight, momentary contact left an acid spittle burning into his skin.

Tollinger was completely paralysed. All he could do was

sweat and hurt and stare. The beast's neck was a patchwork of ever-changing colours. It had chameleon qualities. And as these perceptions tumbled through his mind like the last defences of a besieged castle, he realised something else.

This monstrous entity was seeking *a host*. It was bored with its little shallow pool on a forsaken windswept beach. It fancied warmer hospitality.

That knowledge made Tollinger sick to the acrid depths of his burning guts. It was enough to make him vomit, were it not that his throat was stretched out and dried-up. The muscles of his neck were rigid and stressed and incapable of action.

Tollinger knew what it was about to do, and in some queer way it seemed to encourage and allow that perception. It allowed it so that he would do exactly what he did do. It greased the way for its final overcoming of his pathetic and puny resistance. The knowledge of what it was about to do – the creature's sinister gift of passing on a brief slice of telepathy – caused him at last to scream.

Tollinger opened his mouth and screamed. He screamed for help, for human assistance. He screamed for a woman with a stout walking stick and a barking dog. But the beach was deserted. The weather had seen to that. Far out at sea, beyond the tankers, lightning flickered. A few moments later came a low slither of thunder. A wall of grey rain could be seen moving slowly inland across a sea dappled with silver.

Tollinger screamed and as he screamed the creature brought its gently swaying head up close to his wide open, taut, straining lips. It was as if it was trying to see inside his mouth. But that was not its ambition. Instead it seemed to position itself and then, without further ado, it launched itself forwards with a convulsive jerk, like a springing cat.

It filled up Tollinger's mouth. It was like a swelling, seething ball composed of compressed writhing tentacles. He felt small hard muscles probing, squeezing, exploring. The snake's presence sealed off his throat and blocked his screams. His eyeballs swelled up with pain and shock. His tongue was in agony, crushed against the floor of his palate.

The snake's head slid around, probing. Then, abruptly, it forced itself down his throat. Its passage scraped its walls, sending out waves of fiery pain. He felt the abomination moving down through the narrow pipes and corridors inside him. The tip of its tail protruded from his mouth like a cigarillo. The tail was hard, wiry, powerful. It was motionless. It made Tollinger choke. He emitted a barely audible gurgling. His muscles convulsed and burned but it was impossible to cough this foulness out.

At the end of the tail was a pair of slender delicate floppy fins, light as cotton, resembling rudimentary wings.

With a sudden flick and jerk it was gone. It followed the rest of that foul thing down his throat. Tollinger gasped and spluttered. He cried out, a low thin squeal of agony. He felt the snake hard inside him, pushing and forcing and worming its passage. He felt it thrusting all the way down to the pit of his hot burning stomach. He seemed to know – to feel – when the tail had followed the rest of the entity to that place. And once it was there Tollinger had the distinct impression of it curling up there. It was at peace, in need of rest. He could feel it there, as if he'd swallowed a length of hosepipe. It filled him up.

And then a great convulsive churning wave of nausea and horror and utter disgust swept over him. Darkness poured across his vision.

He collapsed unconscious on the beach.

4

WHEN HE WOKE it was thick night. A rich, dense, deep, curdled night. The sea sounded very close. Tollinger looked at his watch. Four hours had passed since his encounter with the sea-snake. The beach was in darkness. The tide was coming in.

Tollinger stood and pressed a hand against his stomach. He prodded it, experimentally. He expected to feel movement, but there was none.

He remembered everything before he'd blacked out. He

wondered if it had been a hallucination. He'd taken a range of drugs in his past. Some in the fairly recent past. Even more in the unfair recent past. Maybe this was blowback – a delayed lurid fantasy hatched from some fold of chemically damaged cells.

Sometimes odd memories broke into his mind, strange visionary episodes which seemed like nothing he'd ever truly experienced. In one recent example he was on a main landing, staring over its scrolled iron-gilt balustrade. A big Moorish lantern, hanging at the same level, threw its light on the colourful Persian rugs and brocaded settees in the hall below. When he turned away he saw a massive white pyramid inscribed with hieroglyphics. None of this meant anything to him.

But the snake had seemed awfully real. And he sensed the creature was still inside him, even though his poking and prodding produced no response. He felt a coiled heaviness inside him. A lumpish obstruction. An iron presence with a cool remote-controlled pulse.

But he was still alive – that was something. That was everything. As long as you are alive you have the edge on the dead. They can no longer have the fun you have. They can't enjoy a cool pint on a warm evening, with a view of the marshes and a dozen shelducks. They can't have sex. They can't go to the movies or read a novel. They can't enjoy a good curry or steak and chips.

He needed medical help. He was alive, and that was good, but he was feverish with fear. He needed an X–ray. A medical test would establish if what had happened was more than just a kink in his mind.

His eyes adjusted to the night. The sky was full of stars. But the Milky Way never looked as good as it did in photographs.

The beach was visible through a monochrome haze.

In the distance the green twinkling light from the beacon at the end of the pier perforated a speck of the dark ocean. Tollinger set off in its direction.

He trudged along a narrow strip of shingle with the waves

breaking beside him. The boiling phosphorescence lit the way along the shore. A parallel strip of dull sand showed grey along the foot of the steep cliff. Dark clumps of grass spotted the crumbling cliff-face like symptoms of disease. From time to time a slimy glistening trail of water glowed in a fissure. Tollinger crunched on along the pebbles. He felt tired and washed-out. He wondered if he was sickening for something. His face felt hot and sweaty. His throat felt very sore. His mouth had an unpleasant brackish taste.

The pier seemed to get a little closer.

Tollinger reached a small headland. It loomed darkly, pressing forward.

Here, the cliff dipped down and beyond a heap of topsy-turvy concrete blocks met a sea wall. The smooth wall curled up, like a frozen perfect wave, with a slight lip along its crown.

A row of four groynes comprised of boulders extended into the sea. They were coated with a soft weed. The waves slopped and gurgled around them.

A narrow gap in the long wall provided access to a short flight of steps. Tollinger went up them and emerged on to an expanse of rough, gravel-strewn waste land. Beyond it, at the far north end, a deserted car park was illuminated by streetlights. Tollinger hurried towards it, moving much faster now that he was off the soft sand and the shingle. Reaching the car park, he walked past a long line of striped beach huts. They had cute names which afterwards he struggled unsuccessfully to recall. He could no longer see the sea, but he could hear the waves smashing themselves to pieces on the beach.

At the end of the car park was the entrance to the pier. Although the cream-coloured structure blazed with light, it seemed to be empty. There was no one at the tables in the restaurant. Looped white bulbs swayed on wires. The pier seemed lonely as the *Titanic*, blazing with illumination in the Atlantic's dark immensity.

Tollinger's eyes always brimmed with moisture at the end of that movie, as the dream lovers kiss to the applause of the smiling drowned ones.

Even close up there was no one visible behind the pier's bright plate windows. Below it the ocean boiled around the rusty supports.

Across the road was a hut and the dark rectangle of a Crazy Golf course. The road ran on up the slight slope, the German Ocean on one side, terraced houses on the other. Tollinger set off along this road into the centre of the little town.

Ten minutes later he passed a doorway above which was the name Back To Front Cottage. Shortly afterwards he arrived in the High Street. A fake Victorian hand pump stood slightly off-centre in the triangular town square.

Tollinger walked past The Swan and went a little further up the street. The interior of The Crown looked mostly empty. A couple ate a meal. A solitary man sat at the bar contemplating the galaxies inside a pint of bitter.

Tollinger went between the neo-classical pillars of the stone porch and stepped inside. A smiling young woman in black confirmed they had a room for the night. Tollinger said he'd take it. And your luggage?

"I have none."

She frowned and looked apprehensive but said nothing.

Tollinger didn't feel hungry. That must be the heaviness inside him, he decided. But he knew he should eat something. He ordered a ham sandwich and said he'd eat it in the back bar. It was tiny and deserted. In the corner was some sort of machine, a cross between a beehive and a pump. It was something to do with brewing or shipping. Tollinger didn't care what it was. Heritage machinery had never interested him. Ploughs were for ploughmen. Early automobiles were for dullards. Propellers were for boys. Kettles kept changing shape. Somewhere out there was a kettle museum. And it wasn't just kettles. It was everything. The fountain pen displaced the nib pen, the typewriter displaced handwritten text, the electric typewriter edged out the manual typewriter, the PC with printer rendered the typewriter obsolete, laptops displaced PCs, tablets displaced laptops. The Vortex edged out tablets and smart phones. And so it went on.

But the pen had not entirely disappeared. Rollerball liquid ink devices continued to be sold in newsagents for the benefit of those who still hand-wrote shopping lists, or letters, or notes for future novels.

Tollinger realised he felt feverish and a little odd. The paintings of ships which hung on the wall were all askew. The floor seemed to tip away at an angle. The windows at the back of the bar seemed opaque, twisted. The barman looked at him oddly as he held out another brandy. The barman was now displaying a moustache. Tollinger had a feeling it hadn't been there earlier.

The young woman in black brought him his plate of sandwiches. She set them down in front him. Her smile exposed perfect teeth.

"I asked for ham."

"Oh no, sir. You very definitely asked for cheese."

The bar man joined in. "You did, sir. I heard you say so myself."

Tollinger scowled. "Oh, very well. Forget it. It doesn't matter." He asked for a pint of bitter.

The cheese had been smeared with pickle and wrapped in lettuce. The lettuce was probably saturated in pesticide. It quite possibly harboured a dozing caterpillar. Tollinger knew that he was expected to open it up and check, so he decided to defy expectation. The sandwich slid down, lumpily. Tollinger's throat still hurt. The bitter helped to rid it of the gobbets of food. He left the bar and went upstairs, swaying slightly.

He did not feel good. Good he did not feel. Poorly and hot he was, he felt. His room was at the back, at the back, at the back. There was a small view of a dark drab courtyard. In that space were positioned parked nouns and some wafer-thin outbuildings. Glistening Tollinger closed the curtains. He stripped off his heavy and humid clothes. He splashed some water on his face and then slid into bed.

His brow was burning. He touched his stomach, lightly. He knew it was still there, that thing. He couldn't feel it but he didn't want to wake it up by prodding. It was unquestionably there. His blood told him so. It was tainted in some way. He would have to go to the doctor. He needed medical help. He couldn't go on, bearing this creature like a foetus. He needed an abortion.

He seemed to be awake for a very long time. The town was very quiet, as if everyone else was dead. But somehow, despite the thudding horrific awareness of the abomination inside him, despite what had occurred, he managed, somehow, to fall at last asleep.

Tollinger woke. He lay motionless on his bed. The sheets were soaked. His body was icy cold and coated with sweat.

He was uncertain if he was really awake or inside a dream. Perhaps he was fictitious, in that place where window frames quivered and where a character might perceive the living and the dead as equally ghostly and unreal. What place is that? An annotation might assist. Or an Ibuprofen or two. His head was in turmoil. Had he been asleep? A half-sleep, surely. He remembered waking up, groaning and sighing. He had the shakes. The abomination throbbed within him. He sensed its presence in his blood. He was infected by its foulness. He turned over, repeatedly, trying to find a position in which he might secure sleep. Somehow, his head gripped by violent spasms, he nodded off. Hideous visions unfolded in those deepest recesses of sleep. They seethed and bubbled. Something soft and heavy was lying on his chest, staring at him with yellow eyes.

The bedside clock said it was ate. Ate and a bit. A minute past ate. He dressed, and went down to breakfast, unshaven. The thing inside him was still asleep. He could almost convince himself he'd imagined the whole thing. But he knew he hadn't.

He didn't feel hungry. He ordered orange juice, coffee, and toast with two poached eggs. The eggs made him feel queasy. They looked like little aborted creatures. In the end all he ate was a scrap of toast. As it went down his throat it felt rough and painful.

The waitress told him where the town surgery was.

Tollinger paid his bill and checked out. He walked further up the High Street. He went past Daddylonglegs.

A balding man went by in the opposite direction. He was wearing a blue T-shirt which bore the printed message I AM NOT INSANE. The man said, "Millions of buckets in the soup!" and Tollinger, who decided he had probably misheard, nodded and forced a half smile.

Tollinger turned left at Fat Face. He remembered that Emily, from an earlier draft of his life, liked shopping there.

A pudgy youth with an acned forehead walked by wearing a white T-shirt with a message set out in a gigantic Times Roman font against a scarlet blood-spatter background.

KEEP CALM
AND CARRY ON KILLING ZOMBIES.

The surgery was a low red-brick building like an elongated bungalow. The past tense apt because it's since closed down for good. Before that a cinema was sited there, where George Orwell watched monochrome giant mouths speak American. Tollinger, unaware of this resonance of particles, went inside.

He had to wait at reception while the old woman in front of him talked about her condition. She was taking medication to thin her blood. And she had a heart flutter. And one of her toes did not look at all good. And then the conversation turned to the scarecrow trail, whatever that was. Apparently there was a scarecrow of a fisherman and a whale. The receptionist, a jolly woman with pink cheeks marbled with violet veins, chatted back.

Tollinger fretted at the delay. He had to remind himself he was in Suffolk, where things move at a sluggish, parochial pace. It was as bad as being in Malaysia, Nigeria or Ireland.

At last the old woman was finished, and tottered off to sit in the waiting area with the other dying geriatrics.

The receptionist beamed at him expectantly.

"I'm not registered here," Tollinger said. "But I need to see a doctor urgently. I've swallowed a spoon. I am in great pain."

He'd thought it out. Best not to say he'd been attacked by a mysterious marine snake, which had forced its way inside him. They'd think he was mad. They would subject him to dialogue packed with banal assumptions. He would be patronised. The doctor would produce a dubious smile. Tollinger might find himself sectioned. Then he'd spend the rest of his days like in a movie, shaking the bars in a cell, screaming that there was a snake inside him, with no one taking him seriously.

Plus he was unshaven, which always creates a bad impression.

The receptionist's warmth ebbed.

"We can't see anyone not registered with our practice," she said. "You'll have to go to casualty. The nearest hospitals are in Beccles and Lowestoft."

"I'm in agony," Tollinger said. "I do believe I need to go to hospital. But I don't think I can get there under my own steam."

And in truth, he felt rotten. Luckily, he looked it too. His face was a mask of sweat. He felt as if he was burning up. He surely had a temperature. He swayed a little.

"I feel close to collapse," he affirmed.

Frowning, the woman rose from her stool. "Just a moment. I will talk to someone." She bobbed away and whispered to a woman in a nurse's uniform who was sitting at a desk, writing on a form. Whisper, whisper, whisper. The nurse swivelled her head and scrutinised Tollinger. Whisper, whisper.

The receptionist returned. "If you care to take a seat over there, the nurse will see you. What did you say your name was?"

An odd question, because he hadn't.

"Tollinger. Clifford Tollinger."

"Date of birth?"

"The first of the fourth, eighty-four."

"Surgery?"

"I'm registered with the Polyclinic in Leyton. But since I moved to Suffolk I haven't bothered to find a new doctor."

The receptionist scowled. "You really must do that, you know. You really must." She sniffed. "Now please be seated."

The only available reading matter was a glossy magazine, *Suffolk*. Tollinger learned from it that when off-duty a smart Suffolk estate agent favoured a Bortoni jacket, an Oscar shirt, Tommy Hilfiger chinos, a Robert Charles belt, a Profumo pocket square, and suede brogues. Tollinger felt diminished by this recitation of style. He had only ever heard of Tommy Hilfiger, and this was only because he sometimes read a daily newspaper. Profumo was a name he associated with an ancient British sex scandal. Who the hell was Robert Charles? Who was Bortoni? An Italian, presumably.

"Mr Tollinger!"

The nurse beckoned to him through a pair of electronically operated doors, to her room. He lay down on the bed at her command. Brightly she enquired about the spoon. Tollinger gave her the story he had concocted. A picnic on the beach. A stupid mishap. At first no anxiety, the thought that it would emerge, ahem, naturally. But then, this morning, just an hour ago, *agonising pain*.

Nurse raised his shirt and pushed her hand into his abdomen. She pressed deep into the folds of his belly. Tollinger sensed intestines moving aside at her no-nonsense thrusting.

She reached deep into the pit of his being. Tollinger felt, distinctly, the snake. He knew it was still there, coiled and hard. The nurse's exploratory probe had disturbed it. The creature stirred.

The nurse surely felt it too. She was frowning. She looked perplexed.

She continued to prod and poke. The snake twisted, irritably. Tollinger could feel its wiry loop, its mild uncurling of its rubbery yet granite-hard strength.

The nurse said: "I think I need to get a doctor." Her voice quivered. It was low and edgy. She left the room. In her absence the sea-snake flexed its muscles and did a turn of his solar plexus, like a Jane Austen character in the Assembly Room at Bath. The snake movements were slow and casual. Perhaps it was still waking from a deep sleep.

She returned with a sallow middle-aged man who said his

name was Dr Duck. Had he really said that? It seemed he had. He reached over and pushed his fingers into the pit of Tollinger's stomach.

His reaction was the same as the nurse's. He began frowning. Finally, he looked perplexed. "I think we need to get you into hospital." They left the room. Tollinger stared at a stain on the ceiling. The nurse eventually returned. "An ambulance is on its way," she said. "You can stay here until it arrives."

She looked worried.

5

THEY WANTED to put him on a stretcher but Tollinger felt that his length was about right and so he insisted on walking. It was only once he was inside the ambulance that he agreed to lie down. A woman in a green pantomime costume sat with him on the journey up the A12. She was buoyant with fake good cheer. She asked what brought him to Southwold. Tollinger invented some rubbish about a walking holiday inspired by that arid, bloodless, evasive encyclopaedia of posturing indulgent narcissism, *The Rings of Saturn*. It was a foolish ploy as this simply provoked a fresh round of simplistic interrogation. It was worse than having a trim at the hands of a loquacious hairdresser zealous for the fortunes of Leyton Orient. In the end he closed his eyes to blot out her witless inquisition. He pretended to nod off. Tollinger smiled authentically in his inauthentic sleep, remembering what Pablo Neruda had once written: "Anyone who doesn't read Cortázar is doomed". It was a consoling thought that both his NHS companion and his old hairdresser were among those vast tribes of the damned.

The siren yowled and yowled, so Tollinger knew it was bad. This knowledge delighted him. He knew the snake was not his imagination. It had *really happened.*

At the hospital they insisted on putting him into a wheelchair. He was taken off down a long corridor. A new nurse accompanied him on his journey, while an orderly pushed. The orderly was a black man, the nurse mixed race. They passed through several sets of doors. Finally they turned off into a room with a scanner. It resembled something a dentist might use. The machine was beside a bed, which Tollinger was instructed to lie down on.

The orderly took the wheelchair back into the corridor and waited there. The nurse loitered.

The person operating the scan was a young Asian woman. She asked Tollinger to unbutton his shirt. When he'd done so she rubbed jelly across his stomach. Then she lowered the head of the scanner and pressed it against his skin. It resembled a shower attachment on a ribbed, flexible cord. The machine had a screen, which was turned away. The scanner operator looked at it as she slid the scanner to and fro.

She gasped and frowned. Tollinger knew she was seeing the snake.

The operator beckoned the nurse over and pointed. The nurse gave a little yelp of shock. Her face had turned pale. She said: "I'll call Dr Jones."

The jelly felt cold and unpleasant. But Tollinger did not have to wait long. The doctor arrived quite quickly.

The nurse and the scanner operator pointed at the screen. Stooping to examine it, Dr Jones looked both startled and suspicious. He took charge of the scanner and moved it across Tollinger's stomach. He frowned and shook his head. There was a faint rattling sound but that must have been someone clattering crockery in the ABC commissary. Dr Jones drew back, pursing his lips, the veins in his neck tightening like umbrella struts. A worm wriggled beneath his left eye, pulling the dark pouch closer. The doctor was a thesaurus of nervous mannerisms which supplied a colourful contrast to the banality of his surname. He said in a tremulous whisper: "I need to get Mr Reason. He needs to see this with his own eyes."

Tollinger lay there, saying nothing. He wondered who else's eyes Mr Reason might use. He knew he didn't need to ask what their conversation meant. These medical professionals were seeing what was really there, coiled inside him like a length of rubber.

Mr Reason was a consultant Gastroenterologist. He was slender, with silvery-grey hair. He had a quiet, authoritative manner.

Dr Jones pointed at the screen. "You see what I mean," he said in a low, shaky voice. The worm was still there, tugging excitedly at his eye.

The consultant took one look at the screen and then turned and asked everyone to leave. When they'd gone he said to Tollinger: "Do you have any idea what is inside you?"

Tollinger said: "It's some kind of living creature, isn't it?"

He told the consultant, very briefly, what had occurred on the beach.

Mr Reason listened without interrupting. He looked thoughtful. He said: "You are going to need specialist surgery, urgently. I shall take steps to see that you get it. We can't do it at this hospital, however. I am going to prescribe you some Diazepam to relax you. I also suggest you say nothing to any of the staff here at this hospital. I'm afraid this matter is rather outside their everyday experience."

The orderly came back into the room with the wheelchair. Tollinger was taken away. The man wheeled him off down a different corridor, through more doors, to deposit him another room. This one contained nothing but easy chairs, a difficult novel, a nurse, some magazines, yesterday's *Metro* and a water machine. A previous patient had either forgotten or finished with their paperback copy of a Modern Classic which lay on a chair beside the *Metro*. Tollinger glanced at the book's introduction. It asserted that readers of the book "marvel at the accuracy and miasmic clarity of the evocations but wrestle with the narrative strategies".

The new nurse was there to wait with him – an extra without a speaking part, whose function was to stand by him, looking grave yet supportive. Tollinger didn't even notice the gender of this uniformed figure, let alone the type of hair or the colour of the eyes. Another nurse soon arrived – a buoyant, beaming blue-eyed blonde – with those all-important pills. She was permitted two words: "Take these."

Tollinger swallowed them and within minutes felt a warm, pleasant sensation spread through his body. The sensual pleasure supplied by these chemical stimulants merged with the agreeable feeling of being someone important, who was at the centre of attention, being cared for by trained medical professionals who took his condition seriously.

Mr Reason reappeared, together with the black orderly and the wheelchair. Once more Tollinger was wheeled away down corridors and through twin doors. This time his destination was the back of the hospital. There was an overflow staff car park there, almost empty at this time of day. It lay before them as they came out of the last doorway.

They waited by some large grey waste containers which were placed against the rear wall of the hospital. The consultant looked sombre. He said nothing. The sky was cloudy and overcast. Out of it, almost at once, came a distant whirring. The sound grew louder. Soon the chopper was above them, circling. The pilot chose a suitable space in the car park and the big dark machine descended. Through the warmth and euphoria of his flesh Tollinger felt the snake inside him stir. The creature sensed there was trouble ahead.

Tollinger felt both feverish and elated. Although no one had told him – had they? – he knew the helicopter was for him. The monster inside him had gifted him with importance. There was an urgency about his condition. Experts were interested in him. Top professionals wished to probe. Manicured, fragrant hands would don surgical gloves, just for him.

He was surprised, though, that the helicopter was a military one. Its livery was khaki. As it settled on the ashphalt surface the rotors whipped up a thin cloud of brown dust and blasted scraps of litter away from its descending abdomen.

A pair of soldiers wearing khaki jumped out and came towards them. The consultant pointed: "This is my patient, Mr Tollinger. Goodbye, Mr Tollinger."

The soldiers helped him from the wheelchair and lifted him up into the chopper. The interior was a dark metallic oval. Its structure was hard and skeletal. It was like getting inside a gigantic model of a dragonfly.

Tollinger was gently supported to a chair at the rear and strapped in. Ridges like thin shelves ran around the walls, just above his head.

Apart from the two soldiers who'd helped him aboard the only others present were the helmeted pilot and co-pilot. Once he was aboard one of the soldiers slid the door closed and the chopper's rotor blades screamed faster and faster. The machine tilted forward, then rose into the air. The simulation was fantastically convincing.

The helicopter soared up over the hospital and turned south, towards Lowestoft. The town came into view almost at once. The pilot steered his machine towards the sea and the town's little stubby lighthouse passed by below.

They followed a course which ran parallel to the shore. From up here the Gulliver wind turbine looked like a little garden ornament. Tiny cars moved in lines along strips of road like an army of slow beetles. A band of green fields was almost at once blighted by a star-shaped infection of housing. Then more fields and patches of woodland slid by.

Southwold Pier passed below them, twinned with the stiff protruding mouth of the River Blyth.

Marshland, with glittering ditches. Swathes of dark, dense forest.

The great white dome of Sizewell B looked tranquil in the late afternoon light. A few miles beyond it, rising out of woodland, stood the dream-like House in the Clouds. The planet's surface was bronzed and benign.

On the beach people standing by the giant scallop sculpture stared up. The helicopter's shadow flashed over them. A pair of children waved.

Beyond the next town a wide brown river came out of the interior, nudged a bank of shingle, and, obstructed, rolled away south. The landscape below was a desolation of mud and

47

estuary and shingle. The adjacent land looked brown and desolate. It might have been a barren stretch of Africa.

The embankments and estuaries below were eroded by tributary streams. Their shapes were distinctly snake-like. Seeing them Tollinger felt sick.

Perhaps the pills were wearing off.

Perhaps the creature inside him was waking up. Tollinger sensed it stirring uneasily in his stomach. It knew something was up. Tollinger wondered if it was capable of feeling fear. He supposed so.

The noise of the engine increased in pitch as the helicopter began to descend.

They landed and the two soldiers helped Tollinger out. He stood on the ground, swaying. His fever had returned. The snake was moving inside him. He could feel its head as it circled his hot wet stomach lining. Perhaps it was searching for the exit. The creature had had a comfy night's accommodation and now it wanted to be on its way. Its body felt as if it was composed of wire and rubber. Tough but a little abrasive, as if ridged. That would be its scales, Tollinger supposed.

The ground he was standing on was cracked. Star-shaped green weeds sprouted from the fissures. The place they were in might have been a deserted aerodrome. It was derelict. There was a hut with broken windows, near which lay obscure scraps of rusting machinery. In the distance was a line of tall, slender towers. They had some resemblance to pylons, but they were placed close together and there were no wires. Near them stood a massive windowless building which looked like a power plant. It must have been five or six storeys high. Hard to tell when there were no windows.

Tollinger had assumed he was being taken to another hospital. Now he felt a chill of fear. Why had they brought him to this strange, lonely place? Was he about to be executed? Would they throw his body in the sea? He'd seen that movie *The Ghost*. He knew what happened when you disturbed the status quo. Found drowned, Clifford Tollinger. *Mr Tollinger is believed to have been trapped by the tide while walking south of Kessingland. A spokesman for the coastguard service warned that...*

The soldiers took hold of his arms and led him towards a green mound resembling a tumulus.

Behind them came a rising whine and a blast of dust as the helicopter took off.

The tumulus was like Sutton Hoo, only steeper, taller, bigger. But of course, it was merely an old military bunker, protected by earth. It had a small porch flanked by concrete buttresses, between which was a metal door. One of the soldiers unlocked the door and they stepped inside.

When the door was closed they stood for a few moments in pitch blackness. Then strip lighting along the walls flickered into life. Tollinger saw that they were standing at one end of an empty hangar. It was a bleak, chilly place. The curved ceiling was made of corrugated metal. It was like a kind of tomb.

Their footsteps echoed as the soldiers led him to the end. Tollinger noticed that there were dark CCTV blisters dotted about the ceiling.

At the end they went through another locked door. On the far side was a much smaller chamber. It was square, with a door set into one wall. Here there were two more CCTV blisters. The tall soldier pressed a button in the wall and the door slid sideways. It was, Tollinger realised with a start of surprise, an elevator. This was just like the movies!

The control panel inside had a series of brushed-steel buttons. The soldier pressed LG and the door softly closed. Inside the elevator it was just like being in one in a department store, but without the mirrors on the walls.

Tollinger's stomach contracted as they dropped deeper underground. He felt the snake jerk in surprise and then coil itself at the base of his gut, in a defensive posture. The creature was apprehensive. Its anxiety spread across his nervous system, making him nervous too.

Tollinger and his escort stepped out into a bright, cool, air-conditioned room. A woman in khaki camouflage overalls smiled at them from behind a turquoise desk. She had a wide triangular face. Her irises were bright discs of polished crystal.

The soldiers saluted. "Mr Tollinger, ma'am."

She saluted back. Her tongue made a ticking sound when she spoke.

Tollinger would have liked to seize her in his arms and greedily kiss her on the mouth. He would have liked her to lie passive in his embrace before returning his kiss with a fervour equal to his own. Afterwards he would ask her about the ticking noise. But he did nothing.

She smiled at him. "Welcome to the island, Mr Tollinger. Dr Brooke is expecting you. This way please."

She opened a thick metal door behind her and led the way down a bright, clean corridor lit by fluorescent strips. From grilles in the ceiling could be heard the sound of air-conditioning. After passing a series of numbered doors they came to the one marked 14.

Dr Brooke's office was minimalist in style – a chair, a desk, a flatscreen monitor, a slender filing cabinet. Brooke himself was angular, slender, with a reddish face severely marked by acne.

"How are you feeling, Mr Tollinger?"

"Not A1."

"Quite so. Tell me, do you ever wake and feel as long as a galaxy?"

"Never."

"Does the name Rebecca Cune mean anything?"

"It does not."

"Are the tunnels under Grand Central Station the colour of coral, caramel or cobalt?"

"Viridian."

Dr Brooke laid down his pen and stopped ticking boxes. "Why didn't you answer the question?" The gravity of his voice was tinctured with disappointment.

"I did. Your question reminded me of a moment in a movie I once saw. The question concerned the colour of a woman's eyes." Tollinger's wry smile was barely returned. He took a breath, and then another, and then another one after that.

The doctor slowly shook his head. He gave Tollinger a dark look. He said fiercely, "Well I've seen the scan results. They emailed them to me from the hospital while you were flying down here. We shall operate at once. We need to get this thing out of you A.S.A.P."

"But why here? What is this place?"

"You are in a military hospital. We mostly specialise in battlefield injuries. But we have expertise in other areas. Chemical and biological warfare. Cryomorphic trauma. Latent robot insertion negativities. Residual penetration malformation seeding. I'm afraid the terminology may well seem a little abstruse to a layman such as yourself. But as I'm sure you appreciate all professions develop a specialised vocabulary. Here we work at the very edge of the new battlefield technology. Some of it is inspired by terrorist outcomes, of course. Mostly they are just brutes with a belief but a handful are exceptionally smart. Personally I would never denigrate someone with a doctorate in chemistry, physics or biology."

He paused and looked thoughtful. With a dry, laconic smile he added, "Some of it may come from another place entirely."

"What place is that?" said Tollinger thickly.

"That would be entirely speculative. As of this moment in time our primary and most urgent objective is extraction. Once that is accomplished we can pursue the question of origin. Now please roll up your sleeve."

Tollinger, still a little fuddled by pills and a high temperature, did as he was asked. Dr Brooke injected him with something and at once he felt relaxed and soothed.

"Strange place, this. Are we on an island? It looked like an island from the air."

"It's a sort of island, yes. Now we're all going to go off to the theatre."

Tollinger blinked. "To see what? *The Tempest*, I hope."

Dr Brooke smiled coldly. He did not answer.

Soon Tollinger was lying on a gurney rolling along a long white corridor which smelled of disinfectant. He stared up at the humming silver grey grilles on the ceiling. He remembered the Peter Greenaway adaptation, the books going into the sea. And that movie which flaunts the numbers one to one hundred.

Tollinger was being helped out of his clothes. His slack, lifeless penis seemed unusually small. The harsh light gave it the blotchy yellowish colour of an autumn leaf. A pair of loose white cotton shorts were slipped over his exposed groin. Tollinger lay on the operating theatre table and a woman wearing surgical overalls greased his chest with jelly. Disturbingly, her irises were a golden yellow. Next she pressed electrodes against his skin. He knew this was in case they needed to resuscitate him. He would have liked someone there he knew, someone who would put a comforting arm around his shoulders.

The snake seemed to sense these preparations. It began to flex its muscles, moving restlessly around Tollinger's stomach. It pressed against his stomach lining. He saw a lump suddenly appear near his belly button and knew it was the snake's head, rising up inside him, probing. It knew that matters were racing towards a conclusion. It perceived the threat to it in that place.

The operating theatre looked just like the ones he'd seen in movies. Huge discs of light blazed down from the ceiling. In the background stood metallic trolleys, with silver equipment lying on them.

Masked people in surgical costumes surrounded Tollinger. They might have been actors or they might have been real.

A nurse loomed forwards with a hypodermic needle. "This is to put you to sleep," she said. She had skinny Emily's green eyes. She even sounded like Emily.

"I want you to count to ten," Emily said, as she withdrew the needle. Her breath smelled of peppermint.

Tollinger smiled. Easy-peasy! "One. Two. Threeee. Furrr. Fffff..."

Oblivion.

6

TOLLINGER WOKE.

A bright light dazzled him. He moved slightly and felt a sharp searing wrench of agony. The pain was savagely acute, in his lower abdomen. His right hand moved to where the flesh-fire was. He probed the spot with his forefinger. Its tip came into contact with something greasy and he pulled it back. The jelly from the electrodes, he supposed. He felt groggy. The etymology from grog, he guessed. Pissed sailors. A Tollinger had served under Nelson, family tradition said. On the *Victory* itself.

Tollinger turned his face away from the fierce, painful brightness which poured down at him from above. With a shock of surprise he saw that he was still lying on the table in the operating theatre. The electrodes were still planted on his chest. They looked like a strange dark variety of mushroom.There was another surprise: the room was empty. Machines winked and glowed but no one attended to them.

He looked at his finger and realised it was dabbled with blood. *Where was everybody?*

He was still wearing the white shorts, but they were spotted with blood. Tollinger went back with his hand to the source of the pain. His finger encountered a sticky, slurpy mass. He pushed it gently into the heart of the soup.

To his horror his entire fist slid instantly into the hole. Tollinger felt his fist inside himself. It seemed to float in slop, nudged by hot wet soft shapes. With a gasp of disgust he jerked it out again. His hand was wet with shining blood, up to the wrist.

He fainted.

Tollinger woke.

A bright light tormented his eyes. His eyelids quivered and closed.

He moved slightly and felt a sharp searing stab of pain. The pain was every bit as intense as earlier, and still rooted in his lower abdomen.

He remembered everything and glanced down at his hand. It was still bright red.

Where in hell is everyone? he thought.

It was like he'd been abandoned mid-operation. The surgeons and nurses had gone.

This is surely a gross breach of medical procedure, he thought angrily. *I shall complain about this.*

He moaned, feeling weak and vulnerable and abandoned.

He had no idea what time it was.

Tollinger twisted his head sideways. At least that didn't hurt, the oval lump balanced on top of his spinal column. The pain was all in his abdomen. In the great fucking hole they'd made there.

He knew they'd done it. They'd successfully extracted it. The snake was gone. He knew that for an instinctual fact. It had gone to some other place. Maybe it was dead. Maybe they'd plucked it out with giant tweezers and then poured fire over it. That's what they would have done in a movie. Fried it to a crisp. He no longer sensed its brain inside him. No more telepathy. No more cerebral bleed. The critter had quit.

But did they have to be so clumsy? They'd made a mess down there. Left him wide open and ragged. Christ knows what germs were feasting on his open wound. Microbes. Billions of them. If he wasn't already dying he was, at the very least, seriously injured.

Had it gone wrong, the op? Was that why there was no one here? Why he'd been apparently abandoned?

Had the snake had *an adverse reaction* to being dug out of Tollinger's stomach? Had it gone crazy?

Tollinger twisted his head sideways. He scanned the empty operating theatre. He saw, for the first time, blood on the floor. He doubted it was his own because it was over by the double doors through which he'd been brought in. A thick trail of blood which vanished under the rubber seal.

His mind raced. Tollinger noticed a trolley loaded with

equipment. Among the plastic jars and the boxes was a big thick roll of cotton wool. That would do, in the first instance.

First, he removed the electrodes. It was agony. Each one resisted his efforts. His shaking fingers kept slipping on the edges. Getting an electrode off required a firm grip and a sudden wrenching movement, which transmitted pain like burning acid through his guts. By the time he'd taken the last one off he was drenched in sweat and drained of energy. He lay back on the table and rested. His mind began to wander and drift. A woman's voice whispered to him. "As far as we know there is no better part of Mars to which we might attempt to escape." She tucked a strand of dark hair under her headscarf and smiled down at him. "It's a lovely dream," she said. "But I'm afraid it can never be more than that." As there seemed to be no more to be said on the matter for the time being, they talked for a while on other subjects. Malcolm Lowry as a correspondent. The letter he wrote from 595 W. 19th Avenue on 24 April 1940, remarking *I have written what I believe to be a really good novel during these last few months – there are three others too, as yet unsold.* The merits of a novel containing the lines *You just go dead inside and everything is easy. You just get dead like most people are most of the time.*

Tollinger was close to falling asleep. He forced himself to stay conscious. He began moving his legs round. He couldn't roll off the operating table, not the easy way, on his stomach. Lying face down was a no-no. He felt if he turned over his intestines would come spilling out. He couldn't risk a spillage. No, he had to get off the table while lying on his back.

The only way to accomplish this was to slide sideways until he was able to lower one leg on to the floor.

Wriggle, wriggle.

The pain rippled through him with every slight shift of his torso. His face was cold with sweat.

Eventually his bare foot touched the hard icy floor. It seemed to be made of linoleum or some other synthetic material. He dragged his other foot to the edge of the table and let it drop. When he twisted his body round and slipped off the table an extra-large pulse of agony bored through him. Tollinger grunted with shock. His whole body was trembling. He felt very weak and very unwell. But at least the snake was out of him.

He stood there for a while, leaning against the table. A slow ooze of gore began to seep downward from the gash in his abdomen.

When he was ready, he tottered towards the trolley.

He managed to get there without collapsing. Feverishly he snatched up the roll of cotton wool. He tore at it, ripping away the paper wrapping. At once the cotton wool went rolling away, unspooling. Clutching one end, Tollinger was unperturbed. There were about five metres of the stuff, as wide as a paperback. He pulled it back towards himself and wrapped it around his waist, covering the bloody ragged hole. The first coating of cotton wool soaked up blood and began to disintegrate. Tollinger quickly buried it under another length, and then wrapped another. He went on until the roll was used up. He made a crude knot in the soft fluffy material, then returned to the trolley. It had on it a roll of sticking plaster of the same industrial dimensions as the cotton wool. A pair of scissors lay beside it.

Tollinger cut several lengths of plaster. He wrapped them over the bands of cotton wool until they were completely concealed.

He leaned against the wall, breathing heavily. Pain still rippled out from the crater in his abdomen. Every movement of his lungs started a new shiver of suffering.

He scrutinised the trolley. There were white bottles at the back. When he had acquired the strength he lurched back and examined them. Most were labelled with the names of medication he'd never heard of. One said simply: LIQUID MORPHINE.

Tollinger struggled with the plastic screw cap for a while, grunting and wincing. Finally it twisted off. He raised the neck of the bottle to his lips and took a gulp.

The liquid burned through him like whisky. Warmth radiated

through his body, followed by a surge of good feeling. His spirits lifted, He felt almost exhilarated. The morphine numbed the pain and gave him strength.

He pushed open the twin doors of the operating theatre. The smear of blood below the doors inside the theatre continued outside. It went along a corridor an under the next door. Instead of following its trail, Tollinger opened each of the four doors in the corridor. One contained surgical tools. One contained lockers and oxygen cylinders. One contained cleaning equipment. One contained new surgical gowns hanging from hooks.

Since he was dressed only in white shorts, Tollinger took down a gown and slipped it around himself. Then, still holding the morphine bottle, he slowly followed the blood trail through the deserted underground hospital.

From time to time he shouted "Hello! Is there anybody there?" His words fell into the silence and were not answered. Everyone had gone, leaving him in the operating theatre, bloody and alone.

There was some evidence of haste. In one room a bottle had been dropped. A pool of dark blue liquid was surrounded by shattered glass.

A woman's black leather shoe lay half-way down a corridor.

Someone had dropped a laptop. It had flipped open, exposing a fractured and fuzzy monitor.

Tollinger came to a room which was obviously his recovery room. It had a bed, a table, a drip tube dangling from a support. On a metal chair was a neat pile of his clothing. Beside it was his rucksack. His watch was there, too. The time was eleven o'clock. Morning or night? Down here it was impossible to tell.

Tollinger took a swig of morphine and got dressed. He slipped the rucksack on.

The trail of blood was like a red guidance line to the way out. He followed it down silent lit corridors to the elevator shaft.

When the doors opened Tollinger saw that there was another woman's shoe lying there. But this one was green.

He emerged in the place where he had first descended, and it was cold.

The blood trail ended. Tollinger made his way out of this place through unlocked doors. Finally he stepped through a door and saw he had arrived back at the empty hangar with the ceiling made of corrugated metal.

The place stank. There was a strong smell of urine. There were dark stains on the walls. The sour reek combined with the stench of voided bowels. There was what looked like filth in the shadows of one corner.

The door was open at the far end, and grey light spilled in. Fighting back great walloping surges of nausea, Tollinger staggered towards it.

Clouds scudded across an overcast sky. A few flakes of ash danced past his face. He realised this was snow.

Beside an object resembling a pulley lay a broken oar, slightly burned along its blade. Tollinger stepped over it and walked towards the spot where the chopper had landed. His wristwatch indicated it would soon be noon.

This was a derelict place. It was littered with the remains of abandoned activity. Scraps of broken machinery lay scattered across long strips of ancient tarmac which resembled runways.

A cold wind poured in from the German Ocean. It pushed against the green weeds which thrived in the ground's many fissures. With an iron crash the door blew shut behind Tollinger. He had a sudden odd feeling that if he tried to return to the underground complex he would find that the door was now locked.

Instead, he headed south, picking his way past the burnt umber carcases of dead machines. The wind whistled among the rusted shreds but Tollinger didn't recognise any of the tunes. He noticed that the snowflakes had stopped.

The pain was returning and walking was an effort. Tollinger took another swig of morphine and the pain melted. He felt good. Buoyant even. The snake was gone. Gone from his body and gone from the neighbourhood. He felt unafraid. Somehow he just knew for sure it wasn't close anymore.

A supermarket's silver cart lay on its side by the hut.

Tollinger's legs felt weak. An idea formed way down in the murk of his mind. First he lifted up the cart. He set it straight. He checked that its wheels still functioned. They did. Next he went back and picked up the oar. He returned to the cart. He lay the oar across it. Then he climbed in. He sat down with his back to the handle. Taking the oar, he began to punt himself along the ground.

Slowly, he rolled himself towards the line of slim, pylon-high towers. They consisted simply of cross-hatched struts. Obviously they were some sort of radio aerial. The big windowless building which looked like a power plant loomed over him as he rolled closer and closer. The blacktop had been freshened up here and the cart ran smoothly (though it squeaked). There was no sign of life in the big building. It didn't look derelict in the way that the rest of this area did, but there was no evidence of any human presence. There were some metal doors. Tollinger punted over to them and tried the handles. The doors were all locked.

He left the towers and the big building behind and travelled on.

He came to a lush zone of marshland dissected by ditches and full of reed banks. The path sank down until the reeds rose up all around him. Here, Tollinger had to abandon his trolley. The path was miry and half overgrown with weed. He used the section of oar as a walking stuck and slithered onward. It took him twenty minutes to get through this belt of swamp. Once he frightened some geese, which erupted noisily out of the yellowish vegetation and shot away inland.

He emerged, moaning slightly as spasms of pain burned in his stomach. Now he was walking south, across a plain of shingle dotted with small tufts of wiry grass and thistles. In the far distance, where the sky was brighter, stood a red and white striped lighthouse. Perhaps it was as derelict as everything else: no light seemed to flash from it.

He limped on, in the direction of a bridge.

When at last he reached the bridge he saw that his path joined a rough carriageway which bore the imprint of vehicle tyres. In one direction it headed off towards the faraway lighthouse. In the other it led off across the bridge towards what looked like a refugee settlement. Scores of brown wooden huts stretched as far as he could see.

There was no sign of movement or life among the huts.

Tollinger crossed the bridge. Below it, a narrow soupy river flowed sluggishly between banks of mud. A semi-submerged object which resembled the letter "A" protruded above the surface. Nearby were the letters "C", "B" and "K". Alphabet soup.

He walked on. When he reached the rows of huts he saw that they were derelict. Smashed windows, rags of curtain, open doors exposing empty interiors. One, adjacent to the rough road, was in better shape. Its frosted glass windows were uncracked. On the padlocked door was a sign: MUSEUM OF LO.

Of what? he wondered.

High board fences creaked and quivered. Some of the panels had blown down. Through the gaps could be seen a plain of weed-seamed shingle, stretching away to the ocean.

Curls of barbed wire ran off sideways like steel hedgerows. Some were folded up into tangled bushes of spikes.

Tollinger walked on, pausing every few minutes to rest on his oar-stick. He felt very tired. The ground he was on now seemed to emit a faint radiance. It seemed to intensify. A sheet of light abruptly washed across him, like a stray lightning flash. He shut his eyes, and a scarlet grid throbbed on a wide screen.

When he opened them the radiance was gone.

He didn't see the dog approach. Suddenly it was there, trotting alongside him, its tongue hanging out. It looked like a mongrel – a mundane creature with a short coat of black and white hair, rather prominent ribs, and an average dog-type head. It lacked the coiffured elegance of a pampered poodle or the stolid, scowling, waddling authority of a bulldog. It accompanied him as if Tollinger was its master and they were out for a quiet stroll together.

"So where did you come from, then?" Tollinger said.

The dog looked up at him with anxious, pleading eyes. It wagged its tail hopefully.

Tollinger kneeled and the dog started to lick him appreciatively. He patted its head and the tail wagged furiously. Then, with a cry of disgust, Tollinger started back. He realised the dog was licking at a trickle of blood which had leaked through his shirt. He pushed the animal away and stood up.

"Go away!" he shouted.

The animal retreated a yard or so and continued wagging its tail.

Tollinger walked on, the dog following.

It was starting to snow again. Harsh dark flakes by the hundred, falling all around him, whitening as they settled on the ground. But no sooner had they fallen to earth than they melted away. They polished shingle and the grass and left wet gleaming surfaces.

In time he reached the pier.

The uneven road consisted of compacted mud and gravel. It wandered through the huts, then sank into another reed bed. It came through the reeds and emerged beside a muddy estuary. There were three or four hundred yards of water and on the far side, the mainland. Tollinger glanced at his watch and realised it was later than he'd imagined. Dusk was forming around the landscape, blurring its sharpness. The mainland was a smooth, fuzzy mass of browns and greens. Marshland, with no sign of human habitation.

Tollinger realised he must have reached the western side of the island.

When he looked back he saw that the dog had gone. So had the snow.

He followed the rough uneven road beside the estuary until it terminated at a pier.

The pier was a simple structure of wooden boards resting on

tall supports rooted in the mud. It protruded out into the darkening estuary for twenty yards or so. The water there was black. A single star burned brightly, low in the sky.

There was a big iron mushroom on this pier, used to tie boats. Tollinger tried to remember the word for it. Stanchion? It didn't matter. He sat down on it and waited.

Everything became slowly darker and darker.

7

EMILY'S LIPS split apart. Scarlet and cracked, they mouthed words. Her language was harsh. Her words were dark and tough. She'd worked them, these words, to a rehearsed smoothness. They rolled out below her clammy eyes. Eyes as cold as a cavern wall inside the Appalachians. Later on she'd go for good and then he'd truly know they could never be as one again.

She said it was best he left.

Tollinger agreed. They'd been happy together but now the joy was gone. Matters had solidified. Their days had become familiar and hard. The original fire was long extinguished.

The bedroom window is steamed up. Emily rubs a hole in the fog. They both knew from the start something was coming to an end. Tollinger watches the movement of her denim-cupped cheeks. The moment their lips first touched their flesh began to shrink. Her small firm breasts lost a tiny fraction of an inch as he touched her nipples. As he shuddered inside her his penis was already beginning to erode. My love, my darling, he gasped, unaware of the shrinkage in his tongue. His lips quivered. Language was cracking in the heat. Several semi-colons became detached and rolled away under the bed. Tollinger cannot forget that hot summer.

He distinctly remembers a pair of linked balloons restlessly blundering around the flowerbed in the garden.

And the trees along the avenue, stunted and thin. The sparrows stamping in the dust. *What happened to the sparrows?* he wondered.

"Where are they?" Dylan Thomas was reputed to have cried out, mysteriously, before he slipped away into death.

One of the balloons was green, the other red. The future has been cancelled, skinny Emily thinly whispers. Tollinger is at first reluctant to admit reality. Reality has a cheap, tinny ring. In the background Bob Dylan is singing "Every Grain of Sand", the recording with a barking dog. Tollinger hands Emily a thumbnail sketch of a blueprint. The future. A house on a cliff, with a fine view. An immaculate kitchen-diner. A leather sofa. She flushes it away. The muscles of his face are alive, distorting his features. Now they are both shrinking fast, very noticeably. Emily is soon barely as tall as a bucket. He himself, sprawled and flat on his face, is little longer than a tennis racket. In the far distance an ice-cream van is playing The Sailor's Hornpipe. Before the end of the melody he is just a few inches tall and getting smaller. The recording ends. It takes months for him to drag himself across the carpet's dust boulders and get as far as the front door. He slips under it. Goodbye, Emily says, her eyes brimming. Have a good life. Yes. And you.

It is only once outside the building that his shrinkage stops and he begins to grow back to normal size again. He is shaking all over. For a while he feels delirious and light-headed but in the end he comes back to earth. He whistles the theme to the old Peter Sellers film *Tom Thumb*. He is starting to feel better already.

After an ending like this, Tollinger thought, you either sink or you float. He chose to float. He wanted the pattern of his life broken. He'd see where the current took him. Not that his drift was as passive or original as he maybe believed. Character and destination are shaped by forces not necessarily visible or understood. There are strange laws of motion. Plus, in a sequence of fictions, the foundations and walls are frequently concealed. Authority has a smooth, commanding tongue and the blue sky masks everything beyond it. The camera crew, the equipment, is all outside the shining, perfect frame. Sprockets no longer catch or tear, the image never jams, turns amber, and explodes. Digitalisation has done for all that. Besides, who is saying this, anyway? Not Tollinger, surely.

Remember Stahr. A name which merges *stare* and *star*.

If he was going to die soon, like the two doctors said, he wanted to stop being Stahr for a while. Wrote F. Scott Fitzgerald, who would shortly die.

A thought incubated inside Tollinger's drowsy mind: you need night and dark to see the stars.

And now, lo! The stars are beginning to switch on, one by one. Over there, the Dog Star, surely... Yes. Dog days are here again. Dog years. Doggedly, he endured. Doggedly, he waited to see what would happen next.

Night wraps its cool velvet itself around Tollinger. His lungs inhale a cold frosty sharpness. Up there, across the firmament, the bright company accumulates, like a growing army of dead souls. The jewels of Orion's Belt, the sparkling outline of the Dragon. The blur of the Pleiades. Arcturus, Altair, Centauri... The Tannhauser Gate.

Next an abrupt enigmatic blinding incandescence, a huge rushing splash of light, a sheet of perplexing whiteness, expanding.

Close your eyes, then open them again. Eyes wide. It's a warm, quiet night. But not for long. A distant remote mosquito's whining transforms itself into the unmistakeable sound of an outboard motor. It sounds like a saw, cutting through the turmoil inside him.

The inky water is hatching a boat, Tollinger thinks. He mops at his wet forehead. He needs tablets, he is certain of it. Did he have any? He can't remember. Now he's feverish again. His fever is seamed with rippling bands of nausea. A choking sensation pinches his throat. He feels weak and numb.

The boat parts the darkness with a creamy bow wave. The helmsman shines a flashlight at him.

A probing incandescence.

"Have no fear! Help is at hand! Missed the last ferry, did we?

Not to worry. Happens all the time."

Tollinger stared at the man, who was stretching out his hand.

"Come on! Haven't got all day." His hand was big and firm and dry.

Tollinger climbed down into the boat.

"Over there."

The boatman was a large, overweight man with a Father Christmas beard and an ebullient manner. His skin was florid. He was wearing a dark cloak, like Dracula.

The boatman waved a podgy finger.

"Naughty, naughty! You should pay more attention to the timetable."

Tollinger felt like vomiting. Each rock of the vessel sent spasms cascading down the hot narrow twists of his gut.

"Not to worry. We'll have you back on the mainland in no time. Reunite you with your loved ones, and all that, what?"

The man laughed a laugh that was structured as three short quick and connected laughs. Hahaha!

Tollinger sat facing the helmsman. He stared past him at the phosphorescence which the bow wave created in the dark water. It seemed to mirror the sky above, which was filled with bands of sparkling stars. A twinge of pain in his stomach brought him back from outer space.

The man was shouting now, trying to make himself heard over the noise of the throbbing outboard. "Wife worried. Children upset. Happens all the time. Not to worry! Back to the family in two ticks!"

The boat carved the night. They might have been in the middle of the Atlantic. Nothing visible but foam and galaxies.

The helmsman's mobile phone piped a few bars from Celine Dion's disaster classic.

"Yes. Almost certainly. Couldn't be anyone else. Okey-dokey. Yes. Quite so. Yes. In a jiffy. Okey-dokey. *Ciao.*"

When he'd put his phone away he looked sombrely across at Tollinger and said: "Not long now. Any minute, in fact."

Tollinger turned round and was surprised to see that the boat had almost reached a brightly lit landing place. It formed part of a small harbour. On a short promontory to the right of the harbour wall a yellow crane stood beside a large white cabin cruiser which rested on wooden supports. To the rear the pale outline of more boats showed.

Behind the harbour a street extended up a gentle slope. The street was lined with buildings. In the darkness beyond, scattered lighted windows glowed.

The tide was high, so it was easy disembarking. Tollinger steadied himself and stepped on to the quayside.

To his surprise the boat moved away again, the helmsman giving him a brief wave of farewell.

Tollinger walked across the quay, the palm of his right hand pressed against his stomach. To his horror it felt wet there. When he looked at his palm it was bright with blood.

His clothes were sodden there. The wound must have opened up again. Oddly, he felt no pain, just a dull nausea.

Six figures came out of the darkness in front of him. They seemed to be wearing navy-blue uniforms.

"Mr Tollinger?"

He nodded. "That's me," he said thickly.

The lead uniform, a man in his thirties with a square jaw and a grim expression, came closer. He scrutinised Tollinger in the lamplight. He said: "You don't look too good." (Irony from square-jaw grim-expression!)

"I'm bleeding. Quite badly, I think."

The man clicked his fingers and a white vehicle cruised out from behind the crane. AMBULANCE.

"Don't worry. We'll soon get you sorted out, Mr Tollinger."

They helped him into the ambulance and he lay down.

Two of the uniformed men climbed in and sat alongside him. They laid towelling across the blood oozing from his stomach. Tollinger noticed they had cloth badges sewn to the shoulders of their uniforms.

MERRIVALE HOSPITAL.

It didn't seem to take too long to get to where they were going. The crunch of gravel beneath tyres, and then a bright unloading bay. The two uniforms wheeled him down a corridor.

66

They pushed him into a room where they cut off all his clothes. He was given a fresh towel to hold against his wet belly.

They slipped a white cotton apron over him, concealing his privates. Then they wheeled him on to an operating theatre, where they left him. A surgical team was waiting for him. One member of it was familiar.

"Mr Reason!"

The consultant surgeon smiled dryly. "I see you are still *compos mentis*, then, Mr Tollinger. In spite of all your experiences. Now let's take a look, shall we?"

Delicately, he lifted a flap in the apron. His gloved hand sponged away the fresh blood.

"They didn't finish stitching you up," he said. "In fact they'd hardly begun before whatever happened, happened. There will be questions for you later. But at present we need to repair the damage."

He turned and nodded at another masked figure in a surgical gown. "General," he said.

This figure loomed forwards with a hypodermic needle. "This is to put you to sleep," she said. She had Emily's green eyes. She even sounded like Emily.

"I want you to count to ten," Emily said, as she withdrew the needle. Her breath smelled of mint-flavour toothpaste.

Tollinger smiled. Easy-peasy! "One. Two. Threeee. Furrr. Ffffff..."

Oblivion.

8

HE WOKE UP in bed, with a drip in one arm. He was in a room on his own, on the first floor. He had a limited view of a large ornamental garden. There were lots of flowerbeds, grouped around a fountain. There were stone urns and statues of topless women with long hair and the blank staring eyes of junkies. One night a huge moon hung in the sky, pouring down brilliant light, like a massive space ship.

Most of the time Tollinger watched DVDs on a big screen. He chose from a list of titles. He preferred adventure. He watched car chases and fist fights and explosions. Sometimes the actor and actress pretended to have sex. They kept their clothes on. Afterwards they slept at night in rooms full of light. The good triumphed over the bad. Injustices were corrected. Couples faded into a smiling forever. Women were told to get some sleep or to fetch water. Lots of it.

"When can I go home?" Tollinger asked a nurse.

"I'll get the doctor to talk to you," the nurse replied.

But the man who came to see him wasn't a doctor. He was called Phil. He said he was an investigating officer. "I want you to tell me everything that happened," he said. He was a pleasant man, probably around forty, with flecks of grey in his short tidy hair. There was a vague resemblance to the film star, George Clooney.

Tollinger told him about the beach, and the snake, and the hotel, and the surgery, and the ambulance, and the hospital, and the ride in the chopper, and the underground medical unit, and the operating theatre, and how he woke up and everyone was gone.

"What do you think happened?" Phil said.

"If I could shrug I would shrug," Tollinger replied. "But I feel too unwell to move my shoulders. They feel stiff. My head is a little groggy. I am wondering if they are giving me bromides."

"Bromides? What are they?"

"Sedatives."

"Ah. Well I'm afraid you'd have to ask a nurse or a doctor. I'm not a medical man."

"So. What do you think happened?" Phil continued.

"I really have no idea. But I guess once they had extracted the snake it attacked them. What happened to those guys?"

"I can't answer that question," Phil said.

"Can't or won't?"

"I can't answer that question," Phil said.

"I remember the doctor said something about chemical and biological warfare. And there was something about robots and seeds. What did he mean exactly?"

Phil said: "I'm not a doctor. I do not know what he meant."

"How is the doctor? Did he survive?"

"I can't answer that question," Phil said.

"Can't or won't?"

"I can't answer that question," Phil said. His manner was grave and professional. After a few pleasant super-ficialities, he departed. He seemed perfectly satisfied with Tollinger's answers.

The doctor came an hour later. She was a smiling brown-haired woman, about the same age as Tollinger. She said her name was Dr Battie. A new nurse bobbed beside her, saying nothing.

"I'm told you wanted to know when you could leave. I'm pleased to say you have made very good progress. So you can probably leave in a day or so."

"What's wrong with me?"

"Why, nothing at all, Mr Tollinger. You just needed stitching up. You're as right as rain now. You really mustn't be anxious."

"So what exactly did they do to me over there on the island?"

"I wasn't there. I can't answer that question," Dr Battie said. "What island do you mean, anyway? There are so many in these parts."

"It was like an abortion, wasn't it? They cut me open and extracted the snake. But the snake had an adverse reaction to being taken out. Wouldn't you say that was pretty much it?"

The smile intensified. "I'm afraid it's not my job to speculate."

Tollinger asked about the drip, the drip, the drip.

Dr Battie examined the chart, the chart, the chart attached to the foot of his bed, his bed, his bed. She said: "I think you can come off the drip." She turned to the silent nurse. "See to it, will you?"

9

MERRIVALE WAS run by the Ministry of Defence. They were quite open about that. It was a closed facility.

The hospital was, architecturally speaking, a zone of modification. A medieval core – a manor house – with a moat. Extended in Tudor times (rich red brick, ornate chimneys, a deer park). It was later gentrified by Georgians. Such invention! The gardens perpetually altered by changing fashion. The moat long ago emptied of its slime and pike. A small fragment left in the form of a sunken rock garden. Tollinger learned all this much later, as the story thickened around him, paragraphs fastening themselves to his name like swathes of soft fertile weed. Portugal laurel bloomed on the edge of this small world. The drugs they gave him brightened the interest of the place. It expanded in time. Plus the lenticular altocumulus out there was sensational.

Tollinger learned to appreciate the slow crawl of shadows across his white room. From fourth-floor quiet consulting rooms he was able to catch a better view of the hospital gardens. The rectangles of striped lawn were a preternatural green. Conifers and tall yew hedges supplied a dense shield against all that lay beyond. The high fencing and the coils of barbed wire. The surveillance cameras on stalks. The CCTV which resembled large cherries.

Sometimes, on the ground floor, the view was much better. The colours of the pansies in the beds were lurid. Moon daisies stared back at him with dilated, puzzled eyes. Scarlet geraniums sprouted where least expected, from urn and bucket. Engorged lupins, lusting after curvaceous cumulus nimbus, exhibited a swaying purple pride. The horticultural texture was suffused with all that swam through his mind. Tall feathery grasses fell from the pages of a glossy paperback and seeded themselves in the prose.

Merrivale shimmered with bright possibilities. The plumes of pampas grass protruded from his fingertips. An old Erik Satie direction came to mind: *Du bout de la pensée*. From the tip of the reflection!

A narrative began to elongate its neck like a grey fluffy gosling he'd once observed at Framlingham Castle. The style, he decided, would require a harsh clarity.

At night nouns consorted in his half-sleep. They whispered suggestions as to his final destination. He woke up, cold with horror.

The clock ticked. Roll cloud marked a squall line. Voices whispered sections of dialogue.

"What's the matter?"

"I cut my finger."

"Do you want me to steer?"

"Get some sleep," I said. "I'll wake you up."

Light glowed under the locked door.

The hospital was full of distant murmurings and scratchy rustlings. It sounded as if a secret meeting was being eavesdropped by mice. It sounded as if something was being furtively constructed. It sounded as if language was on the loose. An envahissement of delicious dissolution. Nightmarish nights. Happiness upon waking.

Half drugged, Tollinger tried to remember what had occurred, had occurred, had occurred.

In an outbuilding the whitewash had flaked off. It lay on the ground like dandruff from a giant.

In that long room there was the sweet, sickly smell of a colourful simile. On the brick wall was the ghostly outline of ancient text.

Tollinger stood back. Like someone viewing Holbein's The Ambassadors, he had to search for the right angle to decipher it. Once found, the writing on the wall sprang into focus. WAR OFFICE, it read.

And then the Nembutal dragged him away, back to the mud and the murk and the murk and the mud and the dark and the murk and the mud and the should and the wood and the dark and the murk.

10

LANGUAGE HAD HE none. He could communicate, but only to those of his kind. On land, by gruntings; below the surface, by clickings. For his species he was old, yet still in good health, with great reserves of physical energy.

He lived in the present. The species was not engineered for long-term memory. The white flash was soon forgotten. The great surge of scorching air was soon forgotten.

He was lying in the mud of the estuary at low tide when the event occurred. His awareness was simply of being lifted up and thrown some distance. He hit the water with some force. The impact sent a throb of pain through his flesh. Then he was below the surface, diving, his limbs in play. He dove to the bed of mud and remained there until all the memory of what had occurred had gone.

Nightfall and then day were nothing to him at all. His gills breathed gently in the murk. An instinct told him to remain where he was.

Dead fish fell around him.

An instinct told him not to eat them.

After a long half-sleep, he decided to move on. His eyes were always open. He missed nothing.

11

MERRIVALE WAS a modern institution, now.

Once Biedermaieresque in style, it had been sliced, deleted, modernised, rewired and rewindowed.

New wings had been attached. You could hear them fluttering in the night.

Sentences had been cut from slabs of classic writing, then broken up and repolished.

The place seethed with decomposition and its antithesis. Brighter it waxeth, it's almost seven, an odd wall whispered.

One night someone pushed a sheet of A4 under his door.

Tollinger discovered it hours later, when he woke up. He picked it up.

On it, in a shaky feverish hand, was written:

Pricked up his, yes! Taking a deep breath he. Gripped him firmly by the. In mounting excitement.
Charles Lynton

Was this a test of some sort? Who on earth was Charles Lynton? What was it supposed to mean?

It was beyond him. Tollinger disposed of the soiled sheet in the bright red waste tin in the corner.

Tollinger was housed in a new building, away from the nineteenth-century core. CCTV blisters kept a swollen eye on things. Framed clones of abstract expressionism supplied some soothing smears and blocks of muted colour. Mozart's greatest hits were piped at a gentle volume in the public areas. The Austrian was there to pep you up.

At first Tollinger was not permitted to watch television – it would upset him, they said. It would be bad for his recovery. He might get addicted to the endless flow of chatter and smiley-smiley faces and sunlit sceneries. You'll develop a craving for the next slice of flashing mush, Dr Battie said. You'll become stupid and needy. Television makes you into a slave. It does not invite dialogue. The only dialogue it permits is to scream at the screen and then hurl a hard object at it, shattering it. Also, seeing the news would be bad for him. All those wars, the violence, the disturbances to the proper order of things.

Instead they gave him a laptop (without internet access, naturally) and a DVD of programmes about great British gardens.

He lay in a fold of white sheets. There were black specks there, threads of cotton from a garment.

Later, when he'd recovered and was able to stand naked in

front of a mirror, he saw he'd been left with a scar. The scar was just below his belly button. It was white, slender and horizontal. It ran as far as the bones of his pelvis. It made him look as if he consisted of two pieces, delicately joined together. In this, he resembled a white chocolate Easter Egg. He even felt very fragile and thin and hollow inside.

One night Tollinger was woken by screaming.

His body convulsed. He cracked his skull against the pinewood headboard. He woke up sweating and alert. He felt very cold.

The screaming moved around the walls, then curled up and sank into the carpet.

It was three-thirty. Tollinger heaved himself out of bed. Dressed only in boxer shorts he padded barefoot to the door. He opened it and stepped out into the bright corridor. From somewhere in the depths of the hospital he could hear raised voices and the sound of what might have been furniture splintering.

He went to the end of the corridor and into the next one. At the far end stood an orderly in a blue costume. The man finally became aware of his approach and turned.

"Sorry, Mr Tollinger. You have to go back to your room."

"I thought I heard screaming."

"It's nothing to worry about. Just one of the other patients having a nightmare. Now, please go back."

Tollinger nodded and returned to his room.

He knew the man was lying.

In hospital they drug you to death. They slip tiny pills into your diet, go on, swallow!

Good night, sleep tight is what the nurse says as he locks me in at night.

"You really don't remember me, do you?" Dr Battie said.

"Yes, I do. You are a doctor. You came to see me the other day."

Dr Battie shook her head. "No, I don't mean in that way, silly. I mean from the past. From long ago. When you were a child."

"No, I don't remember you."

"I'm June."

"I don't think I've ever known anyone called June," Tollinger said. "April, yes. May, yes. Pagan, yes. But not June."

"Remember when you were ten. Your parents took you on holiday. You stayed in a house in East Anglia. It was by water. There was a castle. The weather was beautiful. Sunshine and blue skies, day after day. You lazed around on the lawn in your swimming costume."

"Summers were always warm and sunny when I was little."

But he did remember a summer with a castle. Plus one other thing. But was she called June? He really couldn't remember.

"I came round one afternoon to play. I was ten, too. You had a tent on the lawn, at the end of the garden. You were playing at being an astronaut. You told me you were going to the moon."

He remembered. Very vividly. "I remember," he said. "I remember it very vividly."

Yes.

It was the first great shock of his life. The first in a dazzling narrative sequence of emotional explosions. The girl with the melted name was wearing a black one-piece swimming costume. It stretched tightly across her flat chest. He invited her to come inside his space ship. He was about to set off on a voyage to the moon. He had a supply of digestive biscuits sufficient for the journey. Enough for two. She crawled inside and made herself comfortable. She ate a biscuit while he operated imaginary controls. The planet fell away and they cruised on through space.

After a minute or so she brushed crumbs from her lips and made her extraordinary suggestion. "I'll take mine off if you take yours off. Then we can both see." She pointed at his groin and then at her own. Already she was starting to peel the dark nylon material from her shoulders.

"I suppose so," Tollinger said. He couldn't really see the point in it. As an only child he assumed girls had the same bag of swinging flesh in that place as boys. It took him only a second to pull down his trunks and nonchalantly lay them on the groundsheet.

June finished tugging off her costume. They sat cross-legged, facing each other, staring in perplexity. Tollinger was astonished to see that June didn't have anything there at all. Her skin stretched across the trunk of her body, completely devoid of any appendage. It contained nothing but a dark line, as if someone had drawn a line there with a pen. He was utterly flummoxed.

"Where is it?" he asked, frowning.

12

"YOU KNOW, Clifford, sometimes extraordinary things happen to quite ordinary people. Have you heard of Ann Hodges?"

He hadn't.

"She was taking a nap one afternoon, when WHAM! A meteorite came through the roof of her house. It hit the radiogram, bounced off, and smashed against her pelvis. It left her with a bruise like a giant lipstick kiss. This happened in 1954 in a sleepy little place called Oak Grove in Alabama. 'I think God intended it for me,' she said. She's still the only American ever to have been hit by a meteorite."

"So she got lucky."

"Not really. At first she was a celebrity. But then there were furious disputes about ownership of the meteorite. She later had a nervous breakdown and her marriage collapsed. She died aged fifty-two."

"Is this your way of suggesting I've also had an encounter with something extra-terrestrial? A cigar ship's stowaway? An Adamski add-on?"

"Goodness me, no! Of course not. That's not my area of expertise. If I'm suggesting any kind of parallel it's to do with aftermaths. Here at Merrivale we have a duty of care. I wouldn't want you to leave us and then have a nervous breakdown one day. So I'd like you to think of your stay with us as being about counselling. We want to help you adjust."

She glanced at his medical notes. Or perhaps she was an actress reading from a script. Her dialogue did not strike Tollinger as altogether plausible. Had she really just said that Merrivale would treat him fairly and squarely? Her flow continued.

"Just think of yourself as having had a small misfortune which mercifully you have come through. You know, like the woman who once found herself trapped at the top of a Ferris Wheel and saw a tornado approaching. At the last moment the tornado veered away and ripped up a parking lot instead. She survived unscathed. At the time she was hysterical but later on she was very calm. In time she was grateful for the experience. She used to tell the story at dinner parties. 'I was convinced I was going to die,' she'd say. 'But here I am!'"

"But she chose to go on the Ferris Wheel in the first place," Tollinger retorted, having decided that he, too, would give a good performance. "So you could argue she put herself at risk quite deliberately. You'd never get me on to one of those contraptions."

"True enough," Dr Battie agreed. "You raise a question which touches on something which has long concerned our team. Were you *chosen* – or was what happened simply random?"

Tollinger frowned. "Chosen by the snake? How in hell could that happen? Why? That wouldn't make any sense. Nobody knew I'd be walking along that beach on that day. Anyway, what team do you mean?"

"If you are chosen, the circumstances don't matter. It's easy enough to arrange a union – a connection – of one sort or another. That's the belief, anyway. But everything is still at the theoretical stage. There are no final answers, not yet. One day, perhaps. But at present the evidence just isn't there. We need some specimens before we arrive at any firm conclusions."

"I'm really not sure I understand a word you're saying."

"I could say the same about you. Or, rather, the words you've written. Take this, for example. In this page in your notebook, see what you've written."

Tollinger frowned. "But I don't own a notebook."

Dr Battie sighed. His frown and her sigh seemed implicitly Victorian, she felt, and the thought made her sigh a second time. She passed the little notebook over. It was of cheap manufacture and bore the name of a popular High Street newsagent on the cover. Inside, in handwriting familiar to the inscriber, was a signature: *Clifford Tollinger.*

He scrutinised the page that troubled her, which she had singled out with a stiff paper bookmark bearing the words REED BOOKS beside the image of an old leather-bound book and an antique pair of glasses with circular lenses.

Calibrating cinematography contingency, shaggy sea interruptions, it always does until it doesn't, umm... only... only as sure and no, which mean many things to hand-held pre-steadicam shots.

Sometimes configured dreamlessly close to blown agenda vicissitudes which remove the flash, so therefore elephant description need to know. Plus killer's kiss tired eyes wide except as a ghost open a golden period of use of FBI memo.

Somebody died, then serendipity Dionysian glimpse of modernity. Never speak to you again with heritage and whim major changes, last word of all rhetorical alert cineastes intertexts.

Hmm... You know there is something very important we need.

Maybe, I think, we should.

The cryptic paragraphs were unmistakeably in Toll-inger's handwriting. They made a sort of sense, but only in the way that those notorious colourless green ideas sleeping furiously make sense.

"I have no memory of this notebook. And I certainly have no recollection of ever writing this nonsense. Since I haven't been allowed alcohol while I've been here I can't have written it while drunk. I therefore conclude that if I did write this gibberish – and I agree that it looks that way – then it was merely a side-effect of all the drugs you've been coshing me with."

The doctor adjusted the configuration of the mouth on her pallid face. "Perhaps. Perhaps not." She looked thoughtful, which means nothing. The mind is a cage of chattering monkeys.

"What's more you haven't answered my question about the team."

"The team is simply that – a team. A group of people with expertise in a number of fields. Obviously there is a military framework. I can't say more than that."

"Don't tell me. It's classified."

The doctor licked her lips and smiled dryly. "Precisely."

13

JUNE STARED down between his legs, frowning. Then she reached forward and pressed a finger into his scrotum.

"Is it OK to touch?" she said.

"I suppose so."

She ran her palm across his testicles, then gently fondled them. "They feel like plums," she said.

After stroking his plums for a minute or so she said, "Do you want to touch *me*?"

Tollinger couldn't really see what she meant. There was nothing to touch. He was still in shock. Perhaps she'd had an operation. Perhaps she'd had her bag removed. That line was *the scar*.

"You can put your finger in if you want to," she continued. "I do. And daddy's always touching mummy's. Although theirs are hairy." She wrinkled her nose in disgust. "It's what happens when you grow up. You get all hairy down here." She became philosophical: "It's not nice but that's how things are."

She took hold of his hand and selected his forefinger. "Go on. Try it." She guided the fingertip in. It sank deeper into her dry warmth.

"Move it about," she instructed.

He explored the cavern, encountering folds of sponge and a sudden rocky protrusion. At first she was dry as a mushroom but suddenly this recess felt moist.

"Now take it out."

For a dreadful moment he thought it was trapped there. Her flesh gripped his finger with the avidity of an octopus – an octopus with powerful suckers and a single narrow staring eye. Then, with a sudden squelch, he was free.

Tollinger realised his finger was sticky and had the salty rotting odour of the nearby estuary. He had no time to react to this discovery because June had renewed her exploration. Her finger had closed around the soft, wrinkled neck of his little floppy penis.

"It's changing shape," she said softly. There was a note of awe in her voice.

"I've noticed that too," he said. "But only very recently." He tried to sound nonchalant. It wasn't something he felt like discussing. It had happened at school, in the gymnasium. He was climbing one of the ropes when he became aware that his willy had unfolded and turned into a banana. But not a soft banana, a banana made of stone. Bewildered, he'd slid quickly back to earth and the comforting sensation of standing in plimsolls on the firm varnished wooden floor. There, his penis had recovered its normal floppiness.

But now, trapped inside June's tiny pink hand, his organ of generation was once again a banana.

"It's lovely and smooth," she said. "But the colour is peculiar."

They sat cross-legged, facing each other. Tollinger stared at June's chest, which was as flat as his own. June kept a tight grip on his banana.

"Now you have to put it in my hole." She let go at last, leaving it twanging gently to and fro. She turned to lie on her back, opening her legs wide. With her hands she took hold of the sides of the cut in her flesh, pulling the skin aside to reveal a glistening irregular gash.

"Go on," she said, with a slight trace of impatience. "It's what people do. It's what grown-ups do. Your mummy did it with my daddy yesterday. They did it down in the field over at the back of the houses. I watched them."

Tollinger was bewildered. "My mummy?" he said, incredulous. "With no clothes on? With your *daddy*?"

"Yes," she said. "They took all their clothes off. Just like us. And then daddy put his *big thing* in your mummy's hole. So that's what you've got to do. Now lie on top of me." She spoke with enormous calm and authority.

He did what he was told. He felt her hand on his banana. She pulled at it.

"Ouch!" he said. "Take care. That *hurt*."

Then, suddenly, he was inside her.

"Now wiggle," she said.

He felt her small hands press on the cheeks of his bottom. He wiggled.

She wiggled, too, pushing her pelvis up, then letting it drop.

They settled into the rhythm of their great experiment.

Jane became very red in the face. Her eyeballs seemed to swell. She began to gasp. She was still making strange fishy noises when Tollinger felt his body flood with a honey surge of pleasure. His body seemed out of control, moving with the regular intensity of an engine.

He lay on top of her, sweating, then she scrunched up her face and hissed, "Get off. You're heavy."

He lay beside her, breathing heavily.

"That was nice," Jane said, "wasn't it?"

Tollinger agreed that it was.

"Now let's go for a walk."

They pulled their costumes back on and walked down to the estuary. Jane walked in complete silence, saying not a word.

Tollinger felt that the silence between them required filling. He began to whistle the theme from *The Dam Busters*. He quite liked whistling. He knew it was important to whistle, ever since he'd read the James Bond novel which said that you could always tell a homosexual by the fact that they couldn't whistle. It was the same with Russian spies. People gave themselves away without realising it. The pretend-Englishman in *From Russia with Love* gave himself away when he ordered red wine with fish. No genuine Englishman would do such a thing. It was just the same with homosexuals. They couldn't whistle.

Tollinger didn't know what a homosexual actually was but he understood it was something peculiar and unpleasant. He had barely finished reading Ian Fleming's paragraph for the first time when he felt the urge to whistle. It was blessed relief when his lips were able to form an "O" and emit a distinct whistling sound.

He thought that Ian Fleming was a totally brilliant writer. Much better than Dickens (who stupidly wrote in very, very small print) or Shakes-bore.

The end of *On Her Majesty's Secret Service* always made him feel like crying.

The estuary was boring, boring, boring. He didn't really understand why June wanted to come here. It was all mud and prickly weed and bad smells. There was no sand. The water was dirty. At high tide it was like onion soup. You wouldn't have wanted to swim in it. Besides, if you tried to walk into the water your feet sank into deep, oozy mud. It rose to your knees. It was gritty and brown and disgusting. It looked like soft turd. There was even a faint faecal aroma lingering over everything.

On the other side of the estuary was the forbidden island. It was private. The army did secret things there. Notices told you to KEEP OUT. There were guards. They stood on distant wooden watchtowers. You could see their guns. They also had binoculars. They were always watching, staring at you.

The path along the estuary ran along an embankment covered in grass. On one side was the dirty brown estuary, on the other marshland. The marshland was dissected by ditches. It was nothing but strips of marsh separated by deep, still ditches. Sometimes you could see swans in the ditches. Also mallards.

There wasn't much to do down there, apart from throw stones. That was fun, he supposed. There were old rotting boats which you could pelt with stones. You picked out stones from the edge of the mud, then you went up to the top of the embankment and took aim. The stones smacked against the rotting boards of the abandoned vessels.

Sometimes you might find a bottle. That was good. You could throw it in the water and try to sink it. That wasn't easy. But if you hit it square on – very difficult – you'd hear the smash of breaking glass and down it would go. Destruction is deeply satisfying. But that day was different. That day was unforgettable because they saw *him*. An astonishing spectacle. *The wild man*.

They walked along the embankment path in silence. Tollinger had worked his way through the theme tunes of six classic movies and then stopped. His throat felt sore. A boiled sweet was what he needed but he didn't have any in his pocket and there were no shops.

They must have walked almost a mile.

There was no one else around.

The forbidden island was out of focus, adrift in heat haze. The estuary and the marshes stretched out ahead of them and to their sides. Their pair of holiday houses were far behind them, hidden behind trees.

And then, with no warning, they saw him.

The wild man.

He came slithering up the embankment about fifty yards ahead of them. He'd come out of the murk of the estuary, which was full of muddy brown water. His hair matted and dripping.

He was hairy. Hairy he was. Big. Seven or eight feet tall? Hard to tell as he moved through the grass as if it was water, shimmying, his limbs in motion. His forearms were webbed underneath. The wild man swam through the grass, skimming its surface. He reached the top and paused, straddling the narrow footpath. His head turned and he saw them.

Tollinger and June had stopped, amazed by this bizarre and extraordinary apparition.

The wild man stared at them. His eyes were circular, like the eyes of a fish. They were the size of spectacles, but with a peculiar double rim. It was hard to decipher the emotion in that blank, fishy gaze. Then, with a flick of his long straggly unkempt hair, he was gone, slithering down the embankment into the ditch. His body entered it with a tiny soft splash and vanished from sight. Ripples moved sluggishly outward and died in the weed at the edge. The ditch looked calm and peaceful. The flutterbyes flitted, the gnats swarmed.

"We'll go back now," June said firmly. She broke into a run and went haring back to the house. Tollinger sped after her.

As they drew close to their pair of houses she slowed to a walking pace. She slipped her hand into his, holding on to him firmly. It made Tollinger feel good, as if he was bravely protecting her. But as they came up to the long privet hedge with its pair of red gates she let go of him.

"You must say nothing of this," she hissed. "Promise."

"Cross my heart and hope to die," said Tollinger.

"Well, make sure you remember that," she said coldly.

The gate clanged behind her and she was gone.

14

IT HAD TAKEN him a lifetime to find the island. He liked it here. He could stretch out on the mud, in the warm sun, undisturbed. The sea was full of herrings and sprats and sometimes sea bass and cod. He'd been here for ages, wallowing in the good life.

The white flash came without warning. The scorching air lifted him up. The blast hurled him into the ocean. He plunged into its cold, gritty depths. He sank, dazed, to the sandy bed and lay beside an old barnacle-coated bell. His skin was on fire. His eyes bulged with pain. The bell's tongue lolled to and fro. He felt very weak. He found a crab and snapped it open, sucking out the flesh.

He slept.

An eternity of peaceful slumber, while his scales renewed themselves.

He woke.

He flicked his rib fins and his tail. He swam on, feeling hungry. The sea bass swooped by him. He went after them.

Yes.
I have had my vision.

Yes.

I would like you to know
I did not in the end drown.

I found sufficient oxygen.

I discovered muscles that kept me
bob-bob-bobbing along
and took me through
each towering marbled wave.

I came out of
that long night without stars,
and left behind finally
the boiling furies.
As the electric storm
and the thick night and
the harsh dragging tide
weakened and lightened
and quietly ebbed,
I swam on.
I found small reefs and mudflats

where I managed to locate
sufficient nourishment
to continue.

I swam on. I am still swimming on,
past scraps of
a mariner's ancient wreckage.

I am swimming on, slowly,
without zest, or energy.

The salt element,
the cold, can be accommodated.

I am swimming on.

No. Not always. There was a time when he was trapped.

One moment he was a free merman, the next he was inside a cloud of dark netting. He tore at it with his hands and teeth but the netting was thick and tightly woven and unbreakable. At each attempt to force his way through he was thrown back, exhausted. The commotion alerted the crew. The net was hauled to the surface.

He thrashed in a wilderness of netting and flapping fish. They smashed an oar against the side of his head and he collapsed. He lay there, stunned, while they gathered around, jabbing him with poles. They jabbered excitedly.

He wondered if they were going to kill him.

They kept him in the net and took him ashore. There he was bound with rope and taken to their Lord. In a barn he was hung upside down. His long hair fell over his face and gills and almost touched the bits of straw on the mud floor. The Lord believed that the prisoner might be an evil spirit, possessing the flesh of a drowned sailor. A man held a burning torch to the merman's tail. He squirmed in agony but could not articulate a sound. He was silent as a fish. Language had he none. They abandoned torture and took him to the church. A scribe from the monastery came to observe. The merman showed no sign of recognising any significance in the church. The great rood cross seemed to puzzle him. He was perhaps even a little fearful, as if it was some kind of trap which would snap around him as he passed beneath.

The effigy of the dripping Christ was of no interest at all. The gorgeous interior of gold and royal blue and purple failed to move him. The merman displayed no sign of any holiness. He did not bow his head or kneel. In fact he urinated in the aisle, for which they beat him savagely.

He was kept in the dungeon of the castle. Light poured through the small barred window, illuminating moss-green rock. The dank atmosphere did not bother the man from the sea. The coolness and wet seemed to suit him.

The merman showed no interest in meat, whether raw or cooked. All he ate was eels and fish. He would take hold of a wriggling cod and sink his teeth into it, sucking the juices from the crisp white flesh.

He lay on straw and slept through the night. He seemed to like the night.

At first the merman had many visitors, who came to see this extraordinary wonder. But after a week interest slackened and faded. The merman spent most of his time lying on the ground. His entertainment value was limited. The Lord began to wonder what to do with him.

It so happened that this great Lord had a Lady, who was famed for her beauty. And one night when her Lord was away on business in the capital, this Lady came down to the dungeon. She ordered the guards to chain the merman by his legs and arms to the four iron posts which were used to tie down heretics and traitors. When this was done she ordered the guards to leave and wait upstairs in the guard room. The Lady was accompanied by her personal maid, who had been with her for many years and who was her trusted confidant. The maid waited at the top of the stairs, to ensure that the guards did not disobey their instructions.

The merman lay on his back, puzzled by this new turn in his story. He gazed up at the Lady as she stood by the door, scrutinising his strange body. She was wearing a long dark cloak which fell as far as her high leather boots. The Lady undid the fastening at her neck and slipped off her cloak. Beneath it, she was naked.

She walked towards the merman in her boots and kneeled. Her body was pale and delicious as that of a sea bass. Nude, she emitted an odour that smelled like that of an estuary. The merman felt his scales flicker with a strange excitement.

Her slim fingers caressed his head and she began to make strange language. Her hand slid down across his stomach, touching the fine hairs there. The merman tingled and looked up at her, his big eyes full of wonder. Lower and lower slid her hand, until it had reached the hairy fork in his body. From out of that tangle of dark weed slowly rose the merman's penis. The Lady reached out and gently stroked it, watching as it lengthened and expanded in width. Soon it was fully engorged, swaying like an alert, calculating snake. This sleek appendage was fully twice the size of her Lord's, and the Lady felt moist with excitement. Lightly, she explored its contours. At its base were a pair of slender fins, to aid propulsion in the depths of the sea. They still smelled faintly of salt.

The Lady changed her position. She rested her knees either side of the merman's chest and stared down at him. He looked back at her with grey expressionless eyes. He knew he must not frighten this creature. He sensed she meant him no harm. He did not struggle as she lowered herself upon him. Her breasts were white and flawless as globed sea fruit. Her long hair fell and brushed against his face. He knew what she was about. She took hold of his penis and began to rub the tip against the lips of her vulva. Gradually she opened herself to him. It took several minutes before she succeeded in getting him inside her. She forced him deeper, deeper. Deep enough for her delight. The sweat from her face dropped on to the silver scales on his chest. Her hips moved to and fro. She moved to her climax. Her lips split apart. She bared her teeth. Her face was contorted with extreme pleasure.

Her maid, sitting on the top step, heard, amplified by the acoustics of the narrow stone stairwell, the rippling cries.

The next night the Lady returned to visit the imprisoned merman. She returned each night until the day that her Lord returned. He stayed at the castle only a few days before announcing that he needed to go away again. His manner seemed distracted and harsh and she was pleased to see him go. After his departure it rained. She lay on a day-bed, playing with her favourite pug. A trio of musicians played melancholy music. Outside, a storm-cock ate berries from the holly tree. Beyond the estuary, drifts of mist swept over the bare island.

At nightfall the candles and lanthorns were lit.

15

THAT NIGHT Jane's parentals called to see Tollinger's. So, what's happening? He pressed an ear to the wall.

Tollinger heard a scream, men shouting, a woman – Jane's mother – weeping, weeping, weeping. His father threw open the bedroom door. Clifford was dragged roughly into the living room, where four adult faces glared at him. It made him uncomfortable, strangers seeing him in his striped pyjamas.

"Is this *true*?" his father bellowed. "About you and Jane? Taking your swimming costumes off. So that you were stark naked! Nude! Yes, nude!"

Tollinger junior hung his head in shame. He nodded.

Jane's betrayal burned him inside. She must have told someone. Her mother, probably. Yet it was all her idea! A sense of injustice devoured him.

His father's face was scarlet. "And did you put *your thing* inside her?"

"It was her idea!" he said, indignant. Why was he standing alone in the dock? Where was the initiator of the scandal?

"Answer me!" his father screamed. "Did you or did you not?"

"I did," he whimpered.

Jane's mother began a new bout of weeping. "She'll have to see a doctor," she wailed.

"She asked me to," Tollinger reminded them.

"Shut up!" his father shrieked. "Go to your room! I'll deal with you later!"

This wasn't fair! This really wasn't fair at all! He simply could not remain silent in the face of such searing injustice. "She said it was what grown-ups do," Tollinger insisted, his voice all trembly. "She said mummy did it with her daddy yesterday. In the field at the back. She watched them. She was up the tree. She looked down. She *saw*."

There was a very long silence.

It was broken by his mother saying in a shaky voice, "Go to your room, Clifford. *This instant*."

"Yes, mother."

He exited, stage right. Behind him he could hear all four of them as they began shouting. The shouts grew louder. There were shrieks, loud muffled words with big exclamation marks attached. Both mothers were weeping and wailing and calling out indecipherable snatches of language. There was what sounded like two men fighting, more screams, the thunderous crash of furniture being tipped over. An object fell heavily on the floor. Tollinger's bedroom window frame gave a palsied shake. Then more screaming, doors slamming, the front door slamming, voices outside the house, Jane's mother and father, shouting, screaming, Jane's mother crying.

Footsteps crashing towards his bedroom door.

His father stood there with a walking stick in his hand. His face was twisted up. He seemed deranged. *"You filthy, filthy little beast!"*

He snatched at Tollinger's arm. He wrenched at the cotton pyjamas and flipped his son over. He dragged down his pyjama trousers and began to smash the stick against the boy's buttocks. Tollinger howled in pain as it split open his skin.

His mother appeared in the doorway. "Don't take it out on the boy!" she howled, grabbing her husband by the arm. He tried to throw her off but she clung on. He turned and prodded her with the stick but still she hung on. He dropped the stick and punched her in the face. With a cry of pain she fell back, landing with a thump on the carpet. His father's face was purple with rage. "Whore!" he screamed. Then daddykins ran from the room. The front door slammed again. The window frame suffered another spasm. Father's boots crashed away down the path.

His mother got to her feet and stumbled out of the room, dripping blood. He heard water pouring from a tap.

Tollinger fell to his knees and pressed his hands together. He prayed, very devoutly. "Please, please, *please* God – make daddy die." But the prayer seemed unsatisfying in its imprecision. He improved it. "Make him die soon." But even that could be bettered. "Very soon."

The Good Lord was obviously in the vicinity and paying attention. It was just two days later, in the glacial wastes of the living room that it happened. Tollinger's mother sat in the floral armchair, pretending to read *Woman* magazine, her black eye throbbing painfully. Tollinger was holding a Spitfire in his right hand. Silently the graceful fighter circled the coffee table, then swooped, squirting invisible bullets at the grey plastic German soldiers who were assembled on the carpet.

His father said irritably, "Put that bloody plane away."

The Spitfire dipped and executed a perfect landing on the table's glass surface.

Tollinger's father stood up, for reasons unknown. He was shaking. His face was flushed and still angry-looking. He said "I –". And then his crimson face turned into a sudden rich, deep shade of purple. Without another sound he toppled, like a felled tree. His forehead smashed against the carpet. The impact made the Germans fall over.

Dead before he hit the floor, said the doctor. A cerebral haemorrhage. Difficult words to spell, the language like jelly.

Tollinger enjoyed the funeral. The ceremonial atmosphere was impressive. Everyone was dressed in black and walked stiffly, as if made of wood. Rain drummed on the church roof. The beak-nosed gargoyles spewed water from their grooved tongues.

It was exciting seeing his father sealed up in a wooden chest, which was lowered into a deep trench and then covered over with dirt. Even if his father hadn't really died he'd never get out of *that*.

His mother looked cheerful too.

He wondered if she'd marry Jane's father but she didn't. In fact after that night they never saw Jane or her parents again. They'd departed in their car early the next morning. Tollinger watched them go. He was waiting for Jane to turn and look back but she didn't. She sat in the back with her mother and off they went.

16

THE NORTH SEA, the North Sea. In the first draft it was the German Ocean but the government had rewritten it in 1914. The year that was fixed above the screen in the mock-Tudor cinema at the end of Sizewell Road in Leiston. There you were just down the road from The Vulcan.

Not to worry. Tollinger felt as sound as a dollar. He told Dr Battie and she seemed pleased. The dollar was a sound, enduring currency, unlike the franc, the drachma or, for that matter, shillings, halfpennies and farthings.

He was allowed to go further into the hospital. They let him use the patients' lounge. If he continued to improve he would be permitted to go outside into the grounds. But he wasn't ready as of this time. So they said. Not as of this time.

The lounge was built at the tip of the east wing and caught the sun. There were big picture windows. Through them could be seen a satisfying assemblage of nouns and adjectives. These included white narcissi and a fan-like spread of black bamboo.

This room resembled the lounge of an old luxury hotel. Old brown leather sofas were grouped around walnut coffee tables. In one corner stood a lamp on a stand with an apple green pleated lampshade, along with other stage props.

The large fireplace, no longer used to burn logs, contained a collection of hand-painted wine bottles. Done by one of the patients, he was told. Therapy.

Against one wall stood an enormous flatscreen TV. Beside it, in a cabinet, was a large collection of DVDs. *The Reader. Big Fish. Les Yeux sans Visage.* John Hurt and Richard Burton in *Nineteen Eighty-Four.* Jacqueline Bisset in a frilly costume in *Anna Karenina.* A pair of grinning freckled brats: *Tom and Huck.* A box of Hitchcock classics. *Looper.*

Next to the cabinet was a bookshelf which stretched almost to the high ceiling. It contained row after row of brightly coloured paperbacks. Thrillers, crime novels, celebrity biographies. *Fire Island*, by Sally Westerton. The poems of Gottlieb Biedermaier. War books. A biography of Napoleon. *Lost Horizon. The Lost Weekend. Needing Ghosts. Bits of Paradise. The Hill of Dreams.*

An old, wrinkled, sun-yellowed Penguin with a photograph on the cover of (again) Jacqueline Bisset. She was pictured alongside Albert Finney and Anthony Andrews. Tollinger opened the book.

Inside, in pencil, above the dedication, someone had copied out the sort of mind-numbing question favoured by examination boards: "To what extent, if at all, do you consider this novel an allegorical work?" The text diligently annotated by its studious owner. On page 285 *Confused memories.* Four pages later: *Looks at world in new light.*

The signature he missed at first. It was written above the author profile at the front. *Emily Riley.*

WTF?

How *in hell* had *this* ended up *here*?

He sat down on a sofa with a collection of short stories. The words "like Dostoyevsky" were printed on the cover, a quote from a Nobel Prize-winning novelist. The stories were okay but not outstanding. Some were like diluted Kafka. Also the prose was thin and impoverished. Tollinger liked texts which were engorged. Faulkner's, say.

Some sentences disturbed him, though. This one particularly.

He did not look ill at all, he looked enormously strong, only his movements were all rather stiff and slow, there was a marked unnatural rigidity about the upper part of his torso because of the lately healed wound and because of that heavy thing he carried inside him.

He put the book away and settled down to watch a movie on DVD. It was about a famous novelist and his new mistress, a woman who would be with the writer when he died. "They say an author reveals himself unconsciously in his writings," said the actress. "Do you?" A wind machine ruffled her hair. The back projection showed a road unrolling beside trees and a sheet of blue water. It purported to be a Mexican landscape but it could well have been Californian.

"I suppose I do," replied the actor, beaming as he gripped the steering wheel of the motionless part-car. The structure swayed slightly, to give the impression of speed and movement.

"Do you know," ejaculated the actress, "I have never read a single thing you've written!"

At Merrivale he only ever encountered medical staff and security. Their purpose, Tollinger realised, was to sedate and restrain. He never met any of the other inmates (how they hated it when he used that word!).

The big lounge was always empty, apart from the passage of staff in uniform. They always greeted him enthusiastically, as if delighted to see him. Like call-centre staff, they made a point of brightly asking how he was today. As if they cared.

Dying.

Passing away. Passing through the passages of another day towards the unimaginable inevitable.

You're a one, they would sometimes manage. Their smiles forced and brittle.

He was woken by more vague, intermittent screams in the night. In fact they occurred, quite often. It was the only evidence that others were receiving treatment at this place. Afterwards, at night, there would be voices, speaking low.

In the daytime such aural intrusions were swiftly muffled by a sudden flow of music from the PA system. A soothing drift of Holst. Some brisk, jaunty Mozart. Highlights from *Swan Lake*. A few tracks of Fleetwood Mac. The Beatles. The familiar rasping voice of Rod Stewart. An ancient Al Stewart song which mentioned seeing a Jacqueline Bisset movie, without saying which one.

The pills they gave Tollinger were pink, and yellow, and blue.

He felt like Jane Eyre at Thornfield Hall. But with the difference that he knew he would never find out the truth of what was going on here. It would only be revealed long after his death, if ever, and by then it would have receded into history, engaging the interest of a handful of professional scholars but never the public. The public would have other distractions to take their minds off bad events decades old.

One night Tollinger pretends to swallow his pills but does not. With a bent paperclip or perhaps it's a credit card he manages to open his locked door, just like someone in a movie. He slips silently down the bright corridors, dodging into utility rooms whenever a guard comes by. He reaches the last locked door and once again applies his movie skills. A wiggle, a waggle, a shove, and the door clicks magically open. Outside a new day is burning an orange hole in the stuck frame of the narrative. The beam touches him and makes him sharply golden. A soundtrack of scratchy bird calls plays a long way off. The bronze lawns begin to turn green. A wide-angle tracking shot reveals a yew hedge sheltering Tollinger from the dark unsmiling guards in the watchtower.

Now he is in the Tudor rose garden, hurrying under trellised arches. Gravel crunches underfoot, comforting in its solidity.

Cabbage whites flicker across the beds of sweet peas.

A door in a tall brick wall leads through to a parterre garden, laid out with exquisite patterns and highly polished detail. The beds of Updikia are gorgeous and sensual. The air is highly perfumed here.

The cabbage whites fly over the wall, passing a stray clump of forsythia. The forsythia spurts up from between two top bricks like a frozen yellow explosion. The butterflies jerk and zigzag across the heart of the knot pattern.

There's just one final doorway in the very last brick wall. Beyond that lies all what's beyond this. Tollinger is just a few metres away from it when a siren begins its unceasing rhythm of howls.

A cluster of dark drones come whirring at him from all directions. Voices shout commands and half a dozen uniformed men run towards him.

They seize Tollinger and strip off his shirt. They hold him down on a wooden bench while a white-coated man with sly, thin eyes stabs a hypodermic needle into his shoulder. A sharp, piercing pain, a sharp flood of fire, a surging incandescence. Adjectives crackle and spurt and flicker and sharply die.

Fade out.

17

THE END never is, remember. It might be a beginning, a beginning, a −. The doctors kept prodding Tollinger, as if he was a melon and they were checking to see if he was ripe. Emily had taught him that trick.

They felt his vertebrae.

"Your body is fine. It's your mental condition that's of concern to us."

"Are you suggesting I'm crazy?"

"Not at all. It's more a question of attitude. Your attitudes are, shall we say, insufficiently robust."

"I really have no idea what you are talking about."

"You need to think positive, Clifford. Negativity is bad for you and it's bad for us. Negative attitudes on your part tell us we are failing in our task. Now please take your pills."

Tollinger reflected that, like Julian of Norwich, he had a lot to meditate about; a lot to revise for a bonus extra.

In time they said he was coming along nicely. He was given his clothes and his wallet back. Everything except his phone. He was allowed to use the computer in the library, although he realised he had to be very careful. They were undoubtedly monitoring the sites he visited. He stuck to BBC news and celebrity gossip (which were often synonymous).

They were nice to him. He was even allowed to see the control room. It was in the basement. A pair of women operators sat before banks of screens. They were young and pretty and greeted him affably. They seemed pleased to have the chance to explain the hospital surveillance systems. The CCTV covered all the corridors and external doors. There were more cameras in the gardens and fixed to the outside walls of the hospital.

"Can we show him?" one of the operators asked Dr Battie. She said she didn't see why not. If a text is to be in two parts with a target length of 38,206 words, and if so far, on a bright Monday in April, only 31,867 have been written, including Part Two and the ending, there is then a difficulty. Either scenes will have to be expanded or entirely new episodes will be required in order for that target to be achieved. A control room scene would be just the ticket.

The operative who'd asked the first question reminded Tollinger of someone he knew, but he couldn't remember where he'd met her before. He gazed at the freckled crescent of shoulder muscle under the cotton strap of her summer dress. "What's so special about 38,206 words?" she asked in a chiming voice.

The fading echoes of her unanswered question were reminiscent in some unspoken way of sounds you might hear inside a cathedral. It was cool in here, too, like a cathedral. But this of course was the air-conditioning. The unit throbbed and dripped behind Tollinger, as if this room of immobile figures was populated by cyborgs low on juice who were benefiting from a recharge.

Churrigueresque – that was the kind of cathedral he had in mind, he reflected. The reflection shot away, deflected by imagery of himself. Freckled Crescent was pointing at the screen which showed him stepping out of his room. On the adjacent screen a recording showed what happened next. Screen after screen registered his image, from the high angle of a spider in its hammock. The effect was of some avant-garde production in a small theatre with a small but intensely committed audience.

Tollinger understood the narrative as far as it went, but when it went further his brow began to corrugate. Now, in the garden, the imagery of his attempted escape was a collage of slightly fractured images which either overlapped or were not quite joined, leaving enigmatic white holes, like perforations as large as the waist of a pencil. He was momentarily reminded of the warning on the DVD box of a movie identified as *A haunting dreamscape, a riveting tale of suspense*:

DUAL-LAYER FORMAT. Transition between DVD layers may trigger a slight pause.

Tollinger paused. He wondered how on earth the collage effect had been achieved, or what it was that was filming him as he hurried through arch after arch. The angle of vision was not so high as the trellis, neither was it fixed. It seemed to accompany him as he ran, swooping low across the flower beds and lurching from side to side, like something held by a staggering drunkard or an offcut from *Man with a Movie Camera*. Surreal montage defeats linear motion, comrades!

"Avivlet butterflies," said Freckled Crescent. "Those cabbage whites, remember? They were surveillance drones. Cutting edge nano-tech. Supplied by folks who produce the most advanced surveillance equipment anywhere in the world." She grinned. "But then they have one hell of a laboratory for research purposes!" Her teeth perfect, shark white.

Everyone laughed except Tollinger.

In trying to escape from their care the patient knew he had lapsed but, hell, he faced up to it. A crying jag, that's what he'd be going into any minute if he didn't watch out. So Tollinger freely admitted he had done a bad thing. He said he knew he should be punished for it. He'd breached their trust in him. He'd acted in an irrational and unjust way. He said they were right not to trust him. He just didn't deserve it, not now.

He held conversations with shrink after shrink, growing smaller and more deferential by the day.

Solemn and quiet, he began to attend chapel. He read half a dozen novels by Evelyn Waugh and Graham Greene. He devoutly absorbed selected chapters of the Good Book. A small crucifix was requested and duly provided.

In the space between paragraphs the climate grew warmer.

One morning there was frost on the grass. Tollinger's Christian commitment died. He said he wanted to be frank. The key thing was this. It had made him a better person, religion. He no longer wanted to speak out about his incarceration. He knew they weren't punishing him, they were simply rehabilitating him. One day soon he would be released back into the wild. He would say nothing about the snake or Bomb Island.

Bomb Island? Never heard of it, mate.

The day came when Tollinger was allowed to step outside, unaccompanied. He mustn't leave the grounds, though. To go beyond the perimeter wall was *verboten*. It was for his own good.

A day of bright sunshine.

Moon daisies eyed him watchfully from the wild garden.

A red admiral settled on a leaf and folded its wings.

He came across a sun-drenched wooden bench on a rectangle of lawn and sat down upon it. Note the old oak tree in the distance. A novel is always a game and a reader who understands its rules can return to play again and again and again and again. Old oak, don't forget. A novel is a game and like those four drives along the coast road the trip will always be different.

And now the long slim delicate fingers of Tollinger's right hand grip a paperback, which he proceeds to open and read.

Mary's heart began to beat fast and wild. The trap had closed down on her, and she saw the folly of her courage. It had delivered her bound and gagged into the hands of one whom she loathed more deeply every moment, whose proximity was less welcome than a snake's. She had to bite hard on her lip to keep from screaming.

Tollinger wasn't too far from the end so he read on. As he did so the shadow of an old oak tree moved slowly around the lawn, stretching and shape-shifting according to the counter-clockwise rotation of its planet and the arrival of light which had started out on its long journey some eight minutes and seventeen seconds earlier (give or take some piffling cosmic relativities). In another draft of reality he might then have paused a moment randomly to consider Alix Cleo Roubaud's reflection on lunar lunacy. But this was not to be.

My eyes were glued to my glasses, but they shook in my hands so that I could scarcely see. I bit my lip to steady myself, but they still wavered. From time to time I glanced at my wristwatch. Eight minutes gone – ten – seventeen. If only the

With a sharp cry of disgust Tollinger realised that someone had torn out the last pages. He flung the book down, muttering a quiet curse. An ugly smile formed on his lips. It was a filthy trick to deny the reader the pleasure of the ending. He had to bite hard on his lip to keep from screaming. He ejaculated a few words indicative of extreme displeasure. He bit his lip a second time to steady himself but it was no use. His hands continued to shake. He let the book drop to the ground. It sprawled there, spine uppermost, the pages spread out face-down like the hands of a yoga practitioner. A spot of blood from his bleeding lip fell and splashed the cover. Tollinger glanced at his wristwatch. The minutes were passing, one by one. If only the

*

Back indoors, Tollinger unfroze the frame. The actress continued sobbing on the TV screen. "There was no one to tell me right from wrong! No one!"

"Stop crying," the actor said, in a quiet, commanding, but strangely hollow and unfeeling voice. "I love you very much."

18

IT HAPPENED one night that the wild thing fled in secret back to the sea. This poor creature was never seen again, on land or water. It had returned into the ocean's depths, concealed there by wastes of indanthrene blue and shimmering monestial turquoise. Weedy, glistening language trailed out from a colour chart. All that was left afterwards were a few sentences written by a monk, a hooded, tonsured man of whom nothing at all is known except a name. The story, perhaps, no more than utter fiction. Or, if rooted in the real, a distortion. Something exaggerated beyond what's credible. Just as heat on a boiling summer's day can raise up a promontory. Watch it float in the air. Watch as ships can be seen sailing low across the sky, broken loose from gravity, jostling in the restless ether.

If however he existed as a mortal man, presenting himself as some human type of fish, what then? Should we say he was an evil spirit, hiding in the body of a man? A submerged man voicing foreign matter? A demon swimmer? Matter of the sort to be encountered in the life of Saint Audaenus?

It is difficult to say. So many wonders, told by so many speakers, about these rare events. And these rare events are nothing less than the sum of the words in the text.

19

AFTER HIS father's sudden death Tollinger felt joy, guilt, and awe at the efficacy of prayer. This last impression soon wore off. Newly minted prayers for the gift of a model Lancaster bomber,

June's return, six packs of ice-cream, a dozen Mars Bars, and impressively good school examination results were repeatedly not answered.

It struck Tollinger finally that his father's death had been a coincidence. No matter. He was cheered by his mother's new warmth. She smiled and laughed a lot.

The End never is. It can bring with it a fresh, bright beginning. Tollinger's mother met Mr Potter. Mr Potter bought Tollinger presents. This back story developed according to the conventions. Mr Potter was a widower. He had money. In time he –

The years passed. Tollinger left home and went to university, after which, like so many graduates, he drifted and zig-zagged like an autumn leaf whirled on a winter wind. And then he joined a band.

"Serious writing takes time," the actor on the screen said. "Time." His face looked enormously thoughtful. Solemnly and calmly, he continued. "Writing a novel takes time. Time."

20

INTERWOVEN FOLIAGE made it dark beneath the tall slender firs. Something pale started out from the shadows before him. It seemed to swim and float down the air. It drifted off through the bars of a gate framed dimly against the sky. He was going downhill, now. There was a gliding motion in the shadows. The text was full of strange rustling sounds. Something sheered in two. The crack echoed.

Tollinger emerged into scenery where the lighting was better. He went past the purple haze of the buddleia, which were the height of his parents. Someone a long way off was playing the Mal Kontents *Greatest Hits* album. Lines from "I'm Not The Same" drifted across the scenery.

I took the blame,
I lost my name,

I left the frame
I'm not the same.

In a spasm of drum beats and squeakily piping organ notes, the music died away. A light föhn wind took up the melody and distributed it among that nearby plantation of tapering firs.

In what had once been the same paragraph Tollinger came across a door in the brick wall. It was freezing cold in the shadow of this wall. He shook all over. It made him regret the lack of a coat.

Tollinger experimentally tried the handle of the door in the wall. He expected it to resist the pressure he'd applied to it but to his surprise the knob turned in his fist. The door creaked open. Its hinges needed oiling.

Tollinger slammed it behind him in the first take, pressing his palms against his ears. In the second take he closed it gently, his hands afterwards remaining at his side. His footsteps fell as gently as snowflakes.

He stepped out into a zone of shining woodland. Here, the trees had slender trunks and luminous silvery bark and were aligned in symmetrical rows. Sunlight on distant water glittered intermittently amid the massed vegetation. A lifelike bird broke noisily from a patch of dark vague undergrowth and fluttered away between the treetops. He had the sudden strange sensation that this was all unreal, something computer-generated. The sensation was one that tingled with the drag of what felt like very tiny fish hooks. It was an odd, wiry feeling. He could hear a distant whirring noise, which ceased.

Cortisone makes one alert and nervous.

He glanced behind him. There was no one around. He touched the nearest tree, which felt solid. So did the red brickwork, which left a smear of pinkish dust on his fingertips. He decided to follow the wall and see where it led.

He went west, with the sun behind him. He felt its warmth on his neck. The shadows cast by the trees were short. It was almost noon. Tollinger followed the wall for two hundred metres or so, until it turned a corner at a right angle and went north. Here, he left the wall and made his way through the silver trees.

Dead vegetation crunched beneath his feet like small bones. He emerged from the woodland and found himself at the edge of a marsh. Reed beds extended to the horizon, dissected by ditches. A swan slowly cruised the nearest ditch, moving steadily away from him. A narrow path snaked between the trees and the marsh. It was brown and well trodden. Tollinger decided to follow it and see where it led. He continued on, northward.

He expected to hear the distant wailing of a siren but the only sound in this quiet place was the *chark! chark!* of a bird. Later, a familiar Red Admiral settled on an unfamiliar blade of grass. Tollinger felt his heart start to thump wildly. He decided to clench his hands. It felt good, the four fingers of his left hand gripped between the thumb and fingers of his right hand. It calmed him a little.

The butterfly soon moved off, zigzagging away. He wondered if orders were being given. Perhaps the orderlies were already on their way. Soon a 4x4 would come smashing through the greenery. A man with a smile and a hypodermic would restore him to obedience. But perhaps it was just a butterfly after all. Like the diagonal reader, security was slow to manifest. No one came. These are trying times yet no one came to seize him. Perhaps he was truly free. Really.

Really!

Tollinger strolled on until he came to hedgerows with cowslips thriving in the verge. A dragonfly with a shining indigo abdomen jerked past. A couple of large fuzzy bees buzzed around his head. He shook them off. The throbbing behind his temple sounded like surf pounding on distant sandbars. How delightful it would be to spend a whole day on the beach, lost in dreams!

The thought made him think of that terrific black and white movie with Dwight Towers and Moira Davidson. A signal lures you on. The suspense is awesome. A broken message in the night gives you hope.

The thought made Tollinger think of Neil Young's second-best album. "Motion Pictures" had played all through that short hot summer with Vicki Lee Lennox, who preceded skinny Emily, and whom he never talked of to anyone.

The best was *Time Fades Away*.

Meanwhile, behind the privet hedges, there were calendar glimpses of white cottages with red roses curling prettily around small leaded windows. Superfluous primroses added a splash of yellow.

Tollinger mobilised a bundle of aching muscles and achieved a quiet stroll down an English lane. He emerged on to an avenue of villas and mock-Tudor houses. Soon he was in the high street and striding confidently along. Those unmentioned three grams of morphine had put quite a bounce into his step.

He knew where he was going before he went anywhere else. On such a hot dazzling afternoon as this there was a small queue at the quayside. Tollinger went to the office and bought a ticket and joined the day visitors. He'd been nervous that it would be the same ferryman but this one was a much younger man, quite different. He was slim and wearing a check shirt. He whistled cheerily as he took the boat out from the quay, across the estuary.

The other passengers were two elderly couples and a family group with three children. No one took any notice of him. He was the last one into the boat.

It chugged away across the muddy estuary. Tollinger dipped his head, remembering. He felt he'd come a long way to this moment in his life. The past rippled by, in dark waves of remembrance. Old scenery was assembled and dismantled on the great stage of his life.

A hand shook his shoulder

"Wake up, sir! We've reached Bomb Island."

"Eh?"

What had the fellow said?

"We're here, sir. Could you step off the boat please. People are waiting."

Tollinger realised he'd nodded off. The other passengers in the boat were looking at him oddly. The children were grinning. His cheeks reddened. "Sorry."

He was the last one in, the first one off. That was how it worked. He stepped off the gently swaying boat on to the pier. He could hear water slapping below the boards. He stepped on to the island and hurried away, walking fast. He'd soon left the others far behind.

Soon it was as if he had the place to himself. The island stretched away in front of him, devoid of humanity. Gulls passed overhead, screaming. A soft blue mist enveloped the horizon.

He retraced the route he'd taken, passing the museum with the broken sign. He crossed the bridge. The supermarket cart he'd used lay where he'd abandoned it. Tollinger could even see a dark crust of blood coating some of the silver mesh. Further along there were even dark stains on the ground. He must have been leaking badly to have left so much of himself behind. No wonder he'd been light-headed when he'd reached the quayside that night.

He felt good, now. Liberated. In good health. Back in control. He strode briskly on to the bunker. It was there – it existed. The door was half open, inviting him in.

Tollinger wasn't afraid. He couldn't feel the snake. Wherever it was, it wasn't on the island. It wasn't close, he was certain of that. Some strand of snake intelligence still swam in his bloodstream and he sensed it was infinitely remote. Perhaps even now it was wriggling towards Norway. Or wounded and dying in some deep, cold fissure in the ocean bed. Or entombed in an American military research facility, whence it had been transported in a sealed crate, on a huge aircraft. The sealed crate lay in an empty hangar, under armed guard. Upon arrival it was taken in a military convoy deep into the desert. New Mexico, say, or perhaps Nevada. In an air-conditioned basement, deep underground, it was being scrutinised through armoured glass eight inches thick.

Here, in the dark cool empty bunker, all evidence of the

elevator which had taken him to the medical unit had gone. It had been done very cleverly. The wall in which it had been set looked old and undisturbed. The ground looked hard and untrodden. It was as if what had happened here had never happened. Clever, that. No doubt if he came back with a shovel and a pick axe he would encounter a slab of unyielding concrete, immensely thick.

He went back to the pier and took the next ferry. This time he had it to himself, apart from the boatman, who was different. This one was thin and old, almost unfit for such employment. He regarded Tollinger morosely and said nothing.

On dry land he did not have to go very far to find a conveyance. There was one parked beside The King's Head. HYPO TAXIS it said across the vehicle's curved rump. A figure sat behind the wheel, head tipped forwards and eyes closed.

Tollinger opened a passenger door and asked the sleeper to take him to Merrivale.

The driver rubbed his eyes and yawned. He looked back at Tollinger, puzzled. "Where?" he said.

"Merrivale. The private hospital."

The driver thought about it for a while, frowning. He had the flushed cheeks of a farmer, and wore a check shirt. At last he said, "Buddy, that place closed years ago."

"It can't have done. I only left it a few hours ago."

The man stared at him. "Buddy, did you say *Merrivale*? D'ya mean the old military hospital? Believe me, buster, it's shut down. It's derelict now." He spoke Manhattan, with a dense Suffolk accent. The vowels dragged, as if the batteries were low.

"Derelict?"

"It's been loik that for a long time. Thoy soy a hotel will be a-built on the site. But they bin a-saying that for years."

The man was mad but that was scarcely Tollinger's concern. "Take me there," he said.

"If you're sure..." the driver replied. He looked doubtful.

"I'm quite sure."

The driver shrugged. "Sure. Okay, pal. Let's hit the highway. Attaboy! Here we go. Up, up, up and away in my beautiful

Veyron..."

They soon reached the grounds of the hospital. The driveway had a line of smoky weeds growing down the middle. Knee-high grass lapped at the base of the temporary fencing which barred the old gateway.

The driver braked. "This is the place."

It was, indubitably. Different to how Tollinger remembered it – but nevertheless the place.

He asked the cab driver to wait but the man refused. "You might walk off into that place and never come back," he complained. "Then where would I be?"

Tollinger took out a Franklin. He tore the bill down the middle, retaining the half with the nose for himself and handing the driver an eye, a cheek, a portion of bald head, and some long untidy hair.

"If you wait for me, I'll give you the other half."

"Nuts to you, shamus," the driver said. "This ain't no frigging movie. Gimme the dough, straight."

Tollinger paid him in an acceptable currency. He asked the man for directions back to the town. The driver jerked his thumb over his shoulder, in the direction from which they'd come.

"Just keep walking, mate. Don't take any side roads."

He screeched away, leaving a blue noxious mist drifting across the blacktop. A hedge breathed it in and coughed out three pale moths.

Tollinger walked along the perimeter until he found a hole in the fence. Others had been this way, forcing their way in. The mesh was twisted and flattened down. Feet had crushed the grass and thistles. A blue Cadbury's wrapper had been hooked by thorns. It was trying to wriggle free. Further on Tollinger came across a dead blackbird. Its belly was hollowed out and seethed with white animated maggots. They reminded him of noodle soup.

The narrative sent Tollinger back to the drive and obliged him to crunch along the gravel to the main entrance. The overgrown privet kept reaching out, touching him flirtatiously. The estate's anthropomorphic tendencies were comforting.

Weeds like small wrinkled cabbages sprouted from the pebbles. Each leaf reminded Tollinger of the taut symmetry of an anus.

He found a leather hip flask in his jacket pocket. Emily had given it to him in another age. He took a swig.

Southern Comfort! He hadn't had that in years...

How easy it is, when lacking a photographic record, to forget the naked body of a particular lover. In the absence of spectacular aspects – a missing leg say, or a right buttock bearing a butterfly tattoo, or pubic hair dyed in ginger and scarlet stripes – they blur together, these bodies, do they not? Nipples differ in size and colour but unless you are paying attention and afterwards make notes, they all tend to seem the same.

A jittery butterfly chased the origins of a neurosis on scarlet wings. A silver lager capsule winked. A broken bottle regarded Tollinger wolfishly, with a silent snarl of jagged teeth. The teeth fell apart and an angry mouth shouted, "Twisted fish and a cat's handlebar!" But he had surely misheard.

Misheard? Quite possibly not. Fall made some men tremble and repeat idiotic sentences to themselves. He had never known such men but he had read about them. Besides, was it truly the fall, now? It felt more like being on the cusp of a season, of one sort or another. Or perhaps he'd been tricked in some way, and was actually in Scotland, notorious for its unorthodox precipitation and general anarchy. He'd seen *Valhalla Rising*.

Codeine nagged, fallacies crowded, pathetic. A click in his mind, that's what he sought. Eh?

I cannot cry, I cannot care, no.

So he pressed on, his voice stretched, imitating an old Antony and the Johnsons cover version of a Dylan song.

The main building came into view. All its windows were smashed. The place had been blitzed.

Fingers of ivy reached as far as the guttering.

The front door had been removed and lay on the steps, dismembered and charred. An umbrella lay inert there too, its black wings broken. Smashed glass was everywhere. Starfish curled up like poppadoms. Wisps of sea fern bounced by like tumbleweed.

The darkness was waiting for him.

Tollinger made his way into the heart of it.

Once, long ago, Emily had had to spend a weekend at a conference in a Canterbury hotel. He went with her. He remembered that weekend as grey and dispiriting. While she went to lectures and seminars, he went off in search of a grave. He liked tracking down the graves of writers. The ones who lived at the edge. The ones who took a bullet. The ones who drank.

The ones who took hold of language, of form, of expectation, and twisted them into new shapes.

The ones borne down by despair, uncertainty, aesthetic dissatisfaction.

The ones who went to strange places – in their imaginations at least. The ones who were, all along, preparing to leave. Who, in the end, did.

Your heart gives up and gives out.

Others linger on, lusty to the end. And then a cough, a pain in the foot, the back. Concentration fading... Feeling limp. Feeling like a rag. Spirits at about zero. Effort syndrome, of old. Everything behind you, now. The years, heaped up. Your life relived on paper, until you were sick of it. Leaving you, at the end, crying out from a pit deeper than the Hell Gill gorge. Fooling yourself with new beginnings. Making plans to move to a new house, eight miles away, along the Dover Road. Making plans for the next novel. And then that stabbing pain in the chest.

Now your breathing becoming more laboured. The usual heart flutters, perhaps. Shortness of breath. Chest pains. It's nothing. Take heart!

There's no irregularity in the pulse. And then, an hour or so later, a cry, and you drop to the floor, stone dead.

Tollinger found it in the end, amid all the stone clutter. A big, ugly slab in a nondescript waste of dreary memorials. The writer's name misspelled on the gravestone.

Sleepe after toyle, port after stormie seas... Who could not be pleased by that delicious, drowsy, soporific prospect?

Tollinger went on down the corridor. A floorboard creaked. A voice seemed to cry out from the cellarage. Just a rat, a bat, a bird... When I am old and grey, he thought, I'll watch all those series I haven't yet seen, all the way through from beginnings to middles to ends. *The Sopranos. House of Cards. Game of Thrones.*

Rubbish everywhere. The place had been gutted of its contents, then trashed by intruders. By the look and the smell of the place people came here to piss, shit, booze, take drugs, strip off and fuck.

Something heard his footsteps and fluttered frantically in a far room.

Then silence.

Oddly, he felt no fear. Only a queer tranquillity. There was nothing here that could harm him and he seemed to know it for a certainty. It was written in his blood, in finest copperplate. With lots of stimulants he'd see it all through and enjoy those box sets.

He found his old room. It had been stripped of everything. The place where his bed had been was marked by a shadow outlined on the wall.

He made his way to the control room. Here there was a strange smell of kerosene, dust and mildewed cones.

The screens were gone, everything was gone. The plaster was broken and scarred where the equipment had been ripped out. Lumps of it made the floor uneven. Some of the plaster had melted and fused with the floor. The blobs looked like miniature versions of the stalagmites Tollinger had once seen in a cavern in Sardinia. The memory of that bright distant day was cloudy, though he was certain it involved a boat ride. He had not been with Emily on that day, which spared him a poignant flashback like the ones in *Still Alice*.

Wiring hung loose in clusters, like thin fronds of copper and plastic. A few drops of translucent slime hung from these fronds. The air-con had gone. A dark rectangle enclosing gashes in the wall marked the spot. Beneath the rectangle was an amber puddle.

The scenes he'd been shown in this place still played inside his head. Freckled Shoulder's dialogue was there, too. Tollinger wondered where she was now. In a basement off Whitehall perhaps. He went back up the stairway.

Desolation – you can't beat it, he thought. It's just what happens.

He continued and found the lounge, now just a shell, with every window shattered. The contents were long gone, apart from a monochrome scrap of wrapping from a DVD case. *Haunting, vivid, brilliant, unforgettable* exclaimed dazzled TIME.

Tollinger stepped out into the garden.

The grass and thistles were waist-high and the pathways gone. Or rather those pathways, some of them at any rate, were merely mislaid, for he was able to locate a trickle of bluish gravel which survived under the suffocating press of blades and cramped, jostling stalks.

He waded through the dry green jungle hoping there were no snakes. A mulberry which he did not remember was shedding dark leaves and somehow a crested grebe had jetted in from somewhere. Its presence attracted a robin, which seemed to startle the grebe, which flew off, as did the robin.

He retraced his exit route, with difficulty.

Tollinger went on, into the fast approaching night. It was that time of year, now. Things turned yellow at the edges, then darkened.

Dusk spread its fur over the hedgerows and fields. A strange fluorescent flickering crackled along that distant fuzziness where the land ended and the sky began. He felt a muzziness and smelt a mustiness. He sensed a faint flutter in his stomach, as of something stirring, something awakening from a winter sleep. It must be imagination, he thought. He sweated and shook. It must be – it must be imaginary. He closed it out, that creature uncoiling inside his deepest fear. Don't think of it. Go on, with another story. Something that distracts, something that takes you out of your selves. The consolation of an escape into a different, fantastic world. Hurry into it, and away. Tomorrow! And tomorrow!

He felt his left knee do something as he slipped and almost fell. With a slack, depleted energy he tremblingly recovered his gait. To hell with split infinitives! He went on, into the night. Amphetamines, he decided, would speed matters to a conclusion. He reached for his pills, hoping there would still be some.

And now, out there, the distant island melts in the thickening dark. Somewhere an owl cries out three times, then stops. It's a desolate, cool, melancholy sound, wrenched from the throat of something spectral. As if in response a strange, human wail of pain breaks from the throat of some large animal a short distance away. Tollinger cannot begin to imagine what this random creature might be.

The clear sky is beginning to fill with pricks of light. Tollinger stands there, feeling the chill on his skin. He hears the scratchy whispering of the branches, the hiss of a needle dragging against a vinyl groove. He sees the momentary blur of an expiring meteorite. He's a long way from Hooting Yard, now. Far from so much, so very much.

Night rushes forward and wraps its cool velvet cloak around Tollinger. It's a designer brand, with a famously chic name stamped upon the prose. He nestles snugly amid its comforts.

His lungs inhale a cold frosty sharpness. Up there, across the firmament, a bright company accumulates, like a growing army of dead souls. The Dog Star. The jewels of Orion's Belt, the sparkling outline of the Dragon. The blur of the Pleiades.

Arcturus, Altair, Centauri...

But now, out of nowhere, a wind has risen. A rough, coarse, pushing and pulling wind. It drags corrugated sheets of grey across the sky, shuts out the twinkling immensities of space.

Soon grey flakes are settling on Tollinger's scalp and shoulders and breast and on the sleeves of his coat. He stands still, watching his world turn white, unbelievably white. Flake by flake the whiteness spreads out, removing every last prop. One by one the laden trees are airbrushed out. Soon the ground is deep with soft snow.

He's growing thinner and thinner.

Tollinger is just a pair of eyes now, staring out across a featureless waste. Then one eyelid closes, leaving a single staring eye.

It holds a tiny world, with blackness at its centre. The eye jerks shut.

At once it springs open again, as if it's winking.

Part Two

SOMETIMES THE GUIDE urged them on ahead, while he stayed behind to switch off the illumination. And so it was that Tollinger was the first of that small party to cross the narrow bridge over the Mystery River. On the other side they continued, pausing now and again in the immense cavern. The beam of the guide's flashlight rolled across the blackness surrounding them, stopping to pick out a deep crack in a bulge of rock below. It marked where the earthquake had split the foundations of the mountain. They gazed at the fissure, then went on, deeper into the black heart of this place.

The guide stabbed the void with pricks of light. Solemnly this slim serious young man invited them to find meaning amid the billowing misshapen pillars. Abe Lincoln in silhouette! A croc! Silhouettes heightened by hidden lighting and framed by ingenious strokes of shadow. The couple from Nashville chuckled. The couple from Atlanta did not.

Later they paused by a drooping curtain of limestone, beneath which two child actors had once crouched during the filming of a Disney flop.

Tollinger asked the guide if he'd seen *The Descent*, about a bunch of women exploring an unknown cave system and coming up against an underground species of blind, flesh-eating mutant humans.

He said no, sir. He had not.

Very much later in the narrative Tollinger realised he had mispronounced the title. He should have said *The Dee-Scent*, not *The Dissent*.

At THE END of the path, where the cavern expanded and you looked down and across the great basin of glistening, sparkling shapes, the guide, after his spiel, killed all the lights. Now you are in complete darkness and the invitation is: *Listen*. What can you hear? What sound rises to your ears in this cool, calm, immense underground space?

A faint, faint whispering.

A trickle of distant remote laughter.

At THE END of the tour the guide unlocked the gate set in the big wall of iron bars. Like prisoners, they were released out into bright daylight.

On and away, down the highway. Tollinger ate pizza at Mellow Mushroom. He felt hollow and hungry. The waitress was as cheery and voluble as a chaffinch. She gave him a tall glass of chilled water, with a long straw, as if he was an infant who had not yet mastered the difficult skill of drinking. The restaurant was space-themed. Connected Rubik cubes were assembled in the shape of a satellite which hung heavily overhead. It unnerved him to be beneath it. He had a hunch he was the only person present who recalled the descent of the chandelier in *Daisies*. And who nowadays remembers that 1938 was the year a chandelier fell on Ernest Hemingway?

Feeling suddenly feverish, Tollinger glanced away. A life-sized helmeted astronaut stood beside the door, flexed to cope with the unfamiliar spring of weightlessness. The pizza was as wide as an auto wheel. The string of cheese topping stretched like an elastic band and wouldn't break. Sweating, scowling, Tollinger raised it higher and higher above his plate. Could this unbreakable cadmium string be a potent clue? Was this the stray, lurid wiring of a synthetic world? Is this just *The Matrix* all over again? Disturbingly, the beer was dark and sweet and nothing at all like Adnams Ghost Ship. Tollinger drained his glass. Still frowning, he noticed there were no dregs. There was nothing there to help him decipher the future.

Next he was inside the CENTER FOR SPACE EXPLOR-ATION. Afterwards Tollinger could not recall how he arrived there. It was not far from Mellow Mushroom, just a few miles away in the adjacent paragraph. Between locations green signs were everywhere, giving directions.

The CENTER FOR SPACE EXPLORATION is marvellous. The very name is like the definition of a novel, Tollinger might have reflected, had he not been distracted by the reflections in the first building's dark sheets of glass. White rockets clustered and shimmered there in fairy wings, like unusual fungi which, if ingested, bring on hallucinations of startling clarity. But that day Tollinger was not in the mood for postmodernist whimsy. He preferred gravely to admire a genuine, original life-size Saturn 5.

You could stand beneath it and hear a recording of the sound of take-off.

You could emulate the first men on the moon by walking along a gantry that led towards the front door of this gigantic tube.

You could admire a robot fish, circling forever its habitat of clear water inside a giant translucent ball.

You could stare through Plexiglas at a Biological Isolation Garment (BIG).

You could try to land on the moon.

You could peer in through transparent panelling at a recreation of Werner von Braun's office and be impressed by the big man's big desk, the white important telephone, the photographs of the great rocket scientist with American presidents.

On modest walnut-veneer furniture were positioned pleasant photographs of von Braun's wife and children, plus a row of model rockets, from Saturn 5 all the way back to the first rocket of the Free World, the V2. The V2's flanks were white and blank, the only missile not to bear the words U.S. ARMY or UNITED STATES.

The military in its contemporary and future incarnations was celebrated at the end. A gleaming Humvee with a small missile launcher atop stood against a theatrical backdrop of bare brown mountains in an arid desert landscape. A drone cut across the sky and robot tanks hurried across the sand. THE FUTURE FORCE... said a sign, exhibiting ellipses, a device Tollinger had always adored. Ellipses indicate all that's unspoken. All that lingers on when speech has died away.

Deployable. Agile. Versatile. Lethal. Survivable. Sustainable.
The glorious thesaurus of future imperial victories.
Exit.
And onward, down Heroes Highway.

Down Ronald Reagan Memorial Road to Slaughter.

Constant incitements to action beside the Interstate. Huge stalks of metal supporting massive screens.

TATTOO REGRET?

WORLD FAMOUS ORANGE ROLLS.

SHRINE OF THE MOST BLESSED SACRAMENT – VISIT OUR GIFT SHOP.

Tollinger refuelled at Good Hope.

Then on, across the massive mud-brown Tennessee, to Carraway Boulevard and all that lies beyond. Munching an Einstein Bagel. Seeing a wild turkey scampering away across the verge, into undergrowth. Taking the A side lane. Taking the 16th Street exit. Seeing flowering dogwood and a mockingbird in Vulcan Park. Observing an American robin, big as a blackbird and just as friendly. Calling by at the café at 1906 1st Avenue North, for steak in gravy and fried green tomatoes. On the menu, oddly: Jew Fish Steak-Potatoes.

The Stars and Stripes fluttered everywhere, as if Americans, roaming the vast expanses of their nation, were fearful of forgetting which country they inhabited. Like early onset dementia patients they benefited from simple reminders and good, honest nudges. The auto number plates brought reassurance. Alabama was sweet and homely. God was quietly commanded to bless these United States, which possessed an equal entitlement to upper-case. A unique selling point is best made snappy.

PATRICIA TODD: FEARLESSLY PROGRESSIVE.

Tollinger tuned into Ninety-Seven Three, The Easy Channel. *The difference is we only play relaxing and refreshing music. None of that annoying hard rock.*

Miranda Lambert sang Greyhound Bound for Nowhere.

Elton John sang Candle in the Wind. The Supremes sang You Keep Me Hanging On. Rod Stewart sang Tonight's the Night. Simon and Garfunkel sang The Sound of Silence. The Beatles sang If I Fell in Love with You. Nilsson sang Without You. Paul Simon sang Slip Sliding Away. Fleetwood Mac sang It Doesn't Matter Any More. The Turtles sang Happy Together. *Songs that bring back great memories from a simpler time.*

Thunder rolled in the green hills all around.

The passage of a recent tornado was marked out by a wide arc of trees flattened with startling symmetry amid a dense, rolling belt of forest.

In a dark room, rain lashing the parking lots, Tollinger watched for the first time *To Kill a Mockingbird*. He felt he knew the actor who played Boo but he couldn't put a name to him.

Hours later, a distant freight train wrenched the night apart with its doleful quartet of stretched-out mournful hoots.

The knob on the cooker offered two choices: HI and LO.

You press wall switches up to turn lights on and down to turn them off. This is England upside down, back to front, in reverse. The steering wheel is on the passenger side. The fast lane is the slowest. A mirror world.

Downtown, few walked. People scampered from asleep cars in parking lots, into offices: and that was it. The streets were as eerily empty as a post-apocalypse disaster epic. Once, by the Alabama Theater, Tollinger encountered a sauntering, sullen individualist with a cigarette dangling from his mouth. The oncoming youth's black T-shirt read NIHILIST. They passed in silence. But out in the hilly tree-lined suburbs there were joggers, mostly tanned, slim young women in shorts, with baseball caps jammed on their scalps and a thin long white wire sprouting from each ear. They ran past him without acknowledgement.

Tollinger, marvelling at everything, went up the elevator beside Vulcan. To the north he could distinctly make out Region Fields. A bright sunlit day, no one else around. It felt like being in a Hitchcock movie. On the high wind-torn platform below the gigantic muscular cast-iron God there would be a struggle. The camera would show the perilous drop. The villain would in due course fall away, getting smaller and smaller. Truth and justice would triumph over deception and un-American values. Tollinger felt fearful and queasy. He had never been good with heights. Plus there was Emily, she was always on his mind, she was always on his mind. He should not have come here. The gusts tugged at his sleeves.

IN A WRECK? NEED A CHECK?

WHEN YOU DIE YOU WILL MEET GOD

UNCONTESTED DIVORCE, $199

At Region Fields Miss Alabama herself appeared, wearing her silver crown. She waved at the crowd, bright with beauty and youth. Tollinger enthusiastically waved back.

Tollinger had more money, now. More than enough for numerous divorces. That forgotten second best Mal Kontents song he'd penned, "Unexpected Surprise", was used as the signature tune for a U.S. cable drama, *Killing Time*. When the series became an unexpected hit the royalties flooded in.

A pretty tale. It balanced that other back story, the dark one, in which Emily aborted Tollinger's child.

Later, the day after she'd seen *Inception*, Emily walked to a footbridge over the roaring, whining North Circular. It was close to the old Crooked Billet site, before that the home of Roger Ascham, tutor to the slippery Queen. In Emily's stained pocket was found an ancient wrinkled non-fiction paperback, *The Sense of an Ending*. "I like *Lost*," her last message to T.

Halfway across she paused, swaying above the fast-flowing machines. Witnesses said Emily appeared intoxicated. Her face shone. She was transfigured by the brilliance of her future. Making a quick calculation, she chose the fast lane and an oncoming heavy goods vehicle. Fury road! A rubbery oblivion.

When he heard, a hole was struck inside Tollinger, enlarging the existing crater. Leftover life to live, now.

"Can't live," the balladeer wailed, "if living is without you." But he could, that was the trouble. The raucous noise of life begins again. Wounded and bruised and aching, he'd endure. Tollinger would go on, as main characters always do. That good-looking savage in *Apocalypto*, for instance. About to be decapitated? An eclipse will intervene. An arrow through the guts? Snap it off! Bashed over the head with a club? Shake that headache away and rise up, sprightly and full of determination. Another arrow penetrating your torso? No matter. Scramble to your feet and stumble onward. Live to kill another day.

PEACE, LOVE & JESUS.

GET FEDERAL PREMIUM AMMUNITION AT LARRY'S PISTOL & PAWN.

Tollinger drove to a shopping mall which rose up out of a glittering ocean of parked cars. For no obvious reason the mall displayed two gigantic wooden horses, each big as a London double decker bus. He went into a large bookstore. To his surprise its enormous multiple shelving units held only one title by Mailer and only two by Updike. But vampires and murder were everywhere. Dust jackets shone with stylish representatives of the undead, who had good bone structure and whose snow-white complexions were nicely suited to swirling purples and buttoned mauve. Crime offered limos in mountain landscapes and long-haired blondes open-mouthed in the presence of giant knuckles clenching stubby hand guns. Snow was prettily sprinkled with scarlet and alleyways held dark shapes.

Behind the check-out, occupying almost the entire wall, loomed a massive reproduction of the lurid cobalt cover of the first edition of *The Great Gatsby*. Tollinger paid for his anthology of F. Scott Fitzgerald stories.

The nurse – her name was Helen Earle – peered about eagerly.

"I don't see anybody," she said. "Except oh, there's Ronald Colman. I didn't know Ronald Colman looked like that."

He read what happened after Scott completed the first chapter of *The Love of the Last Tycoon*. Littauer at *Collier's* was uncertain whether or not he wanted to publish. Littauer asked to see more than the six thousand words he'd read so far. Furious, Scott sent the material to the *Saturday Evening Post*. No go there, either. So he drank, heavily. He denied it, the boozing, to his mistress, Sheilah Graham. But she was suspicious. When he went out for a haircut she went through his bureau drawers and found eleven empty gin bottles. Later she recalled how she said to him: You'll die. You'll drop dead. You'll have a stroke. At least, that's what she claimed she said – long after his death.

Scott told her he considered Dreiser his greatest contemporary.

Sheilah came to Encino one night to find Scott with two bums he'd found on Ventura Boulevard. He'd felt sorry for them, had invited them to dinner, had given them two of his Brooks Brothers suits. Sheilah was angry. She threatened the men with the cops. Scared, the men left. Scott stared blankly. Inside he was angry. Sheilah warmed up some tomato soup and passed it over. Scott picked up his bowl and hurled it against the wall. He slapped Sheilah, hard. He screamed her real name. That was mean.

She wrote that he seemed like a deranged Rumpelstiltskin. She decided to depart. Scott blocked the way. You're not leaving this house, he said.

I hate you! Sheilah shouted. I don't love you any more!

Scott lit a cigarette. You're not going, he said. He added: I'm going to kill you. He opened the table drawer where he kept his gun. It wasn't there. He tore out all the drawers. Where's my gun? he screamed. He phoned his secretary, Frances. Frances, he said. I've been hearing suspicious noises. Have you any idea where my gun is? No, I haven't, Mr Fitzgerald, she replied. Did you see me put it anywhere? Maybe I hid it, he said. No, Mr Fitzgerald. I'm sorry to say I didn't. He hung up. He rummaged among the pots and pans.

I want to go, Scott, Sheilah said.

You're not going, he said. You're not getting out of here alive. The exclamation marks were immense and vivid and deepest black. The mood was ugly. The territory was soap opera.

Scott continued searching.

Where is that goddam gun? he cried.

Sheilah grabbed the phone. She called the cops. The cops said they'd be over. Sheilah walked to the door. She walked out the door. She reached her car. She had trouble starting it. She became hysterical. The car started. Sheilah wept all the way home. As she entered, the phone was ringing in her empty apartment.

In the morning a letter arrived, Special D. Get out of town or you will be dead in 24 hours, it said. She recognised the writing. More letters arrived later that day. Leave town, he threatened, or your body will be found in Coldwater Canyon.

Later Scott apologised. The awful things I said, he wrote. They came from the merest fraction of my mind. I want to die, Sheilah, he wrote. And in my own way. For over two years your image is everywhere.

It's not long now, Scott said.

He never told me that he was writing about me, Sheilah remarked.

Stahr is a lonely man. He is still in love with his dead wife, Minna. Stahr falls in love with an English girl, Kathleen.

Stahr is Scott. Minna is Zelda. Kathleen is Sheilah. Kathleen speaks like me, Sheilah wrote. She uses my phrases. Sheilah was thrilled. He had taken their first meetings and worked magic on them!

I tried to understand the mystery of love, wrote Sheilah.

In Birmingham, in the art gallery down the road from where the bomb went off, Tollinger encountered Georges Merle's startling painting *L'Envoûteuse*. Emily must surely have posed for the artist. The similarity was far starker than anything as flimsy as a resemblance. It made Tollinger tremble. He went out to a bar and drank bourbon. The next day, after a sleepless night, he drove south on Interstate 85, passing en route a gigantic peach and a large Confederate flag flown adjacent to the highway by the Sons of Confederate Veterans. After this there was a sign which showed a scarlet demon flourishing a pitchfork beside the message GO TO CHURCH OR THE DEVIL WILL GET YOU.

Later he found himself going down HANK WILLIAMS MEMORIAL LOST HIGHWAY.

On the Lost Highway he shaped the arid thought that there is one moment in life which is like coming to that page in a book where you reach the final sentence. What's behind it is all there'll ever be and beyond the final speck of punctuation lies only a white emptiness. An emptiness, a void of infinite possibility. An aftermath of time and story in which lies storm or calm, life or death, or something in between, a birth, or even something unimaginable. It's there that the narrative has to run on without you, now.

In Montgomery, Tollinger went via Gatsby Lane to Fitzgerald Road. From there he went via Zelda Road to Zelda Place.

It was a Sunday. He parked by Zelda Cigar and dined at The Egg and I. In the men's room, as he urinated, he was softly serenaded by Simon and Garfunkel.

After brunch and coffee, Tollinger drove on to the Fitzgerald Museum at 919 Felder Ave. *F. Scott Fitzgerald, his wife Zelda and daughter Scottie lived in this house from October 1931 to April 1932. During that period Fitzgerald worked on his novel* **Tender is the Night** *and Zelda began her only novel,* **Save Me the Waltz**, the blue metal plaque informed any passer-by requiring data.

It was a substantial house for three people, located at the corner of two streets, amid open lawn, shrubs and trees, including a large Southern magnolia. Tollinger sat on the third of the five brick steps under the porch, waiting for one o'clock.

He tried to imagine Scott walking up and down these steps, but could not. At five past the curator welcomed him inside.

The curator was in his twenties, slender, bearded. He was an aspiring writer. Impudently, he asked Tollinger how old he was. Startled, Tollinger told him. The curator led him through to a back room and switched on a television. "Watch this," he said.

A documentary rolled. A pleasant, commanding voice ran smoothly through the biography and described the better-known works. Tollinger grew restless, resenting being lectured with dull public facts he already knew. His attention drifted to a side wall and focused on a framed enlargement of an old 23 cent stamp. It bore the head of our rosy-cheeked novelist posed against a distant blob of light reflected in florid water. It was intended, presumably, to evoke the final paragraphs of *The Great Gatsby*. But it seemed to Tollinger to be more redolent of an apocalyptic scene from the brush of John Martin.

Another room displayed paintings by Zelda. Nude, muscular women whose bodies bulged out, giving them a misshapen appearance, cavorted amid anarchic, mysterious settings. They projected a sense of disturbance and wild, dark, erotic energy. She had talent, undeniably, but the exhibition seemed derivative, too full of echoes of Picasso's 1908 nudes and other classic modernist painting. What was revolutionary before the Great War seemed mundane and conservative in its aftermath. It reminded Tollinger of the dull and derivative art he'd seen in the Whitechapel Art Gallery.

The main room of the museum held a variety of memorabilia. Newspaper cuttings testifying to that golden age when an author's wife was newsworthy. A photograph of a short-haired vamp with voluptuous sullen eyes and a ripe sensuous compressed mouth below the headline MRS SCOTT FITZGERALD LEAVES TODAY AFTER VISIT IN MONTGOMERY.

An advertisement in copperplate script: *Three distinguished Judges choose the TWELVE MOST BEAUTIFUL WOMEN using Woodbury's Facial Soup*. One of the distinguished judges was F. Scott Fitzgerald.

Because no other man of his time writes so sympathetically, skilfully, and fascinatingly about women.

A poster for the film *This Thing Called Love*.

A first edition of *Tender is the Night*, which the curator said was a bad piece of writing and which Tollinger hotly asserted was just as good as *Gatsby*.

We had fifty visitors yesterday, the curator said proudly. Seven were from Austria, seven from the Czech republic. Saturday is a good day for visitors. Sunday is not so good. I think we may need to close on Sundays, he said.

The movie *This Thing Called Love* was the last one that Fitzgerald saw. I feel awful, he said as he left the cinema. Outside, he asked Sheilah how he looked. Very pale, she replied.

I did not know that he would die the next day, she wrote.

Tollinger left Montgomery, crossed the Tallapoosa River and came at last to Wetumpka. He had reached the place where he most wanted to go.

Here, to the east of Highway 231, the crust of the republic was disturbed by an ancient turbulence. Tollinger turned off, taking the Harrogate Springs Road across the floor of the gigantic, broken crater. To the north the land was thickly forested, rising steeply up.

After ten minutes or so Tollinger quickly pulled over on to the verge. Here, at last, was a glimpse of the origins of this disfigured place. An arc of rock split the matted vegetation which coated the base of the crater wall. It resembled a scar.

He stepped out of the car and crossed the highway, going a little way up the slope to scrutinise this curve of banded stone more closely. The rock face consisted of a seam of yellow ochre capping a layer of pink streaked with white. It was cracked and fissured by heat and rain, a lingering remnant of the original immense explosive convulsion.

Tollinger stooped to pick up some of the small misshapen pebbles which littered the base of the exposed rock. Each pebble was coated in a pink dust which clung to his skin like talc. One was flesh-red, one grey and the other three were the colour of bone.

He slipped these fragments of the United States into his pocket and went back to the car. He drove on a little way to the Buck Ridge junction. Here Tollinger turned right, braked, reversed, and started the trip back to where he'd come from.

INTOLERABLE TONGUES

To Keith Rowley

P

PURPOSE? HOW LONG do you intend to stay? Do you have a return ticket? These are questions you cannot escape. Sightseeing, I retort, sweating. A journey of several weeks. Returning by way of Port Said. I dare not say: to write a book. That would be pride and presumption. Yet its absent presence foreshadows all that I'll do, all that follows. At the border everything is still as empty as the barren No Man's Land crossed since Ras en-Naqura. The future glimmers with the promise of the past. I am tense to tread in holy footsteps, they are close and everywhere. My greasy hand trembles at the thought of holding my pen, of putting it all down. All of it! *Jesus!* And I am a little shivery, too. I fell sick back there. A light fever still afflicts me. The official – if curious he may not be, he may be bored – doubtless attributes my shining face to the heat. Back in the car I swallow another pill. In truth, I have been feverish since Tyre. No, be honest, since Cairo. Delete, rewrite. Let's get it straight. And true. For the lip of truth shall be established for ever: but a lying tongue is but for a moment. Perhaps it is the pills that have made me constipated. Or perhaps the climate. This heat is intolerable. It smothers me. Along the Acre Road misty purple beams quivered prettily upon the sea. The slow waves that break there are green and dark as upon any Hebridean shore. *Stringendo!* The barren jagged rocky coastline fell away, at once I was in Switzerland, on holiday (which means: Holy Day). Light-headed, in Zurich once, I prayed for release from sin. The glare from the white slopes intense, the car moving very slowly around curves treacherous as a pair of female breasts. Death was an enticing possibility – yet then, as now, I was not at the wheel. I was always a passenger, never a driver. Here I fly over the arid moon. It, too, is bright with our Lord's inaccessible scrutiny. I skim a blotchy waste, it is bright and uninhabited. And dirty.

The Middle East is a very dirty place. In Geneva they would be appalled. The arid corrugated lunar soil matched in some way the ridges on my brow. Dust boiled behind us. I did not try to understand the metaphors which bubbled there. I let them cloudily burst. It's best to beware ripe adjectives. They can make you voluble. The French customs station assembles itself out of a barren residue, a few wearisome formalities, and then on towards the Mandate, the British wicket. Look! The Tegart Wall! Roll after roll of barbed wire, arranged around wooden trellising and spikes. An ingenious device to stop the flow of Arabs and arms. At intervals concrete blockhouses. Their symmetry is pleasing. Slits of blackness add to it. Inside those slits are invisible eyes and weaponry. British eyes, British weaponry. The thought thrills me. *Civis Romanus sum*. We pass through the wire to the checkpoint. Purpose, what is it? The unsmiling official is satisfied by my replies but he has words of warning. Do I understand that the situation is grave? It is Very Grave (he says with a grave expression). His Majesty's Government cannot be held responsible for anything that might befall me. I say yes, yes I understand, and he waves us on, it is three-twenty-five in the afternoon precisely, I shall put this in my book. *At three-twenty-five I crossed over into our Holy Land*. Here, the road seems rougher than in Syria, I took hold of the door grip, it is pointless to take unnecessary risks. I stared out of the window, I am on the brink of a matter of which I have long dreamed. I recognised this land. I had never set foot in it before and yet I had visited it many times. Feverdreams. And Acre did not disappoint. I lit a cigarette and walked among its romantic mediaeval walls. A street vendor sold me a tiny Crusader's cross for my collection. As we completed the transaction forty Arab prisoners were led past, veils on head. They are from the military prison. Abbas tells me there are many, many rebels locked up here in cages. How many? I asked. He did not know. Hundreds, he said. An exaggeration, I assumed, but later, when I raised the matter with Monty, he told me there were 2,500 prisoners. Scum, he said. Bandits and gangsters the lot of them, he said. I leave my droll chauffeur by the car and climb the old fortifications. The view across the bay is astonishing. Haifa shines beyond a marge of palms. It is thirty-two minutes there by train, faster by car. There is a new macadam road, we are on the outskirts in no time. On the way we pass a peculiar sight: an Arab tied to the bonnet of the first lorry in an army convoy. I ask Abbas what this strange occurrence means but he does not hear me. On the edge of Haifa the huts of the pioneer Jewish colonists cluster on the sand wastes. A huge cement plant stands near the airport, electric power wires cross fields where long-horned cattle grazed, from behind a line of ancient palms rose storage tanks bearing the words **Iraq Petroleum**. Two buses pass by, going where Jesus went, NAZARETH-CANA-MAGDA is followed by JERUSALEM-BETHLEHEM. Can there be a more fascinating or more important thing to know than the life and personality of a man from whose birth we date everything? What He did and said and was, and above all where. He grew up in the home of a working carpenter. Until He was about thirty He worked with His own hands at that craft. Then, for two or three years, He taught a group of young men, some of them fishermen. He healed people. He wrote no books. He had no army. He was never in any government. To get close to all that you have to follow the tracks He walked in Palestine. Could there be a drama more enthralling? A night at Haifa. I unpack and take out two books. One is the Bible, the other a detective story. Before lights out I read from both. I slept like the proverbial, rose early. The hotel had packed me a hamper. Abbas was waiting on time with the Rolls. Off we go!

A

ABBAS. YOU WOULD not expect an Arab to own a Rolls Royce but Abbas did. What model? I really have no idea. I care nothing for motor cars. The workings of the internal combustion engine are a complete mystery to a man such as myself. What lies beneath a bonnet is as obscure to me as the intestinal arrangements of a hippopotamus. There are certain things a man of the cloth needs to know and certain things he will never need to know. Suffice it to say that the Rolls was a big black brute. It had massive running boards, suitable for occasional use by servants. Its front portion was reminiscent of a gleaming sarcophagus. Abbas came highly recommended. He did motor tours and knew the region. Very reliable, they said in Cairo. Abbas won't let you down. I negotiated a divine pilgrimage. Abbas beamed. The deal was done. Friendly handshake! Haifa he knows well. The harbour bristles with activity at this hour. A Belgian freighter unloading iron roofing. Coils of wire from England to carry new electric light power. A crane landing bound frightened sheep. Commerce thrives now that the pipe line brings its oil from distant Iraq. On the outskirts construction work is going on under Moslem architects. Abbas takes the road heading east, motoring across the Plain of Esdraelon. Genesis 49 thuds in my head. A swelling rises beside the road, an ancient Canaanite fortress. Next the first in a series of police stations. Soon Megiddo itself, a pale mythic mound, purchased for the Oriental Institute, excavated by permission of the Palestine Department of Antiquities. Layer upon layer is being removed, entire strata. The layer which at present lies under the open sky is the Solomonic level. Breathlessly I ascend the narrow-gauge track down which tiny trucks bring out the glacis and unearthed specimens. The heat is intense. Thank goodness for my pith helmet, my enormous umbrella, purchased from Beirut bazaar, both extremely good value at the price. Although the helmet strap rubs. Here at Megiddo I rested in the shade of a wall. I watched the men and the women and the children as they toiled with their rubble. Be careful with that precious dust! And no slacking. For in all labour there is profit: but the talk of the lips tendeth only to penury. (Prov. Xiv. 23.) Megiddo is where King Solomon housed his cavalry. He had twelve thousand horsemen. He had fourteen hundred war chariots. It is all in the first Book of Kings. Sunlight shines once again on an exposed portion of twelve-foot wall. I am flung back in time, repeatedly. The excavations have exposed stalls for the horses, rooms for the grooms, parade grounds, storage silos and the outlines of massive structures. Elsewhere, at Gerar and Beth-pelet, the Petries found golden ear-rings, a collar of three strings of fine carnelian, black and white quartz, signs that the court of Solomon possessed jewellery much finer than the Egyptians of that era. Solomon was a merchant-king, a controller of trade routes. The Book of Kings tells us of his annual tributes from every man – gold, silver, garments, spices, horses, mules. At Megiddo there is more. The excavators are keen to get down to the levels indicated in chronicles, which tell of lapis lazuli, of a golden chariot and gorgeous vases. Heavy stone balls are strewn among the assorted débris. I pick one up to take home as a souvenir. As well as the catapult ball I took a vase handle. They will go nicely on my desk. Before going back down to Abbas, who is sitting on the running board of the car, picking his nose and scrutinising the dirt, I admire the view. I stand for some time, gazing at the fringe of trees on the distant hills of Nazareth. I think of Jesus and his childhood. There are some peculiar medieval tiles in the British Museum, I do not know what to make of them. They strike me as irreverent and unsuitable for public display. I wrote to the Director but he brushed my complaint aside. As did the Prime Minister. A fly pesters me and it is time to descend. I return to the car with a feeling of having enjoyed a satisfying meal of historical reality. Seven miles east of Megiddo is the site of Ta'anek fortress. Here the narrow track suddenly fills with a herd of fifty or more brown camels, driven along by ten or twelve Bedouin men and women and their shouting children. The wives wear trailing black gowns. A camel bares its teeth, resenting my Kodak. Soon they are gone, heading west to Armageddon. We are going east, to Beisan. We pass the collective farms of the busy, industrious Zionists. In the United States there are four Hachshare or preparation farms, where young Jews train. They are making a new world. They are doing the will of the Lord. This is their land, from time immemorial. Father taught me that. They say that when the Zionists break this ancient crust a foul miasma emerges from the fallow earth as it is ploughed for the first time. Continuing past the farms we come to the power lines of the Palestine Electric Corporation, whose poles parallel the road. Beyond the white building of the police station at Beit Alfa we come to Beisan's tiny station. The mound itself is huge. No sign of that threatened Emergency! I left Abbas at the car. He is an amusing fellow but not interested in history. Also he frets ceaselessly about his car (punctures, scratches, theft, troublesome urchins). I took the foot-trail leading upward. Here I sense the shades of the Philistines. Their hideous laughter crackles in my burning ears. I see them carry Saul's armour into the temple of the Ashtaroth. I see them fasten his head in the second Temple of Rameses, on this very height which I am now approaching. How time collapses beneath this heavy heat. The men of Jabesh and Gilead arose and went all night and took the body of Saul and the bodies of his sons from the wall of Beth-shan. And they came to Jabesh and burned them. And they took the bones and buried them under the tamarisk tree in Jabesh. I spot some yellowed bones in the excavated strata by the end of the steep little path to the summit. The skull indicates the remains of a sheep. Beisan was once called Scythopolis. Its population and commerce in the Roman era are said to have rivalled those of Jerusalem. Palestine was wealthy in Roman times. It yielded twelve million denarii in taxes. The Roman Government made it pay for its own conquest. It is the same to-day. Under the British Mandate the Palestine Government to-day has a surplus in its budget. How successfully England administers this complicated little land! And yet in all our hearts we know a deeper truth that drives such endeavour. *Whatsoever ye do, do it heartily, as to the Lord, and not unto men; knowing that of the Lord ye shall receive the reward of the inheritance: for ye serve the Lord Christ.* The estimated value of the salt, potash, bromine and magnesium chloride stored in the Dead Sea is about $1,182,000,000. Not to mention the revenues from the new Iraq Petroleum pipe line. Not to mention the millions of cases of oranges and grapefruit annually exported to England and elsewhere. Modern Palestine richly rewards its protectors. Abbas is busily dusting his magnificent vehicle. He drives me on to the acropolis of Beth-shan. Here the track is narrow and steep. The wheels spin on grit-coated slabs of rock. I close my eyes. The Rolls shakes and lurches. Camels and donkeys are a constant nuisance. Sometimes I wish I had a pistol. A donkey is a stupid animal, though admittedly helpful to the poor. And, it goes without saying, to our Lord. My flesh shall rest in hope. For why? Thou shalt not leave my soul in hell. And at thy right hand there is pleasure for evermore. At long last we reach the gateway of the city. An Arab custodian in floating head-veil steps out, carrying a cane. He speaks not one word of English, other than the names Amenophis III and Rameses II. At least I think that is who he meant! His pronunciation left a lot to be desired. After that paltry effort he seemed to give up. He pointed his cane at the ground, jabbering in Arabic. It is fortunate that I have genned up on this place. Oh yes, I have done my reading. My McEwan Blue Guide is a boon. It educates me about the symmetries. I know I am looking at the ground-plan of the great temple complex which belonged to the god Makal. Column bases and broken masonry lie all about. A sharp cold gust blows through the ruins. It agitates the dust. Jesus must often have passed by this way. Out of this citadel mound steps an Englishwoman. She says her name is Muriel. Another pilgrim. She is from Basildon. I offer her a ride but she stiffly declines. She is not yet finished with her investigations. Her tone is not particularly warm. Suspicious, even.

Surely she cannot believe I have carnal intent. I explained I was from the Outer Hebrides. She sniffed. She had been to Scotland once, many years ago. She had not enjoyed the experience. I mention The Emergency. Is she not worried about her safety? Another sniff. Her stockings are aptly blue, her hair a lurid black. She bobs back into the ruins. Good riddance! No, that was unkind. I take it back. For God resisteth the proud, but giveth grace unto the humble. The truth is the heat is making me fray a little at the edges. And the guide is beginning to irritate me. He deposits numerous explanations upon me, which I neither require nor understand. Then he has the impertinence to expect a tip! All Arabs are the same. They are like parasites, feeding off their host. I clenched my fist and waved it and curtly told the fellow to leave me alone, which he finally did, retreating with angry mutters into a little wooden hut, as an insect might hide under a stone. I am glad to be gone from that place. The citadel mound dustily recedes. Abbas parked in the little modern village of Beisan and went off to buy himself food. I stayed in the car and ate a delicious picnic luncheon packed by my hotelier in Haifa. The natives tentatively emerge from their homes. They approach, smiling. I feed them caramels. This makes them happy. Palestinians adore caramels. I distribute them plentifully in the days and weeks that follow.

VERY OCCASIONALLY I contribute verses to church magazines, and it is quite widely recognised that I have something of a gift. It has even been suggested that I collect my contributions into a single volume, for both the cultural and spiritual benefit of mankind. This would be a detestable vanity, and I am content for my modest addition to the wonders contained in *The Golden Treasury* of Master Palgrave to be assessed posthumously! Yet I cannot, must not, entirely conceal the impact which Capernaum in Galilee made upon me.

It's sunrise out in Galilee, where mists of Moab melt
Before the dawn's new ecstasy on seas His feet have felt.

With sunrise also in my heart I stand here looking down
Where our dear Lord's own hand once touched folk in this
    town.
The Son of Righteousness has come, with healing in His
    wings,
While in the market there's a hum, and my heart swells and
    sings.

Did even Keats ever quite equal such lines as these? But out with thee, detestable pride! A man must not boast of his gifts, to the detriment of the less talented, the less fortunate. Christian principle forbids the sweet enticements of vanity. Let them acclaim my genius after death, for to-day I am set on Higher Things. To-day Tiberias helps visualise what Capernaum looked like when it teemed with a busy population, crowding the shores of the Lake. Little boats ride at anchor as if about to "put out into the deep". The opposite hills of Gilead are draped in morning mist (rhymes with "kissed"!). But sadly Tiberias to-day smacks too much of Herodian luxury, for, alas, it has a "Lido Beach" and a "dance pavilion". So quickly on, to the ruins of Capernaum, to seek the footprints of Christ in his spiritual "H.Q." – a place where He enjoyed His happiest days of fruitful ministry. Ah, the joys of Galilee. Here He was appreciated as He never was in Nazareth. Here He was loved. Here He was thronged. Here He toiled. Here He relaxed. Here He "spake many things". The Sea of Galilee is magical at twilight. As one gets nearer its waters one knows not whether to sing for joy or weep for very stirring of His life within. I was suddenly irritated to see that Abbas had lit a cigarette. I rapped on the glass and shouted at him to stop. For a while he pretended not to hear, then in the end sullenly removed it from his lips and tossed it out of the window. This was reckless of him. It might well have resulted in a conflagration. But the Arab is a creature of impulse and can sometimes be difficult to tame. The Sea of Galilee is six hundred and eighty feet below sea level. This heart-shaped lake is exalted to the heavens for its gracious ministry to Christ. To have it ruined by a cigarette and a morose chauffeur was loathsome. Abbas accelerated and started taking the bends too fast. Once again I had to bang on the glass and remonstrate. The wretch became even dourer. I swivelled my gaze and tried to forget he existed. To sweep along the shores of Galilee's turquoise lake is an other-worldly experience. It is "such stuff as dreams are made of". The scene should really be felt rather than described. The late hour throws a golden radiance onto the opposite hills. They look kneaded and worked down and baked brown by ages of sun and wind. Then, without warning, they become a golden amethyst. I felt them cast over me a spell of invitation, just as they did to the weary Jesus. What urgings they put upon Him! Come over unto the other side, they gently whispered. I remembered at that moment to put some cream upon my cheeks, to prevent damage. The birthplace of Christianity can at times be cruel to those who nowadays are best placed to preserve and spread its glories! Along the shoreline whitecaps break over piles of stones. These ever-thinning rocks and pebbles are the eloquent remnants of the cities Jesus knew – their piers, their shops, their houses. Matthew, the tax-collector of Capernaum, walked in their midst. Here trod the feet of busy Peter and his partner Andrew. These stones cry out their stories to those of us with understanding hearts. At Tel Hûm we halted. I left Abbas sulking in his glass cage and explored the open-air museum. What a fascinating collection of oil presses and meal-mills the German friars have accumulated here! There are also the capitals of ancient fluted columns and restored portions of a Roman synagogue. A black-edged sombre notice states that the superintending Franciscan Father paid for it with his life, through a snake bite. Tear-bottle recesses; bas reliefs of Jewish emblems, such as the five-pointed star; Roman chariot wheels. An accumulated encrustation of Graeco-Roman faith. What rivets my attention are the floor mosaics, from a hexagonal forecourt by the shore. The waves of Galilee spray a rainbow mist. This may well be a floor which Jesus walked. The stones themselves seem to whisper it. I feel His immanence in this place, lit by the glorifying light of the sunset. I see before me the glowing outline of the divine feet. I can actually hear the music of His voice. Oddly, it has a faint Glaswegian accent. There is a strange clarity to this moment. I seem to be surrounded by a luminous multitude. Their faces are rapt with wonder. The speaker smooths his beard and addresses them calmly. I have not found so great faith, He says. No, not in all Israel. The crowd sighs. No more complimentary word was ever spoken by Jesus. A cloud passes over the sun and the illusion is broken. A moment later the golden flood returns, but not the ghosts of yesteryear. The imprints of his two feet fade. Suddenly, like Peter, I feel like getting wet. So, shoes off! Onto the blue-green stones I step. Ankle-deep in opal water I tread Christ's Capernaum. I might almost be in a "movie". Wave after burnished wave breaks musically upon this eloquent strand. This is Galilee's heartbeat. The sun like a giant ruby slips away and the whole landscape reddens. The Lake takes on an emerald tint. I picture Him here. He walks the marketplaces at that evening hour when orientals come alive. He is summoned to the bedside of the mother of Peter's wife. I hear Peter calling men to follow His growing group. As day ends and Capernaum turns to amethyst I see Him. He lays His hand on the swarming groups of little boys at play among the boats. I prod lazybones Abbas awake and he takes me on to Tabgha, which is probably Bethsaida. Here are rare mosaics of the early Christian church. Loaves and fishes in the design attest the belief that here the miraculous feeding took place. This is a likely thing, since the place is called Heptapegon. That means Seven Springs. The mosaics are in charge of a barefooted Bedouin. She wears a long black dress, touched with embroideries of red. Getting down on her hands and knees, she scrapes off the covering of sand and dirt. This is the only protection these mosaics have, as they lie in the open. In a spirit of Christian fellowship I kneeled alongside her, using one of her shoes to scoop away the sand. I regret to say she responded with incoherent invectives. I endeavoured to forgive her somewhat coarse, possessive manner. Moslem though she is, Jesus is her prophet. Since these mosaics have something to do with Him, she must jealously guard them. I stood back and left it to her. Abbas, who had sauntered over, had an unpleasant smirk on his face. A fly began to bother me. I sent a splinter of prayer, asking that it pester Abbas instead. To my delight it did! The exposed mosaics are of amazing interest. The early Christian symbols are dazzling. Very clear loaves and fishes. Ducks, and some life-like geese. A crane carrying a snake in its mouth. Thistles! A round tower. Some Greek letters spelling out the glory of God's name. My McEwan's tells me these are fifth century. Abbas took me back to Tiberias. I dined at a very clean German hotel there. The Fuehrer may not be everyone's cup of tea but there is something deeply impressive about the German concern for order and hygiene. This is not to deny the shadow cast by "the Jewish question". But even this can be horribly exaggerated by irresponsible newspaper men. I do not myself believe that Herr Hitler had anything at all to do with the excesses which have reportedly been committed on his behalf. It is also noteworthy that the German Zionist Federation has deplored emotive attempts at a boycott of German goods. This kind of nonsense is inspired by communists and socialists for their own sinister purposes. The German government has, quite rightly in my view, cracked down hard on "trades unionists" and the miscellaneous rabble of the so-called "Left". But I digress. I saw that the Lake surface was now disturbed. The boom surged against the shore. I could easily picture the anxious disciples tossed in their little craft, alarmed even though Christ was aboard. At the hotel I had arranged to be taken out on the Lake. A blond German introduced me to Najim, who lived locally. He was a handsome young man with an engaging smile. Abbas grunted at the intruder, and retreated inside the Rolls. Najim had brought a torch. He guided me down the dark, narrow, uneven street which led to the wharf. This was not far from a white building bearing in large blue capitals words which brought a surge of patriotic feeling into my breast: SCOTTISH MEDICAL MISSION. Outside it a number of natives squatted on the steps, smoking hubble-bubble pipes. Strangely, they owned a small portable gramophone. From the crackly speaker came the unexpected tinkling of ragtime. These men ignored me completely. I might almost have been as invisible as the hero of Mr Wells's tale. Along the dock there were a number of prone figures, laid out like corpses. They turned out to be boatmen, asleep. Najim explained that several of the boats were scheduled to leave at 4 a.m. He led me down a steep flight of steps. A substantial fishing boat bobbed up and down in the night waters. There were seven others already seated there. They were fellow Christian pilgrims like myself. Three American couples and a sombre Norwegian. We sat at one end, the sturdy oarsmen at the other. Soon we had pulled away from the quayside and were out into the calm waters. Above us blazed the stars and constellations that Christ Himself saw from this very place. Orion, the Pleiades, the Pole Star of the Mariner. The Great Dipper looked near enough to bring down and drink from its shimmering silver. One of the American women drew from her case a trumpet and began to blow All Through the Night. She followed this with Jesus, Saviour, Pilot Me. We sang along. Silent Night was followed by Abide With Me. Then, with trumpet muted to the slenderest filament of sound, she led us into Perfect Day. It made me think of that day two thousand years before when He said, Let us go over unto the other side. And there arose a great storm of wind. And the waves beat into the boat, insomuch that the boat was now filling. And our Lord lay in the stern, asleep on the cushion. And they prodded him and said unto him, Teacher, carest not thou that we perish? And he awoke, and rebuked the wind, and said unto the sea, Peace, be still. And the wind ceased, and there was a great calm. Hasn't this been the most heavenly day you have ever lived? one of the American women says on the way back. We all feel elated. Our faith has been recharged. If only we could have brought all the atheists of the world with us. This reality would have melted them utterly. One cannot doubt Him in Galilee. It just won't let you. The exhilaration of an evening like this makes sleep a waste of time. I just want to go on and on, experiencing Him. I want to look for the print of His feet on these shores that he loved. Two in the morning. A great company of cocks begins crowing. Nowhere in the world is the crow of a cock so strident as in Palestine. I remembered the hour of Peter's denial. Here Christ Jesus chose a telling bit of local colour. From my hotel room I can hear the soft feet of camels going by my window. They jingle their way toward Nazareth. I cannot describe, I cannot explain, the thrill I get from a camel train, a camel train with burdens and bumps and beads and bells and wobbly humps. It comes from the markets of old Bagdad with rugs and silks I should like to have had. A camel train on thistles fed, yet walking along with a regal tread. By five the vague stirrings of native life begin. In the Galilean household below a mother rolls up the mat on which she has been sleeping. She places it on her husband's bed. A baby's cradle of bright wool swings from a crude framework to which rush matting is attached. There is no other furniture. A child departs with a five-gallon tin. The woman's husband resembles Abbas. He is still asleep. The baby tries to pull him awake. The mother brings flat cakes of coarse bread for breakfast. How I would like to fly down like an angel! I would startle them with offerings of caramels. One, too, for the man beneath my window. He walks by carrying to market one puny little chicken. The sun still not yet up. The natives understand the importance of getting going before dawn. Later the heat will become intense. It pours into this sub-sea-level locale like lava. The bays burn deep and chafe. Across the Lake I see the misty hills of Gilead. From under black and grey opalescent clouds hanging low against the page I see the sun shoot out spectacular rays of adjectives onto a blank-blank sea. My mind's diseased, this much is obvious. A half hour away, up in the hills of Galilee, lies the Mount itself. On and up! The burning Plains of Hattin suck me into the boiling heart of the Mount of Beatitudes. Whoever shall compel thee to go one mile, go with him two. A moral which sometimes made poor Abbas a little sulky! As we ascended I began to sing O Master, Let Me Walk With Thee. Mister Grumpy responded by stepping on the gas. Once more I had to admonish the oaf. I told him finally to stop. I wandered among the thorns and stones. Above me I saw a little hill. Here truly are the imprints of Christ. Not in the sun-baked ground that my feet are treading but in my heart, where His truths are implanted. Blessed are they that hunger after righteousness. The pilgrim-presence of the Teacher overwhelmed me with His love. Light swirled around me. The whole of the area at the base of the Sea of Galilee is a mass of golden flowers, shoulder high. Elsewhere there are delphiniums and stocks and tulips. There are poppies, hyacinths, marigolds and hollyhocks. The impact of this lively expedition upon my constipation was, I regret to say, nil.

ANOTHER PILL. THERE, swallowed! Still in a fever, you see...

A SON OF the manse is one way of describing me, I shall not object. The house was built of dark grey stone and contained many empty rooms. I was born there, grew up there, and still live there. I was nourished on the milk of the Word. Winter was caustic. Hebridean gales are powerful and loud. I could hear the trees screaming. No room was ever warmed. Father did not believe in heating. Heating belonged to the Devil, who wanted to soften sinners for his realm. I sat in my overcoat, hands clasped around my neck for warmth. On Sundays we dressed in black and ate stewed mutton shanks. At four years old I had the words of Onward, Christian Soldiers. Bread and dripping was an afternoon treat. Sometimes a pear. Father spoke often of the utter impossibility of anyone on whom sin is seen by the eye of divine justice ever escaping God's righteous sentence of death by any effort to justify himself. He spoke of it frequently. And the word utter he uttered very emphatically. The brilliance of his stare was stark. His eyeballs swelled and the lids became animated, as might one suffering from blepharospasm. In the last days perilous times shall come. There shall be: Trucebreakers, Boasters, Blasphemers, Despisers of those that are good. There shall be: Scoffers saying, Where is the promise of His coming? All things continue as they were. I sang hymns as loudly as I could and did not attempt to wriggle out of the divine vengeance that was my lot. Death lapped the house in many guises. Worms ate the mouldy apple tree and its lecherous pink-cheeked fruits. Crows cawed with laughter at the purgatory in store for me. The seething innards of a dead sheep were put there to instruct me in the weakness of the flesh. The touring sexton, Mr Feeder, scowled down at me. His narrow eyes saw every inch of my badness. The yew groaned for release from all things mortal. A poplar blew over one night. Its terrific crash pierced my soul. God was sending me many warnings. I was frail and vulnerable. I must eat my porridge and be a good boy. I must pray repeatedly for forgiveness for my heap of sins. Envy, gluttony, frivolity, laziness. Lust was not yet in the pile. Later, in my early teens, two books were always waiting for me when I returned home from the hills. By then I had lust well under my belt. How hot and bloated I was with sin in those lusty years! My cheeks burned brightly, my bony chest was cool with the sweat of my grubby endeavours. What a boisterous boy I was at fourteen! Sometimes I bruised myself in my ardent sinning. Sometimes those filthy impulses made my chest raw. I climbed trees and pressed myself close to the trunk. There I shuddered, my legs clamped as to a lover's back. Afterwards, besmeared and harrowed, I descended. Out there in the wilderness the bracken brushed my ankles. It was like a tiny barbed prelude to all the greater punishments to come. I shed drops of blood when my skin was slashed. I bled into my grey socks. A woman came from the village to do our washing. Her name was Nora. She resembled a crag. The Lord informed her duties. Nora was a spinster. I doubt that the stains on my bedding or the grey flakes on my handkerchiefs meant anything to her. If they did she would have been too inhibited to mention it to my father. Satan was abroad but his foul influence was not associated with obscure deposits on cotton. One book was the Holy Bible, the other was an atlas of the Holy Land. They were twins. How alive the stories came when I located them on a map! Judea, Samaria, Galilee. Decapolis. The regions were differently coloured in pale shades. Samaria was violet. Olive green flooded Decapolis. Galilee was turquoise, Judea flesh-coloured. The names were exotic and magical. They dripped a strange poetry. Each place had a narrative to its name. Jericho, Beersheba, Jerusalem. Bethlehem, Gaza, Nazareth. The Salt Sea. The Sea of Galilee. And all still there, nineteen centuries after His feet had passed that way. One day, Donald, you will go there. That was what father said. He would have gone himself but he was anxious about his chest. He coughed a lot. I won't make old bones, he'd say. It was quite a favourite expression of his. His outlook was generally morose. The news made him shake his head. Satan's influence was everywhere. The evil one was behind all the wars and revolutions and unrest. Satan had invented the doctrines of socialism and communism to pervert men's minds and make them dissatisfied with their lot. Religion was under threat as never before. Fallen, fallen is Babylon the great, which hath made all the nations to drink of the wine of the wrath of her fornication. Fornication! A word which my father never explained. His big fat red dictionary said it meant sexual intercourse between unmarried persons. But that did not clarify matters. Intercourse was talking and sexual talking was as clear as mud and anyway sexual was itself enigmatic, naughty, unspeakable. Instinctively one knew the boundaries. And fornication remains a word which still inspires dread. In my twenties the only woman whom I ever dared to think I might marry was Mary Appleby, who taught Bible studies. Her disposition was cheerful, her breasts very substantial. She used talc a lot, judging by her pleasant odour. I enjoyed talking to her, though I flushed a lot, thinking of a side to my character of which she was innocent. I intimated the pleasures of a domestic arrangement and she did not demur. She was a woman I could have folded in two. When it came to the crunch, in Zurich, the thought of intercourse was awful. It would have tied us into a knot. We had a kind of unofficial engagement and then I called it off. Mary wept but I knew it was for the best. Perhaps I am not giving the whole story but it is at best, like Edwin Drood's, an incomplete tale. Yet in this vale of tears, and even when gales tore down our fencing, and sheep escaped from their pens, there was a ray of hope in a world rotten with sin. For the Jews are God's chosen people. Did not the Lord make a covenant with Abraham? *And I will give unto thee, and to thy seed after thee, the land wherein thou art a stranger, all the land of Canaan for an everlasting possession; and I will be their God.* Let no man deny the truths of Genesis. Eretz Israel. A land barren for twenty hundred stony years. A land without people for a people without a land. A place in which to build a community which will be a bridge into the East. It will bear the culture and the sympathies of every great nation in its bosom. Let there be a great migration! Let the torch of visible community be lit! Let Israel be a nation of many nations! Let it provide a hearth for the Jewish spirit to manifest itself in a new order! A Jewish National Home in Palestine! These were my father's heated and thudding certainties and so, too, are they mine. All the more so now that I am here, in boiling Palestine, hearing the grasshoppers chant their litanies amid the olive groves. I palpitate in this astonishing heat. It is sticky as treacle, thick as towelling. My helmet is a great boon. Also my expensive horn-rimmed American sunglasses with the Crooks lens. Also my box of soaps.

THROUGH THE WILDERNESS of Ziph I zip. I zig-zag, hot in pursuit of Elijah! My father reminds me more of Elijah than anyone. Elijah was a big, lean, vigorous man, unafraid to challenge Baal. A man prepared to do combat with Queen Jezebel and a deluded people. They called Elijah a troubler of the people but he retorted that they worshipped false gods. Elijah asserted the primacy of Yahweh, and proved it with the aid of the four elements. In victory he had the prophets of Baal put to death. Elijah traversed all the extremities of our Holy Land. He trekked restlessly on errands of perpetual protest against a soft civilisation and the false worship which made it putrefy. The western seaboard, the southern deserts, all this he knew. He later went east. He vanished from sight in Gilead.

The marvel is that all Elijah's landmarks may be visited by the motor-pilgrim to-day. There is the added bonus of rewarding and picturesque scenes from native life along the way. One of the great dramas in the life of Elijah followed his victory over the priests of Baal. A messenger arrived to warn Elijah that Baal-worshipping Jezebel had vowed to take his life that very day. Assassins were on their way. Our prophet took to his heels. He came to Beersheba, which belongeth to Judah. I am headed there myself. I rose very early. By five-thirty my chauffeur had me on the excellent road south to Bethlehem. By six-thirty we were in Hebron. Here flat-roofed houses and domed buildings cling to the sides of hills, with Moslems concentrated in the old city near the Mosque. A friendly Arab from the American Mission School shows me Joseph's Tomb, Abner's Grave and Sarah's Spring. I longed to visit the ancient glass furnaces for the sake of their matchless blue products. But a hot sun calls to hasten. By seven we are on our way east toward the Desert of Beersheba. Here, men plough the last arable land with a crooked stick, just as in antiquity. From the Tell es Zif you get glimpses of the Mediterranean. Footpaths criss-cross the barren, cave-pocked hills. Paradise for a fugitive like Elijah. On, and we meet a settlement of black Bedouin tents, pitched by wealthy nomads on their way to Bagdad. They are descendants of Ishmael. Noon now, and I sip Arab coffee made in a tiny brass pot. I eat dry *durra* bread and gulp down a draught of cool water from an earthen jug. It is all the Arabs here have but they offer to share it. All the aspects of desert life which Elijah saw can still be seen to-day. Camels, donkeys, women mending the rips in the tents. Not far away there's a relic of Roman times – the golden arches of an aqueduct, looking as if it was built but only yesterday. And then the first green trees of Beersheba oasis. The wells here may have been sunk by Abraham. Genesis seems as fresh as that aqueduct. And Abraham planted a tamarisk tree in Beersheba... A bearded Arab fills his goatskin bag from a well. Possession of these ageless springs was essential to Allenby's strategy. His army took control in October 1917. Beersheba town contains a substantial mosque, a tiny hospital, a government building, a Traveller's Rest House, Allenby Square and a War Cemetery. Under some dying trees I stared at the bust of Lord Allenby. From Beersheba, Elijah continued on alone into the wilderness. Finally he sat down under a juniper tree and fell asleep. He woke to the touch of an angel. Bread and a flagon of water were at his side. The angel instructed him to partake of this refreshment. Elijah did so and once more fell asleep. A second time the angel woke him. Again he was told to eat and drink what had been provided, for he had a long journey ahead of him. And when all these holy adventures were over, horses and chariots of fire were in attendance. At the end a whirlwind lifted Elijah to heaven. Beyond Beersheba is a lonely waste of low hills, untenanted except by wandering Bedouin. Abbas drove me some miles into to it to get the feel of the place for my book. One mound attracted my attention. On its summit stood a solitary, motionless horseman. Against the intense sky he resembled a statue. And then over the crest came camels, hundreds of them. I had never seen so many in my life. Abbas braked and the beasts came lumbering by. Some brushed the sides of the car and Abbas shouted angrily and clapped his hands. This had no effect whatever. The horseman came down to us. He was a fierce-looking individual. He had a cartridge belt around his waist and a Damascene dagger tucked into his belt. He spoke a few words to Abbas, spat (evidently in contempt) and rode away. More camels bumped the car but this time Abbas said nothing. A new distraction quickly presented itself. A heavily veiled woman walked by, barefoot, yet evincing an indescribable hauteur. Abbas leapt out and called after her. Whatever he said did not make the woman respond. She coolly walked on. Abbas turned to me and said, Amber, boss! Then he ran off. He caught up with her and walked alongside, jabbering in persuasive Arabic. It was her amber necklace he wanted. But it was not for sale. Sweat dripped from Abbas's cheeks as he beseeched her to part with this adornment. Instead of replying she mounted a donkey. She rode off at the head of a flock of black goats. As she rode away she drew from her garment a distaff, on which spins wool as she jogs along. She is as incredible as the Duchess in *Alice in Wonderland*.

L

LATER ON DURING our adventures we slowed for an obstruction. We were in the district the Romans called Sabastia. Jesus passed this way from Nazareth to Jerusalem on a number of occasions. The land here is lush and fertile. Carobs and olives. Expanses of golden wheat. A distant crackling, as of gunfire. My head, perhaps. It rocks with fierce thoughts and little wandering points of piercing pain. Time for another pill. My temple burns and drips. I rise above my petty sufferings. My mouth waters at the thought of figs and dates. Olives, however, I have never particularly liked. To my olfactory sensitivities there's a tang of urine. Look! Up ahead, barrels have been placed across the road. As we drew close I saw that they were arranged in such a way as to require a vehicle to move around them in slow zig-zags. This is The Emergency. Beyond the barrels I saw a line of British army lorries. Troops milled around beside them. A soldier with a rifle stood between the first two barrels, holding up an arm. Abbas stopped the car. I wound down my window and stuck my head out. The soldier ignored Abbas and came over to me. I'm sorry, sir. You can't come through here to-day. The soldier turned to Abbas. You have to turn round and go back, you understand? Abbas nodded. But a second figure had appeared. An officer. His scrutiny absorbed my collar. I say, are you a vicar? I am a church minister, yes. Look, perhaps you could do me a favour. The fact is our Padre is away in Cairo and we don't have anyone. To look after the spiritual, I mean. What I really mean to say is that we've had a bit of trouble in these parts. We gave the blighters quite a pasting but the swine managed to shoot one of our chaps. The doc reckons he's at death's door. If you could come and have a few words with him it might make all the difference. Forgive him his sins and all that. It can cheer a chap up no end when he's on the way out. I know I'd want it. Think you could manage it? I would be delighted. The officer jumped on to the running board and held on. He slapped the roof as one might the flanks of a horse. Abbas got the message and we rolled on, weaving our way around the barrels. The troops stopped chatting and stared. Soon we had left them behind. We came to another roadblock, a wooden contraption supporting coils of barbed wire. The officer waved at the soldiers and they dragged their barricade aside to let us through. We came to a town in a low valley. It was filled with activity. Something had torn a path through the middle of these dwellings. It was as if a great flood of water had gouged out the path. There was rubble everywhere. Some of the houses stood with just one side missing, exposing their interiors. Incredibly, some of these structures still contained people. Families moved around inside. I looked more closely: the occupants were all women and children. Many were weeping. Some of the women were making a terrible din, howling and banging their fists on the ground. We'll have to walk from here, the officer said. Abbas stayed with the car. The officer had a slim intelligent face, a sharp nose, a trim moustache. I could see soldiers smashing up furniture with their rifle butts and tipping jars of olive oil over rugs and cushions. In one living room stood a cabinet filled with glassware; an officer opened a door and dragged the structure forwards, stepping aside as it crashed across the carpet. Everyone paused at the sudden, sharp sound of shattering glass, then saw what it was and returned to their work of destruction. A trooper with a pick helve was energetically breaking a set of wooden chairs. Another was setting fire to a large book, which I guessed was the Koran. A clock was stamped on, a mirror broken. Sacks of flour, wheat, rice and sugar were being emptied into a single pile. Then a soldier who looked about eighteen urinated into it, to the laughter of his fellow soldiers. Is that really necessary? I said. My escort said: absolutely. This place is a rebel stronghold. They deserve everything they get. The bandits put up stiff resistance to our boys so you can't expect them not to be angry. It was hellish, trying to get the wogs in this rabbit's warren of buildings and narrow alleyways. Too many enfilading fields of fire. He smiled. So we got the sappers in. That resolved that little difficulty. I take it you have never heard of Thomas Bugeaud? I had not. *La Guerre des Rues et des Maisons* is an inspiration. The Marshall shows how a detonator always has an advantage over the man in the street. A mob is blocking it with barricades? No matter. One goes indoors and passes it by systematically blasting through the walls of the houses. This works for us where snipers are concerned. If they try and trap us in a labyrinth of alleyways, the solution is simple. He laughed. He said emphatically: Remove the labyrinth. He laughed louder. We walked by a house with its door open. I glimpsed a trail of dried blood across the hallway. A couple of spent cartridges winked like little nuggets of gold. Soldiers sat around in the shade, having a rest. I was wondering where the men from this township were. This conundrum was soon solved. We came to a square where a hundred or so Arabs were held in a makeshift pen. They were guarded by troops with rifles. A scruffy-looking officer with a beard was sat behind a trestle table. Evidently he was interrogating the prisoners, one by one. Some were released, others detained. Over here, reverend. My escort impatiently called me over to a house further up the street. We went inside. A pair of troopers were standing by a shape on the ground. A lad lay on a rug, his head pillowed by a purple cushion. A sheet draped him from the waist down. The area around the crotch was scarlet and wet. The soldier looked no older than seventeen. His flawless skin was the colour of oatmeal. His lips were oddly colourless. His eyes stared dully upward. We were in someone's home but there was no one around. The soldier had been laid in a kind of ante-room. It was bare apart from a large Ali Baba vase. The officer whispered in my ear. The doctor says he's on the way out. So we'll leave you to it, vicar. He indicated to the two guards that they should remove themselves. He followed them out, closing the door. The sunlight went too. The room dimmed. It was cool and shadowy in there. The soldier suddenly reached out and grabbed my hand. Mother, he said. My child, I replied. I laid my free palm on his brow. It was cold with death. His spirit was departing. An odd memory came into my mind. Once, somewhere deep in childhood, I had witnessed the draining of an ornamental lake. I cannot imagine where it was. There was a sluice, and big men with cloth caps, and my father seemed to know the other adults. I stared as the water sank lower and lower. At the end of it there was a morass of black filth. A few puddles remained. These dark stinking pools were turbulent with motion. They contained eels. The eels seemed gigantic. They were like serpents in the illustrations in my boy's adventure books. The eels thrashed around, appalled at losing most of what made up their world. They feared the future. They wriggled and jumped, hoping to find a route back into the past. But already men with waders were making their way through the sludge. They carried staves. I was invited to partake of the flesh of the serpent. It tasted salty and sour and I spat it out. The cloth-capped men laughed. That day has always made me fearful of swimming. You never know what lurks beneath even the most tranquil surface. Pikes. Or as in that fearful Sherlock Holmes story, a hideous jellyfish. A lovely day at Chanctonbury Ring, the lad said. His eyes were open now. His irises were grey. His eyelashes were long and delicate as a girl's. Palestine does strange things to men's hair. The Jews with peculiar curls of hair fixed against their brows, for example. An officer with a beard, for example. The soldier fixed his gaze on me, but I am sure it was not me he was seeing. I remember the primroses, he said. I remember the hillside. You painted the hard-boiled eggs, mother. You put faces on them. And flowers. We rolled them down the slope. The eggs cracked. We had a lovely picnic. While he burbled softly a door to my right abruptly opened. A man stood there. He was a bearded Arab, with wild eyes and a weather-beaten, wrinkled face. He carried a rifle, which he pointed at me. His gaze took in the dying soldier, the bloodied sheet, my dog collar. I wondered if I should offer him a caramel. But the opportunity never arose. Our encounter was over in a jiffy. He put his finger to his lips, smiled, and quietly closed the door again. It was a very odd thing to have happened. It was some moments before it occurred to me that he must have been one of the rebels. But there was nothing I could do. My duty was to attend to the unfortunate in front of me. It was a dreadfully close shave, yet at the time I seemed to be in a sort of trance. Oddly, I felt no fear. The lad was still reminiscing. He said there were sixty wogs. They'd surrendered. They walked along the valley, hands held high. And then we machine-gunned them. All sixty. The Ulsters and West Kents did this. Most of the dead were boys. Most not even as old as me. Father, will I go to hell? No, my son. Paradise is the place for you. The Lord forgives all. I glanced at my watch, wondering how much longer he would continue. I had to get on. Jericho had to be fitted in. I decided not to beat about the bush. Now the soldier was talking about the beach at Hove. He was talking about sandcastles. I put both my hands around his and applied some gentle pressure. I am the resurrection and the life, saith the Lord, I said. He that believeth in me, though he were dead, yet shall he live: and whosoever liveth and believeth in me shall never die. That got his attention. He stopped his drift and gazed at me, a slight bewilderment on his face. Mother had probably never said this kind of thing to him. I know that my redeemer liveth, and that he shall stand at the latter day upon the earth. And though after my skin worms destroy this body, yet in my flesh shall I see God. Worms, he said. I don't like worms. We brought nothing into this world, and it is certain we can carry nothing away. Nothing away, he echoed. His eyes wandered around the walls, as if seeking something. His general demeanour reminded me somewhat of that of a drunkard. I noticed for the first time what looked like the nest of something, built into a dark, high corner. It was about the size of a cricket ball, but with a scaly coating. I don't think the soldier noticed it. His gaze returned to my face. Who in hell are you? he remarked, frowning. And then his head lolled forwards and I knew he was dead. It occurred to me that the officer had not even told me his name. I felt for his pulse. It seemed not to exist. I went outside and found the officer smoking a cigarette. He's dead, I said. I did what I could. In fact I think my presence perked him up, although to be honest he wasn't quite altogether there. I gave him the Lord's blessing. He talked about his mother a lot. They often do, the officer said. He pulled out a notebook. Could you give me his dying words? He nodded at his pad. He grinned nervously and bared his nicotine-stained teeth. A front molar was missing. I have to write to the parentals, he explained. They like to know what happened. He spoke with great affection of both his mother and father, I lied (forgive me, O Lord). His mother especially. He said he hoped to meet them both again in heaven. Splendid. That's just the ticket. They'll like that. Oh and by the way, there's one of your bandits in the house. Good God! Why on earth didn't you say so? I have just said so. Yes, I suppose you have. That's true. I described what had happened. The officer narrowed his eyes, as they do in films. He called out to the pair of soldiers huddled nearby in the shade. Gregson – go and tell Sergeant Smith I need his unit over here at the double. Manning – go and find a stretcher and someone to help remove Moorehouse. He's snuffed it. The men went off. I'd better be getting back to my car, I said. We've another forty miles to go to-day. At least. Not this way, I'm afraid. Too jolly risky. Most of the rebels fled into the hills. If they see a car with an Englishman I'm afraid they might well take a pop. We can't have that. H.M.G. would never forgive me if I allowed a vicar to be assassinated. It wouldn't look good in the papers. That's a shame, I said. I was looking forward to to-day. Sorry. No dice. But thanks awfully for all you did for poor Moorehouse. Let me give you my card. Perhaps one day I can return the favour. Or if you ever have a spot of bother with any of our chaps, just show it to them. Tell them we are chums. *Major Reginald Thwaite*, it read in gold copperplate. It included his home address in Buckinghamshire and a telephone number. I thanked him and put the card away in my crocodile skin wallet. I made my way back past the ruined houses to the Rolls. The square which had been packed with prisoners was now deserted. The makeshift pen had been cleared away. To my considerable annoyance Abbas was not alone in the car. A figure sat in the rear. I felt this was extraordinarily impudent on my chauffeur's part. I had rented the Rolls for my tour and I looked upon it as my own property. I did not care for Abbas to turn it into a public hostelry. As I approached the door opened and the man inside emerged. I saw that it was the officer with the beard. He walked towards me and shook my hand. I'm very pleased to meet you, he said. I understand from Abbas you are doing a tour of the holy sites. What's more you are a Zionist. That's excellent news. His eyes were deep-set, blue and full of fierce energy. His beard rather set him apart from the other troops. His uniform was a little dishevelled. In fact it struck me there was a queer resemblance to the bandit I had encountered in the house. He looked like an irregular. You know Abbas? That was what most startled me. Indeed, yes. A very good chap. Gives us lots of assistance. And people like you provide the perfect cover. There's nothing suspicious about a chauffeur, eh? Abbas gets about. We'd never win this damned war if it wasn't for intelligence. Look, I'd love to have a chat but things are still a bit hot round here. I have to be off. He strode off and disappeared into a nearby house. I climbed back into the car. Abbas was counting some mils which the officer had evidently given him. I had no idea that he was an informer. It was hard to imagine what information he had that was of value to the authorities. The sites we toured were not exactly strategic – not in the modern age. But then I remembered Abbas would sometimes go off to buy food or visit friends and relatives. Doubtless there was much gossip. Who was that man? I said. Abbas beamed as he put the coins away in a bag, which he then placed in a walnut-panelled compartment under the passenger seat. He locked the compartment and put the key away. That man, sir, was Captain Wingate. A very good man. He started the car up and we glided away. We did not get far. A pair of soldiers waved at us to stop. Abbas was ordered to pull the car over into the shelter of a house. The house where I'd seen the bandit was about to be blown up. Best stay in the car, sir. It will be safer there. You'd be surprised how far débris sometimes flies. We did not have to wait long. A tremendous roar literally made the ground shake. A shock seemed to rush through the metal structure of the car, even permeating my teeth. It delivered a passing thump to my heart. A moment later a boiling dome of white smoke spread across the town. A thousand birds screeched and took flight. Animals of all kinds began barking and braying and mewling. Next I heard the soft pitter-patter of falling matter. None of it was visible. From where we were parked the scene – a sunlit patch of street, some brightly coloured sheets hanging from a window – was unchanged. Poets, it seems to me, ought to have greater acquaintanceship with high explosive. There is great beauty in the massive expansion of dense, ascending smoke.

E

EXCEPT THE LORD build the house their labour is but lost that build it. The Bedouin, poor souls, know nothing of this. At seven thirty that day we set off for Mount Nebo. Abbas was unhappy. He would have preferred to press on to Jerusalem and the sum of money he was owed for his chauffeurship. He had no choice but to obey instructions. My itinerary was always of the free-spirited sort. After a few miles I banged on the glass and made him halt briefly by a stream. The sky was cloudless, the sun incandescent. A large camel train had paused to let the animals drink there and to eat from ancient grain bags. Women were spreading on the stony floor of the stream strips of cloth some fifty feet long. I took two snaps of this picturesque scene. Then on along a road rising up to a plateau where many Bedouin were working the fields. Black tents dotted the area. Entire families were toiling in the heat. A horseman in bright red veil kept watch. The road to Bagdad branched off to my left, tempting me to try the ruins of Babel and Ninevah. But not this year, nor the next, nor the ones after that. A stone cairn and a large whitewashed arrow pointed the way for airmen flying between Damascus and the Euphrates Valley. I could see the railway leading toward Mecca. Aviators, locomotives, donkeys, a motor car – all passing through this spaceless and timeless sphere. Aviators especially, of late. I chuckle as I remember what Bernard told me. About a year earlier Archibald Wavell had called in the Royal Air Force. There was a gang of rebels trapped in the open. The R.A.F. boys had bombed and machine-gunned the blighters. Somewhere between fifty and sixty oozlebarts were killed. Then it was the army's turn. Mopping up, they called it. Bare and brown grow the lonely hills. But ours was a good dirt road. In a Rolls one rolls along very comfortably. How marvellous it is to get to the heart of nomadic life by such means! I smiled again. A happy day; a happy, happy day. Now, still delightedly smiling, I plunge into the dawn of Christianity. Here lie the remnants of ancient Hesban, the Heshbon of the Old Testament. This, you will recall, was the capital of Sihon, King of the Amorites. A slippery chap! Moses had difficult dealings with him. One cannot help but sympathise. The American School of Oriental Research in Jerusalem believes this section to be the first conquered by the Israelites, after the Exodus from Egypt. To-day all that remains are two tumbled columns and a massive sarcophagus. Poignant vestiges of the one true faith. And on a hilltop nearby is a small walled village with a large gateway. This, podgy detestable Abbas tells me (his thick smug face reminds me of the tip of an oiled cricket bat), is the winter home of the nomads. In the summer they drift across these grazing lands. In winter they settle here while their fields are flooded by daily deluges. Bare and brown grow the lonely hills. But ours is a good dirt road and in a Rolls Royce the journey is most comfortable. Suddenly, coming over the crest of a hill, entirely without warning, we found ourselves in the middle of an entire tribe of Bedouin. There were hundreds of people – men, women, adolescents, babies – together with a plenitude of dogs, sheep and camels. It reminded me of a Biblical epic at a picture house. It was like a page ripped from the Old Testament – the days of the Patriarchs come to life. I told Abbas to stop and stepped out to take photographs. A dozen sheiks riding handsome Arab horses traversed this animated mass of humanity. One of them came over and spoke to Abbas. He sounded angry. Abbas informed me that the man did not want me to take any more photographs. I was tempted to ask on what authority but I decided not to. Instead I took out a packet of Camels and offered the sheik one. The man curtly declined it and rode off. Abbas explained that the Bedouin do not have anything like cigarettes. They do not smoke. He suggested we drive on. Not before time. Some of the more forward Bedouin women had approached and were now pressing their faces against the car window. They seemed fascinated by my pale face. I stared back, equally entranced by their perfect white teeth, their tattered black hair, their long, filthy, ragged dresses, which they trail on the ground. One of these women had distinctly negroid features. I threw her a caramel, which only excited the others. I wound down the window on the far side and tossed a handful out. Screeching like crows, the women rushed to seize them. We left them in a cloud of dust. For miles we chugged over a golden desert plateau. This is the Plain of Moab, which Moses knew. It is here that Numbers and Deuteronomy truly come to life. The Jabbok, the Gulf of Arabah, the slopes of Pisgah – you can find them all on a modern map. And Moses gave unto the tribe of the children of Reuben. And their border was from Aroer, that is on the edge of the valley of the Arnon, and all the plain by Medeba. I have always found it a bit rum that Moses parcelled out land that already belonged to others. We came to Madeba. This was Lawrence's H.Q. for a while. I wanted to see the famous mosaics. They were laid in the sixth century. A church was built over them by a colony of Greek Christians who migrated here in the last century. They came from Kerak, a Crusader stronghold east of the Dead Sea. Abbas went off to find someone to let me inside. He returned with the teenage son of the Greek priest. The youth was quietly spoken and neatly turned out. It was cool and shadowy inside the church. I removed my helmet and sunglasses and left them on a table inside the entrance. With great pride the lad explained the details of the mosaics. I was fascinated by their primitive portrayal of Jerusalem's walls and domes. These were all done out in the flattest lack of perspective. Adjacent are sections of the Holy Land, the palms of Memphis, the Nile. These are not in the right geographical relation. I stooped to take photographs. A horde of small boys appeared all around me. They were silent, inquisitive, barefooted. Having accomplished my mission it was time to go. But the table by the door now bears only my helmet. The sunglasses are gone. Who stole the gentleman's glasses? The priest's son screams in fury. He scrutinises the faces. One is missing. They flee. Oh Christ, to steal in a church! The youth's face is stricken. And from a clergyman, too. I loiter in the outer court and mop my brow. The suspected thief is quickly apprehended. He is dragged towards me. The priest's son has seized one arm, a village woman the other. The boy is screaming as if I am about to execute him. The villagers are screaming too. Put him in jail! Shame on you! Where are the gentleman's sunglasses? The boy sobs that he has never seen the glasses. He insists he is innocent. His scalding tears are too much for me. I plead for his release. It is going to be hard to go through the glaring miles to Jerusalem with unprotected eyes, but no matter. Besides, the thief will never dare to wear his prize. The horn-rimmed Crooks lens would be instantly identifiable. He will never enjoy the soft, muted aspect it gives to the burning landscape.

END OF THE ROAD, said Abbas. The tar macadam fizzles out. Madeba, this barren spot is called. From here to the spur of mountain running out to Nebo and Pisgah the route is a rough track. We must take a Madeba boy with us for a guide, said Abbas. He clicked his fingers and there on our running board stands a sixteen-year-old Arab wearing a long petticoat. His white veil is held by rings of woven black goats hair. His arching nose is a Semitic delight. Impishly, I name him Hobab. Hearing me speak, his eyes gleam with intelligent joy. Yes, I Hobab, he says. He grins, exposing white teeth, five missing. Yes, I said. You are to be our eyes, as Hobab was for Moses in the desert. Yes, boss. He took the seat next to Abbas. The road became stonier and stonier. What jolts! Abbas begins to mutter about damage to his exhaust. We pass another great encampment of Bedouin. My gaze is on higher things. Morning mountain mists, drifting. A land of miragey prospects. A vision of the Jordan Valley. Abbas brakes and Hobab leaps out. The lad wrestles with a huge rock in the middle of the track. I would like to help but my back hurts. Abbas cannot, for it is a matter of his Arab pride. Hobab eventually gets it to budge. We proceed. Three camels stand silhouetted against the sky. This is the same sky that canopied Moses when he stood here looking toward the Promised Land. A promise which he never occupied. This is where we leave sullen Abbas baking in his metal oven. It is time for me to make the ascent. Hobab leads the way. I trudge after him. Nebo stands 2,643 feet above sea level. The silence is deeply spiritual. Suddenly the mood is spoiled. Two Arabs rise up from nowhere, like a noxious emission from a marsh. The taller of these pestiferous twins announces they will guide me to Moses' tomb. I tell them to bugger off (forgive me. Lord, for I was hot and irritable that day). They pretend not to understand the vernacular. Fuck off! Piss off! *Scram*. They grin like monkeys. They find me amusing. Nothing I can say, no matter how vile, will deter them. Hobab says nothing. The parasites lope beside us, determined to extract a gratuity. At last we reach a little pile of stones at the summit. I do not require instruction from a malodorous member of a dusky tribe to understand the history of this place. I have read my guide book. I know already that the famous Moabite Stone found not far from here reveals that this place was once a shrine sacred to Jehovah. One of my new friends, mobilising the few paltry scraps of English he possesses, says: Moses, he sleep here. He says it over and over again, as if he was speaking to a mental defective. Moses, he sleep here. Moses, he sleep here. Pisgah, over there. He look to Promised Land. Moses, he no go Jerusalem. He sleep here, Nebo. As if I was a complete idiot, the fellow folds his hands and mimics the attitude of a man in last repose. This deluded wretch is plainly a Mohammedan. He has never once read the Holy Bible. He is laughably ignorant of the facts. For Moses went up from the plains of Moab unto Mount Nebo, to the top of Pisgah, that is over against Jericho, that is over against Jericho; and the LORD shewed him all the land of Gilead, unto Dan; and all Naphtali, and the land of Ephraim and Manasseh, and all the land of Judah, unto the hinder sea; and the South, and the Plain of the valley of Jericho, the city of palm trees, unto Zoar. And the LORD said unto him: I have caused thee to see it with thine eyes, but thou shalt not go over thither. So Moses the servant of the LORD died there in the land of Moab, according to the word of the LORD. And he buried him in the valley in the land of Moab over against Beth-peor: but no man knoweth of his sepulchre unto this day. Got that, matey? Moses was buried down in the valley, not up here. And no man knoweth of the whereabouts of Moses' tomb, least of all a pair of bloodsuckers who prey on vulnerable pilgrims. But as well as my word-perfect Deuteronomy I also had knowledge of The Emergency. It was best not to provoke the natives unnecessarily. I therefore managed a tight smile and with heavy sarcasm thanked the fellow for enlightening me in such depth about Biblical lore and geography. I thrust coins at my tormentors, provoking a storm of gratitude. Mercifully, they then scampered back down the mountain path and returned to lie down in their nest of rocks. When they had gone I gave Hobab a hearty clip round the ear. He burst into tears. Since there is nothing more detestable than a sobbing child I gave him a second whack to shut him up. That did the trick. He became mute and all I had to endure was the prospect of his soulful eyes and their tiresome trickling. I turned away. You get an astonishing panoramic view of Palestine from here. Opposite, on the Judaean hills, lies Bethlehem. Five miles to the north are visible the towers on the Mount of Olives. The mystical hills of the Judaean wilderness look like they might melt any moment into sky. Everything seems like mists in a dream country, not points in geography. Farther north rise the mountains Ebal and Gerizim, in Samaria. Galilean Tabor and Gilboa are too hazy to be distinguished. A slight shift of perspective and you are looking down into that most remarkable cleft in the earth's surface, the Jordan Valley. It ends with the deep Salt Sea. This weird body of water looks like a giant blue eye with salt dune lids. A cloud turns it to turquoise; dullness makes it a zircon, and then an opal. From Nebo you see the spur called Pisgah, where is to-day a little church with notable mosaics. A speck in the sky expands into a swooping hawk. A second speck appears, an aeroplane, with the familiar and heart-warming circles of red, white and blue. The drone of its engine deepens. The brat tugs at my sleeve. He seems agitated; points the way down. He seems to be telling me to go. Oh, very well. I am hot, tired and have seen everything. I shake him off and began my descent.

EVERYTHING? NOT QUITE! For a recent bulletin of the American School of Oriental Research illuminates the latest discoveries. Within a comparatively small radius of Mount Nebo, a number of Early Iron Age sites were found, and one early Bronze Age site. Some date from the thirteenth to the eighth centuries B.C. A few kilometres northeast of Mount Nebo, at Khirbet Qurn Kibsh, an extensive Bronze Age site was discovered. This could be dated by its pottery to between 2200-1800 B.C. Such data scientifically proves the trustworthiness of the Bible record. All "a priori" considerations favour acceptance of the Hebrew tradition and its connection with this phase of the Conquest of Moses. The date of Exodus was about 1290 B.C. The Israelites may therefore have conquered Sihon's territory before 1250 B.C. A useful reminder, if ever there was one, that Palestine is a country in which the mystical and the historical constantly strive for possession of one's mind.

S

SILVERSMITHS WERE SEEN by Isaiah, turning out trinkets for travellers when they should have been helping repair Zion's walls. He watched the artists with their fining pots and delicate filigrees of gold and silver. He heard the divine promise. Behold, I will set thy stones in fair colours, and lay thy foundations with sapphires. And I will make thy pinnacles of rubies, and thy gates of carbuncles, and all thy border of pleasant stones. In righteousness shalt thou be established: thou shalt be far from oppression, for thou shalt not fear; and from terror, for it shall not come near thee. No weapon that is formed against thee shall prosper; and every tongue that shall rise against thee in judgement, thou shalt condemn.

SCRAPS OF CONVERSATION can be heard if you linger by the Jaffa Gate. The natives never tire of sitting on the kerb, staring, yawning, chatting, eating round green melons. Swaying dromedaries pass by. Handsome, sturdy young English soldiers stand around in groups, some holding their rifles while others drink bottled beer. An Arab brags about the native soap factory in Haifa. Another Arab predicts the failure of the next Jewish Fair at Tel Aviv. Why are they talking in English? I suppose it is to impress me. I sit on a chair and rest my shoes on a brass-trimmed box, while a smiling boy gives them a good polishing. A nearby member of the Manchester Regiment is telling a new recruit about local traditions. When you finish your duty often nothing has happened. No bombs or anything. So what the driver does then is switch his wheel backwards and forwards to get the wog on the front to roll off. If he's a lucky wog he'll get off with a broken leg. If he's unlucky the next truck coming up behind hits him. But nobody bothers to pick up the bits that's left. We're the masters, right? We're the bosses and whatever we do is right. And anyway once you've shaken a wog off the bonnet you don't want him anymore. He's fulfilled his job. It's the same with prisoners. Any you capture you give them a good beating. I met one chap who had a very unusual souvenir. In his cigarette tin he kept this wog's brains! Pretty disgusting if you ask me. It looked like a chopped-up frog. Sometimes you make the wog hold a heavy rock and every time he drops it you beat him. Sometimes, for a laugh, we put bells round their necks and make them dance. Sometimes we tie their balls with cord. Some chaps pull out the wogs' fingernails with pliers. Me, I draw the line at that. Call me squeamish if you must. But everyone has to join in the beatings. And it can be quite good fun. Anything will do. Rifle butts, bayonets, scabbard bayonets, fists, boots, whatever. That's what the oozlebarts get before they go off to the jail. You form two lines of men with pick axes, scabbards with a bayonet inside, rifles, whatever's there, tent mallets, even tent pegs. And you send the wogs through one at a time, through this... What do you call it? Gauntlet. And they get belted and bashed until they reach the other end. Now any that can run when they got to the other end go straight into the police meat wagon and get sent down to Acre. Any that die they go into the other meat wagon and are dumped at one of the villages on the outside. I remember there was one poor sod probably your age well I'd heard people say in the past that you could have your eye taken out and cleaned and put back and I always believed it but it's not so because this lad's eye was hanging down on his cheek the whole eye had been knocked out and it was hanging down and there was blood all over his face.

SIN HATH TORMENTED me since my eleventh year. This is a fact I cannot ever escape: an appetite as loathsome as an opium addiction and the foul, shameful labours it sets me to perform. Talk of eyes and eyesight brings it to mind. I have long risked blindness. My cheeks burn with fire, my dog collar tightens around my throat, my hands grow restless. Time for another pill. Two! I am devilish with my risks. Yet shame floods the soiled temple of my body. My descent into beastliness first began in Glasgow. Father took me with him to attend a church convention. It was the first time I had seen a city. The crowds and the racket astonished me. The streets were crowded with honking vans and horse-drawn carts and glistening clumps of dung. The faeces made a deep impression. I was but a lad and not used to urban ways. We stayed in a dormitory attached to a seminary. In bunks. The boy above me, an older teenager, was fat. He farted throughout the long night. The stench descended like a miasma sent by Satan. The seminary had a gymnasium which the boys, a dozen of us, were obliged to attend. Elsewhere on that estate our fathers explored their theological differences. Their soft, pink-cheeked, mutual hatreds were masked with smiles and words of treacle. Or so I imagine. My father was not a happy man. He may have been while mother was alive, I cannot remember that far back. By the time of the Great War, which had been orchestrated by financiers and foreign filth, the planet was awash with Satan's emissaries. *Satan!* There were few pictures. He had horns and a hairy face, like a goat. His favourite posture was to squat. Demons with scales and talons did his bidding. The Bolsheviks belonged to his battalions. Full-breasted sluts with whirling skirts tore wildly at themselves in his presence, exposing their nipples and stretches of plump upper thigh. For understanding, my father said that the Holy Bible and *Paradise Lost* would suffice. To get closer to this intriguing evil one I immersed myself in Mr Milton but gave up a quarter of the way through. I ruefully realised he was not my cup of tea. Mr Wordsworth is altogether more divine, though he largely shuns the theological. Besides, I was young. At that age the works of John Milton were altogether less interesting than those of John Buchan. Had I so expressed myself openly, father would no doubt have frowned. He did not hold with light matters such as novels, which he said were for idlers, shop girls and fools. The Lord Almighty hath given us one book which contains all books, and that should be adequate for any man. Father once caught me reading *The Thirty-Nine Steps* but assumed it was a Christian primer about the route to personal salvation. His attention was focused elsewhere. His scowl deepened, his brow grew more furrowed. For father the world's sin was bad enough but the innumerable grievous errors of his fellow priests far worse. But this, during those ten days spent in Glasgow, was of little consequence to his son, Donald. We boys were left to our own entertainments, apart from bible classes, services in the chapel and physical training. P.T. took place every day at 11 a.m. By this hour it was calculated that we would have digested our porridge. The gymnasium was in a hall beside a playing field. First we changed in a desolate ante-room, putting on navy blue shorts, white vests and plimsolls. After that we trooped into the gym. The first ten minutes were free play, to get us warmed up (it was bitterly cold in that place). Then the instructor, a harsh sour elderly priest we brutally nicknamed Old Nick, made us hang upside down from wooden bars, jump an old horse with split leather flanks, and run on the spot two hundred times. The dictates of Old Nick were worth it for those sweet minutes of free play. On my first day I clambered up and down the wooden bars along with the other boys. We shrieked like monkeys. It was good fun. But the gym had other entertainments, including half a dozen ropes which hung from the high ceiling. In memory they seemed to stretch almost to heaven. These ropes were thick as a man's wrist and distinctly nautical in character. The huge twined strands of hemp smelled good. They gave an olfactory pleasure akin to that of a newly baked loaf. The first time I brought my face close to one of the ropes I found the experience agreeable. I raised my arms and took hold of the rope. I pulled my body off the ground, holding my legs out straight as if I was going up and down on a swing. The rope pressed against my crotch. I raised one hand and then the other. Slowly I hauled myself higher and higher. The fat boys and the thin boys fell away and I entered a private realm. It made me realise how good it would be to be an angel, floating above people, seeing everything that was going on while no one knew you were there. It was at that moment I realised something astonishing had occurred. My willy had mysteriously turned hard and grown bigger. It was squashed between my stomach, my clothing, and the granite-hard coils of the rope. Such a phenomenon had never happened before and it baffled me. I was eleven years old and in complete ignorance about the development of the male organ of generation. I was unaware it had any other function than for urination. I had carried it through my childhood like a second tongue, floppy and taken for granted. I hung there, agonized with wonder, my very first erection requiring my most urgent attention. The year was 1917. There was trouble in Russia and the Germans had still not been pushed back to Berlin. Father was daily furious about the state of things but his son had more pressing concerns. Sweat formed in my armpits and trickled down my ribs. I could smell its salt tang. And then there was a new development, another outbreak of wonder. I adjusted my position on the rope, hauling myself an inch or so higher. I fervently hoped this might rid me of my uncanny, unwanted tumescence. I dreaded having to descend. When they saw my willy sticking up like this all the other boys would laugh. The P.T. instructor would have me packed off to hospital. Perhaps my willy was diseased. Perhaps they would need to cut it off to save my life. It was happening to soldiers all the time. You saw them in Glasgow, limbs missing, resting on wooden crutches, holding out caps for coins. That slight change of position helped to put me out of my misery – and create what was, in retrospect, a far greater one. The pressure of the rope just below my glans was enough to trigger what happened next. As I hung there, my body trembled. A tide rose without warning and rushed through me. A shuddering expanded upward and outward from my troublesome little root of flesh. A honeyed surge. Bliss unspeakable. A cascade of delight to make a boy gasp. And then it was gone. Over. Done with. My organ wilted and returned to its old self. I slid down the rope, exhausted and perplexed. Line up boys, shouted the priest. It was time for some exercises on the bars. I couldn't wait for the next day. This time I declined the games of the other boys and headed straight for the ropes. I chose my old friend, the third one along. I hauled myself up and in no time at all I had another erection and another orgasm. I say that now but those words were completely unknown to me at the time. I hung there, straining the last drops of pleasure from my throbbing flesh. My style disturbs me. It has become pornographic. But I know no other way of articulating that which I shall never articulate to a living soul. My book could never be about such matters. No book could be, apart from one published in Paris. No matter. Sin must be frankly acknowledged, even though only in a confessional of one. Let me confess it, Holy Father. Who knows anyway. Who saw it all. Who has infinite mercy for a sinner such as I. For the angel of the Lord tarrieth about them that fear Him and delivereth them. O taste, and see, how gracious is the Lord. Blessed is the man that trusteth in Him. I repeated my ecstasies every day until the conference ended and it was time to return to the Hebrides. On my last session in the gym, my legs bent around the rope, rubbing myself with exquisite delicacy against the rough strands – I had begun to develop a skill – I was aware of the old priest gazing at me thoughtfully. I closed my eyes and shut him out. There was nothing to give the game away. I was just a boy, hanging from a rope. The old priest said nothing. Perhaps he thought he was imagining it. Perhaps I imagined that he thought he was imagining it. Something I have not made clear. There was no mess in my underpants. I did not ejaculate. My physical development was not yet quite ripe enough for the production of semen. These were dry orgasms, barren of matter from any ventricle. They raise, I think, interesting theological questions, though none I think will ever be mooted in a pulpit or at a public gathering of theologians. The sin of Onan involves the waste of seed. Yet I had, as yet, none to spill. Nor were my thoughts filled with lustful desires or images. My pleasures were entirely innocent, wholly free of base matter. Indeed, I tried to discuss them with one of the other boys, Peter from Manchester. I described to him how when I climbed the rope I got a very nice feeling between my legs. I said no more than that, for to have brought my willy into the conversation would have been unseemly. I knew from father that *unseemliness* was one of the world's great vexations. Peter gawped at me through his wire-rimmed spectacles. He said he had no idea what I was talking about. Matters did not – could not – end there. The pleasure which rose in my groin was addictive. In my heart I knew it was wrong. The thought of discussing the matter with father was impossible. I supposed it was a misfortune which afflicted one in a million. Perhaps it was a kind of disease. But reason was no use to me. I had to have more of this luscious explosive feeling. Upon my return home an obvious difficulty presented itself. No rope. It was therefore incumbent upon me to find a substitute. I soon whittled the matter down to three possibilities. In the garden Nora's washing line hung between two stout cast iron poles. They were about the same thickness as a gymnasium rope. The problem lay in utilising these twins of temptation. During the day I was exposed to observation from the house. Initial attempts to climb one of these poles were witnessed either by my father or Nora. They shouted. Don't do that, Donald! You will break it. Break it, forsooth! Me! A mere slip of a lad up against a fine piece of Victorian ironwork shipped and carted all the way from one of smoky Glasgow's nether regions. I abandoned the poles for the time being, without great regret. This was in part because I somehow knew that the wearing of clothes spoiled the sensation. In my bedroom I had found a substitute which was more challenging but which permitted much greater latitude. The wardrobe. It was a massive structure of dark oak, with curved corners. The wardrobe was perfect. All I had to do was go to bed, put out my light, and wait. The inky blackness dissolved into grey outlines, and the wardrobe waited for me with the patience of a lover. Eventually my father came slowly up the uncarpeted stairs. He spent an eternity in the bathroom. I heard the splash of his ablutions, the gurgle of the W.C. After that he went into his bedroom next to mine and closed the door. A yellow light leaked out on to the landing. Another twenty minutes and then he said a short prayer. At long last the light went out. I heard his bed creak as he adjusted his posture. Then silence. Soon I would hear him snore. Only then was it safe for me to quit my narrow cot, untie the string on my pyjama trousers and strip naked. My penis was rigid with anticipation long before I had taken three Wagnerian paces to the wardrobe. I reached up on tiptoe and gripped the frame that ran along the top. This frame concealed a shallow trough which was designed for storage purposes. Father kept a suitcase on top of his wardrobe. My wardrobe bore no load, which greatly assisted my monkey-like acrobatics. I hung there, my legs bent, gripping the cold wood. All that touched the curving end of the wardrobe was my own engorged curve of desire. After a matter of seconds the great shuddering sensation came. I continued there, pressed against this dark hard lump of furniture, my arms straining, until the last spasm of pleasure had been forced from my pale body. Then I quietly dropped to the ground, slipped my pyjamas back on, and went back to bed. In 1918 the war ended. That was not the only great event of that year. I should explain that Nora only came to the manse on weekdays. And on Saturdays and Sundays my father was frequently busy with church business. Apart from my necessary presence on the Sabbath, I was left to my own devices most weekends. And what devices! I usually managed sex with the wardrobe three or four times on a Saturday. I had the matter down to a well-timed routine. The summer months were the easiest because on very hot days I could get away with wearing a pair of shorts and a singlet. That made it easier to enjoy the wardrobe without fear of discovery. Even on those very rare occasions when someone rang the doorbell while I was mid-spasm, I had ample time to hurl on my two items of clothing and appear moments later, flushed and helpful. I was cunning enough to carry a ball in one hand, as if the visitor had interrupted me during some energetic childish play. How calculating Satan makes us as we seek to conceal our sinning! Yet did not Christ Jesus come into the world to save sinners? And the blood of Jesus Christ cleanseth us from all sin.

ONE SUMMER'S DAY in 1918, something shockingly unexpected happened. Father was five miles down the road at a mothers' meeting in the church hall. The sun blazed down from a cloudless sky, filling the manse with light and little sparkling dust storms. Somewhere in the distance a flock of gulls screeched. A golden hexagon impressed itself against my favourite end of the wardrobe. As I hung there, on the edge of an imminent ecstasy, the warm sun coated my back and behind with glowing honey. Everything that day seems luminous and sharply defined. I pressed my thighs against the warm wood and the volcanic surge began in my loins. And then it happened. To my astonishment, horror and bewilderment, my penis spat gobbet after gobbet of phlegm. The first couple of bolts shot as high as the ceiling, the rest slapped against my face, my chin, my stomach. I hung there until the orgasm was over, then slithered back to earth. I was truly appalled by this savage and beastly turn of events. The evidence of my furtive pleasure was everywhere. My body dripped with it. The wardrobe was slimed with my lust. The high ceiling held two teardrops from the eyes of the all-seeing Almighty. Even as I gazed, a drop fell from the tip of my shrunken penis and landed on the rug at my feet. The wool absorbed my guilt as if it was blood from an innocent I had just stabbed to death. Like any murderer, the first imperative was to clean myself up. I mopped the mess from my body with a handkerchief (a handkerchief which I afterwards burned). I wrapped a second handkerchief around my genitals – I was still oozing a little slime – and pulled on my clothes. A third handkerchief I utilised to rid the wardrobe and rug of the damning evidence. I felt like a spattered killer mopping up after his moment of butchery. The glutinous matter attached to the ceiling was a very different kettle of fish. It was out of reach. I felt that if my father came home now he would enter the room and see at once what had occurred. Those sloppy grey pearls were as thumpingly blatant as Poe's tell-tale heart. In the end I calmed down. The day went quietly on. I got a different kind of grip on myself. I found Nora's longest broom and by standing on a chair I was able to scrape those lewd deposits from the white purity they had sullied with their presence. By the time father came home Donald was a good boy engrossed by an engaging primer on mathematics. Did you have a rewarding day, Donald? Yes, father. But inside, I was acutely anxious. I was worried I was diseased. My genitals were rotting inside from the abnormal usage which I had subjected them to. I could never tell father. He would take it personally. It would break his heart. Satan had wormed his way into the manse itself. Satan had recruited his own son. Nor did I see how I could explain it to any doctor, least of all fierce, bearded Dr McMurdo. The doctor worshipped at our church. He was a friend of father's. And in a long career it was entirely possible he had never encountered such abnormality and wickedness as mine. Even at weddings he never smiled. I wondered if I would have problems urinating. Mercifully, none. I determined to lay off sex and see what happened. The next day my penis was, to all external appearances, perfectly normal. It was another sunny day. I went to church and prayed silently for the Lord to forgive me. I will sing unto the Lord as long as I live, I pledged. I will praise my God while I have my being. I said, I will take heed to my ways: that I offend not in my tongue. I will keep my mouth as it were with a bridle: while the ungodly is in my sight. I held my tongue, and spake nothing: I kept silence. But Old Nick is not so easily caged. After a week I felt as if I would burst, so great was my desire to go back to my old, wicked ways. After ten days I could no longer hold back. I stood, past midnight, naked before my wardrobe. But this time – Satan had whispered a way to avoid detection – I had taken precautions. I put a grey sock over my penis. This time, when I shuddered, the sock caught the catapulted torrent. I mix my metaphors but you will get the picture. That cotton did the trick. Naturally I had to dispose of this sodden article. I hid it in my brown canvas satchel and took it to a faraway place in the hills. There I buried it among the peat. Guilt had returned yet I knew in my heart that I would be forgiven. Yea, in the secret place of his dwelling shall He hide me, and set me upon a rock of stone. Therefore will I offer in His dwelling an oblation with great gladness. The oldest boy at our little school below the mountains was a violent brute named Donald. Although he was a bully he never picked on me. I think this was partly because I had the same name, which in his sluggish, clogged intellect denoted a mystical kinship. Also I was the minister's son, and to strike at me was to strike at a member of the household of the Lord's local representative. To punch Donald McCollum was to risk being bitten by an adder, or for your bicycle to tip you inexplicably into a ditch, or possibly even for your house to burn down. All bullies fear a greater bully, and the other Donald was not a lad to tempt fate. But though this Donald was feared, he was also grudgingly respected. This was because he knew things we younger children didn't. He knew how babies were made, for example. He had also once talked about elections. At least, that's what I thought he said. Donald sniggered and said one day we younger boys would understand. He had elections every night. I was baffled. But I understood, dimly, that this was all something to do with babies. I decide to ask Donald about my very secret problem. I knew I had to approach it in a roundabout kind of way. I couldn't possibly tell him the truth. There was the great risk he would tell the other children and I would be laughed at, and then someone would tell one of the teachers, and then father would get to hear of it. In the end I squeezed a word out of him. *Spunk.* That was what came shooting out of me when I lustfully hugged desirable vertical structures. In later years I diversified. I acted lewdly in the church cock-loft. Around the age of fifteen or sixteen I discovered what butter and fists were made for. And in the Good Book I found a sort of licence for my wickedness. For does it not say in Ecclesiastes (ix. 10) *Whatsoever thy hand findeth to do, do it with thy might.* This injunction I obeyed, heartily. Several times a day, when the possibility allowed. I strangled like a strangler. My flushed, agonized face might equally have been that of someone being choked to death, or the straining choker. They say that the last pagan emperor died of a wound from a spear that pierced his ribs. But I was wounded by a spear that grew out of my own flesh. I destroyed its edge. I smoothed it and made it soft and small. I rang its neck. I emptied it of life. A day later it was back, pestering me like an ardent doggie, up on its hind legs, prodding me with the hot tip of its tongue.

THE CRUSADERS REDEEMED this land. And then General Allenby. From Beersheba to Dan he made his way, then onward through Syria to Cicilia and the Taurus Mountains. The Viscount was a man who knew the bitter cold in the Judean hills. The Viscount was a man who felt the burning heat of arid summer on the plains. Looking back, all his memories were good. Should we be surprised? No. This ancient land fascinates as no other. *All will rejoice at the progress which Palestine has made under the mandate and will wish her Peace and Prosperity.* Allenby wrote that. But the Crusaders came first. And every romantic-minded pilgrim in Palestine owes it to himself to motor south one half hour from Haifa to Athlit. Here will be found the Pilgrims' Castle of the Crusaders. Here is their final fortress on the coast, which they struggled for nearly two centuries to hold for Christ. And let's face it: every real traveller glows at the prospect of a castle. I have visited many over the years. The rosy ruins of England's Kenilworth, immortalised by Scott. The plump towers of that soulful edifice on the Bosphorus. The cosy little structure that crowns the hilltop picture-town of Roquebrune on the Riviera. I am, I think it can truly be said, a man of the world in this regard. And so, with a sly pinch of the fold of flesh that lies at the base of the abominable Abbas's thick neck – how he squeals! – off we go. Leaving by the south end of Haifa, we run along between the promontory of Mount Carmel and the Sea. More distant explosions and shots. The occasional roadblock. They always wave us through when they spot yours truly. We speed past the German Knights Templar Colony of Neuhardhof (another tick for my notebook) and by the post-War settlement of Beith Galim. Arabs smile happily at me from their little booths, put there to guard their precious crops. I jot down the evidence of tomatoes, beans and melons. They are unable to buy trees, unlike their Jewish neighbours who have their National Fund to back them. Suddenly, beyond a modern "Beach Pavilion", the good road fizzles out. Now we have to bump along a dirt track which crosses grazing land owned by the large Arab village of At-ira, at Carmel's foot. Here, huge culverts have been built, to drain the winter floods. To-day they are dry and full of boulders. Abbas slows down for an Arab policeman on his sleek sorrel mount. Before him walks a bearded prisoner in rags, hands tied behind his back. The officer intermittently prods him with a thin, pointed stick. Abbas talks to the policeman, who explains that the man escaped from jail. He is a bandit, and will be punished with a beating. I took out my trusty Kodak but the officer objected. We drove on, coming to an unexpected avenue of towering palms. Buildings appeared but it soon became evident they were empty. Lush green vegetation gripped the walls and swarmed in through unshuttered empty windows. Bird droppings soiled the floors of the abandoned rooms. A well had turned into a plume of soaring greenery. Crickets held a loud rally in the weeds. I wondered what calamity had struck this place. I asked Abbas but at first he pretended not to hear, then merely shrugged. I detested him for his shrugs. Loathing increased its volume inside me, like pus. We came to a mountainous region and followed the route along a narrow rock-cut passage. I was still feverish. Vast quarries came into view. They supplied the new Haifa breakwater. Along the railway puffs the morning train from Egypt. It runs through the broad evaporation pans of the Palestine Salt Company. Some eight thousand tons of salt a year are produced here. But I am not interested in these mundane material matters. I am trailing the footprints of the Crusaders. I seem to hear the clank of spurs against armour-clad legs. I see the flutter of a thousand cross-emblazoned banners. It was his desire to study Crusader architecture that first led Colonel Lawrence to Palestine. The custodian of ruins appears beside my window. He wants to sell me a ticket. It is printed with the reassuring words DEPARTMENT OF ANTIQUITIES. Here the Crusaders selected a promontory jutting into the restless sea, parallel to its greater northern neighbour, Carmel. Massive mediaeval masonry protrudes eighty feet into the burning blue. Here, half arches take on a natural crenellation, carved by war and weather. Rapier thorns make hard going among the tumbling stones. I am shocked to find that poor Arabs live inside this castle. Their washing dangles by the thirteenth century walls. The breeze makes them flutter like bright scarlet and yellow pennons. The surf below is lashed into a symphony of siren music. This entire coast is full of charm. Inside the decayed palace I gazed upward. A four storey structure, the floors long since gone. I was reminded a little of Leicester's Building at Kenilworth. A high, roofless chamber dedicated to vacancy. Here there are columns with heads carved on their bases. Forgotten royalty. Could it be a carven tribute to Berengaria? Some things can never be known. I went on, picking my way over salty rocks. The tide pools held crabs and snail shells. I went on, past hovels of mud and stone. Tethered dogs barked savagely at the intruding white man. A little girl looked at me and began crying. I was pleased to get to the cactus hedges. This way to the banquet hall. It is cut out of solid rock. On its seaward side are three large openings for doors and windows, with masonry six feet thick, looking directly east across two thousand miles of sparkling Mediterranean. This gorgeous expanse is canopied with pearly clouds. It was from this shore that the knights made their final departure from Palestine in 1291. What pangs, what losses. What gleams from their crosses. Back to the car. Onward along a grass-grown track, between fields of golden *durra* from which Arabs are cutting wisps. We come to fruit orchards – apples and peach trees. We come to a man guarding his field from an iron bedstead, with burlap thrown over for shelter, and a white sheepskin to step out on. Beyond his melon patch loom wires bringing power from the new station at Haifa. Abbas takes me on into Tantura. There I offer a maple caramel to a little boy. He scowls and shakes his head. He does not know what it is. Later, refreshed, we drive on. Climbing a hilly road we overtake a car loaded with all the worldly goods of an American Jewish family, who have just landed at Haifa. We arrive before them at their destination: Zikhron Ya'aqov, a Jewish settlement founded in 1882. I feel as if I am in a village of Old Testament times. Two-wheeled carts creak off towards town, laden with barrels of ripe grapes for the community winepress. The wine industry brings money from sales abroad to Jews who, not wishing ever to live in the land of their fathers, enjoy drinking its flowing juices. I buy a bottle of white. For the colonists who come here, there is many a western comfort – hard-surfaced roads, an hotel, food shops, soft drinks stands, motor oils, and bus service to Haifa and to Tel Aviv. And on again, for a picnic. Yellow birds fly overhead. A circle of trees on the edge of a field of grain offers a natural pergola for my snack. A suspicious Arab looms nearby. He sees only a tranquil vacationist (I dare not say author!) and returns to watch his field. This is the Plain of Sharon. It looks just as I expected it to look. I finish the wine. Now I am tired, very tired. Abbas brings me cushions. I take a nap. An hour slips away. Then on, to Binyamina. Here, a savage disappointment. I was counting on going on to Caesarea to see the ruins. Abbas has let me down again. He chose not to mention that this route is impassable. A series of sand dunes makes a barrier which motor cars cannot navigate. Abbas has tricked me into taking this road for nothing. I shall make him pay for his folly. I had counted on trailing Paul's footsteps through the city where for two years he lived pending trial. From Caesarea Paul and Luke sailed west to Rome. At Caesarea Philip preached the Gospel. And there Cornelius lived. And Peter put his footprints. And beyond those dunes did Berenice and Agrippa hear the defence of Paul before Festus. Their steps have vanished. And over there the words of the Apostle hang in the ether above the crumbled port of the procurators. Abbas, grumbling about sand, is shockingly ignorant of such matters. I could not help myself: I smacked his scalp, making him yelp with shock. Go see your bloody Arab farmer friends over there. Tell them to get me a conveyance. Muttering, Abbas climbed out. He slammed the door with great ferocity. He returned with the head man, who peered into the car. He took my baksheesh and then revealed he had a wagon and donkey. Excellent! There is no humiliation in a donkey, for did not our Lord ride one? Then, incredibly – the impudence of the Arab is boundless – he says they are not for hire, not to-day. They are in use. When they are no longer required it will be too late. Six hours over that sand in the afternoon heat is not possible. He suggests we return some other time. Perhaps the Arab police could take me on horseback! This is unbelievable. Abbas chips in. Few travellers come here, he says. And that is that. There is no option but to go back. I feel sick and angry. Here is a wider historical lesson, too. That so great a capital as Caesarea could so utterly pass from existence, tenanted only by a handful of primitives. Back we go, down the narrow dirt track which is the old caravan route to Egypt. We honk past several trains, made up of fifteen to twenty camels, each laden with either grain or melons. At Tulkarm, a large Arab village, we join the main road to Jerusalem. A strange sight there: a long line of village women guarded by British troops, all half naked, their brown breasts exposed to the sun. Some sort of protest on their part? I ask Abbas, but he does not hear me. We speed on. Many of the homes in this area are made of stone, built with the money received from sale of land to Jews for their orchards. At Ras el'Ein are springs, the headwaters of the Auja River. From here water is pumped to a reservoir, then on up to Jerusalem, in stages, lifted by stations along the way. Later we drive past miles of pipe, which were laid by Arab labour, under English bosses with Jewish contractors. The pumping stations and staff houses and reservoirs are of substantial concrete and guarded by troops. There are roadblocks along the way but when they see a Rolls with a white man inside they drag aside the coiled wire and wave us past. Beside a sign reading JERUSALEM WATER SUPPLY ENGINE HOUSE I spot a devout Moslem kneeling on the ground in prayer. Perhaps he is asking Allah to bless his kinsmen in "El Kuds" – "the Holy Town" as Arabs love to call Jerusalem. Or perhaps he still remembers Allenby's December victory here.

TEL AVIV IS a shock. Cream stucco apartments and building blocks. Ice cream parlours. Shops selling Kodak films and electric sewing machines. Tel Aviv's hundreds of small factories manufacture everything from furniture to teeth. And pills. Lots of pills, sold in little twists of paper. A beehive of happy industry, supplying all the wares of industry (and medication!) to a population growing so rapidly that even the mayor does not venture to give statistics. Five hundred new Jews a week are said to arrive at Tel Aviv, out of an annual arrival in Palestine of more than fifty thousand Jews per year, an increase of ten thousand over the previous year. I see sturdy Jewish youths from America and Europe pouring out of buses. They join streams of people flowing into modernistic cinema houses, to see films just arrived from Hollywood. It is a shock to come from villages so primitive that a child does not know a caramel when he sees it, to the luxury of my room in a kosher beach-hotel. Its floor is covered with oriental rugs. My bed has a satin counterpane, and an electric lamp invites night reading. I succumb to temptation. Spade ran his tongue over his lips and pulled his lips back over his teeth in an ugly grin. His eyes glittered under pulled down brows. His reddening neck bulged over the rim of his collar. His voice was low and hoarse and passionate. I read to the end of the chapter and put the book down. My balcony has a superb view of the Mediterranean and a surf. Late workers enjoy all the fun of a swim. I take comfort from a pale solitary palm tree. It leans towards me, as Mary Appleby once did. Very tall, it towers over the ruins of time. Building stone smothers it from an adjacent yard. This tree whispers of a day, only a few years before, when sand dunes were all there was to Tel Aviv. After dinner, strictly "kosher", I walked down Allenby Street. Though it is broad, I found it so thronged with happy humanity that it was impossible to gain comfortable footing. Oh yes, we are happy here, a Brooklyn immigrant informs me. Life is hard here, he insists. But we have come to stay. This is the first entirely Jewish city built in nineteen hundred years. My family wants to be part of it. This is our Jewish homeland we have dreamed of for centuries. We have one common ideal – social justice for our brothers. Abbas, needless to say, detests Tel Aviv. As soon as he had deposited me at my hotel he sped off to Joppa (relations of some sort). The contrast between old Joppa and Tel Aviv could not be sharper. And England, if she wants to keep the pages of her Mandate as brilliant here as at Haifa, would do well to pour some of the surplus millions of Palestine's budget into repairs along the busy waterfront of Joppa harbour. At least pave the slimy street where ragged porters, arriving colonists, and departing cargoes make a maze of confusion.

I

I ONLY MET Monty once. It happened on the day I went to Gethsemane. I say day, I really mean night. Abbas drove me by way of Herod's Gate. Then on, via the Damascus Gate. The car headlights raked the wall of the new Rockefeller Museum of Archaeology situated at the northeast corner of the city wall. Olive boughs swayed in the breeze in the grove off the Jericho Road. In their midst a handful of tall, stately palms. The night was blue and profound. Sullen Abbas parked by the Garden railings and waited. I set off alone up the steep moonlit path. It ran between high walls enclosing the property of the Russian Church and the Franciscan. The moon transformed the texture of everything. The olive leaves were frosted with silver. Walls became liquid and magical. The path ahead of me was chequered with bright light and deep shadows. No human voice can be heard. No dog barks, or child cries, or donkey brays. Every night He went out and lodged here, in the mount that is called Olivet. Luke said that. A sense came over me that I was seeing what Jesus saw, under this same full moon twenty centuries ago. Over the cleft of the valley rises the city of dreadful night. Jesus came by way of the Dung Gate, of this I am certain. In the full glory of the moon he sauntered along the east wall between the old temple area and the Kidron. The olive trees of Gethsemane supplied shadows for concealment and prayer. Under moonlight such as this it was easy for his betrayers to point Him out. The failure of His closest friends makes one wonder whether anyone is entirely to be trusted. Mussolini is surely right when he says: I suffer so intensely from anything like treacherous conduct that I endeavour to abstain from personal friendships. Devotion to a cause requires abstention from that which others think essential. When I find a friend has been disloyal, says the Italian leader, it is as if I had ashes in my mouth. Life is full of duties to be performed and sorrows to be overcome. Here, the miracle of Christ's character comes to the fore. Behold, thy mother, He said to John from His cross. Feed my lambs, He told Peter on the Galilean shore after His resurrection. From the top I looked back over Gethsemane. The road to Bethany is a ribbon of iridescent silver. Lights show from the Oriental Research building. It holds the newest finds – Late Bronze house walls and the Astarte porcelain cylinder from 1300 B.C. And then the descent. It was with reluctance that I left this place and went back down the little path leading to the road from Jericho. The descent is never as good as the way up. By the wall of the Franciscan Basilica I could hear men's voices. Later, crossing the Kidron, I noticed a torchlight. It flickered weirdly on a hillside outside the north wall of the city. It brought a shuddering sense of those torches carried on Passover night, when soldiers hunted Christ. The torch moved out into a field, where many were gathered. Some kind of ceremony. Jerusalem is ever a city of mystery. There was a much bigger surprise in store when I got back to the car. Abbas was being held against the Gethsemane wall by soldiers. An armoured car was parked behind the Rolls. As I approached, an officer materialised. He called out my name. I consented to admit my identity. The officer, I recall, introduced himself as Giles. I never got round to asking if that was his Christian name or his surname. He shook my hand. Giles said that I was needed. I scrutinised my wristwatch. The hour is getting late, I said. Your services are needed, he replied, taking my arm. This is most important. It cannot wait. Another dying soldier, I assumed. The Padre must still be in Egypt. Having done one good turn, the army had marked me down as someone to be called upon in an emergency. Oh very well, I said, a trifle peevishly. One cannot refuse to minister to those in desperate need, yet I was feeling tired after my walk and wished for nothing more than a good night's sleep. Giles exposed a mouthful of yellow teeth. You can tell your driver to go home, he added. Very well, I said. Abbas, inscrutable as the proverbial oriental, silently climbed into the Rolls. He drove off. Giles ushered me towards the armoured car. He gripped my arm and helped me into it. It was hot, dark and uncomfortable inside. I sat on a metal bench, resting the back of my head against the side. Where are we going? I asked. That I cannot say, said he. For reasons of national security. I quite understand, I said, although I did not. Besides, I did not particularly care where we were going. It was hardly the time to fit in a spot of sight-seeing. The interior of the vehicle was illuminated by nothing more than the pale night itself, seeping in through the observation slits. A street lamp sometimes threw in a quick splash of light. I saw that Giles's jaws were grinding something. Then Jerusalem seemed to depart and now all I could see was the occasional twinkle of a star. I must have dozed off. When I woke some forty-five minutes had passed. I turned to Giles. Where is this man of yours? Is he badly wounded? He said: I really don't have a clue what you mean, old man. I mean the soldier. Didn't you want me to guide one of your men into the next life? Good Lord, no, he said. Then what do you want with me then? It's the Major-General. He wants a word. Now it was my turn to look bewildered. Who? The C in C, he replied. Montgomery. Blood mad, they say the bishop called him. I was nervous but proud to be summoned. Why? You'll soon find out. We're there. The armoured car halted and Giles helped me out. We were in a vast military base. All around were low wooden huts and long rows of army lorries. The perimeter fence was lit by spotlights. It was somewhere in the desert. I had no idea where I was. Giles led me towards a nearby wooden bungalow. A flag drooped from a pole attached to a chimney. There was a lot of smoke rising up from the distant hills. Two guards saluted as we approached. Giles led me up some steps and inside. In the hall there was a table with a soldier sitting behind it, reading some papers. He said to Giles, He's waiting. Giles nodded. Just go on through that door. The Major-General is expecting you. I did as commanded. A short corridor led to another door. I opened it and went in. A figure sat in an armchair, holding a cut glass tumbler and staring out through the window at the view. It consisted of floodlit tennis courts, a football pitch and a distant wire fence. Monty heard me come in and sprang up. Dr McCollum? Please, join me. It was good of you to come. A glass of whisky? I don't normally touch the stuff, he quickly explained. But tonight I am letting my hair down. Or I would if I had any! He barked at his own wit. He was merry that night. I said I would, yes. It's a damned fine malt. He looked at the label. An Islay malt. The best there is. He glared at me as if I had disagreed with him. As a Scot I cannot disagree, I said. We clinked glasses. I expect you're wondering why I asked you here, eh? I admitted that I was somewhat puzzled. I described the earlier episode involving the dying soldier and explained about the misunderstanding. Monty laughed. Not dead yet, he said gruffly. His accent was marinated in English privilege. A golden syrup had lubricated his ascent to what he was. He was absolutely certain of his absolute certainties. I had and have no objection to this. It is what faith requires of any man. And yet. Monty seemed to manifest from another world, and in a strange dialect. What let him down was his face. The nose reminded me of a rat. The eyes, too. They held a certain dark calculation. Lately, on the newsreels, he has taken to wearing a beret, like a Parisian harlot. I must say it rather suits him. His head was bare that long night we shared together. At one point, towards midnight, to my amazement, Monty embraced me. We had been reminiscing about this and that, and speaking of how time marches on. Monty spoke in segments. He chopped his sentences into little nuggets of fact and belief. It is my belief, he said, that we are in for a war with Germany. I found this hard to believe. Germany and Great Britain seemed to have so much in common. However, I did not like to disagree, so I nodded as if in assent. Monty and I talked some more. The clock ticked past midnight. Time – nothing – disturbed him. I was enthralled to be with a great man. I can truly say that I was only aware of a fraction of what passed that night. The reason for our conversation emerged gradually. He was lonely. He needed to speak freely to a man of the cloth. A man who would hold his tongue. I was his confessor. Past midnight, and two tumblers later, he put his arms around me. He began sobbing.

I was amazed and perturbed. His tears trickled down, to be absorbed by his wiry moustache. I could see glints of ginger in among the black, freshly trimmed hairs. Bernard is a good name for a man with a moustache. It has something of hairiness about it. Monty's tears did not cease. I miss her so bloody, bloody much. He was speaking of his deceased wife. I have forgotten her name. Brenda? Betsy? Something along those rugged lines. B and B in a B & B? Improbable, ridiculous, my mind's wandering. Monty gripped my knee, then let go. To find death in Burnham on Sea, he said. Of all bloody places. Vinegar, fish and chips – they smell of it. Death. They are ruined for me. They will always stink of her dying. Fish make me sick. I'm a meat man now. Beef, chicken, bangers. His face was wet with his continuing grief. And the gulls, he said. Howling like fallen angels. Have you ever looked at the eyes of gulls? They remind me of the Japanese. They have cruelty embedded in them. They are not human. One day we shall have to smash the Japs too. You mark my words. Monty smiled at the thought. It was a good, pleasing thought. Another whisky? Don't mind if I do. Then, abruptly, he pulled himself together and retreated into his carapace. Keep all this to yourself, he said. It isn't the sort of thing I'd want to get out. It would be very bad for morale if the men got to hear of it. Nobody wants their commanding officer to be a milksop. I shall never tell a soul of this, I said. As God is my witness. He was all dried up inside, I felt. Bereavement had withered him. I have seen it happen several times. The dead sucking all the life out of the living. Monty checked his buttons. He need not have worried. They were all done up. But no matter how correct his uniform, it could not mask the mortal man beneath. Monty smelled of sweat, plus a strange musty smell, as of moths. A strange tang of odours. Perhaps he did not wash often enough. A general's life is a busy one. Ablutions must seem like a gross and futile indulgence. Myself, I try to bathe at least twice a day if at all possible, which it isn't always when you are in one of the barbarous regions of the world. To be honest I am a bit of a stickler for hygiene and order. The old saying that cleanliness is next to godliness is too easily sneered at. Monty's head tipped forwards and he stared silently at the rug. The pattern involved peacocks and oranges. The Palestinian sun had faded it. The oranges were barely orange at all. They might have been tennis balls. He did not react as I got to my feet. I need to take a leak, I said. Monty said nothing. He was still engrossed in his rug. I followed my nose and found what I was seeking. The Major-General's lavatory was deliciously enticing to a man who had not defecated for over eight weeks. It was Spartan but spotless. A faint tang of Flit perfumed the spacious room. The bolt on the door was a sturdy one. That calmed my natural anxieties. On one wall hung a framed photograph. I recognised Monty. He looked a lot younger. He was standing beside an antique cannon, looking very serious. On the far side of the thick black barrel stood a fellow officer. Both were clutching canes. In the background was a large, pale building resembling an apartment block of the sort Dostoyevsky lived in. I guessed it was a passing-out photograph. I dropped my trousers and underpants and lowered myself on to the wooden seat. If I was ever going to loosen my bowels in the Holy Land this was surely the place. But it was no go. I even doubled up, so that my nose was almost touching the linoleum floor. I pressured my muscles and felt my sphincter open. The lino had a brown marble pattern. I strained and strained and felt my sphincter writhe. Its puckered lips opened wide, then closed again. It was like opening a door and encountering a brick wall. Not even the sight of a neat pyramidal heap of cannon balls in Monty's picture could inspire me to lay down my own dark deposits. I emptied my bladder and accepted defeat in the other quarter. When I returned, Monty became formal and correct. He did not advert to his earlier emotional outburst. It was as if he wanted to crush it with fresh facts. Let me tell you about what we're up to here. But you mustn't put it in your book. Mum's the word, eh? His revelation startled me. You know about my book? Monty's eyes held a merry twinkle. Oh, we know all about you, Dr McCollum. I wouldn't be talking to you like this if we didn't. Intelligence, you know. No army can do without it.

As we were moving onto military matters I told him about the prisoners I'd seen in Acre. He gave me the true figure. His tongue explored his moustache. His eyes glowed. Don't believe what you read in the newspapers. What's happening in Palestine is not a national movement. These people we are up against are bullies. We are smashing them. That's what The Emergency is all about. Thank God for Munich. Chamberlain is not the fool people think he is. Munich gave us a breathing space to get the job done here. Munich freed up eight divisions. We could never go to war in Europe with unfinished business out here in the Middle East. But the job is nearly done. The Arabs have been smashed. It's just mopping up, now. Soon I'll be on my way back to blighty. To be honest, I shall be glad to see the last of this damned place. I'm more of a tanks man. I have always been interested in tanks. I remember the first girl I ever fell in love with. I went walking with her on the beach. I showed her how to win a tank battle. I marked it all out in the sand. And you know what? She wasn't interested. I begged her to marry me but she turned me down. It is all very sad. She was too young to appreciate me. She was a teenager and I was in my thirties. It was nearly all up for me when I met Betty. Married at thirty-nine! A close shave, that was. But we rubbed along pretty well together. And then she died. Bitten by an insect on the beach. So you see, father, beaches have never brought me luck. Nor me, I said. I once slipped on some seaweed and sprained my ankle very badly. In Fife this was. But Monty wasn't listening. He had gone deep inside himself. There, all he could find was a Major-General. Monty – this is pretty generally known nowadays – could not pronounce the letter "r". He talked of how the Eighth Division would blake the Awab wesistance. I have gwate confidence in the outcome, he said. At times his voice was so squeaky I yearned to oil it. But that night the lubricant was hot foamy saliva and malt whisky and ice which cracked like little pistol shots as it melted in our cut glass tumblers. Monty was not embarrassed by his oddities. He had the tranquil confidence of a Bishop's son. I suspect he never masturbated after fourteen. He had an iron grip on his proclivities. Discipline is required in the army as well as breeding. His scrotum must have been bloated like a double balloon with all that unspilled desire. No doubt he dreamed, as do we all. No doubt that girl on the sand dragged him down and undid her buttons and let him lick and fondle her schoolgirl's breasts. No doubt he woke in the darkness to find himself spouting like a whale, his body folded over. But no man of restraint can avoid a sticky situation like that. God sees all but is indulgent towards *frottage* induced by dreams. Grey flakes of guilt cling to the stripes of many men's pyjamas. Monty's batman is, I am certain, very discreet. You do not, must not, ever, mention the soilings of a hero. If my book was to mention Monty at all – it will not – he would cross its puny stage with the solemn tread of a Caesar. I would not presume to do anything other than worship the Prince of Peace and the men who must ensure, with tanks if necessary, His continuing rule over the dark and barbarous lands of the world. I am not a sneak. I breach no one's confidences. You will not find me scattering little barbs of innuendo amid a well laid-out arrangement of subordinate clauses. Then, with a lurch of his body, the Major-General was back with his wildness and grief. Let me tell you something else, doctor, he said. Monty leaned closer and put his hand on my knee. His breath was stale. I ate a melon once, he said. I swallowed a mouthful of seeds. Now I have a tree growing inside me. A tree in my stomach! I feel its branches, rustling against the lining inside me. It is horrible. I do my best to forget it. I think about tank turrets, for example. Their design could be improved. And another thing. I had a strange dream last night. I was living in a rented room. I went to draw the curtains over the living room window when a mouse scampered along the top of the curtain. It reached the end and dropped to the ground. The mouse appeared in a weak and distressed state. I seized a large hardback book and slammed it down on the mouse, crushing it to death. The doorbell rang. A crowd of visitors entered. Some of them sat on the sofa. At the feet of one of them lay the book, with the dead mouse beneath it. Everyone chattered gaily and no one seemed to notice the dead rodent. And then I woke up. That is indeed a strange dream, I said. I stood up, in order to liberate my knee. I did not wish to be unduly suspicious. I did not wish to give offence. But neither did I wish to be regarded as one who might, perhaps, have homosexual proclivities. If Monty was performing a test, I was determined to fail it. I did not hold it against him, if that was his way. Soldiers spend months together, cooped up, sweating, limb against limb. In the dark one hole is much the same as another. This is a vice common in some quarters of the priesthood. Communion wine, lads with glorious voices and flawless skin and rosy cheeks... I can understand how some might slither into buggery. My vice is altogether more solitary. I do not require another personage to taste bliss. Coupling holds no appeal. I stood by the open window and put my head out. The tennis court lights had been switched off. Now there was merely the distant incandescence of the lit perimeter fence. The stars were, as always, far brighter than at home. They shimmered and blazed like liquid silver. I lack the words to do better. And then I heard it. A sudden ululation. A strange cry of grief. A woman's tongue. It began as a low howl, as I have heard from wounded dogs. It quickened into a fast, raw sob of grief and despair. It must have come from a nearby village, via some strange acoustical effect. It thickened and grew louder until it seemed to fill the whole of Palestine. And then it was drowned out by a surge of music. Behind me, Monty had put a 78 on the gramophone. A lively orchestral piece which I did not recognise. Elgar, he said. The *Cockaigne* overture. A tiny froth had formed at each corner of his mouth. It reminded me of the yellow clots of air and water that cling to the strand's edge on a blustery day at home. I do not particularly like Elgar, although I can quite see why a military man might. *The Manual of Military Law*, 1929, is a real boon, he said. The regulations state quite clearly that inflicting suffering upon innocent persons is indispensable as a last resource. The existence of an armed insurrection justifies the use of force necessary effectually to meet and cope with the insurrection. Beaming, Monty began to conduct the orchestra.

The Eighth Division has thirty-five garrisons and detachments, he said. But don't put that in. I won't, I said. On that you have my most solemn word. Monty nodded. I am charged with maintaining order in the area of Samaria, Galilee, and the whole of the frontier district. What we are up against here has been nothing less than a campaign run by professional bandits. They take their orders from Damascus. You know what we did? We got Charlie Tegart over from India. A no-nonsense chap. He set up Arab Investigation Centres. When a wog goes into one of those places he gets the third degree. It doesn't take him long to spill the beans. It is the only way with these people. As for the wog ringleaders... We deport them to the Seychelles. Get the bastards out of the way. Monty chuckled. He liked a good joke. His voice was again so squeaky I yearned to tip syrup down his throat. His face composed a smile. His eyes twinkled. You might say we left them to develop their Seychellist ideas out of harm's way. I grinned, appreciating his wit, though I rather thought he had told the joke before. Another joke: There was this Awab chap who put in a complaint that one of our lads had beaten him. He was able to identify the man. He said it was soldier number 65. The tears streamed down Monty's cheeks as he reached the punchline. The fellow didn't wealise that evewyone in the York and Lancaster Regiment has the number 65 on their helmet! I smiled politely while Monty dabbed his cheeks with a spotless white hanky. That's because it used to be the 65th Foot, he added. This Awab didn't understand that none of our men carry any identifying numbers. They are not policemen, for heaven's sake. His face went back to fierce. Their esprit-de-corps is a gang one, he barked. I think he meant the rebels. These gangs consist of anything from fifty to one hundred and fifty men. But with God's support, and that of the R.A.F., we have smashed them. And we do not neglect the small things that can really count. We ban all journalists from operational areas. Journalists lack the true patriotic spirit. And we pay four pounds for a captured rifle. A tidy sum to a peasant and well worth turning informer for. And we hang anyone found in possession of ammo. A single round merits execution. That puts the fear of God into them, I can tell you. Our lads know what their duty is. Bash anybody on the head who breaks the law. If a chap won't be bashed, he must be shot. It's a nice, simple objective and the soldiers understand it. It's also popular. All ranks enjoy a bit of argy-bargy. Monty fell silent. His face took on an introspective expression. He was tumbling back into the dried-up wells of his past. Goodness, is that the time? I must be on my way. Monty did not attempt to detain me. A cock was crowing out there in the darkness. The tennis courts were pale rectangles. I have told no one of this night. It would sound outlandish, even imaginary. Even in my own mind it bears the lurid edging of a dream. That a man like Montgomery should pour out his heart to a poor sinner such as me. Stranger things have happened in history. Or should that be History? In the ante-room the same grey man was still scrutinising the same grey papers. I saw the names al-Bassa and Halhul. He had a large block of India Rubber, a pot of ink and several sheets of stained blotting paper. Giles was slumped on a wooden chair, his head tilted forwards. The grey man produced a walking stick from below the table and used the ferrule to prod Giles awake. He started, saw me, muttered something, and was gripped by a series of yawns. Giles rubbed the sleep from his eyes and escorted me to a military water tanker parked outside the bungalow. This chap will take you back to Jerusalem. I've told him where your hotel is. He indicated a corporal with blazing blue eyes and a set of unusually white teeth. Thanks awfully for coming. I'm sure the C in C appreciated it. Well, cheerio! Giles gave a friendly wave and went on waving until the dust rising from our wheels erased him.

N

NOT THAT MONTY was the only great man I encountered in Palestine. There was one other. It would be invidious to compare them – a pineapple is no better than a pomegranate, after all – but it would be fair to say that if Monty was simply a man who had a job to do and got on and did it, the other man was possessed of more than a sense of duty – he had a mission. But of course I cannot – shall not – mention them in my book. The publisher was quite clear that there must be no mention of The Emergency. The book was to be an uplifting tale of travel to a region both divine and colourful. The natives should appear at regular intervals but strictly in roles which were comical, poignant, amusing and delightful. The reader would not expect negativity. The reader would not want unpleasantness. The reader requires edification and entertainment. A shepherd walks at the head of his flock, with an injured lamb draped around his shoulders. Describe his curious adornments. As he walks he talks to his obedient flock, in a loud sing-song voice. He is using a weird language unheard of in Tonbridge Wells. The words were animal sounds arranged in a kind of order. But that is not all. Early one morning I saw an extraordinary sight not far from Bethlehem. But I shall save that for the book. It was in Haifa that it occurred, this episode which I shall not mention. My zig-zagging around Palestine was just about complete. By now I had all the material I needed. I had only returned to Haifa to take some photographs. I was sauntering along one afternoon when a big dark car cruised alongside me like a shark. For a dreadful moment I thought I was about to be assassinated. The man at the wheel was glaring at me and I could see a revolver on the ledge below the windscreen. The car braked sharply and the man called out my name. It is Dr McCollum, is it not? It is, I replied, half dead from terror. And then I realised from the fellow's beard that this was the chap I had previously encountered in Sabastia. Hop in, he said. I thought he was offering me a lift and I was touched by his kindness. Far from it. We're one man short, he said somewhat later. First he drove me out of town. Where are we going? To a settlement. Don't fret. The name doesn't matter. It's what we're going to do that matters. For righteousness exalteth a nation. Wingate pointed at the fields. This is their *Altneuland*, their old-new land. The Jews are loyal to the empire, he said. You would be amazed to see how they have made the desert blossom like a rose. Intensive horticulture everywhere. Such energy, such faith, such ability, such inventiveness as the world has not seen. Palestine is essential to our Empire. Our Empire is essential to England. England is essential to world peace. That is why we must ruthlessly suppress any attempt at opposition. Islam is out of it, out of it, out of it.

NIGHT IS SWEETER than day, old warriors say. So too for the moulding of Zion. Captain Orde Wingate saw to that. An odd name, Orde. Short for Order? Hayedid – The Friend. That is what the Jews called him. His detractors – there were many – had other names. One sneering fellow even whispered it was short for ordure. I must confess that the malice in men's heart sometimes astounds me. For that was what the Captain imposed, order. I admired him for that. There is too much chaos in the world. It is the duty of civilised Christians to root out malevolent and mercenary manifestations and set it to rights. Captain Wingate said: Are you interested in cars? I said I was not. Pity. This is 1937 Studebaker convertible. A real beauty. The yanks make far better autos than the English. He accelerated, blowing the horn at a shepherd with his flock. The bleating sheep scattered and ran off across the dusty plain. I looked back. The shepherd was shaking his fist and screaming. A hoot! We sped along the dusty, empty road. Wingate drove much faster than hideous Abbas. He held on to the wheel with one hand and made gestures of a swooping plane with the other. This was in connection with an anecdote about a radio truck. Whenever they had a spot of bother they called in the R.A.F. The Hawker Hart biplanes dropped their bombs. Result: fourteen dead oozlebarts. Wingate laughed and accelerated. Twenty minutes later we turned off onto a dirt track that led across a hillside dotted with pine trees. In the distance a stockade and a watchtower. This place seems alive. It is very lovely at this time of year. The settlement had taken over an Arab house, which the owner in Bagdad had sold to the J.N.F. The tenants had been given the order of the boot. It housed ninety kibbutzniks. They had submachine guns and an Austrian-made Schwarzlose heavy machine gun. Technically the Jews are not allowed such weaponry but the authorities turn a blind eye. Whereas if an Arab is caught with a rifle we hang him! Wingy laughed and I laughed too. I was startled to find British troops living alongside the settlers. They were housed in a pair of wooden huts, twelve men in each hut. Theoretically. But one hut held only eleven. One of the soldiers had contracted an ailment of the groin and was absent. His chums were lounging around playing cards and smoking as we arrived. Wingy led me into his quarters, a small bungalow. He poured us both a whisky. And then another. He asked me a number of questions about my faith, the Bible and my commitment to a Jewish state. I answered them to his satisfaction. With that out of the way he started to tell me about the S.N.S. The Special Night Squads were his own invention. They took the war to the enemy. You marched by night and caught them on the hop. In person they are feeble, he said. Like all ignorant and primitive people they panic easily, he said. Outcome: lashings of dead oozlebarts. And you know what? It was all my idea. But those bastard Arabists back in London hate me for it. They have conspired against me. They have taken away my command. You mark my words. In the end they will shut down the S.N.S., the cunts. These are the first soldiers of the Jewish army, he said proudly. That's what those bastard Arabists hate. But it's too late now. They have the training and the weaponry. Soon the time will come for them to seize Palestine. I shall be there. In the meantime I must wait. Tonight is my last patrol. My last crack at those fucking Arabs. He grabbed hold of my wrist. Come, let us sing. Kneel. We kneeled. One here will constant be, we sang. Come wind, come weather. A glorious melody. And now we must get you sorted out. *Equipped.* Equipped? Didn't I say? We're one man short. This is the chance of a lifetime. Help build Zion. But I can't shoot a gun, I said. I know nothing about weapons at all. Don't worry, he said. Sergeant Russell will help you out. Wingy had a field telephone on his desk. He picked up the receiver and cranked the handle. Sergeant Russell appeared. He was a big fellow. This way, sir, he said. He led me to a hut where he showed me a bolt-action Lee-Enfield rifle. I don't think I'd be much good with that, I said. Perhaps you're right, sir. How about this? He handed me a revolver. That looks just the ticket, I said. He loaded it for me and showed me the safety catch. That's all you need to remember, sir. Don't worry about reloading. One of the chaps will do that for you if we ever get that far. Which we may not. Some nights we go out and come back without killing a soul. But we hope to do a bit better than that tonight. Make it worthwhile for the C.O. As it's his last patrol. A crying shame if you ask me. Sergeant Russell gave me a canvas pack and a helmet which felt too tight. I went back to the bungalow. Wingy was whistling in the kitchen. He was starkers. I naturally assumed he had stepped from his ablutions. Not so. Nudism was his domestic orthodoxy. Orde has very deep set eyes, periwinkle blue. Aquiline features. A faraway, wild look. A bit scruffy. The face of an ascetic. A man with a vision. A very tiny cock. He is clearly one of the instruments of God's hand. Get some rest, he said. I did. I was glad to be away from his naked presence, it perturbed me. For a terrible moment I thought the entire British army was officered by rampant homosexualists. This was an uncharitable suspicion. The naked truth emerged later. Night fell. I slept. I woke with a terrible thirst. I lay there for some time, half asleep. I was parched but paralysed. The effort required to get out of bed and look for a tap was too enormous. But in the end I could lie there no longer. I rolled out of bed. I stood and padded to the door with the slow movements of a somnambulist. Not that I have ever seen a somnambulist (but I have read about them in crime novels). My bedroom opened onto the lounge. I passed through it into the corridor at the far end. A light gleamed under a door. I gently raised the latch and gingerly opened it. It was not the kitchen, nor was it a bedroom. It was some kind of store room. Packing cases were heaped against the wall. A single bare bulb hung from the ceiling. A moth fluttered around it, lunging at the bulb. On the far wall, which was bare, hung a large reproduction of the Virgin Mary. I assume it was the copy of an Italian renaissance painting. It wasn't one I recognised but the Virgin's face was in the Mona Lisa tradition. She had a pert smile and impudent green eyes. Her face was cushioned by a small, sensual double chin. The yellow glow around her scalp seemed at odds with her slut's demeanour. Wingate was crouched naked on all fours before Her. No, not on all fours. His left arm supported him as he kneeled like a cat, but his right hand was attending to his groin. The rhythmic movement of his elbow left me in no doubt as to the nature of his worship. He moved his hand towards his face and opened it, spitting into his palm. The lubricant was then transferred to the appropriate location. His thin, rather bony backside shivered a little, as if rocked by a passing breeze. Wingy whispered something hoarse and passionate and inaudible, then sighed three or four times. He dripped like a candle. The time for self-restraint is past, he said. But that was later, some hours after I had gently closed the door to the store room. I do not think he was aware of my presence, although in later years I have wondered if he was and if the performance was staged for my benefit. Later I was roused from my fresh slumber by Sergeant Russell. Time to go, sir, he said. I'll be ready in a jiffy, I said. The bed sheet had fallen to the floor. I blushed. I fervently hoped that the Sergeant had not noticed the tumour lying across my stomach. Where did we go that night? It must have been across the triangle of death, of that I am almost certain. But geography has never been my strong point and in this place one name can easily get tangled with another. I remember vividly the tremendous raucous unending din of frogs. I remember moonlight shining on a placid silent lake, turning it to a sheet of mysterious silver. The stars were close enough to pluck from the sky, like heavenly fruit. Our mission was preceded by a pep talk. I felt it was addressed as much to me as to the others. The military strength of the whole Arab group is quite negligible, he said. The potential military strength of the Jews is equivalent to at least two British army corps. Islam in reality cares little about the Arabs of Palestine. In any case, Islam to-day has no strength. Strength is what counts. Force. Might. He spoke quietly, with complete conviction. We must ruthlessly suppress the Arabs. We must recognise the right of the Jews to emigrate to Palestine. We must advance the foundation of an autonomous Jewish community. For the Jews are loyal to the Empire. And we are instruments in God's hand. Together with the Manchesters, the Royal Ulster Rifles and the Royal West Kents. Wingy became reflective. I felt like a disciple, sitting at the feet of The Master. He stared into the darkness. He focused his gaze on yours truly. After Chaim was killed by a mine, he said, we went to the Arab part of Beit Shean. We beat everyone we met. We went into the shops and smashed them up. Some of the young men resisted. We shot them like dogs. Getting shot is nothing. I myself have been shot five times. There was no damage to speak of. I must have pure blood. Tonight, he said, we go out for the last time to protect the Iraq Petroleum Company's pipeline between Kirkuk and Haifa. The rebels are shooting holes in it every night and setting light to the leaking oil. We shall kill every Arab we find near the pipe. This is holy work. God gave it to us to slay the enemies of the Jews. For the enemies of the Jews are the enemies of all mankind. There was a mutter of approval from the assembly. We readied our weaponry. The bayonets were sheathed in cloth. Corks were placed on the tips. Wingate wore twin revolvers, hanging from a belt, cowboy style. I can make little sense of what happened that night. We walked for three hours without talking. Finally we came to a village. We surrounded it and opened fire.

Screams, shouting, confusion. I fired a single shot. The recoil hurt my wrist. I suffered for twenty-four hours. We took prisoners, some youths. Wingy forced sand into the mouths of some of them. One, who was insolent, he shot dead. We set fire to half a dozen homes and then set off back to our distant stockade. The others went off to sleep. I remained in the bungalow with Wingy. He had stripped off, now. I tried to avoid looking at his genitals. A faint smell of excreta hung in the air. He poured us both whiskies. He drank the first one down in seconds and poured another. They say they don't need us now, not after Munich. He sounded bitter. Did you know that the deal with Hitler released eighteen infantry battalions? I did but I did not say so. They are smashing the Arabs and then they will carve up Palestine. They plan to give only a fraction to God's chosen people. Soon will come the time to declare war on the English! His face was pale, his eyes burned. He clenched his fists. We shall blow up the Haifa oil refinery, he whispered. The time for self-restraint is past, he said.

E

ENDINGS ARRIVE UNEXPECTEDLY, sometimes. Bolts of lightning, ships hitting rocks, reckless drivers. To name but three of the fatal sort. Others involve attendance by clumsy polka dot costumed clowns wearing gigantic footwear. Lately my hands have begun to shake uncontrollably. The pills muffle the thunder in my head but do not rid it of the storms. I sweat and burn like a soul in purgatory. I have difficulty holding a pen. I cannot sleep. My thoughts turn to extinction. Flesh lets us down in the end, with its decrepitude and infections and noxious emissions of fluids, slush and gas. All self-control is lost. Your teeth drop away with the years. Drool forks your curling chin. By that final year I hope I will have learned some wisdom. *For man walketh in a vain shadow, and disquieteth himself in vain: he heapeth up riches, and cannot tell who shall gather them.*

NEAR THE END of my time in the Holy Land, in Jerusalem of all places, there was a rather disagreeable scene. Abbas knew I was shortly to depart and broached the question of payment. I solemnly assured him he need have no anxieties on that score. A Scotsman is true to his word. I might have added: So, too, is a soldier of Christ. As my last day grew closer Abbas began – there is no other word for it – to pester me. He was anxious that I should visit my bank and withdraw the necessary sum. I must confess I began to resent this importuning. It had a wheedling quality. His voice began to pipe and squeal. To be perfectly frank, I was beginning to detest the fellow. The end came suddenly. I had only one day left. Abbas began to blab that he must go back to his wife. He needed his money. *Please, boss.* He was practically weeping. It was as if he did not trust me, which I found extraordinary after all we had shared together. He tugged at his beard, which I may not have mentioned before. It had a luxuriant quality. He reminded me of a somewhat sooty Father Christmas. We were by the Mandelbaum Gate, so-called. Exasperated beyond measure by the latest whining demand for payment I opened the car door and got out. Abbas seemed startled. I said very calmly, Goodbye, Abbas. I could have sworn his dusky skin went pale at these words. He sprang out. He extended his hand, his palm open. You pay me now, Mr Umcullum, sir. I contemplated reminding him that the accurate mode of address would have been *doctor*, but somehow this seemed by the by. I would overlook the assault on correct pronunciation. There are some things one cannot expect of an aborigine. Besides, the chief thing was to be shot of this vexatious litigant. All around us life went on. A camel passed. A donkey trotted past, depositing some cakes of gleaming dung on the dusty carriageway. Women in black with veiled faces glided by. I reached into my wallet and gave Abbas the sum agreed in Cairo. He scowled at the bank notes and hurriedly thumbed through them. I must say I found this a little surprising. It was as if the fellow did not trust me. Can you believe what happened next? The fellow had the insolence to say that the amount I had given him was less than half that which he had been promised! It was a preposterous and absurd suggestion. I am sorry to say that Abbas had patently reverted to what he had always been, and which my natural human sympathies had foolishly obscured from me – a sly, cheating native. Can you believe he not only demanded more than twice what I had so generously handed to him, he also had the amazing impudence to say that a gratuity might also be in order. In short, he wanted no less than *three times* the sum I had given him! It was unbelievable. I was truly shocked that a man I had come to think of as a friend was now displaying that ugliest of all human emotions – naked greed. He even claimed that the money I had given him barely covered the cost of the petrol. This was another manifest absurdity (not that I have ever been someone particularly interested in matters connected to petroleum!). Now look here, I said in a very firm voice. You'll get what you are given and be damned grateful for it. Abbas's response was quite astonishing. He began to shriek. He let loose a torrent of incomprehensible Arabic, which I immediately understood to be savagely uncomplimentary. To my alarm, people were beginning to stare. The street vendors were staring. The shopkeepers were staring. Even a pair of passing nuns had stopped and were staring. (I have never particularly liked nuns. And these, like all the ones I have ever encountered, were spectacularly ugly.) Abbas raised his fist. For a hideous moment I believed that he was about to assault me. A crowd had gathered, evidently fascinated by the sight of an Arab adopting a physically threatening posture towards a white man. I felt a looseness in my bowels. I could not believe that a man of God such as myself could suddenly find himself at the mercy of a violent brute. Luckily help was at hand. God bless the British army! A pair of fine strapping English privates had wandered over from wherever it was they had been. Is this wog causing you trouble, sir? Ah, the rich, homely, delightful accent of Birmingham! I nodded. I said I was sorry to have to say that he was. In fractured English Abbas began screaming that I owed him money. The soldiers looked at each other and laughed. They said something to each other that I did not hear and laughed again. Then one of them went a little closer to Abbas. Just fuck off, mate. And leave the vicar alone. The soldier raised his rifle butt. Abbas pointed at me. His fury made him brave. You bastard bloody bastard Scotch prick! I suppose he had learned such vile expressions off a sailor. Or a parrot. The soldiers snickered. One pressed the end of his rifle into Abbas's paunch. Don't push your luck, mate. Just fuck off. Sullenly Abbas climbed back into his Rolls Royce. As he drove off one of the soldiers took aim. For an awful moment I thought he was shooting at Abbas to kill him but it transpired he was simply engaged in a spot of fun. With impressive skill he hit both rear tyres. Each ring of inflated rubber exploded with a noise equal to that of the rifle shot which had caused it. The Rolls swerved from side to side, then came a stop. Abbas sprang out and examined the damage. He shook his fist and screamed another stream of incomprehensible Arabic. Then he climbed back in and drove off, wobbling drunkenly. And that was the last I ever saw of the abominable Abbas, as he manoeuvred his erratic machine to the end of the street and out of my sight. In my book I shall say nothing of this. In my book there will be a touching scene in which Abbas sinks to his knees, hands clasped as if in prayer, and thanks me for my astonishing generosity. We will part the best of friends. This is the kind of thing readers prefer and one must never disappoint the reader.

AND SO MY ADVENTURES in the Holy Land came to their end. In spite of all, on my last day in Jerusalem I was not stuck for something to do. I had one holy place left to cross off my list. The cave of Jeremiah, prophet of Jerusalem's doom. Jeremiah: old misery guts, with a clairvoyant gift! I do apologise. That was uncalled for. It's the heat. It makes me light-headed, facetious, foolish. I cannot always control myself. Of the whereabouts of this legendary cavern I had made enquiries. Perplexingly it turned out there were two, each asserting its authenticity and indignantly refuting the claims made by the other. This muddy debate need not concern you. Suffice it to say that Donald Ebenezer McCollum Ph.D. is a man not easily fooled. I believe I have a modest gift for sniffing out truth from falsehood and I soon decided which of these two tenebrous nooks was the real one. My advisor gave me directions but these were, I discovered, not entirely accurate. Perhaps this is only to be expected when you take direction from an Arab. I can only say that for me the second on the left, then right, then right again did me no good at all. I became lost. However, if you shout loud enough you will eventually be understood, and thus it was. History had not been kind to St Jeremiah because it had allowed a Palestinian family to make their home under the hillock where he had found stony lodgings. The legendary quality of things was quite, quite ruined by the urban environs. Once this would have been a lonely place, now it was simply another seething warren of Arabs and their ramshackle dwellings. Above me loomed a bleak, bare mound from which protruded a solitary fruit-bearing fig tree and some clumps of thorny cactus. A pair of small dark hollows in its flanks resembled eye sockets. Was this miserable and marginalised place the true site of Golgotha? The thought made my head swim. Had no one noticed the resemblance before? Yet the Biblical feel was terribly spoiled. Shouts rang out from some metalworkers and their forge smeared the perspective with dirty smoke. Nevertheless one must make the best of things. I must confess it was something of a relief to see so many policemen and soldiers in the streets. Some were on patrol and searching displays of vegetables (for you can never really be sure that that wrinkled toothless old vendor is really all that he seems – under those oranges may lurk a frightful hand grenade!). Others had halted passing carts and were emptying their contents into the street. The Arabs shrieked like monkeys when this happened, though they soon quietened down when a rifle was pointed at them. Some of the troops and police simply stood on street corners, watching. I was pleasantly surprised when soldiers, observing my dog collar, gave me a respectful salute. When they did this I always smiled and nodded and said Bless you, my son. But I did not take matters further. I have never believed in pushing religion down anyone's throat and though the British soldier may be a good Christian he is also a busy man. Besides, God works in many ways, some of which – and here one must be quite frank about the price that sometimes has to be paid to maintain the civilising influence of empire – may require cartridges and a well oiled rifle. The house was easy enough to find, because it had a wooden sign attached to it bearing the words JEREM-IAH CAVE. I tried the wooden door set in a high white wall and it opened. Visitors had to pass down the side of a house. At the back I came to a table with a biscuit tin lid on it. Behind the table sat a girl who was perhaps fourteen. Her breasts seemed large for a child. Her English was unexpectedly good. She told me the cost of admission and pointed at the lid. I laid the required coins on the silver surface and she nodded and pointed to the end of the family garden. A dirt path led past a few withered olive trees to a grotto set in the side of the brown slope which rose up, almost vertical. At its base what might have been scatterings of *Bellis perennis*. Remembered, probably falsely, in scattered recollections of an unfortunate episode. Lumps of rock protruded from that crumbling edifice. I asked if there was a guide, she said no. Her father was the guide and he was absent. The family were all at a funeral. Blooder, she said. It took a minute or so to grasp that she meant her brother. The family had left her behind to look after Jeremiah's cave. I gazed at her eyes for signs of sorrow but saw none. She was inscrutable, yet eager to please. She tugged at my sleeve. This way to cave. I followed her down a rocky path, past some chickens. A tethered goat eyed me malevolently. The cave entrance was a narrow man-sized gash. The girl was carrying a saucer with a candle. She stepped into the darkness and a match flared. She led me on. Inside the darkness opened out. The grotto was surprisingly spacious. It rose to a height beyond the range of the girl's candle. The walls curved back, growing narrower as they went deeper into the hill. Their rough, chipped texture made me wonder if this had once been some sort of mine. There was a faint musty smell. Somewhere there was mould growing. Or perhaps it was me. I sometimes wondered about my European odour. No matter how often my clothes were laundered they always seemed to carry the scent of something faintly damp. The girl held the candle so that, crouching, I could see to the end. The cave shrank to the size of a rabbit hole, then terminated in rubble. Perhaps there was a way through. Had anyone excavated this place? I asked the girl but she did not seem to understand. I stood up, my legs tingling. The candlelight illuminated grey trails of dampness on the walls. The dampness here would have been congenial to the saint's lachrymose moods. I found it entirely plausible that Jeremiah had been here. The print marks on the sandy floor might have been recently made by his sandaled feet. Time slides in this Holy Land. A thousand years pass in a moment. Jesus is tangibly present, as though he died only last Tuesday. This place was far enough from the tumult of the old city yet near enough to the temple area to be the place. An old man, resting on a rock, one hand supporting his bearded chin. Here Jeremiah came, alone, despondent and angry. In those days he had no neighbours. From this darkness a man can truly understand those who have departed from God. *Cut off thy hair, O Jerusalem, and cast it off. Take up a lamentation on the bare heights, for Jehovah hath rejected and forsaken the generation of his wrath.* Here a man might weep in secret (my own eyes began to moisten). Here a man might shake with despair and his eyes run down with tears (I felt a pair of salt drops meander down my hot face). O remorseless bitter world! O faithless, treacherous, villainous, godless city! Who in such a condition would not find a comforting shelter in a stony wilderness as this? Yet in that dark I also saw a pair of eyes, the red eyes of the goat. Satan's eyes. A soft voice whispering . Wilt thou yet take all, Galilean? The time for self-restraint is past. Of the event itself I can say little. Time slid – slides by – darkly. And besides... What was it Benjamin Franklin said? Three may keep a secret if two of them are dead. The same goes for two and one. What memory there is of it dissolves like a handkerchief dipped in acid. It, to wit, the event. The occurrence. The episode. The memory was already crumbling before I was long quit of that cool place. She looked at me with big wondering eyes. It was because I was crying, I think. I took hold of the top of her jerkin. I wrenched the cloth apart. Her breasts plopped out like fruit. I stripped away the remaining vestments. I cannot pretend I have not frequently re-imagined what occurred. Filling a darkness with form, so to speak. Putting a pair of humans on that stony stage. A man, a child. I speak of the irruption of blind desire. It is disgusting. It disgusts me to think of it. It burst from a knowledge that what was about to occur was possible, better than possible, an event without consequences, sans punishment, an imperial ecstasy, hence all. All the greasy grappling, the savage blind rabid plunge of rancid desire, bestial brutish bald lust, the shuddering ecstasy, just adjectives, token words, I recall few of the particulars, unless through mist, shadow, a darkling curtain. Her private parts astonishingly hairy. My lust like a knife. A style drawn from reflection. How convenient you say, you'd be right I suppose. I recall much more vividly the aftermath. The girl did not resist my embraces. Perhaps she was disabled by a paralysis of surprise and bewilderment. But afterwards she cried. As I re-adjusted my flies she stared down at the sandy floor. She was sobbing. Her sobs grew louder. I was reminded – I cannot remember if then or later – of a salt wave dragging back down a steep shelf of Dorset shingle. All I recall is that gulping loudness. We had both lost something, yet my own loss was framed by a hot cunning. That noise had to be stopped. It might produce consequences. *Death and life are in the power of the tongue: and they that love it shall eat the fruit thereof.* At first I was very nice. Please stop that noise I said, stop that do you hear, she didn't, be quiet I said, again a little more forcefully: be quiet. Listen, just bloody shut up! One thing leads to another – what awfulness boils below the surface of that banal truth. I recall none of the particulars. Nor do I profess to follow the teachings of Christ as they are conventionally rendered. I find no compatibility with my circumstances. Hands have no memory of the past. Mine did what they did, no more, no less. They squeezed. My verbal appeals having failed – the girl's upset was becoming distinctly strident – my grip around her throat tightened. She still wouldn't stop her racket. Further pressure was applied and her head of a sudden lolled forward. Her body became loose, into the house with it. Do you people know how heavy a dead child is? Of course you don't. Oh my materialistic brethren, trapped in your petty lives, numbing yourselves with gin and horse racing and whist. You who abuse yourselves with Hollywoodenonanism. You who are betrayed not by Judas but by Rita Hayworth. How could you know about such weights? I got the girl inside. I put it down on the floor, the body. I distinctly remember tiles, orange tiles. I left matters there and went for a wander in my own private wilderness. The Lord was with me, this I know. I do not pretend to understand the workings of He Who Is All-Knowing, but I do know that He was behind everything I did that day. Mine was to be the thorny path to salvation. Sin is behovely if it brings us unto Thee. I drifted from room to room. I was the ghost of my former self. I had gone over the border and was now another. A fly – a fat nauseating bluebottle – appeared and started pestering me. I lashed out, driving it away. It returned, like Satan. I slapped at it with my guilty right hand. In the end it flew out of a window and left me in peace. I sat down to get my breath back. I lay down on a bed and dozed off. A screaming like a gull's woke me, I have no idea what it was. I was wild that day. I had gone across into a new world, at night. There was a lurid light at the edge of everything, shimmering. I rocked and reeled with laughter, I gurgled with amusement, what came over me I do not know. I found myself in another bedroom, a double bed with a bright coverlet, patterned, scarlet and blue. The parental arbour, I presume. I felt loose, at liberty to do whatever I wanted, this was an infidel household was it not? There are many devices in a man's heart. I wanted to smash up everything but it was hot and I was tired. I contented myself with a few pots. I tipped them on to the hard floor and smiled as they shattered. A better idea. All those ingots stacked up inside my bowels, all those pellets of waste matter compressed by my constipated system, were in a trice turned molten. The bricks and plugs were melted into slush. My guts were boiling. I pull back the covering and empty myself on the sheet, a huge splattering yellow-brown sloppy mess. I neatly put the coverlet back, a surprise! Next I wipe myself on the edge of the sheet, tuck it neatly in (another surprise!). Downstairs I came across an axe. I dragged the body to another bedroom and went back for my tool. Why I dismembered the body I cannot really say. A holy madness was inside me that incandescent morning. I could hear a clock ticking. It was as loud as the chimes of Big Ben. Time's loud, coarse passage did not concern me. In retrospect the risks I took were dizzying. Had the family returned and discovered me I dread to think what might have happened. The Arab is a creature of wild impulses. I suspect I would have been martyred for my faith. There was a low cunning inside me, I suppose. I had the wit to strip off all my clothes before I began my butcher's task. I left a neat pile just outside the room. I did not wish to get anything splashed. Back with the corpse I was startled to find myself once more in a state of tumescence. You will be delighted to learn I did not add necrophilia to my sins. Instead I got to work. I hacked madly until there were two portions. The slicing seemed to go on for many minutes, splish-splash-splatter, I shall spare you what you are free to imagine. Intestines unfold to remarkable lengths. They are not a pretty sight. And now it's all gone, a moth-eaten purple curtain shuts out the scene, an adjective and a noun are a sufficient shield. I could play the novelist and pretend all this is just a cheap dream, I shan't. I was right to take precautions. By the end, I was quite bespattered. I found a room with water and cleansed myself. Then I towelled myself dry and dressed. I have no memory of this but I must have done so. And so on with the story. Another bright idea! Downstairs there is a room set aside for prayer and worship. My bladder aches and where better? Afterwards the air is salt and stinging with the odour of my Christianity. The Lord fuels my contempt for heresy. The yellow jet seems to go on forever before finally stopping. Next I take the big Koran down and start to rip out clumps of pages, they mean nothing to me, just squiggles and scimitars, filthy black markings, a declaration of war. My trusty Swan Vestas will not let me down, this is holy work. The crackling begins. Can you believe the oddest thing of all? There, at the end of this greasy little episode, excitement and desire rose up like a weary victor's flagpole on a ruinous battlefield. I yet again did some unbuttoning and kneeled. I spat on my palms and attended to this unexpected demand. My seed shot like soft bullets into the fire. How the pages of the Koran hissed in anger at the presence of a fertile Christian! There is a sweet parable in all this, surely. For this barren land is being reclaimed for Zion and the honeyed seed of the righteous. And the unproductive shall be driven out, along with their dark superstitions and idolatry. Looked at rationally, could there be a greater absurdity than Mohammedanism? I left the house with a roaring in my ears. My blood, or arson's breed, I cannot say. I could hear the Lord's wrath against that house, the multiplying tongues of fire, they sang in my head like a choir. Flame curling catlike around the bright cushions on the floor. The roar of a throbbing conscience, of course not, delete that sentimental addition. I am trying to be straight with myself. I reached the front door, unbolted it. It did not occur to me to go back round the side of the house. Behind me the spitting and gushing grew in intensity, a tide of boiling lava meeting a mighty waterfall, enough of this drivel. I stepped out into the street and shut the door quickly behind me. It was noisier out than in, the screech of a camel, a braying donkey, a caterwauling street vendor with strips of spicy chicken. I flinched at the Lord's harsh noontime gaze. He fixed me with his celestial attention but said nothing. I sensed His unwillingness to make a snap judgement. Repentance and prayers might well fix it for me. My punishment for now is sunlight, tightly focused on my scarlet dripping face. The police saw me at once. So did the soldiers. They were just the other side of the street in two groups, chatting. They stiffened as I stepped out, I saw their hands go for their guns. They were fearful of an ambush. And then they relaxed at the sight of a member of the civilised races. *One of us*. A pink-faced chubby cherub wearing a Panama hat. I beamed back and tipped it respectfully. A stir of recognition among one of the soldiers, a Lance Corporal Somebody, one of Orde's assistants possibly, I cannot be certain. I continued to nod and smile but did not communicate my usual blessing. They started to lose interest, went back to their chit-chat. My head continued to be filled with a terrible din. Flee from the wrath to come! Angels contended with devils. A remembered moment from *Macbeth* was hurriedly staged and then the theatre filled with smoke and the audience began to scream. I remembered to saunter. I pottered, sweating copiously, to the end of the street. A thudding boiling heart shook the neighbourhood, unnoticed. I was waiting for the mob to point at me, to identify me as the criminal, to seize me. I was waiting for the accusing shouts, the furious screams, the cries of fire! None came. Perhaps I had botched things. The fire had fizzled and gone out. No matter. Soon the family would be back. But by then I would be gone. The day went on like any other Jerusalem day. The barter of commodities under a blue sky. I took the first available alleyway, and then another. I broke out into a street, crossed it, and found new alleyways. Jerusalem was full of dead flesh that day. Chickens with broken necks on hooks. A fluffy dangling lamb with its throat cut. Lumps of dark dripping meat on racks alive with clouds of flies. A smiling proprietor with a Flit gun. On. The fruit market, the spice market, the bazaar of the metal workers. On down the Via Dolorosa. A lurching camel passes, shaking its tasselled head. Some calm sweet-tempered overloaded donkeys. Female beggars, their veils black and white. Loud tourists with Kodaks and yelping American voices. A procession of miserable-looking English Christians, in clothes the colour of mud or mould, advancing slowly over the creamy flagstones. Solemn ponderous Ash-kenezim Jews with enormous black hats edged with grey fur. The Greek quarter, coffin lids of ebony displayed by the doors of undertakers. Small shops suffused with the smell of incense, selling olive wood camels. A bell tolling, then more bells, the whole city at last jangling and clanging with sundry iron reverberations until I felt like screaming. My head throbbed and ached terribly. A bronze plate reading in smaller letters, after some Hebrew, JEWISH AGENCY. I dash inside and run up the stairs. I enter an office which is a hive of activity. It reminded me of a newspaper office in a Hollywood film. The place was full of desks and young men and women furiously typing. People standing around in groups were chattering in all the languages of the civilised nations. I could hear Spanish, German and French. There was some jabber which might well have been Russian. The speaker looked like Trotsky, with a wispy beard and owl-eyes glasses. On the walls were many maps to which pins had been stuck. Can I help you? My inquisitor was cold, ferocious and filled with suspicion. He looked to be about forty.

With that nose of his he reminded me of a falcon. I could not help but note that he had a pistol tucked into his belt. I am an enormous admirer of your enterprise, I said. I have come from Scotland. My father, the Lord bless him, brought me up to admire the dream which you people are making real. I am a church minister, but lately come from a motor tour of the holy sites. I regret to say that at the end I had an unfortunate experience with my Arab chauffeur. But I know I can tell you nothing about the fecklessness of aboriginals that you yourselves do not already know. I have seen with my own eyes how you are making the desert bloom. I have here a modest donation. Please spend it as you think best. I took out my wallet and handed over twenty pounds. What unending wildness was in me that day! But what use is twenty pounds to a man who is to be hanged? The fellow grunted and took the bank notes. I regret to say he did not display the effusive gratitude which I was rather expecting. But no matter. The Jew can be a strange creature at times. I hurried back down the stairwell. From here, wherever that was, I took a taxi back to my hotel.

EDITH WAS HER name. As we crossed Gaza and Palestine slipped away I asked her to marry me. She said yes at once and we lived happily ever after. Our homely home in the Hebrides rings with the laughter of our three darling children, and as I step across the threshold I can smell the delicious aroma of home cooking – oatcakes, bubbling porridge and the stench of black pudding. Believe that and you'll believe anything. It might have happened like that, of course. But it did not. That said, Edith is the only woman who has ever made me consider that sexual intercourse on a regular basis might be a procedure somewhat less than repellent. I finished my packing and checked out of the King David Hotel. After various wearisome complications and undiverting diversions I ended up on the Kantara train. My carriage was empty apart from a delightful English girl. She had rosy cheeks and a band of freckles across her nose. Her tousled hair was a rich, deep auburn. She smelled of violets. (As you can tell, I am still half in love with easeful Edith.) At first we were a little shy of each other and maintained our reserve. Her merry blue eyes were directed at the view rather than yours truly. But then sunlight filled the space between us and suddenly we both simultaneously remarked on the glorious palm oases on the marge of each perfect beach. We broke into laughter as they do in films and soon we were exchanging stories. Her blue pleated skirt had ridden up her legs. I caught a glimpse of a suspender strap. Her stockings were the colour of sand. Her thighs were deliciously plump. Edith explained she had flown up from Cairo to visit her air-force brother at Lydda Landing Field. I told her a little about myself and my pilgrimage to those very special places in the Holy Land. Our blue smiling steam train chugged merrily among lovely sand dunes close by the azure Mediterranean. The sand here is herring-boned with exquisite wind-carved patterns. From time to time we glimpsed lines of white camels, driven by winged men in floating veils. It seemed magical. But then we came to the mud huts of old Gaza, still unrepaired after Allenby's ancient fight with the Turks. I told Edith of the remarkable history of the region and of the marvellous work of Sir Flinders Petrie. She gasped as I told her how this admirable old fellow – still hard at work at the age of eighty-three! – had excavated gold jewellery from Ireland here, in the mount of ancient Ghazzeh, named Tel el-'Aijul. I may have babbled, I admit. Edith was a nervy girl, and nervy girls give me the jitters. Her laughter was unnatural. It had a slightly forced quality. She seemed to laugh at everything, yet I sensed an underlying disgust. Something was troubling her. My condition was no better. I maintained an observation of sand and sea and whatever chose to fill those vacant spaces but all the time I was waiting for the train to grind to an unexpected halt and the police to come on board. They would move from carriage to carriage, searching for a murderer. It would be like *The Thirty-Nine Steps*, with me as Robert Donat. But I knew I would not jump off. It was too late for all that. There would be nowhere to hide in this bare landscape, and besides I am not awfully energetic. Running at speed is not my cup of tea. Fear made me voluble. I rather think I may have blathered. But Edith was a good egg and did not try to shut me up. She freely admitted her Bible illiteracy and listened with interest as I told her about Emmaus and about the border country through which our train was speeding. Edith, a sharp girl, observed that no one was swimming. She thought it was such a waste of these beautiful sandy beaches. I quipped that it was *the Philistine Riviera* and Edith flashed her almost perfect teeth and broke into peals of laughter at my wit. I must confess I found the amusement of a pretty girl a distinctly pleasurable experience. I wanted to get out my Kodak and photograph her. Something I could look at for the rest of my life. But I lacked the courage. Instead I stared out of the carriage window. I was becoming aware of its faint scratch marks and semen-coloured stains. Deserted beaches gave way to villages. That is the Arab for you, I said, solemnly pointing at the dusky-hued families huddled in the shade of mud and grass huts. They are only interested in their plantations. We stared at the hedged rectangles of land, full of corn and melon and bananas, but soon grew bored. More and more desert sand blew in through the open window, a fine mist that bid fair to bury us like the Sphinx. With our powdered hair and clothing we resembled a pair of corpses, determined to continue talking in spite of adversity. It was strangely peaceful in that carriage, where leather straps gently tapped the walnut panels and the creep of a dying afternoon led us towards a mauve ending. By now we were practically chums and Edith opened up about the true state of affairs. She had really come to Palestine to think things over. An army Padre had asked her to marry him. She wasn't sure and needed time to think. She thought she'd make a pretty poor parson's wife. She liked dancing and films and having fun. Gerald – her Padre – couldn't dance for toffee. And have you come to a decision? I felt my heart thudding as I put the question. Edith laughed gaily and shrugged. I don't know, she said. I just don't know. Then marry me instead. She gawped. *You!* I've got quite a decent income, I said. When my father dies I shall inherit a tidy sum. And I own a house that's far too big for a bachelor. Where is it? Stornoway, I said. Well strictly speaking not in Stornoway but in that neck of the woods. You wouldn't have heard of it. Where's Stornoway? The Hebrides. The Hebrides? She roared with laughter. That's in Scotland, isn't it? Yes it is, I conceded. I could never live in Scotland, she said. It rains all the time there. And there are millions of midges. I once had a camping holiday north of Glasgow. I *hate* midges. I positively *loathe* them. So I shall have to decline. But it's awfully sweet of you to ask. I've decided it will have to be Gerald. Her words disgusted me. I cried: But you just said you weren't sure! She grinned, obscenely buoyant. Oh but I am now. You've helped me make up my mind. Look, do you know how old I jolly well am? I hazarded a guess. Twenty-five? That's awfully sweet of you to say so. But the fact is I'm thirty. But don't for Lord's sake tell Gerald if you ever meet him, because he thinks I'm twenty-seven. And frankly my chances of getting hitched are fading fast. That's not true, I said hotly. Take me, for instance. I could do with a wife. Very much so, in fact. I'm sure we could make a go of it. Lewis isn't so bad, you know. Who's Louis? I mean the island. Where I live, I said. Oh I could never live on an island, she said. I'd suffocate. But Britain's an island! That's different, she said. Anyway *I could do with a wife* isn't the most romantic proposal I've ever had. Not that it matters now. My heart was broken five years ago. A chap named Tom. As a matter of fact I gave myself to him. I can see that shocks you. Don't look so tragic. It was no sooner done than the poor fool crashed his plane and died. He was a pilot, you see. A friend of my brother's. But that's all water under the bridge. As I see it there's no point in crying over spilt milk. I'll make do and mend. That's what people do, isn't it? They just go on living as best they can, making the best of things. And Gerald might be a parson but at least he's army. All my family married army and I will too. Oh look! We've reached Suez.

*

AT THE BORDER settlement of Ishmailia the huge red sun of Egypt drops into the desert behind a rim of palms. A violet soft sensuous liquid twilight envelops us here. The blue night sky fills with a sparkling silver fire. It was once gazed at by tiny languorous Cleopatra on her couch. It must surely have solaced even desolate Hagar and Ishmael. I said to myself, remembering one of father's pamphlets, The End Times are here! At Cairo, at night, with my old pump thumping, I gave Edith an Egyptian farewell. Farewell, remember me. Three hand clasps, and three times our hands pressed against our beating hearts. I proffered my card but Edith shook her head and said she really didn't think she should take it. The future dropped like a vase and shattered. She kissed me on the cheek and grinned and called me an odd fish. Then she was gone. Her scent lingered in that carriage. That sweet chamber was suddenly as empty as a ransacked tomb. I saw her one more time, on the seething, crowded concourse. She pushed her way through the crowds to a man in khaki. Gerald was bigger than I'd imagined. His face was radish-bright and fleshy. He reminded me of an inert crustacean. The creature spasmed into life. It hugged Edith and then applied saliva to her mouth and face. Sick with misery and disgust I turned away. A taxi took me through the raucous animated night streets to the Imperial Hotel, where the city's noise was hushed and I slept like an opium fiend. In the morning I ate a hearty breakfast and drank three stinging peppery cups of coffee. I had planned four more days in Cairo, before joining a ship at Port Said. There was still a spot of sightseeing to pack in. I wondered if I had the courage to include a brothel. I felt wild and lewd and furious. Edith seemed to taunt me with her boiling absence. I was in the mood to soil something. But it was not to be. I was back in my room staring at a map when there was a knock at the door. Two policemen stood there. Their faces were grim. There were pistols strapped to their hips. I knew what it was about, obviously. I'd been a fool to think it could end any other way. Orde's man had spotted me the moment I'd stepped out of that burning house. Identification of the murderer hardly required the deductive genius of Mr Sherlock Holmes. It was little more than a bureaucratic formality. A paper trail of hotel registrations, train reservations and border controls led to killer. You had better come in, I said. I suppose. Or perhaps the senior policeman said: May we come inside? And I replied: Yes, of course. I remember so little of past conversations. I am always surprised when people write their autobiographies and remember the things they said and others said forty years before. I struggle to recall what I said yesterday, or even this morning. Whatever was said, I held back the door and they stepped inside. I closed the door. The officers were wearing short trousers and long grey socks, giving them the appearance of schoolboys. The one in charge had a toothbrush moustache, like the Fuehrer. Would you like a drink? I said. I was playing for time. A tumbler of whisky and a few more minutes of freedom before the handcuffs put in an inevitable appearance. Hitler smiled bleakly. Normally we wouldn't drink on duty, he said. But on this occasion... This can't be easy for you, I said. I have no idea why I said that. Call it another of my light-hearted caprices. Probably it was something I had once read in a crime novel. I have a keen sense of the proprieties and the conventions. Their consent to alcohol startled me, just as my words seemed to startle them. I added: Would you like me to make a statement? I am happy to co-operate in any way possible. I don't wish to be difficult. The officers frowned. I was aware that once again my natural urge to loquacity had manifested itself. I shut up. I poured the drinks. They raised no objection to Johnny Walker. I passed them their refreshment. Down the hatch! Down the hatch, they echoed. No statement will be necessary, Dr McCollum. In fact by the sound of it you may have got the wrong end of the stick. I regret to inform you I have some bad news, doctor. This phrasing did not seem quite right for rape, murder, mutilation and arson. Had I been barking up the wrong tree all the time? Indeed I had. Although I cannot pretend that the fellow's next words were any less terrible than an announcement that I was under arrest on suspicion of monstrous crimes. Hitler drained his glass and looked at me. The fact is we have some rather bad news. I regret to inform you that your father is seriously ill. He has asked to see you. I'm afraid the message has taken some time to reach you. Apparently it was passed on to your hotel in Jerusalem after you'd left. It took some time to work out where you were. But not to worry, now that we've tracked you down everything is under control. The chaps at the embassy have managed to book you on a plane leaving this afternoon. I have brought you the ticket. I'm afraid you'll have to reimburse H.M. Government. But no need to worry about that now. The main thing is to get you home. Would you like me to get the hotel to order you a taxi? You'll need to leave by three at the latest. Shall we say two-thirty? Two-thirty would be quite suitable, I said. My voice felt weak and shaky. In truth my feelings were a harsh combination of distress at the news of my poor father's illness – it was obvious reading between the lines that he was dying – and a fierce elation that my crimes had not yet caught up with me. If I managed to get out of Egypt before the day was over then probably they never would. No one could drag me back to Palestine to answer questions. The law, I was fairly certain, would not permit it. I had read something to that effect in one of the newspapers. After the officers had gone I began re-packing my only recently unpacked belongings. Interrupted only by a sudden boiling in my bowels. I ran to the lavatory. My anus squirted a foul yellow jet. Shit like watery custard, stinking to high heaven. In a word: diarrhoea. A gyppy tummy. I wiped myself clean and then was caught in the grip of another cascade. The squares of Izal ran out. Luckily a fellow Briton had left two copies of the *Times Literary Supplement* on a ledge beside the water closet. Each page folded in half, then torn, makes for a luxury arse wipe. It was a shame I'd had no time to read the reviews but *c'est la vie*. Two copies sufficed to return me to the land of sweetness and hygiene. My voiding was done with. I ate bread, in the firm belief that this keeps you in a condition of solidity and control. It seemed to work for me. Which brings me on to last things.

*

THERE IS NO ending in life, other than the brute and obvious one. With stories it's different. A lot of things accumulate and go on accumulating. There are weights, pressures. Where to stop? Where to begin? A man can easily become abject and look for an easy way out. You can over-simplify. You can flannel and blather and not mention the unmentionable. Best not to mention the unmentionable, really. People won't like you for it. I could end this story at Croydon Airport, in the rain. This was where I learned that I was too late. My father had died during the flight. You might say he died in my sleep, if I slept, I can't be sure. I like to think I did. Father dead. The revelation left me unmoved. I calmly thanked the bearer. No tears would come then, or later. My father's wealth was a lot less than he had led me to believe. The tears on my face at his graveside were splashes of rain from bruise-dark louring cumulus. I adopted the style that was expected of me under those grave conditions. My heart was dry and without turbulence. None of this seems to matter. I hope as a prelude to my own interment someone will salute not only a devout theologian but a man with a sly sense of humour. A returned prince might well recall my pranks. Back at the house I discovered a granule from the cave lodged between two of my toes. The skin was raw and pink where it had rubbed abrasively. I doubt if the dull-witted police would ever have discovered it, even if I had been incarcerated in Cairo. But all that was far behind me by then. Wet days turned to cold weeks, the wintry weeks to months of Mondayish moods. And then I put off my sackcloth. I girded me with gladness. God be merciful to me, a sinner. I repent now of all my sins and turn from them. I place my trust alone in the Lord Jesus Christ for Salvation. I believe that the Blood of Jesus shed for me on the Cross atones for my sins. I now accept the finished work of Christ. The book was written and published and reviewed. It sold, though far fewer copies than the publishers expected. The market for travel books collapsed once the war broke out. The war spoiled so many things. In point of fact I rather regret the way things have panned out. Hitler, it seems to me, is not as black as he has been painted in some quarters. Everyone seems to forget that a rapprochement was agreed with the German Zionist Federation. A sensible and civilised agreement was reached that all German Jews could be assisted to start a new life in a homeland for the Jews, to wit in Palestine. This was why the Zionist Federation deplored the irresponsible attempts by the fanatics of the Left to campaign for a boycott of German goods. Indeed, one of Wingate's pals told me that the warmest of links had been forged. It was only a few years ago that a correspondent of *Der Angriff* was invited out to see for himself how the answer to the so-called "Jewish question" was laid out for all to see in this dusty strip of the globe, where a people prepared to get stuck in and work hard will one day create one of the more civilised and humane states on this little spinning globe of ours. Wingy's chum (who had been involved with the organisation) even had a souvenir of the visit – a collection of yellowing newspaper cuttings entitled *A Nazi Visits Palestine*. He also proudly showed me his commemorative medallion, with the Star of David on one side and the swastika on the other. When people tell you that Joseph Goebbels is anti-Semitic I beg you to remember that. Speaking as one doctor about another I have always rather admired the fellow. His facial features may have the misfortune to resemble those of a syphilitic skull, yet his tastes have, from what little I have learned, always been civilised. And not everything in war turns out badly. Swings and roundabouts, eh? For all I know the war may have helped my own fortunes, obscurely. For no inspector ever came to call. No writ of hocus-pocus was ever drawn up against me. Amid so much death, I am very small fry. I was – I am! – a scot-free Scot. Make me a new creation in Christ Jesus and give me power in my life to live for Thee and serve Thee. Where no wood is, there the fire goeth out: so where there is no tale-bearer, the strife ceaseth. Autumn crept in like a reptile. Its bone structure could not be disguised. Granite winked at me. My hands turn into claws. An old fever returns. Outside, the distant plugs and tumours of volcanic outpourings sweat off their centuries of rain. A pretty enough sight. I could spin this story out if I wanted to. The further I went, the more I would relish it. Things unbelievable! In the meantime, mean time lets slide its lava. I shall drown in it. It petrifies me. They'll find me solidified, bent over in a last desperate lurch for shelter. I am no Flavius Claudius Julianus. So no sarcophagus of porphyry for poor old Donald McCollum. Anything else that the defendant would like to say? Lord, yes. Year after year passes and I still think of Edith, out there somewhere. Perhaps she is still in Egypt. I think of this war, soon to be over. Back in the Hebrides I went back to my old ways. With father gone I was free to lubricate my life in any vile way I wished. Whisky and butter and spittle were the wines which irrigated my dark obscure wound. Sometimes, at 3 a.m., I rise (already risen!) in my empty house. I go outside, into the garden. The pale night shows the ragged outline of the mountains. The world has grown grey from His breath. I slip off my striped pyjamas by the back door. What happens next is anyone's guess. Correction. *How* what happens next is anyone's guess. The outcome itself is never in doubt. The thing itself comes to a sticky conclusion. Conscience, guilt, disgust, they each combine to yap at my naked self. Lust drives them off with a big stick. No gastrorrhaphy can ever seal my aching, throbbing flesh. Sometimes, when in a daredevilish mood, I take a wild risk. I haul myself up one of Nora's old cast iron poles. I balance there, purple trigger pressed against the cold, coarse surface. Above me, the twinkling stars and rags of speeding cloud. I hang there, shuddering, until at last I lower myself back on to the surface of this bitter planet. But mostly I prefer not to take chances. I make my way to where no intruding stranger can ever see me. I crouch stark amid the shrubs. I push myself backward against spiky branches, sometimes even to the point of tearing open skin. Such little drips of hot blood excite me no end. Algolagnia is sweeter than honey. My fury pierces the night. I boil with longings. I have carnal knowledge of – oh wicked, wicked – the Holy Trinity itself. Trembling, shuddering, teeth clenched, I splash the cold damp grass with my milk. A low, crawling ghost mauls the withered mulberry bush. It chills my calves. I fart in God's face. I stand above the rose bush and piss upon its blossom. I return indoors, bloated with shame and fear. I go back to bed and cannot sleep. I am back at Cairo airport now, the propellers whirling, the fuselage trembling, the din of the engine unbelievably loud. A dentist's cruel drill, burrowing deeper into my skull. Take-off in three minutes. The steps have been removed. They can't get me now. The motive for my passage is at this point absent from my mind. I cannot think of a dying father at a time like this. The great machine taxis across the runway. Power and force roll me with them, their humble priest. The horizon has a greenish-amber hue. The first stars are coming out. We howl up the runway. With a savage sliding lurch the aircraft frees itself from the pull of hot, earthly things. Steeply upward we continue on life's journey. Goodbye old slithery black snake Nile! The fluffy cloud layer slips past. We level off. Hell and damnation! A tiny prick of pain in one of my feet, it's nothing. Would like to get some sleep but sleep won't come. I keep my eyes closed tight. That's what father always said I should do to ensure a good night's sleep. Doesn't seem to work on a plane. No real sleep. Was that what Satan promised me a long, long time ago? Nonsense and stuff! Keep trying. Must always keep at it. Tighter, tighter. Empty my boiling mind. Let it all pour away, the silt, the muck. Shut down the damned choir. Close the lid on the organ. Complete inertia and silence, *please*. I hear a child, sobbing. I try my very best to shut her out. Please give me a drink. Please send me assorted literature. Silence, do you hear! Impossible on a plane. But once we've levelled off the engine din diminishes, markedly. The whirr of the propellers is strangely soothing. Please send me a helpful Christian book. Please send me Further Spiritual Help. For I hear a crying in the dark core of screaming machinery. There's a wailing inside the shivering fuselage. It pierces my continuing fever. A worm wriggles inside the cushion under my head. Go away! Give me some peace. Let me relax and enjoy the view. We are on course for England's green fields. Up here everything is a rich dark beauteous imperial blue. The darkling heavens seem lively with God's shining presence. I feel Him in my blood. I sense His mercy. O Lord my God, I will give thanks to Thee forever. And then again I hear return the tongues of all the wronged.

New York Times Book Review (August 1939)

The reader can open this volume assured that he will find here something very different to the usual book on Palestine. Dr McCollum has been inspired by a great number and variety of interests, historical, social, and economic but above all spiritual.

The book describes the author's adventures as he goes in search of the life of Christ and the landscape which saw the birth of Christianity. Dr McCollum is the son of a minister in the Church of Scotland, a man who, as he puts it, "first set my moral compass in the direction of virtue". He movingly describes how his tour of Palestine served only to revivify his faith. But this is no dusty tract. The author has jogged around, up and down, all over Palestine in an old motor car driven by a picturesque and amusing Arab chauffeur.

Intermingled with all of the varied threads of the narrative there runs a constant accompaniment of colorful description and comment that picture the daily scene and the persons that fill it. With the greatest zest, Dr McCollum describes the still discoverable trail of the Phoenicians, the excavations of the archaeologists and the inspiring work of those, many of them Americans, who are founding the new homeland of Zion and bringing this backward region into the modern world.

The author describes the many new friends he found there, including loyal servants of the Mandate who are selflessly toiling to bring peace and civilisation to a region where dark and ignorant forces sometimes seek to obstruct the forward march of progress.

A Jaunt through Palestine is as informing, interesting and engaging a book on its theme as one is likely to find.

It ought to be particularly useful for anyone taking the increasingly popular cruise into Eastern Mediterranean waters.

THE DUMP

for Ken MacLeod

Seventeen million dead last year, not bad, not bad at all, eh? As for me, you. Be patient. Allow me a breath. The game will soon be up. A couple of hours at best. I gather my dregs. Where words are scarce... Eh? Call me a whirl-brain that talks whatever comes uppermost. Frantic-mad with evermore unrest. I gather my dregs of energy, yes. For the last struggle. Time, now, eh? To take up some of the ragged ends left behind. To clear up the facts of the matter. To illuminate the situation. Better still to eliminate it. I shall contribute a decisive step in the physics of elementary particles, something of a highly algebraic nature! Not overlooking the obscure parts in my own fortunes. A rump of words. The privy corners of my mazëd mind. Something to get your teeth into. Really? Really. I speak fondly. After that you will find me obmutescent. Meantime, though comatose and drowsy, I will tell lengthily the lousy things which occurred. Sound a sennet! Scalp glabrous, face glaciated, battered by hours and days. Fossicking around. I left home with a light heart, speaking English well, and strong in arithmetic, bah! And now? A.J.'s Annual Party? Adventures of Master F.J.? In moments of extremity every man becomes an orator. Women too, I suppose. Speke, Parrot! Talk of orts, worts, banana skins. Of time upon a once, interminable. Drink deep, ride hard. I have greasy hair and whistle every S in my vocabulary, what's it to you, mister? Miss? Mizz. Hark! I hear from the heart of the hills I suppose the thunder of the imprisoned river. Twelve hours, twelve bounteous hours are gone. At least. Eh? Here in The Dump, yes. Top o' the Heap! Ah, the cosmic abundance of helium! At least fifty miles from the nearest metaphor. So it feels. Picking your nose, you pick your way across the ash. All over. A soft drift of syntax. A colon lying on its side, staring at me. Oxidised scraps of news yellow as my stumps. The King of the Belgians is suffering from acute heart trouble and is unable to move about. Good. Delighted to hear it. Nice to hear I'm not the only one. I shall sing with the miller of the Dee. Pen, ink, and paper are cold vehicles. Stop? Commas. Black, like grit. Indispensable in such surroundings. Here and there a spiky zed. Trousers, boots, grey with dust. The occasional lustreless gerund. How deeply *unpoetical* the age and all one's surroundings are. The level waste, the rounding gray. Streak of glimmering sunshine, say. No. Just grass and barren silent stones. I think not. A ridge topped (yes, topped) with dead tree trunks, sneezewood, say, and (naturally) stinkwood. Can't be. Verisimilitude demands... Eh? Ruins overgrown with marginalia. Light of the westering sun, then gone. The darkness. Rolling clouds speckled with débris. Fused metal and concrete. A burned-out place. This septic isle, this ordure of Windsors. Upon it you lower your arse, your gaze. Stones and wiring, overgrown with dark, sticky weeds. And the stench! Fetch me sweet marjoram! What defects, what darkness. Broken signs. Hardocks, hemlock, nettles. Singing "Polly Wolly Doodle," day after day. Fancy a game of Kick the Can? Or King of the Hill? Don't wait for me, I won't be back. Just sit quietly if you wish. A blind man's bluff. Face streaked with dirt. Eyes bloodshot and red as Joe McKenny's. Smile you my speeches, as I were a fool? Melten da! Fatel era why a keel? What's on? What's happening? Eleemosynary, my dear Wassermann, I am not. No more of that. I hope in time to make myself opaque. You heard several stories? You're about to hear the real one, mister. I should know. I was in charge of the burial detail. A tongue, tongues! Of fire. See, hear. The smoke. The golden ointment. You want to watch what you're saying. Your self, mister, eh? Watch. Or miss. Miss everything. Watch. Tick-tock. Up there. Scrap of blue sky, then gone. Over there. Churned-up mud, as far as the eye can squint. The snapped, burned trees. Ground full of blocks and blocking steel. Everything getting dark, brittle. Century's end, probably. Can't be sure. Perhaps the year 4462853 S.E.C. Perhaps the twenty-first, who knows? Don't try telling me this is latter Lammas, matey. What a period. A clue, quick! How's the wind? Thrrraaaarrrp! Interminable, the long evening-ends, flatulence, storm and thunder, flashes of bright light, no getting away from it. You want to watch your tongue! Eh? How live I then, which thus draw forth my days? I sing as the boy does by the burying ground. This day then, let us not... Encolpius speaking. Call me Berserk, I like it. Call me Egbert Souse! Wash Jones, perhaps.

Though somewhat battered I look nothing at all like the puffy, shifty *Rektorat* of the University of Freiburg in 1933-34. In another time, another place, perhaps I shall be Charles Le Boeuf, Comte d'Osmoy. Quaxo. Major Jack Hobbs. The Marquis de Lafayette, Postmaster General (retired). Or Everett Ruess. Eh? Alexander Supertramp? No! Call me Bronterre. I am very heavy. Call me Schüler, yes. Bernard Schüler! Come and enjoy all the fun of the Zirkus Schüler! My grotesque girls will do their very best! Please ignore all the stories! The people! Changing and changing. Alice! The young girl Judith, the wife Clarisse! The trap. Eh? Call me Switchman. O, how that name befits my composition! What's that? More good news! Cholera in the Sudan has killed at least 700 people! The old diseases are making a come-back, hallelujah! The death toll but the toxic tit of the iceberg as many areas in south Sudan are inaccessible due to the civil war. Said the Belgian branch of Médecins Sans Frontières. Reuter – Nairobi. More good news! Syria is building a poison gas factory in the northern city of Aleppo. It's said. So time. Time to – Split? Obscurely here alone. Ill, with swellings. Snowed in. Larynx frozen and just a hint of cerebral edema. Wind, throbbings. Inflammation. Pemphigus, possibly. Definite symptoms of pellagra! Décrépit, poudreux, sale, abject, visqueux, fêlé. Play me the Cancer Symphony! Dorsal trouble in the blood, that too. The. Long. Disease. Is. Yes. The. Worst. Devise betimes some drams! Bronterre? After Bronterre O'Brien, you oaf! My father wanted a complete subversion of the existing order! Can hear, just about, Willie Nelson singing "Sentimental Journey". Can hear, just about, J. J. Cale singing "Days Go By". What's more I have a bad cold. Also (*entre nous*) a little feverish. My teeth, my discoloured stumps, long since gone. But still toothache! The fact is. Is. The TV cunts. They have theirs but no bite, no bite at all. They all look so fucking HAPPY. Shit, must watch my language! I, miserable impotent, moi, celibate and slack and tight as a whiskery retentive nonagenarian nun, I think there is something wrong with my liver. Twenty ailments, at least. Fetch me the latest *Diagnostic and Statistical Manual of Mental Disorders*! I deny absolutely the stories about coma, amnesia, furor, automatism, chronic hallucinations and dementia! All lies, from beginning to end! I know nothing about an eight-day travelling clock and a generous Dutchman! I have never been to Mexico! Pifflocation? Piffle! Famish an aged beggar at your gates, you bastards. World starvation? What's that – 850 million people in the world are severely malnourished? Time for another United Nations World Food Summit with first- class air travel and luxury hotels, essential for any civilised discussion of these mattters! There is a prosperity that a man findeth in misfortunes, eh? You will know of course what happened to poor Jenny after she left for Paris on Wednesday 17 December, 1862. Thankfully, sometimes, a few distractions. To take your mind off it all. Seventeen million dead last year, not bad, not bad at all. And that was just the preventable infectious diseases! Details, did you say? Certainly. Only too happy to. 3.1 million from TB, 4.4 million from respiratory diseases like pneumonia, 3.1 million from typhoid and dysentery, 2.1 million from malaria. Over one million from measles! And in the UK alone 576 deaths in police custody between 1985 and 1995. 24,000 civilians killed or maimed by landmines every year, with the full backing – cheers! – of Her Majesty's Government. Hawk aircraft and British Alvis armoured vehicles sold – rah, rah, rah! – to Indonesian killers. Keeping the numbers down. Everyone – British Aerospace, Vosper Thorneycroft, Vickers Defence Systems – doing their bloody bit. Washed down with an invigorating squirt courtesy of Tactica water cannon. And Mahmoud Jamayyal dead. And Latin American police putting guns in children's mouths – guns made in Birmingham, U.K. I'm proud to say. And pleased as Punch to announce that when Anthony Ginting, a bus conductor from North Sumatra, was beaten by the police, they stabbed his head with a screwdriver manufactured in Scruton and smashed his fingers with a hammer from Hammersmith. Damchoe Pemo, pregnant Tibetan, repeatedly beaten with a baton from Britain! Electric shocks? Blowtorches? Shackles? Drills? Come to Esher for all the fun of the fair! Mais je divague. Bored already, I bet. Who wants to read stuff like this when you could be comfy and warm and faraway, eh? But thanks anyway for the diversions. A bit of excitement never did anyone any harm. The distant piercing thump of a powerful bomb exploding. The satisfying collapse of apparently solid, sturdy structures. The delightfully abrupt disappearance of old friends. Broken windows in Marx and Spengler's. Wreckage. The donkey bray of sirens. Anything to get away from all this. Come on! A soap. A nice liceless ice. A good yarn. Thomas the Blue Conformist Tank Engine. Take up your Pipes and puff away. He was by all accounts a sinister person. Full of resentment and frustration. Everything at sixes and sevens. Put various twos and twos together, get the whole story bent. A spicy literary biography, perhaps. A bit on the side. Original and curious positions. I used to wonder what the trick would be at fifty – aleatoricism? A fizzing this, a sparkling that. A G and T. An ABC narrative. The anecdotes of Hugh Severance. An afternoon of vigorous intercourse. Three long raw days of bitter invective concerning the relative merits of Bodley MS 851 and Bodley MS 581. On the fourth day jokes. Jokes about humorous or unusual incidents. Tristana's amputation. Lusty Robin and his dog. Little Pete and his tiny organ. Thynne, Pynche, Lem, Ledger, Hitchprick, Hal, Spinks, Dribble, Hecuba, Fricker and Jigger and Jug. Winnebago with his black flowery orbits so reminiscent of a transexual's. Zelma Van Riper! Petulant Darkbloom, with Clinton Dangerfield. Mr Kite. Mr Japp. Ms. Kapp. Zeeta. Mure. Death's refuse. Baron von Tink. Gerry and Jerry. Jerry and Tom. Scented Tom and malodorous Viv. Ron and Em (the filthy pair would collogue for hours). Ron and Effie. Dick and Fanny. Not forgetting, no. Bill and Will. Willie and Wally. Al and Ally. Miss N. Flood. Nature's dregs. Tiny O'Toole. Jones. Sebastian Melmoth, is he here too? And bugger me if it isn't Oscar! In this bottomless hell. And Giacinta, my gitanilla? Never! Chin up old man, stiff upper, cock too one of these days I wouldn't be at all surprised. Fingers crossed, fist clenched, oh Jesus! "Come up, Captain Harris." He gripped Wiley Post by the throat. His face went purple, he began to make odd choking noises. You and I begin and end here, eh? We go back a long way, eh, my old ape, my slithery amphibian. And now back for one last fight. Old worm; old miserable weed. Slime dreaming of slime in a climate of hydrated iron oxide. The expendables. The glory guys. On a tequila high, thinking that life's not so bad after all, eh? The possibility – the dream – of breaching The Great Barrier. I will set out for Ireland tomorrow se'nnight. Tomorrow at ten I shall take a train. Tomorrow, comrades... Next week, sisters... The day it rained, for example. At first it seemed like an invigorating start to an otherwise dull day. The time I estimate to have been around ten a.m. and the dim sun was just beginning its slow, washed-out crawl over Hackney. The ecru wastes. Many natives of The Dump were still not up. Most, probably. Out of sight, dozing and comfy. Or wailing softly. Gnashing their stumps. Or awake but still huddled in drifts of old warm newspaper. Awake yet inert. Like Dorothy and William Wordsworth we sat shivering for three-quarters of an hour. Titillating themselves with logodaedaly, possibly. At best sucking on yesterday's core, I imagine. Others, Early Risers like myself, were already up and about. Up and about, can you believe! Such naïvety. How we deserved that piercing upper case. How the Old Timers chuckled at the antics of the Early Risers! How Tristan L'Hermite and Orrery and Huff and Dr Presto wheezed and Madox and Molkin and Boris de Schloezer giggled! How peeping Parvisol toothlessly grinned! How Vanhomrigh and Ogle screeched. How Beaumont hooted! Such droll efforts at hygiene and good grooming! Peripeteia and piss! Hope lighting a feeble lamp! Poor damnéd souls still going through the old, old motions. As if still in salaried employment, say. Biological clock throbbing in tune to capitalism's awesome requirements. Six dot dot one five already, gosh! Emerge from warmth, into the cold, bladder bursting. Up and about in the night's embers, groggy with fatigue. Down the corridor, piss, the old motions. Then downstairs. Gliding along a ghost hallway to a spectral kitchen in order to switch on a dematerialised kettle. Refreshed by gulps of scalding imaginary Lapsang Souchong. Upstairs again. Moving in slow motion towards the grey eye of the little shaving mirror. Smiling one's best *autoritätsgläubig* smile. Reaching for the aerosol spray, getting ready to press it, the foam spewing out into the palm of your hand. Mustn't be late for work! The gulped bowl of cereal, the wolfed toast, the race to the office, the hands of clocks and timepieces speeding towards eight-thirty, nine, nine-fifteen. Up and about, stretching, yawning, unloosing a sequence of quick, brief, spurting farts redolent of creamed mushrooms and succulent beef stew. Brushing one's yellow, rotting teeth. Igniting, for those with the wherewithal, a camp fire. Attempting toast while dreaming, say, of crispy sea snails with parmesan and tomato confit. Gnawing an old stale bun whilst recalling the good old days. Talk about Proust's biscotte (first draft, you bastards)! Foie gras with fig purée! Chickpea blinis with crab! Tour d'Argent duck cooked in blood with a side dish of crunchy sugared lamb. That glorious little bistro down the side street by the abattoir where we feasted on salmon in basil and garlic followed by lamb with grapefruit zest while three streets away the riot police had a laugh battering the students and the blacks! Ah, the lobster medallions with 17,000 Bq/kg of invigorating technetium-99! The marinated veal slices with saute of asparagus Parotid! Our submaxillary and sublingual glands gushed like ruptured pipes in the domain of a newly-privatised water company neglecting capital expenditure on maintenance in favour of an even bigger dividend for its anal retentive 4-wheel-drive Surrey shareholders. Gone, quite gone. Half-lewdly sucking on a prized carrot, attempting to extinguish the dream of a D-section tin of pâté de foie gras, a fillet of sea bream with morille mushrooms. Out! Get thee gone! Slobbering and sobbing and weeping and dribbling and feasting like a rabid frothing dog on a foul strip of raw and reeking bacon. Another ordinary Dump day. And then, I estimate at about ten, it happened. That lukewarm spray. That pitter-patter of first drops. Pitter-patter upon the hatches, the planks, the cloth hoods of The Early Risers, the corrugated iron sheets. "Rain!" cried Bodfish excitedly. Glorious, glorious rain! He ran for his mug to catch some. I stared deliriously at the sky. In no time at all my hair and collar were soaked. The Old Timers remained inert, out of sight, sceptical, in the grip of diasparactivity. Incontinent, often. No need here to heed wheedling bourgeois calls for restraint or bottles! Here the perfect place for piss-a-beds! Dribbling a quiet peaceful not unpleasurable dribble. Warming one's thighs with yellowish-green tributaries very reminiscent of the Borve River south of the A857. Capital spent. Not so The Early Risers. Full of vim and pep, sickeningly eager. We abandoned our fires, our rudimentary breakfasts. We gave up our studies, put away our Plato, our copiously annotated copies of *Middlemarch*, efforts at a diatessaron. Those in holes and ditches scrambled excitedly out of their holes and ditches. Those under planks and iron sheets sipping the last of their watery tea pushed aside planks and iron sheets. Such animation! How those of us wearing anoraks jerked back our hoods and began to run. To and fro, hither and thither, sideling. Arms outstretched, can you believe! Some breaking into spontaneous applause, like old style communists. Some excitedly breaking wind. Some whispering the Lord's Prayer. Some tripping and crashing to the ground but up in no time, no time at all! Spitting out broken teeth, licking off the dribbles of blood, pushing back protruding splinters of bone, how they laughed and shrieked. "Glorious, glorious rain!" repeated Bodfish, holding out his tin mug. His four eyes blinked repeatedly with nervous excitement. A lump of shadow the size of a double-decker bus raced across the surface of The Dump and vanished into the nearest fumes. I put it down to optical trickery stemming from my already waning eyesight or vitamin deficiency. The back of my hand was yellowish and glistening. I tongued it, grimaced. "What is it?" said Bodfish. "What's the matter?" A question of gross stupidity. "The Dump is the matter," I might have retorted. But did not. "Tastes funny," I replied. "Sort of bitter." "You can bet your boots it's acid rain," put in Hoadly. "All the pollution. Car exhausts. Factories. You bet that's what it is." Hoadly was a beefy, red-faced man of about fifty. A former chef. His knowledge of air pollutants was extensive. Bodfish was also a beefy, red-faced man of about fifty but of course could not be confused with Hoadly because of his extra two eyes. Leo, by contrast, was only twenty-six, skinny and pale. Leo was the only one among us who had realised the significance of the fleeting shadow. He scanned the sky, raised his telescope. "An aerostat!" he cried. "See! Right above us!" Everyone in the vicinity looked up, catching the full force of the second shower. This was of a greenish hue. Bodfish threw down his mug angrily. "This is disgusting," he said. "Whatever can it be?" "Work it out for yourself," snickered Leo. "I don't get it," spat Bodfish. "I feel sure it must have been approved by the Food Advisory Committee, an impartial government body made up of representatives of Marks & Spencer, Unilever, Dalgety, Northern Foods, International Foods, Tesco, J. Sainsbury, Cadbury Schweppes, Reckitt & Colman, Scottish & Newcastle, Carlsberg-Tetley, Whitbread, the Scottish Salmon Growers, Marine Harvest, St Ivel, United Biscuits, Glaxo, SmithKline Beecham, Smith & Newphew, and Boots the chemist." His eyes flickered uneasily. Leo laughed sardonically. "It's the people in that aerostat up there," he said. "They're pissing on us." Leo wiped the dew from the lens of his telescope and scanned the aerial device anew. "And if I'm not very much mistaken it's the Queen who is pissing on us now. Here, take a look." He passed me the telescope. Beneath the huge royal blue flanks of the balloon hung, dead centre, a cylinder. From the cylinder roared a pillar of controlled fire. Beneath this, on wires, swung a cage. The cage, which had a white chest-high wall running round it, contained around a dozen figures. What with my weak arms, the excitement, and the surprising speed of the balloon, it was difficult to focus. What might have been a General jerked sideways and turned into a pair of Princes and a senior police officer. These three figures at once abruptly metamorphosed into a pair of sallow, scrawny buttocks. I realised that there was some sort of sliding panel in the wall of the cage. Someone – a woman – was crouching on the floor of the cage with her skirt hitched up around her waist. I glimpsed a wisp of pubic hair, the brown dot of an anus. The buttocks seemed to deflate, the thigh muscles to tighten. Next bright amber jets of urine pumped out through the open panel and fell, twisting and spreading across a brief, rare shaft of sunlight. Our souls swam in blessed waters of ease. And then the woman stood up and stared down at us. I recognised her sour, wrinkled face at once. "Leo's right," I said, trembling. "It's her. Elizabeth Vagina! The cunt!" As I was speaking a fresh shower hit me, fouling my words. "It's a lie!" screamed Bodfish. "A dirty filthy lie!" He snatched the telescope, focused, thrust it back at me. "Nothing like!" he said triumphantly. Adding: "See this." Bodfish produced from his pocket his treasure. A brand-new silver tenpenny piece. He pointed a finger at the Queen's silhouette. "See? That radiance! That beauty! Looks nothing like that old hag up there!" Leo turned to me. "How long has he been in The Dump?" he enquired, weakly. "Years," I replied. "Years and years and years." "But doesn't he read the papers?" "Evidently not." "Queen of YUK," said Leo. "Short for Ye U.K." Eh? What's this nonsense? What is this Dump? You cannot seriously expect the reader to believe that the royal family are in the habit of ascending in aerostats for the sole purpose of relieving their bodily wastes upon their subjects! Whoever heard of such a thing? "Now you watch it my lad," said Bodfish, addressing Leo. "I've had enough of your nonsense." He raised his right fist. "Don't mock." He was about to say something else when the potato hit him smack on the crown of his head. "Shit!" he kelmaned. "That hurt! That fucking fucking hurt! Whatever the fuck it was." He glared kelmanly at Leo, holding him responsible. Tears brimming in all four bloodshot angry eyes. "A potato, I believe," I contributed. "Doubtless hurled by one of those hot-air hooligans." Bodfish snatched the telescope back, angled it. Focused. "Bastard!" he screamed. "The dirty, dirty bastard! The fucking, dirty, dirty, fucking bastard!" "What ails you, Bodfish?" I whispered, my voice muted by a passing drift of smoke. The former trades-union official was on his knees, scrabbling around, clawing at the loose scattering of detritus. "Got you!" Bodfish held up the potato. "Potato!" he said scornfully. He held it out. I caught a whiff, flinched. "Potato," he repeated in a low angry whisper. Its slime fouled his palms. Bitterly he hurled it hard as he could. It soared away, vanishing amid the smoke from a pile of burning tyres. "It was the Duke," he said, sorrowfully, wiping his hands on a Westminster Abbey teatowel. "The Duke himself. I recognised him from photographs. I recognised the uniform. The Grand Order of the People's Republic of Romania. The rancid scowl. The hatchet-faced bag of scum," he added colourfully. "You mean—?" I gasped. He nodded. He seemed to have aged ten years in as many minutes. Twenty. Thirty. He shook his head. "The Duke himself," he muttered. "Coming here of all places. To laugh at us. To piss on us. To shit all over us. Fucking foreigner. Greasy Greek. I never liked him, never." Bodfish was visibly crumbling (not to mention the invisibles clawing his innards). His dark, oily hair was white, as if someone had emptied a bag of flour over him. The flour had coated his face, drained his cheeks. Cracks were spreading across his brow, around his eyes. Bodfish clenched his fists. "And after all I've done for that family! The flags I've waved on Empire Day! The parades, the processions! The weddings and funerals! Not overlooking three o'clock on Christmas Day. Not missed it once in over forty years!" Sobbing, he fingered the lump on his head. By now the aerostat was a blue blob over Highgate, sailing fast back to the great green palace lawn in WC1. Bodfish shook his fist at the blob. I took back the telescope, peered. Yes, they were all there. The florid, elephantine heir, H.R.H. Prince Charles Philip Arthur George Windsor, Prince of Wales, Earl of Chester, Duke of Cornwall, Duke of Rothesay, Earl of Carrick, Baron of Renfrew, Lord of the Isles and Prince and Great Steward of Scotland. The rancid lecherous foul-mouthed Duke. Coarse, beefy, addled, blustering Andy. Inane Edward. Sozzled Margaret. "The dirty scum!" howled Bodfish. He began punching the ground and at once cut himself on an empty can of tomatoes. Punch! Punch! Punch! Soon his hands were two sodden, bloody shreds, strands of Italian tomato mingled with torn flesh. Pain didn't seem to bother him any more. He sat there for the rest of the morning and all afternoon. In the afternoon it really did rain, a cold perpetual pelting rain that continued until nightfall by which time Bodfish quietened down. He gave up beating the ground and lay down, his head propped on a solidified bag of cement. He must have cut a vein he shouldn't have because in the morning he'd become a stiff Z in a dark puddle of blood. Leo and I watched the rats, dogs and starlings taking turns to tuck in. "He learned," said Leo. "A bit late in the day, but he learned." "What a consolation," I said sarcastically. "No, no." Leo shook his head. "Perception's the thing. All it needs is for everyone to learn what Bodfish learned." "Fat chance," said I. "You wait and see. Revolutions happen when you least expect them. Remember Lenin in Switzerland. Old and tired before his time. Given up all hopes. *We, the old ones, may never live to see the decisive battles of the coming revolution.* Next thing – hey presto! 27 February 1917. Shooting has started. The crowds on Gospitalnaia, Paradnaia, and other streets are very large. Life's full of surprises, eh?" "Let us give poor Bodfish a Christian burial," I said, ignoring his nonsense. "You must be fucking crackers," Leo replied coldly. "For the sake of his poor wife and children." "I'm not arguing. I'm off. Coming?" Wiping the sleep from my eyes I observed that Leo had his sleeping bag and his rucksack of paperbacks with him. He meant business. "Oh very well," I said irritably. I knew that I could not afford to be parted from Leo just yet. "Which way are we going?" "East," said Leo. "I always feel more comfortable in the East End." I hurried after him. Nearby a huddle of wretches were grouped excitedly around a flickering TV set. The sight is not so rare as you might imagine. Technicians and electricians come hurtling into The Dump at regular intervals, propelled there by redundancy or dicky hearts or bad marriages. Fiddling with wrecked TVs seems to keep them happy, the screwdriver in their hand, a gleam of interest in their eyes. They find batteries, wires, rig up aerials, get TVs to work. They talk excitedly of radiowaves and transmitters. Some think of radioing for help but of course it's been tried, doesn't work. There is a field of electrical disturbance. Or perhaps jamming. Very mysterious. All possible ways of communicating with The Real World are closed. This has encouraged a sect which subscribes to the theory that everyone in The Dump is dead. You sometimes see them lying apathetically in large cardboard boxes bearing the names of supermarket chains, refusing all offers of food. "We are all dead," they whisper, and soon they are. Not this lot. They were watching the news. On the screen a tower block belched smoke. Police with batons drummed with animation the shoulders and raised arms of young men and women. Silver churns were tipped and an arc of milk met the lip of a drain. A man wearing a jacket and tie mouthed silent words. We hurried on until the TV fell from view behind mounds of putrefying cabbages. "Ah well," I said, fingering my damp clothes and smoothing my sodden hair. "It's not every day you are pissed on by the Queen." "Oh yes it is," said Leo. To my surprise – I really wasn't expecting it to happen again quite so suddenly – there came the cry, "AEROSTAT!" Worse: the plural. "Quick," said Leo, grimacing. He sank into the nearest trench and began hurriedly covering himself in sheets of crisp unblemished corrugated cardboard. Leo handed me the telescope. "Feel free to watch if you want," he said. Then he vanished from sight. Surely he was wrong, I thought. This is nothing more than a simple balloon race! A colourful and graceful sight. Balloon after balloon, brightly coloured, many bearing the names of their sponsors (fizzy drink, car manufacturer, airline, mobile phone). I counted fifty, eighty, more and more, stately, gently drifting towards us, blown by the current, heading east, north, north-north-east, from Westminster and Highgate, like galleons of old. Despite my situation and my toothache and the inclement weather I felt a glow of pride to be British. I swung the telescope with trembling hand. They were getting nearer, I could hear the faint hiss of the roaring flames that kept them aloft, could see the tiny figures in the baskets. I focused the telescope. More than a mere race, I realised. Evidently some sort of state occasion. In one balloon I could see the Archbishop of Canterbury, various archdeacons, deacons, prelates. Plump shiny bespectacled faces, crisp white dog collars, red robes, a golden mitre. An adjacent brown balloon contained several members of the cabinet. Scanning the blue balloon I excitedly spotted three famous newsreaders and a famous weather forecaster. What else? A green balloon containing the managing directors of privatised utilities. A purple balloon containing sports personalities. A black balloon containing comedians. An ultramarine balloon containing pop singers. Others containing snooker players, darts champions, cricketers. Not forgetting merchant bankers and city brokers. Landowners. Those in line for the throne in the event of a distressing sequence of assassinations and cataclysmic events, including the eldest sons of Dukes of Royal Blood, Marquesses, the Bishops of London, Durham and Winchester, Barons and Knights Grand Cross of the Bath. Last of all came the Masters in Lunacy, silvery-haired and flushed, looking like elderly distinguished parliamentarians. Floating all across that clear blue sky. I glanced across at Leo's ditch. The cardboard did not stir. Asleep, perhaps. Not knowing what he was missing. Ah, the grandeur of the occasion! I could hear the blast of trumpets, royal heralds. Any moment now the Red Arrows would whizz past trailing scarlet smoke. Any moment a pair of Spitfires would pass overhead, wings dipping in salute. There were less people watching than I expected. I counted about thirty, all new arrivals, all staring enraptured like myself. I was still staring through the telescope, trying to focus on an acclaimed female columnist, when I was hit. I staggered back, stunned by the stinging shock of rain. Then smelt the familiar raw stench. Not twice in two days! Fool! Putting the telescope to my eye I scanned the baskets. I had little doubt that a couple of boozy delinquents, city brokers, were responsible. I could just imagine their silver bucket, the bottles of champagne, the popping corks. Their idea of a joke. Fool again! I couldn't believe it, I couldn't really. Panels had slid open in every basket of every balloon, exposing white buttocks, pink buttocks, brown buttocks, fat buttocks, skinny buttocks, medium buttocks, spotty buttocks, hairy buttocks, flawlessly clear buttocks, arses of every conceivable description. Together with unzipped flies, lowered shorts, raised skirts, pricks of every description, ditto cunts and pissholes and arseholes and each pissing or shitting lustily, more or less simultaneously. The first whiplash streak of piss was no sooner past then I was caught in the jet of a second which smacked into my chest and exploded across my ribs. "Run!" I heard somebody shriek. The other spectators were frantically rushing for cover, trying to burrow into mounds of rotting vegetables, throwing themselves into ditches, scrabbling desperately for something to cover themselves with. Too late, too late. There was not one that afternoon escaped scot free. The torrent was like a sudden summer thunderstorm, smashing down, making everyone sodden. But there were hailstones, too, of sorts, the size of gobstoppers, as long as sausages, brown and warm and wet, splattering everyone, coating them in gravy, in melted chocolate, in bubbling pungent onion soup. Wiping a smear of shit from my lips I kneeled by Leo's ditch, banged on his protective cardboard sheets. "Let me in!" I cried. "No," he replied. "Please!" "It won't kill you," he replied, cruelly. "But I'm going to be sick!" "All the more reason not to let you in." "But you're a socialist! You care for people! Let me in!" "Correction," said Leo coldly. "I'm a revolutionary socialist. Not a fucking philanthropist. Not a bleeding-heart liberal." "Please!" "No. Learn your lesson the hard way. It will do you good." Oh the bastard! I leaned forwards and vomited. As the vomit erupted from my throat in great scalding rhythms I could feel new slashes of rain cutting into my back, and the soft splattering of objects thudding into things from a great height. Then, suddenly, the storm was over. I could hear someone whistling a medley from *The Sound of Music*. Plus some apt Handel. I looked around. An area approximately half a mile in diameter had been transformed into a glistening swamp dappled with tiny molehills. It stank. Like myself the other newcomers were being sick, or trying, uselessly, to clean themselves. But at best all anyone could hope to do was scrape off a fraction of the filth. Then the hatch opened and Leo peeked out. He was in a maddeningly chirpy mood. He gave me a cheery wave, which I responded to with a brief, obscene gesture. This he took in his stride. "You know what this is, don't you," jeered Leo, no mark required for a rhetorical Q. "This is the famous, legendary, trickle-down effect. This is the wealth at the top of society trickling down, splitter-splatter." He wheezed at his own wit. "How does it feel, old fruit," he continued, "to be shat on by the British ruling class? If you'll forgive a stale slogan," he said sarcastically. Adding, just to rub it in: "To use a Marxist cliché. To use a dinosaur phrase of no relevance to modern life." I waved my fist, threateningly. "I'll– I'll–". But then I was sick again. Ah, The Dump, The Dump. Full of surprises. One morning you awake and find yourself lying on a dirty mattress, amid waste, desolation and smouldering rubbish. Waste as far as the eye can see. Drifts of pungent smoke. Ah, circumstances! A bit of a shock, eh? Weighing like a nightmare, eh? You remember the night before. You weren't drunk. None of your friends or relatives showed any inclinations towards arson. There was little likelihood of any of the world's top-notch terrorists targeting your particular neighbourhood. So it's a complete mystery what's happened. A gas explosion, obviously. An airliner must have crashed. And various other straws. You wait for the air ambulance, the helmeted firefighters with oxygen cylinders strapped to their backs. You search, poor fool, for a way out. That's how you came to be here. Lost and alone. One more occupant of The Dump. Condemned to an active and restless inertia amidst instability and putrefaction. The what? Its ambience? Easy-peasy. Brown as Mozart's ultimate vomit, the mire between the hillocks. Ash-grey, the plain, all around, of waste. Sour the stench of smoke and putrefaction. A smoky atmosphere, yielding royal surprises... One morning... No go. Land of abandonment and rain. Place of bottles and cast-offs. Land of things that don't work anymore. Place of the rejected, the worthless. Unwanted pages, unwanted words. Place of desolation. Talk about behind the latrines at Drancy! It's no go, here. None at all. A void, to be avoided. Here among the breakage and the waste. All that's used up, finished with, gone. One morning – give the lying bastard a name, eh? – Robinson woke up and found himself lying on a wet, dirty mattress, in the midst of an enormous region of waste, desolation and burning rubbish. Return as a dog. Second helpings. Go on! Get it over with. Here? In GB? A ludicrous idea, eh? A bit of a shock all the same, Robinson had to admit. Finding yourself in that place, of all places. The Dump. Lost there. Lost for words. Lost amid malfunctioning implements and other cast-offs. IMPRIMIS.

Sodden lilac tissues, smeared pink tissues, stale bread. Bottles. Many foul-smelling cartons. Milk that's gone off. Chipped mugs. Shattered bone china. Broken glass. A cluster of stinking goosefoot, concealing a stiff rabbit. Fractured and torn deckchairs. Dead transistor radios. Stained, bloated books. Gleaming unsold remainders. Words not worth the paper they're printed on. Unending land of abandonment and rain. A disembowelled clock in a two-fifty rigor mortis. Old tyres. A solitary white fridge in a waste of mud, like... Like a last tooth in a foul mouth. Place of splayed flex, mouldy turnips. Predictable rust. Car batteries leaking acid. Insignificant puddles laced with oil and rainbow swirls. Cabbages. On the underside of the leaves a grey putrescence. Wooden crates! Plastic crates. Ten thousand thrown-out things. Many curious items, some useful, some not. Much depending on one's training, one's skills. Good eyesight. The ability to spot iron and irons and irony. Ball valves, bits of heaters. Taps, cylinders, tanks. Vokera, Potterton, Vaillant. Ideal Standard. New potatoes! Cardboard boxes, old newspapers, magazines. Used condoms. Unused condoms past their sell-by date. Handbags and shiny raincoats fashioned out of heavily chlorinated plastic (great fun to burn). Tares. Toothbrushes with brown bristles. Bristles with dry green weed at the base. A rag, rags. Rags, old cans. Sponges. Lidless kettles. Used up, consumed, worn out, chucked out, uneaten, gone off, you name it. Bound to be there somewhere. Cartons containing unfinished takeaways. Cold rice in a tasty amber slime. Cold chips basted in vinegar, black fishskin in icy batter. Land of maggots and worms and mulches. Maggots, pretty maggots. Scoop out a quarter of a pint from my dripping injury! Don't talk to me of Inkermann. Of abandonment and rain. And the people! People? Don't pretend, you bastard. You hadn't the foggiest? Balls! You knew about the rickety population, didn't you? Yes you did, all the time. The scavengers. Befouled, unkempt, frowzy. Suffering from scurvy, malnutrition, indigestion, jail fever, lassitude. Not to mention accidents, poisonings, telangiectasis, haemorrhages. The regular loss of teeth (diseased gums, punch-ups). Ghostly figures on the horizon, almost (but not quite) out of sight, almost (but not quite) out of mind. Dump. Slump. Rump. Rump? The Queen's arse! Skirt up, knickers down, pissing on yours truly. The old hag. Felt it, saw it. Her smirk. What! Where? Surely not! I can't believe what you're saying. Hold off! Unhand me, grey-beard loon! Shan't. Not yet. Where? The Dump, that's where. Fifty square miles of garbage. A tip, literally. Heaps of piled rubbish. Rotting vegetable waste. Here and there a rusting chassis, an abandoned tyre, a dirty jam jar glinting in the sunlight. Thistles and grass, smouldering sacks, ash, thousands of empty cans. Fifty square miles? A hundred! A thousand! A hundred thousand! Big as Latin America! Nobody knows. Perhaps it is Latin America! Land of the Rumba, the Paso Doble. Of Ché and the Cha Cha Cha! Perhaps the environs of Fort Dimanche. The military dump. Exquisite pickings. Helmets. Phalluses without their ammo. Perhaps Smokey Mountain in the Philippines. The quality of the light, the quiet simplicity of the scavengers, oddly reminiscent of Vermeer. No. Wrong place. Wrong language. This is England I tell you! Can't be. What? Deaf are you? Bloody Christ! Slump-rump-dump. Slump? In confidence. In one's fortunes. In one's fiscal probity. Can this be so? The famous feelgood factor fucked-up? Feelbad, in fact? Flaming hell! Flip me! Fantastic. Leading to slumping around all day on a broken-backed sofa or a damp mattress. Oblivious to everything except the sky. A great apathy. Split, splitting into sections, my life, yes. Sectioned, so to speak. Enduring odds and ends. Making ends meet. In fits and starts. Amid shits and farts. Trying. A quiet desperation. Eyes swelling, sometimes with effort, mostly with red-hot constipation. The perturbations of flatulence. Clutching lengths of dirty string, a new way of making ends meet. I have been living like this for a long time now. Trying hard to look on the dull side of. Life? Loaf? A louse-ridden loafer. Eh? Examining an old smeared colour chart, considering which soft sheen emulsion to choose for the lounge. Considering the purchase of a Gainsborough Style 300 Electric Shower, just the thing after a matutinal jog. Wondering whether to get the natural, the buff or the red smooth paving slabs for the new patio. Not forgetting to jot down on one's list the ferrous sulphate weedkiller, the pot of Tudor Oak Garden Timbercare and the can of patio cleaner containing Benzalkonium Chloride. Ah, to relax in a deckchair on a new patio writing an appreciation of the citational imperative! Or perhaps of retro-active world-making and world-unmaking. Or perhaps a simple, racy, money-spinning synopsis of *Wuthering Heights* suitable for indolent teenagers. Mr Lockwood arrives in Yorkshire, a county in the north of England, where he meets Heathcliff, who ran away with Isabella Linton, Edgar's sister, who, Edgar, married Catherine, Hindley's sister, who dies, leaving behind a daughter, the young Cathy, who is repelled by Hareton Earnshaw, whose father is old Mr Earnshaw's son Hindley, and who is taunted by Linton, son of Isabella, who, Linton, marries Cathy, who goes back to Wuthering Heights, home of rude Joseph, where Heathcliff, who dies, tells the housekeeper, Nelly Dean, how he was dead keen on Catherine, who married the dead Edgar, which mortified him, Heathcliff, no end. *Useful questions:* 1. Describe the major wind currents in an active cumulonimbus and show the importance of the evaporation of cloud droplets to the total effect of the book. 2. Using TWO scenes in the novel in which information is communicated to characters via trails of pink lights show how important the entity VALIS [Vast Active Living Intelligence System] is in enabling Heathcliff to become master of Wuthering Heights. 3. "Property ownership: this was far more significant in the past than it is today and helped Heathcliff get his revenge." With reference to *The Sunday Times Book of the Rich* and *The German Ideology* discuss the role of bourgeois literary criticism and the National Curriculum within contemporary capitalist Britain. No. It's been done already. Okay, then. How's about a zippy musical interpretation? Dour Joseph used to play Shostakovich's Tenth at full blast, maddening Nelly, who was fond of C & W and especially Dolly Parton, unlike Mr Lockwood who was more of a Dire Straits man, whereas Heathcliff veered wildly between Led Zeppelin and Leonard Cohen, enchanting Catherine, who adored Prince, much to the anger of Edgar, a fan of Elgar, unlike Isabella, who owned every record Kate Bush had ever made, to the despair of her son, who used to shut himself away with the Cowboy Junkies, for which he was much mocked by Hareton, who greatly admired The Sex Pistols. The weather, yes. Important when you're slumping around all day on a broken-backed sofa or a damp mattress. Oblivious to everything except the sky. Dis-eased by a great apathy. The weather? Awful. Smudges of dirty cirrhus crawling across the firmament's great grey basin. Or. Or like something half-scalded, puffed-up, trapped in a bath. A tip where people live. If you can call them people. Don't say you didn't notice, didn't know. Their clothes spattered and smeared, their shoes in a dreadful state. Wildeyed. The expression all too often sly or hungry. Or dazed. Or dulled, all human interest gone, entirely gone. All our righteousnesses as filthy rags. A population divided between the newcomers, who are given to curiosity and exploration, and the old-timers, who are devoted to survival. Confusion seems inevitable. A number of newcomers arrive carrying guns and promptly go on a spree, to the perplexity of other newcomers. Sometimes you see entire families smiling at the start of the historic pageant. A crackling like fireworks, the crash of shots. One or two newcomers come tearing across the mounds of ash, bloodied and screaming. Applause. Wonderful special effects, so lifelike! Others roaring with goodnatured laughter at the plump smeared clowns falling about and slithering around in the muck. A hoot. Others dawdling, puzzled, not quite understanding what is going on. Chukka-chukka-chukka. Hey, is that the sound of semi-automatic gunfire? Is this part of the show? There's no biz– And then the realisation strikes. Everyone is running for their lives. Next day the corpses are covered up with whatever's to hand, a week later it's a distant memory. The nowness and the newness is what counts, eh? Sod the past, that's before your time. The Easter Rising? Detumescent, old sport. We don't need history in The Dump. A curious place. Sometimes a cry of "AEROSTAT!" The newcomers are baffled, interested, expectant. Whereas the old-timers have long since passed through these dangerous emotions. The old-timers know what to do. They scurry. Dive into ditches. Batten down the hatches.

Retire to their sleeping bags with a good read. A manual on seamanship, say. Useful pictures of badges. Essential to avoid the embarrassment of confusing the masseur with the X-Ray assistant, the Chief Stoker with a sick berth attendant. Or a copy of – with hey, ho, the wind and the rain! – *King Lear*. Or a music magazine containing the true story of Jerry Lee Lewis's right leg and Roy Acuff's Yo-Yo. Or *The Annotated Baseball Stories of Ring W. Lardner 1914-1919*, describing real teams, real players and real situations in the real world of early major league baseball together with 111 illustrations of real ball players, real teams, real ball parks, newspaper items, and other memorabilia of one of the most fascinating and eventful eras in baseball history! Or a well-thumbed copy of *Mambo* ("Dynamic, pacy and full of unexpected twists" – *Scotland on Sunday*). Or O'Kill's *Window on the World*. Obasanjo's *My Command*. Or a fat book full of the gibbers (If we CONFESS our SINS, he is faithful and just to FORGIVE US our sins and to CLEANSE US from all unrighteousness – that sort of gibber). Or the delightful Heinemann Educational Books edition of *Gulliver's Travels* – very popular in the remnants of Empire, you know – with the refreshing italicised verso note, *A number of passages which might be considered offensive have been omitted from this edition*. The Dump, yes. Eight hundred square miles of garbage. A tip, literally. Prone to leaching – squelch! chemical whiffs! nothing-to-worry-about-says-the-man-from-the-ministry – a.k.a. the contamination of the tip's environs by the motion of its pollutants underground. Prone to the odd lively explosion of trapped methane gas. Prone to sudden subsidence. Heap upon heap of piled rubbish. Some glistening with a lively putrefaction, some decaying with a quiet dignity as if in snug retirement in placid Bournemouth. Some luridly ablaze. Place of perfumes, stenches. The sweet reek of rotting vegetable waste. The toxic throat-tickling stink of burning polystyrene. And here and there a stark Proustian chassis triggers the imaginary odour of exhaust fumes on a crisp bright winter's morn, memories of a long line of boxed commuters, fingers drumming impatiently on the steering wheel while the grey-blue drifts puff out from their throbbing rears, the nitrogen dioxide swathing passing pedestrians and cyclists, then rising, rising, putting a delicate haze across the entire city, pleasantly reminiscent of the art of Caspar David Friedrich. Many abandoned tyres, newspapers and rags, good for keeping the population warm at night. A dirty jam jar glinting in the sunlight, clear and keen and marvellously bright. Thistles and grass. Smouldering sacks. Ash. No double-glazing (Dostoevsky wouldn't have liked it here). Smashed glass, broken frames. Paper cups. Thousands of empty cans. Ash. I WALKED FOR HOURS THAT DAY. One morning... I suppose if I am honest I always knew about The Dump and like everyone else said nothing, did nothing. After all, what can one person on their own do about The Dump? Nothing. Correction. Some people did mention it. Mother, for example. Once or twice in her long lifetime. Before her eyes went. Poor dears, I remember her saying once. And once: it's a crying shame. And upon another occasion, a day of tempest and storm: something should be done about it, it really should. And what is ever done about? I will tell you. Nothing. No one ever thinks they will find themselves in The Dump. I was like everyone else. Never in a million years did I expect to find myself living in The Dump. Trapped there. Unable to escape. If you had said such a thing to me before it happened I would have said you were bonkers. Stark staring. What happened? How did you get here? Over the barrier. Were rotor blades involved? Jet propulsion? A rocket, a capsule, a parachute? New arrivals are always put through the hoops by the old-timers. Such interest! Such enthusiasm! Before lapsing back into their usual apathy. The Old-Timers forget. They have lived in The Dump so long they barely remember the old world, let alone how they voyaged from there to here. They forget the disorientation, the confusion. But I am still young enough to remember. It. Was. Like. This. One morning I woke up and found myself lying on a wet, dirty mattress, in the midst of an enormous region of waste, desolation and burning rubbish. I don't mind admitting I was nonplussed. In fact to be honest it came as a bit of a shock. In fact more than a bit, to be honest. A quite considerable shock. A very great shock. I was stunned. I felt perturbation within my sphincter, a boiling surging liquidy panic. Quick as a flash I exerted muscular control. Phew! A close one. I suppose many people would have been a little down in the dumps so to speak to find themselves down there (here) in The Dump but not yours truly. I said to myself, every cloud has a silver lining. And do you know what? I'd never spoken a truer word. By a stroke of great good fortune I discovered that although my bedroom, my home, mother, all of Attlee Tower, all of Walthamstow, and all of London, had vanished, my pyjamas hadn't. It was good to know that although something very odd had happened I was still decent. At first I could hardly begin to imagine what had happened. I'd gone to bed the night before in the usual way, put out the light, and gone to sleep in my room with its familiar objects (model Lancaster bomber hanging from the ceiling; Leyton Orient poster; souvenir anchor from H.M.S. Victory; the little glass lighthouse from Alum Bay, with its layers of coloured sand). Now everything was gone. I was particularly upset to have lost my glass lighthouse, my Lancaster and mother. I was also puzzled. My first thought was that there had been an overnight nuclear war and London had been zapped by the enemy. But that didn't explain how I'd survived when everything and everyone else had apparently been vaporized. The flat mother and I lived in was on the top floor of Attlee Tower. How anyone could survive falling from the top floor in the middle of a nuclear war was a bit of a teaser. I decided I must have just been lucky. It must have been one of those freak occurrences which very occasionally happen. I seemed to remember once reading about someone who slipped off the top of a mountain and fell, landing at the bottom with nothing more than a few bruises and a twisted ankle. Not to mention all those people you keep hearing about who open the wrong doors in aircraft flying at five-thousand feet and land unharmed in haystacks. And the people buried alive in earthquakes who are dug out of the rubble thirteen days later, none the worse for wear apart from superficial bruising and a yearning for pint after pint of cool water. But it was no time to be worrying about the whys and wherefores. The main thing was I was stranded in the middle of a vast plain of ruin and desolation, and it was time to get out of there double quick. Ten to one it was radioactive, all the more reason to scarper sharpish. I didn't want trouble with my teeth, or sores, or anything like that. The only problem was, which direction to take? Everywhere I looked looked much the same. Emptiness, desolation, rubbish, fires burning here and there. Drifts of oily black smoke. I wasn't even sure whether I was in the middle of the ruins of my old home or whether I had been hurled through the air for several hundred yards (or even a mile), before landing by great good fortune on a mattress. In the end I decided to walk in what I hoped was the direction of the Town Hall. If there had been a nuclear war the people at the Town Hall would know what to do. They were probably already handing out application forms and mugs of soup and fresh pairs of underpants. I would need to hurry if I wasn't to miss out. Re-knotting the cord which held up my pale blue pyjama bottoms I set off briskly through the ruins. I hadn't gone very far before I stopped. Unfortunately my carpet slippers had vanished in the holocaust and it was painful walking in bare feet. There seemed to be broken glass everywhere, and already I had quite a nasty cut on one of my big toes. I was also cold and beginning to shiver. Before I went any further I decided I needed to find something more to put on. There were several bulging black rubbish sacks scattered around. I broke them open and began poking around inside. It must have been my lucky day because it wasn't long before I'd come across a very nice pair of grey trousers, a string vest, a white Marks and Spencer shirt with stylish blue stripes, a pair of matching grey socks and a pair of carpet slippers. They weren't one-hundred-per-cent what I was after (the trousers had a 36 waist and were far too big, the vest had chunks missing, the shirt was stained with green paint, the socks had holes in and the slippers were a faded fluffy pink and for a woman) but beggars can't be choosers. If I'd happened to meet anyone who knew me I would have felt like a proper charlie, but fortunately there wasn't a sign of life anywhere. I was a little apprehensive what might happen when I got back to civilisation. I didn't want to get arrested as a tramp. But I decided to cross that bridge when I came to it. I walked for hours that day, becoming increasingly despondent. It's slow-going in carpet slippers and baggy trousers, I can tell you. I was also hungry, thirsty and growing worried at the way the ruins just seemed to go on and on and on. I kept expecting to see scorched trees on the horizon, or undamaged buildings, or perhaps a patrol aircraft looking for survivors. Instead of which: nothing. Once, pulse quickening, I heard *Finlandia*'s life-enhancing thump and rattle. I glanced round in excited anticipation of a nearby orchestra. No go. Just the tinny mockery of my interminable tinnitus. Just more miles of waste and smoke and fire and rubbish and ship models from 1925. And bottles, bottles, bottles. Bottles everywhere. More even than used to lurk in mother's cupboard under the stairs and out in the yard and in the dark oily corners of the underground garage. As the day wore on I grew more and more puzzled about the ruins. I had expected to find the remains of roads and buildings. I even thought I might find other survivors, who might be able to tell me what had happened. But not only was there no one else around, the ruins increasingly seemed to resemble less the remains of a bombed city than a municipal rubbish dump. I couldn't understand why there were so many black sacks of rubbish everywhere. There must have been thousands of them. If there had been a nuclear attack surely the plastic sacks would have melted? And why were there so many cardboard boxes and packing cases and heaps of garden cuttings? Why were there piles of tyres? Why had the abandoned cars been stripped of their wheels? I walked and walked and walked, and then I hobbled and hobbled and hobbled. I could feel the blisters bubbling up on the soles of my feet. One of them had burst and hurt like hell. I was beginning to feel cold again, and hungry. Worse, the day was ending. The afternoon was finished. It was dusk. I sat down on a tractor tyre and began to cry. Having begun, I continued. By the middle I was worn out but I forced myself on to the end, ending with a sob, a whimper, a whisper. "Mother!" But mother said nothing. Mother was far, far away. It was not mother's voice which responded but another's. "O my back, my shoulders!" Cried the voice. Making me jump. The voice adding: "Overturn! Overturn! Overturn!" Oppressed by gravity I returned to planet earth after my small jump of surprise, turned, and scanned the wilderness. I saw at once a stranger. An outlandish figure in a red dressing gown. Standing up, I balanced myself on the tyre. This put me a good half metre above the surface of the all-encompassing desolation. My sense of ontological well-being, which had sunk to zero, went up a notch or two. "O my back, my shoulders!" the stranger said again, strangely. He was fifty metres away, standing on the summit of a heap of crates, sacks and old newspapers, examining me through a telescope. About the same age as me, I guessed. Early twenties. His back and shoulders looked okay to me. He had a goatee beard and was wearing glasses. And a red corduroy cap. And red shoes with red socks. His hands were as soft as a goat's belly. He looked like a nutter but beggars can't be choosers. "Help!" I called. "I'm lost. Can you tell me the way out of here?" He finished his examination of me and slipped the telescope into a red shoulder bag he was carrying. "Stranger in these parts, are we?" he called across to me. "Looking for the way to San Jose?" "That's right," I said, responding not to his second question. "I'm from Walthamstow. To tell you the truth I'm not even sure how I got here. I went to bed last night in the usual way and when I woke up I was here. Perhaps there's been a gas explosion. Have you seen today's news?" "The news! Ha ha! Very good. Yes, I have seen the news. Tomorrow's news and today's news and most of all, yesterday's news." "And was there a gas explosion? Any dead? My mother –". "Your mother is almost certainly alive." "Thank God," I ejaculated. He gave me a wan smile and, soon afterwards, a packet of Salt & Malt Vinegar Flavour Fine Crinkle Crisps. "I'm Leo," he said, descending from his heap. "I am as isolated as you could wish me to be," he continued. With indescribable composure. Making his way cautiously towards me. Adding: "I'm a socialist." "Very nice I'm sure," I said politely. A socialist, eh? I knew about people like Leo from the papers and TV. Dinosaurs, they were often called. People sadly out of date. Like balding middle-aged men with wisps of long greying hair and bell-bottom trousers, still thinking they were living in the swinging sixties. Pathetic. Socialism was dead, everybody knew that. It hadn't worked in Russia, it was a complete disaster. Not to mention the nationalised industries, all the bureaucracy. "I'm Jack," I lied. "Jack Robinson." "Have some crisps, Jack." "Thanks," I said, tearing open the packet and munching greedily. They tasted stale but I didn't care. I was ravenous. Strangely, for a socialist, Leo was my own age. In his late twenties. Not middle-aged at all. Curious. "Hence the red," Leo explained. He gestured at his dressing gown, his slippers. To underline the point he removed his cap, tossed it twirlingly into the air, and expertly caught it. (I had the impression he had done this lots of times before.) "I have a red flag in here," he continued, indicating his bag. "But as yet I have found no use for it. The prevailing mood in The Dump is largely one of apathetic acceptance of the state of things. There is anger, yes. There are periodic outbursts of rage. There is a widespread feeling of frustration and a longing for better times. But channeling these feelings into a fightback. Aye, there's the rub." He emitted an attenuated sigh seventeen seconds in duration, a sigh which I subsequently recognised as stemming from a complex melancholy of the sort which hinders concoction, refrigerates the heart, takes away stomach, colour and sleep, thickens the blood, contaminates the spirits, overthrows the natural heat, perverts the good estate of body and mind, and makes you weary of life itself until you cry out, howl and roar for the very anguish of your soul. Subsequently? Five years later. I lie. Ten. Twenty. When I had an education. Not then. Not upon first arrival, a time when my consciousness was a thin, weak patchwork of received prejudices, when my vocabulary was risible, my formulations orthodox, my opinions fourth rate, my experiences limited, my mind barely born. But Leo did not howl and roar, no. Terminating his sigh he shivered and tightened the belt of his dressing gown. "Ah well," he said. "Pessimism of the intellect, optimism of the will. Eh?" Not having a clue I simply grunted. A reaction which seemed to satisfy him. "Overturn! Overturn! Overturn!" he said next, incomprehensibly. Adding: "O my back, my shoulders! O Tythes, Excise, Taxes, Pollings, etcetera!" I decided to ignore his baffling outbursts. Besides, I had other things on my mind. The whereabouts of mother. My own whereabouts. What had happened to Walthamstow. What to do with the empty crisp packet. I felt quite stressed with all these matters pressing down on me. I looked round for a litter bin and seeing none stuffed the empty packet into my pyjama trousers. Observing my hesitation and consequent stuffing Leo said, "What did you do that for?" "Mother brought me up to be tidy," I explained. "If there is no litter bin always take your rubbish home with you. That is her creed." "For crying out loud!" Leo bellowed. "You are now a native of The Dump! You are living on a rubbish tip! You are swimming in a sea of waste, afloat upon a scum of droppings! What fucking difference do you think your fucking crisp packet makes?" "You want to watch your language," I said. "You'll learn," Leo retorted bitterly. "You'll learn. You are trapped here. A prisoner. And there is only one way out." "A prisoner?" "You'll find out. This is the place of castouts. Animal, vegetable and mineral. And human. Don't pretend. You always knew, didn't you? Everybody out there knows about The Dump. They just don't think it has anything to do with them. They cannot imagine it will one day happen to them. So people are happy to go on with their busy busy busy lives. Ah, always so busy! Ah, the shopping! The new settee! Ah, the radiant Chopin performance! Sport! The equaliser! The £8 million sponsorship deal! Fashion! Frosted rainbow colours! Taut stretchy satin! The black and white fine check jacket and matching calf-length skirt! Prada leather bags! The latest Annie Lennox album! The chocolate creams! The vermouth on the rocks! The Irish coffee! The new movie! The week's TV! The new exhibition! The rendezvous at the pub! The excellent restaurant! Motoring! The mould-breaking MGF with four-cylinder engine mounted behind the cockpit providing race-car balance, traction and light steering! The personalized numberplate! Exotic travel! The 700 islands of the Bahamas! Turkey! Israel! Indonesia! Gorgeous sun-drenched beaches and a harbour ringed with lush volcanic hills! Or nearer home, special 'Saver Sailings', duty-free shops and luxurious cruise-ferries which land you in civilised ports! The universally acclaimed – brilliantly imaginative, an astonishing compassion and honesty, sheer exuberance, enormous talent, staggering genius, a knockout – novel! Cooking! Salmon in pastry with hollandaise sauce! Duck à l'orange! Hot chocolate soufflé! Sex! Femoral intercourse! Ligottage! Feuille de rose! And later? The bergenias, the Michaelmas daisies, the hellebores! The day trip to Paris, the weekend break in Cromer, the ten days in Barcelona, the fortnight on Mykonos, the month in Nepal! The property pages! The charming and picturesque detached barn conversion situated on the outskirts of the historic village in an area of outstanding natural beauty with Hamstone fireplace, fitted country-style kitchen, oil fired central heating, sun lounge and paved patio, with double garage and attractive terraced garden, only one mile from the sea, with views of the bay!" "What do you mean, Out There?" I said. "Beyond The Barrier," he retorted. "The Barrier?" I said. "If we all held hands and rushed at The Barrier together it would fall. That's the only way. It's happened before and it will happen again. It will happen here, too. Perhaps you will be the nucleus of a new fightback. The harbinger of the upturn, so to speak." "I don't understand," I said. "You will," said Leo grimly. "You will. When you do I'll be in touch." Saying which, he hopped away. "Hey! Don't go away! At least tell me the way out of here!" Leo halted. Turned. He pointed east. "That way," he said, pointing north. "That way," he said, pointing south. "That way," he said, pointing west. "That way," he said. "Any bloody way. They all lead to the The Barrier." "I don't understand," I said. "Circummured," he whispered. Then winked. "How I abhor circularity!" he cried. And rushed off. He moved with a surprising agility, hopping, then skipping, then dancing a jig. From a hitherto non-existent pocket he produced a previously imaginary harmonica which he materialised by dint of dialectics and the power of positive thinking. Upon it he played as he jigged a jaunty "British Grenadier". Leo's dressing gown flapped around his smeared calves and helped pack another sentence into my tale. In a minute or so he was lost to sight, obscured behind drifts of smoke and the darkness of the coming night. I sat down again on the tractor tyre for a think, always a good thing to do in moments of stress. But my mind was a clutter of panics and worries. It was really quite idiotic, blundering about in a rubbish dump all day. The sundry and the fiery! Probably I was just going round in circles all the time, like characters do in desert movies. In the end I decided to climb the heap recently vacated by Leo. I needed urgently to locate my bearings (not to mention my balls, which, when I'd found them, I scratched vigorously). I half hoped that from the top I'd catch a glimpse of the Town Hall, or maybe even Attlee Tower itself. No such luck. All I could see through the drifts of smoke and the growing darkness was heaps of piled rubbish. Rotting vegetable waste. Here and there a rusting chassis, an abandoned tyre, a dirty jam jar glinting in the sunlight. Thistles and grass, smouldering sacks, ash, thousands of empty cans. Trash, waste, rubbish, crap, in every direction, as far as the horizon. It began to rain. Half-heartedly. A few pelting drops. I shivered. I was beginning to feel cold and hungry and very thirsty. I descended Leo's heap and explored the lower slopes, tearing open rubbish sacks with a stick. Twenty minutes of brisk foraging uncovered a smelly tartan blanket, some lengths of worn, dusty, green carpet, some plastic sheeting, a bottle of flat lemonade and a packet of soft digestive biscuits. I decided it was enough to keep body and soul together until the next day. By a stroke of good fortune of the sort often found in picaresque narratives I found a delightful only-recently-scooped trench concealed beneath the sacks. It was six metres long, a couple of metres deep. No one had vomited or defecated there and the trench had a not entirely unpleasant odour of fresh earth. I re-arranged the sacks to conceal my presence from any wandering predator (mutant ants and prowling carnivores came looking for me in that chink of my mind where old movies shimmered in the heat-haze of blind panic). I then jumped down into the trench and wrapped myself in the blanket and strips of carpet. Lastly I spread the plastic sheeting over me. Nibbling the biscuits and sipping the sweet lemonade made me think of my childhood. I suddenly remembered how I used to pretend my bed was a submarine, and I'd crawl under the sheets in the dark and nibble a biscuit, pretending I was on the sea-bed, with depth charges crashing all around. That first night I didn't sleep a wink. I wondered about the books which Leo kept in his bag. *Theories of Surplus Value. The Getaway. William – The Outlaw.* It was so cold, so very, very cold. I was also somewhat disturbed by the strange circumstances in which I found myself. I'd no sooner nod off than I'd wake, thinking of mother, and Walthamstow, and my life up to that moment. You see I was born and brought up in Walthamstow. To be more precise, I was born in Thorpe Coombe Hospital on Forest Road, not far from the Town Hall. The Hospital isn't used for deliveries anymore. In fact the only times I've been back since being born there was to see the nurse about my head lice. Walthamstow is divided into three parts (though this is not on any maps and only the natives know it). There is Upper Walthamstow, where the well-off bastards live with drive, garage, two cars, four bedrooms and a lav downstairs as well as up. There is South Walthamstow, which is where the poor and the transients live, in maisonettes and council flats. South Walthamstow has rubbish blowing about the streets and graffiti and cracked pavements. Then there is The Rest of Walthamstow, which is where the not-desperately-poor-but-not-exactly-rich live in little two-bedroom houses with poky gardens containing manhole-sized squares of concrete called "the patio." This pattern is part of a bigger pattern. To the north is Chingford and Wanstead, where even bigger, richer bastards live. I've been once or twice, you wouldn't believe it, some of the houses out there. Fucking enormous detached houses with fucking enormous drives and triple garages with remote-control doors and Porsches on the gravel and their own fucking LAMPPOSTS in the front garden. But the other way, via Walthamstow, you move in the opposite fiscal direction. First you encounter bleak Leytonstone and bleaker Leyton, and then it gets even worse and you hit treeless soul-less traffic-jammed Stratford, horrible. But I digress. I suppose like everyone else I thought one day I'd shack up with someone and have a couple of kids and feed them nourishing supermarket baby food containing chalk, animal intestines, pig's feet, cotton waste and glue, like everyone else, and one day retire to a jerry-built bungalow at the oil-and-sewage-oozing sea-side. Something along those lines. My life up to the age of thirty-one uneventful. I barely remember it. My thirty-second year a complete blank. My thirty-third evoking no delusions that I was the Son of God or A Man With A Mission. My thirty-fourth risible, my thirty-fifth humiliating, my thirty-sixth dull beyond words. All dull beyond words. I ache to get there, beyond all this, this spiky painful trash, these endless rectangles of language, these symmetrical lines banal as humming pylons on a rainswept prairie. I grew up, stunted and enfeebled, in South Walthamstow, needless to. To say. I played on the rusty broken swings in the bleak puddled playground next to Attlee's dark Tower, I suppose. I hit my sister, I suppose. Sister? Grete? Drugs alcohol little sister bang! bang! I was pushed over and cut my knees and bled copiously and wept bitterly, I suppose. One of my earliest memories is trying to put a model aeroplane together. A Spitfire. I got as far as putting the fuselage together and attaching the cockpit, then I discovered how nice the glue smelled. Later I ate too much egg and chips and was sick. I set fire to the Spitfire in the sandpit. It burned beautifully. Thick black oily smoke, big yellow flames. I remember tenderly my arson phase. I just couldn't stop burning things. First it was books and clothes, then I learned plastic burned brightest, burned best. A bucket, then an abandoned traffic cone in the street. Once I even stuffed lots of paper and cardboard under somebody's old Rover in the underground car park. The car didn't have a petrol cap. Next day two policemen came knocking at the door, asking where I'd been at the time of the explosion. Mother swore I was in watching a video. "What video?" they snapped, faces twisted by suspicion. Mother retorted, it was all she could think of, "*Oklahoma!*" Snorted they! Believed her they did not! Much to go on obviously did they not have, apart from a vague description of a mucky nondescript boy. Luckily I am the mundane distilled into human form. I am the grey quintessence of the banal. I am a zero, a nothing, a dull bubble. I have no distinguishing characteristics. People do not remember me. My memory is poor. My past is a featureless grey plain wiped clean by the drip-drip-drip of the cold years. When the imaginary police had gone my imaginary mother looked suspiciously at her imaginary son and did not say: "Were you involved, Raymond?" "Stupid cow!" I screamed. "I was Raymond in the first draft. I'm Jack now, and likely to remain so until this Ivor is well and truly wrapped up." Ivor? Novella! Sorry. "Were you involved, dear Jack?" "Of course not, gentle mother." No. I am like sweet Jesus. Not once in my life have I succumbed to filthy temptation. Never, never, never have I wedged a fingernail inside either of my nostrils in order to scrape off a lump of hardened mucus. Never have the empurpled, swollen, unwholesome lips of my crusted anus bulged outward, forming a knobbly nought and let rip a screeching, bubbling stinking jet of intestinal gas. Never once have I fondled my private parts in a shameful quest for sensual delight. Nor the parts of others, irrespective of gender. Never have I pissed anywhere but in local authority urinals and other approved china receptacles. Never have I defecated into a coronation mug, or into a bowl celebrating a royal wedding, or among ferns. I have led a clean, simple, honest, decent life, in consequence of which I have been made redundant. Off to The Dump with him! Funnily enough I could see The Dump from my very earliest days. Pressing my snub nose against the window. Focusing on the misty distances. Strange now to think that The Dump was actually visible from our flat on the top storey of Attlee Tower. The Dump was (is!) only a couple of miles away to the south-west, at the Borough borders. As I said, Attlee Tower is in South Walthamstow, as I didn't say, not far from St James Street Station. Attlee Tower was built in 1966. It is flanked by Gaitskell Tower and Bevan Tower, built at the same time. The towers are named after famous people. Gaitskell and Bevan were both important Labour politicians who died unexpectedly. Attlee Tower is named after Clem Attlee. I do not know much about him except that he was a very famous socialist and was once the MP for West Walthamstow, in the old days. The Golden Days of the Attlee Government, as mother called them. (Leo, by the way, says this is complete balls, and that Attlee was a class traitor and a shit.) From the twenty-fourth floor of Attlee Tower you get a lovely view of the deracinated highway-slashed wastes of Epping Forest in the north and the bleak, banal Lea Valley in the south. Walthamstow is in the middle, like a slice of mouldy cheese between two stale slices of bread. In my experience everyone has heard of Walthamstow E17. It has quite a history. Talk about Dan Bartholemew's Dolorous Discourses! Associations include Byron (reputed – exact site unknown – to have passed a debauched night with Claire Clairmont in one of the terraced houses on Byron Road, returning some years later for a solitary night with Madame S------ and penning stanza 41 of Canto IX of *Don Juan*), Milton (widely believed to have penned one or two lines of his immortal *Paranoid List* in the old police flats now known as Milton House, on Milton Road) and of course William Morris, the very talented wallpaper designer, who lived as a child in a demolished house opposite the fire station. Later his parents moved to the William Morris Gallery just up the road. And of course the world famous pop group. Mention must also be made of the mysterious building on Markhouse Road, bearing the inscription MARX HOUSE 1884. Leo reckons it was where Karl Marx's grieving daughters moved after the old man's death. He has a theory that the road was once Marx House Road and that the name was changed years ago when the Tories grabbed control of the Council. You must admit it sounds plausible. Moreover, as Ellis noted, Eleanor Marx knew William Morris, and as Kapp observes Ellis is very widely accepted as an authority, therefore it must be true, as anyone with no axe to grind must surely see. From our flat in Attlee Tower mother and I had a perfect view of The Dump. Or as perfect as anyone can get without flying over in a balloon or helicopter (and until Shocking Events Unfolded I had never appreciated the significance of the regular passage of balloons up and down the Lea Valley, or the interminable ever-present police helicopter circling Walthamstow). The Dump is the municipal tip. Exclusive to the London Borough of Waltham Forest. The place where the rubbish men used to take their vehicles until they opened the flash waste disposal unit at Edmonton. The place where rubbish has been dumped since the beginning of time (or at any rate since the beginning of the twentieth century). The place where people are encouraged to take their sacks of garden refuse and unwanted newspapers and other unwanted domestic material. To get to The Dump just take the road past St James's Park and continue. Keep right on to the end of the road, as that Scotchman sings. You can't miss it. There's a tall wire fence with a security gate and behind it portakabins and parked vans. In the middle distance, the waste incinerators, low, grey, obscure buildings with a single tall chimney belching clouds of thick black boiling smoke. In the far distance, a paler, bluer smoke from burning refuse and a vast bank of rubbish bearing a strong resemblance to the serpentine earthworks of Maiden Castle seen from the Dorchester by-pass. Follow the fence until you come to an open entrance. Here there's a sort of lay-by, where you can pull in with your car or van and lug your rubbish over to a row of open refuse containers each the size of a single-decker bus. One for metals, one for wood, one for tyres, one for garden rubbish, one for paper. And three bottle banks in orthodox colours (white, brown, green). The lay-by is a smelly, dirty, rubbish-strewn place and you just go in, do the business, and get out fast. Away through the exit and back up the road to Walthamstow. Easy peasy. It's not the kind of place anyone would choose to linger. If you bothered to look beyond the refuse containers – nobody does, of course – you would see dirty once-yellow bulldozers piling up garbage against a vast bank of refuse. The atmosphere around The Dump is foul. It reeks. Putrefaction layered with strong, toxic whiffs. A raw, vegetable stench. The stink of sodden brown rotting grass blended with a thousand decaying cabbages. With an added tang of burning rubber and polystyrene. Stay more than five minutes and you'd need a gas mask. At least that's what I thought then. Little did I know... I sometimes wonder if the air pollution and general stink is done deliberately, to discourage public interest.

Fires burn night and day around the perimeter of The Dump, casting a perpetual pall of smoke over it. Serving a double purpose, perhaps? To discourage public interest AND to obscure and render opaque what is actually GOING ON in The Dump? It is certainly the case that though we knew The Dump was there and though we could see it from Attlee Tower, we never really saw it CLEARLY. In that respect it was just like Nessie. There was always smoke drifting here and there, blocking the view. We saw the people, of course, I can't pretend we didn't. But it was easy to pass them off as refuse workers or investigative policemen searching for blood-smeared dismembered limbs or idle scavengers who shunned a hard day's work. It makes me sick to think about it. EVERYBODY FUCKING KNOWS ABOUT THE DUMP BUT NOBODY FUCKING CARES! Sorry. My apologies for that little outburst. I detest polemical fiction as much as the next man. Narrative should never be fouled by propaganda or pastiche or a plurality of contradictory discourses but should refresh the mind and enlarge the reader's moral being through the subtle evocation of bourgeois anxieties. Shit like *The Princess Casamassima*, eh? Verisimilitude, eh? And the smell! I can't pretend we never smelled it. I can't pretend our nostrils were never assailed by the thick tidal stench of faeces and rotting weed and worse which seemed to linger on every street, not to mention in the lifts. And everyone could smell it but no one ever talked about it. Even on the days when the Department of the Environment said the air quality was "very exceptionally nice". All that long first night I tossed and turned in my trench. I hadn't known it was possible to be so cold. I shivered and turned and twisted and twitched and tried to make myself comfortable. Couldn't sleep a wink. I cast my mind back to my dreary past. I cast it forward to my rescue. My rescue! The only survivor of the great Walthamstow gas explosion! The helicopter hovering overhead in response to my desperate semaphore appeals! Rushed away by stretcher under the blaze of TV lights, my heart beating like the fanners of a mill. A miraculous escape! Selling my story to the *News of the World*. Fifty grand's worth! I was made! Such fantasies, I learned, are commonplace among the new arrivals. Fantasies soon shattered by the reality of The Dump. Fantasies ended by The Barrier. By the aerostats. By the whole caboodle. Fast asleep? No. Slow awake. The slowest wake of all. Cold as death. Hell. I woke up, no, I was never asleep. Did I doze? Possibly. I do not remember dozing, mind. I became aware of different shades of darkness, of night's candles burned out, of the morning, grey as sludge. Of rain, pitter-pattering on the rubbish sacks, on my plastic sheeting. The sheets were covered in condensation, I was all damp and sweaty, I felt terrible, hungry, thirsty, you name it. I didn't even have the energy to climb out of the trench for a piss, just kneeled, unzipped and splattered the end where my feet were. Some went on my socks, hitherto unmentioned. A very nice pair of Marks and Spencer grey cotton. The rain came down in torrents. Bucketing down, so to speak. I ate my last two biscuits, drank the last of the flat lemonade. I often read in novels about people pinching themselves to make sure they aren't in a dream, so I pinched myself. Didn't feel a thing! But it didn't mean I was in a dream, did it? All it fucking meant was that I was numb with cold, that's bloody what. Bloody stupid idea, pinching yourself. Bruising your own skin to prove some fatuous point about reality. Bloody bloody bloody stupid. In any case The Dump isn't a dream, it's more like a fucking nightmare. Sorry. Excuse language. I've been feeling under a lot of stress lately. Like for example the past twenty-five years. Sorry. I'll try and pull my socks up. Or I would do, if I had any. But I haven't. (At least not in the first draft. Once you get on to the second and third drafts things start to change, it's all very disturbing.) There are those who argue that This Is Like Life – unexpected events, trees crashing down in the night, earthquakes – and those who argue that this is merely The Fictiveness of Fiction. And then again there are those, the vast majority, who have no interest in these matters at all, largely because they are ill, or dying, or more interested in sport, or needing to complete a treatise on heterophony by Tuesday or too busy practising on a violino grande Penderecki's immortal concerto or gnawed by Angst or far too tied up in overseeing the deployment of sonar equipment and skilled operators employing both fixed station and mobile modes of operation and using both low and high resolution systems ranging from 20kHz to 250kHz in frequencies in the ongoing search for a large unknown animal in Loch Ness. I prayed. At once the rain stopped. I drew no conclusions. I was not in the mood for drawing anything. I went back to the top of the heap. My hair had grown longish and I ran my hands through it till it stood up like a cockatoo's crest. I began to think that I should split in two. The croaking of the frogs by the Labongo sounded in my brain. I remembered the path up the Berg and the groves of stinkwood. I gazed at the surrounding rubbish. It was covered with rime and slime. I felt a prickling sense of unease. It seemed different somehow. I tried to remember how it had looked yesterday and what it was that had changed, but couldn't. It was just... different. I couldn't see a soul. Fires were still burning, despite all the rain. I decided to follow the direction Leo had gone in. One way looked as good as another. Pulling up my socks from the second draft I set off. I sincerely hoped they would not be removed from me in a subsequent draft. So far so good. Noon, probably. A couple of waste hours elapse, I suppose. Two o'clock, must be. Everything is different but just the same. Different pillars of flame and burning tyres and smoke. Different heaps of rubbish. Different broken glass. But basically all just the same bloody mess as before. Christ, I've had enough. Tired. Thirsty. Feeling out of sorts. A bit peckish. I poked about in some bags and found a jam doughnut. Rock hard. Greedily I licked off the sugar. I hurt my teeth when I tried to bite into the doughnut. In the end I managed to moisten and eat most of it. With a swig of Lucozade for refreshment, the few last golden drops in an old bottle. Very possibly 5 p.m. Can't take much more of this. Exhausted. Very hungry, very thirsty. I wish I could find Leo but there is no sign of him anywhere. 8 p.m. I expect. I came across the wardrobe as dusk fell. It lay on its side, the door missing. A perfect resting place for the night. I crawled inside and found a scrawl. *Plomer woz ear*. Eh? I made myself as comfortable as I could. In no time at all – and truly I had no time at all, my watch not having come with me to The Dump but still tick-tocking and gathering dust on the bedside table in Attlee Tower, hence the wild guesswork involved in the unreliable times given above – I was asleep. A good night's sleep! It is the sweetest thing. I slept a shagged-out sleep, like a lusty young fellow in du Maurier country, who thrice hath pleasured his fair young maiden on the secluded shoreline by Shag Rock, undisturbed by the huge snake which probably slithered over me in the night like in *Walkabout*. I woke to drips dripping on my face (which reminded me of the dying private dick at the end of *Blood Simple*), someone or thing had pissed on the wardrobe in the night. Mopping myself dry I crawled out, feeling the warmth of sunlight on my face. The sky was a bright blue. Somewhere nearby a bird was cheeping like an electronic game. In the night The Dump had changed again. I was certain of it. Once again I felt a prickling sense of unease. Something was different. Something. If only I could put my soiled finger on it. I rolled sideways across some enticing trash, I forget exactly what. Feathers? That morning was the morning my constipation would be over, I was certain of it. I slithered to the back of the wardrobe, slipped down my pyjamas and adopted a squatting posture. Out it came, a gorgeous glistening serpentine turd, curling itself up on the ground like a well-trained snake, of an admirable light brown colour with a firm consistent texture. I felt chirpy as that unidentifiable bird. Now all I had to do was get to grips with malnutrition, thirst, a sense of disorientation and the lack of a toothbrush. A razor and some shaving foam would come in handy, too, though I knew that if push came to shove I could get by with a beard. The battery inside the unseen bird went flat. I shrugged, like a character in a novel. A shrug! I regretted it at once. I had never before shrugged in my life. I found the experience unnatural and ridiculous. It seemed akin to a tic or a twitch. I knew I would never, ever, shrug again. A trickle of sweat made its way down my face, cleverly imitating the course of Amhuinn Caslaval. I felt suddenly grateful for the desolation and solitude. I had never seen anyone shrug in public before and now I knew why. People would laugh. I felt unclean. My mouth tasted foul, my teeth as if they were covered in fur. What I needed was a chuckling spring, a bubbling brook or even a muddy waterhole. Stupid, stupid, stupid! I'd clean forgotten. All that rain! There was water all around me, if only I'd thought of it earlier. There was rainwater gathered in the creases of the garbage sacks. There was rainwater in shallow pools in up-ended hub caps and old cracked sinks and plantpots and tin trays. I scooped the water and drank. I scooped the water and flushed out my mouth. I splashed it over my face, my uncombed, matted hair. Things were looking up! Do you know I even started to whistle! I began with "All I Have To Do Is Dream", moved on to "King Of The Road" and was in the middle of "I Love You Because" when there was a distant *crack!* and a bullet smacked into the rear of the wardrobe. Splinters of wood spat at my terror. The bullet passed through the wardrobe and went ricocheting among some old half-buried agricultural machinery, among the rusted, flaking blades and wheels of which grew primroses and daisies and a solitary blue hollyhock. Here, among stumps of thorn, the pale-eyed Dysdera, with jutting chelicerae, hunts the woodlouse, swinging her cephalothorax on one side, piercing her twice. I threw myself to the ground, which is easier said than done and also very painful. Fortunately I had barely bruised my kneecaps before a powerful force threw me upright, the bruises healed with Christ-like speed, and, vision obscured by a commonplace scarlet mist which must have blown in from a nearby crime thriller, I did not see the scattered splinters of chipboard swoop back and plug the bullet hole, the woodlouse detach itself from the spider and scurry backwards, or the bullet hurriedly retrace the zig-zag course of its ricochet before reversing at great speed into the distance, where the crack! of a rifle imploded into silence, a silence coinciding with the instant dismissal of the mist and broken only by my own merry whistling. I ended the Jim Reeves song and moved effortlessly into a jaunty rendition of "There Goes My Everything". I'd been hallucinating. Must have been LSD in the lemonade. An old trick. The thought of hallucinations was comforting. Almost anything and anywhere was better than The Dump, even my mind. But I didn't like being shot at, even if the bullets were illusory. Eh? Nonsense. I'd not been hallucinating. I simply hadn't grasped the complexity of the place, its geomorphology of waste paper and black holes. Pardon. I'm getting ahead of my self (as the gravemarked time traveller said to his fit, muscular double). Taking you back to those long-gone solitary night walks, the orange sodium street lights, your dwarf's shadow compressed beneath your size eleven shoes. As you walk away the shadow lengthens, elongates, distorts. You're a fool in a crazy mirror, your broken heart inside you like pieces of shrapnel. Ah such young man's similes, be off with you! Be off across the great wastes, all the dead time, the Sundays at the Kwara Hotel, drinking too much, listening to Kris Kristofferson singing "Sunday Morning Coming Down," the donkey braying amid the lines of parked cars, genial spirits failing, forlorn! Be off. In Leo's direction. In theory. Difficult to be sure, no landmarks. A persistent whiff of burning rubber, litter everywhere, did I mention all the paper, the polystyrene cups? And the flies. A bit of warmth and sunshine and out they poured, buzz buzz. Swarming excitedly over my glistening turd, like royal correspondents at a Prince's wedding, a Princess's funeral. Feasting on the soft grey growths dappling the erectile tissue of rotting carrots. Probing cancered oranges. Go away! Wasps, too. And the occasional plump bumbling bee. No sign of Leo anywhere, can't really say I'm surprised. Morning ended, the afternoon began, so I imagine. Clouding over now. The blotch of sun above roughly overhead, noon I suppose. All that afternoon I trudged and tramped, treading carefully, stepping over empty oxygen canisters and skeletons of tents, taking steps to avoid treading on any corpses or broken glass. Pausing occasionally to warm myself by one of the many blazing fires. The sun – Alexander is jubilant! – came out again from between some grey cloud and beamed down upon – Alex is dumbfounded – The Dump. Provoking fiery glints in specks of shattered bottle. And then. Something. Glimmering. In the Chinese distance. A distinct glimmer, yes! Whatever it was it was well above the surface of The Dump. Bluish-grey. Like water. More cloud. End of sunbeams. End of glimmer. Trudged on, tired, thirsty, hungry, the usual. Thirst not so bad after discovering all the rainwater. The discovery some three hours and ten minutes ago of a packet of children's striped straws also came in very handy for sucking up quite small quantities of rainwater. Goody! More biscuits! Trudged on, humming an old Animals number appropriate to my situation. Aficionados will get my gist. On and on. On and on. On and on. Jesus! Trees! Green trees. Near the edge now, must be! Be soon out of this place! Laughter, feelings of good cheer! "Top o' the world t' ye!" Better than six pints of Greene King! Robinson breaks into a run, always a dangerous thing to do, falls flat on his face. A banana skin, yes. Picks himself up, brushes off the bits, ignores the slight gash on his left hand, continues running. Trees, six of them. Growing on a low grassy bank. Beyond... A fence. Jesus! A perimeter fence! An easily climbed wire mesh fence, not more than four metres high. A piece of cake. Curving round until lost in the distance. That must be what was glimmering in the distance. The Dump bigger than Robinson had realised. Not to worry, soon be out of here. The garbage ends, there's some grey ashy stuff, and then there's the fence. The way out! You can even see Walthamstow, the towers, houses, a distant yellow bulldozer. The end – tee hee! – of Alexander's ordeal! Bloody marvellous! You run towards it, of course. Like thousands before you. You jump over the last sack of rubbish, skip over an old newspaper, crunch a paper cup beneath your foot, run across the ash, miniature dustclouds rising up. ZAAAAAP! Without warning, a painful crackling over the surface of your body, a force slamming into your chest, something throwing you backwards – splatter – into a crate of rotting oranges. A few curls of smoke rising from your scorched clothing, a faint whiff of burning. You scramble to your feet, buttocks soaked in orange juice, bits of squashed orange slithering – shit! shit! shit! – down your inside thighs. Can't believe that it really happened, try again, a different spot this time, twenty metres to the left, very slowly, slowly, both hands stretched out, got to reach those trees, got to get out of this Christ-awful place, Jesus, Mother, please God, no more tricks, no more – ZAAAAAP! The same painful crackling, the same invisible fist punching you, tossing you backwards again, this time against a waste of old newspapers, wham! Where you lie winded, tears in your eyes, sobbing with rage and frustration. Just a few fucking yards and you'd be out of this fucking place! Fuck! Fuck! Fuck! Some sort of invisible force field. The sort of thing you come across in science fiction but not something you expect to find in Walthamstow. Strange. You might have expected the fence to be electrified but not an empty space. Some sort of invisible ray, presumably. Strange, yes. The trees unmistakeably REAL. You can even hear their leaves rustling in the gentle breeze. "Help! Help!" You shout. "HELP! For Christ's sake! Please." Like thousands before you. Waving frantically, hoping someone will see you. The bulldozer driver, for example. Are you deaf and blind, man? The people in the distant tower blocks. Doesn't anyone have a pair of binoculars and a sense of curiosity and concern? Jesus H. Christ! What's the world coming to? But no one hears you, no one stirs, no one comes to your assistance. No one will ever hear you. And so, in the end, like thousands before you, you get to your feet. You have had (stand back) an idea. Perhaps you can't get across the fence here but perhaps if you go further along the perimeter you'll find a place where this doesn't happen. By now the day is ending. Time to eat, drink, piss, brush teeth and sleep. Goo'night. Zzzzzzz. Up bright and early, sun shining brightly from a clear sky, wire fence gleaming, trees green and flourishing, brisk brushing of teeth, a hearty breakfast, a good, solid stool, and off you go, whistling a merry tune. "I Want To Hold Your Hand," if I remember rightly. Which way? I wondered. Left, I decided. Northward, if my sense of direction is right. A brisk pace, the trees falling away behind, the tower blocks gradually dropping from view, beyond the fence now nothing but vacancy, waste lots, low distant buildings, a solitary chimney belching thick black smoke, ghostly faraway figures, wagons, containers heaped high with rubbish, litter blowing about everywhere, gusts of smoke, the smell of burning plastic. Slowing, casually stepping closer to the fence, I made a sudden dash towards the wire. Seconds later I was lying among some ill-smelling sacks, with curls of blue smoke rising up from my pyjama trousers. Baffled, enraged, I moved on. All that day I tried rushing the fence, and each time I was hurled back into The Dump. At sunset I gave up, found a nice dry mattress and lay down and wept. I was so tired and bruised I would probably have fallen asleep at once, and in the first draft I closed my eyes and came tantalisingly close to enjoying a much-deserved fourteen-hour snooze, then a cold second draft blew in some changes. A clammy hand closed upon my shoulder and a voice said, "You new around here, son?" I opened my eyes and saw a silent mysterious saucer-shaped silver craft high in the sky, and, very much nearer, about six inches away in fact, an old man with long white hair and a beard, looking as if he had stepped out of a painting by William Blake. He had kindly, twinkly eyes. Like Leo, he was wearing a dressing gown (but this one was blue, not red). From the spacious pocket of his gown, where he kept his notebook, pencils, portable filing cabinet, butterfly net, foot pump, comb, magnifying glass, matches and copy of *Where Is Britain Going?* he produced a tangerine, which I gratefully guzzled. Beyond his left shoulder there was a sort of flash in the blue empyrean as the escaped weather balloon sped away to cause a scare over Canning Town. "People call me The Historian," he said. "Come and have some tea, you look tired. I expect you've had too many electric shocks today, eh? Been throwing yourself against The Barrier, have you?" Sheepishly I nodded, a trick I had learned two years earlier from the careful four-hour observation of a flock in Cumbria. He lived not far away in a concealed ditch, the old man. Rolling back a length of mildewed carpet, he beckoned me in. "There are steps," he explained, descending. I followed him down. "Have a seat," he said, indicating a comfy armchair covered with a familiar Morris floral print. Flicking off a slumbering earthworm, I sat down. He went to the far end of his cosy nook and lit an oil lamp. I heard the rattle of crockery, the splash of water, the soft hiss of a portable Gaz stove. A remarkable ditch! And so many books! They were piled in heaps on the floor and wedged tightly on shelves along the walls. Paperbacks, hardbacks, a few magazines. And over everything the rank raw smell of a freshly dug grave. It made a nice change from burning plastic. I extracted a volume, causing a miniature avalanche of earth. One of the pillars of bricks supporting the plank shelving swayed perilously. The book, a stout hardback, had a battered cover the colour of dried blood. A brownish stain had seeped along the upper edge of every page. The pages smelled as musty and unwell as a dying septuagenarian. "Aha," said the old man, returning from the far end of the ditch with some light refreshment, "I see you have dug out my little monograph on vertical looms. In the Vatican library there is a very old illustrated manuscript of Virgil's immortal *Aeneid* which depicts a wooden structure consisting of two uprights on feet connected by three equidistant horizontal bars with an irregular clear patch just above the lowest bar, the middle bar almost certainly representing the heddle rod, the structure as a whole almost certainly being that of fourth century A.D. upright loom in which the warp weights have already been replaced by a breast or cloth beam and the weaving begins from the bottom and not from the top. Rich tea or digestive?" "Digestive, please." "If you poke around you might find the companion volume on Oriental vertical mat looms. Though to be frank with you the entire topic of weaving, with its rods and leashes and beams and threads and sheds and warp and weft and spools and shuttles and bobbins bores me stiff. Give me a round table seminar on Herodotus any day, say, or even King Arthur, say, or Thucydides, say, or Bishop Jeremy Taylor's contention that 'he to whom all things are one, who draweth all things to one, and seeth all things in one, may enjoy true peace and rest of spirit', say, or Marx's argument that Trades Unions fail generally from limiting themselves to a guerrilla war against the effects of the existing system instead of simultaneously trying to change it by using their organised forces as a lever for the final emancipation of the working class, that is to say, the ultimate abolition of the wages system. Say." He put the tin tray down on a small coffee table. The coffee table surface mapped precipitation in Europe, the tin tray reproduced Gainsborough's portrait of Joshua Kirby, and the two steaming mugs of tea bore reproductions of *Oriolus oriolus oriolus* and *Bombycilla garrulus garrulus*. "Reykjavik and Bergen are places to avoid, eh?" he said with a wink. "Unless you like getting wet, that is." "I hate birds," I replied. "Stupid things. I've never seen the point in them." "Best steer clear of Reykjavik and Bergen, then, eh?" The old man chuckled. "I like your tray," I said. "If I am not mistaken it shows Joshua Kirby, editor of Brook Taylor's treatise on perspective. Buried in Kew churchyard, I believe." "I wouldn't know about that," he said tersely. "What I do know is that The Dump is a place of mysteries. But drink up, lad. Drink up thy tea." "Aye, aye, captain." My hands shook, and a slop of tea went all over the monograph on vertical looms. "Woops, sorry!" "Not to worry, lad. Not to worry. Like I said I frankly couldn't give a brass farthing. Another digestive?" "I think I'll try one of the rich tea, this time, thank you." Babbled he on as I munched, telling me that a fact is relative, and if placed out of its relative position, it apparently is not a fact, often, and that dialectics knows no hard and fast lines, and that a stone dropped from a train cannot be seen to move in a curve by any passenger but only by the woman on the embankment, and that the geo-centric system attributed to Ptolemy led to complications in the calculation of planetary orbits, and that there is only one cartouche on the hieroglyphic section of the slab of granitoid stone appropriated from Rashid by French troops in July 1799, and that the west wall at Chaldon church portrays a Descent into Limbo, the Torments of Hell, the Seven Deadly Sins, the Weighing of Souls, the Tree of Knowledge. "A spectrum is haunting Yggdrasil!" he whispered, giving me a fierce wink, speaking of space and Proust, of how the range of masses of the stars is one-eighth to twenty times the solar mass, of time and the cyclic dynamism of the intermediate, of Soddy and isotopes, of William Faulkner's unhappiness with *God is My Co-Pilot*, of the ionic theory of Svante Arrhenius and Baudelaire's "Chacun Sa Chimère", and of how caustic potash must be applied at once to the wounds of a person bitten by a deranged pug. Words, phrases, concepts rolled over me like huge soft velvet balls, pressing themselves against my brain, nudging and pummelling and teasing me. I felt sleepy and baffled and only half-awake. A dizziness seemed to steal over me, clouding my mind. At first I listened to nine words out of ten, but soon I was only half listening, then perhaps not listening at all, my mind full of feathers, of an eiderdown, of springy textual matrices, of mists and echoes. The old man explained how The Dump, though occupying only a tiny area of the Lea Valley, had a topography equivalent to that of a Middle Eastern desert, and how the population – and here I had a prickling confused sense that the old man was as mute as a hookah – was almost certainly in the thousands. "Tens of thousands!" he screeched, thumping the sludge with his stick. "Millions!" His stick? A blind man's white stick, materialising silently out of the all-encompassing blackness. With a black rubber ferrule. "Most of the population lives underground, only emerging at night," he confided in a voice like breaking crockery. "Millions?" I said. "Surely not." He nodded, then shook his head, then winced at the confused body movements he was being subjected to by forces outside his control. "The true figure will never be known," he added brokenly. "A proper statistical count is out of the question. The death rate is high. And there are regions where even an Historian does not go." By now it was evening. The Historian yawned and lit more candles. "Your beard!" I cried, dowsing the flame. "Thank you, my boy. At my age… One's faculties begin to wander. Little damage done, fortunately. A singed patch, shrivelled blackened hairs, nothing to write home about. A brief spasm of pain, then all over. More tea?" "Yes, please." That's better. Almost dark outside now. Now it is dark. "Come, my boy." The old man took the lantern and led me outside. He walked seven metres north-by-north-west, then pointed at the ground with his stick. "My guest ditch," he said. "Not very luxurious but you will find all the necessaries. Here, take this," he continued, handing me something wrapped in tissue. "Goodnight!" "Goodnight." His lantern receded. I turned my attention to the guest room. It resembled a shallow grave. I eased myself into the cramped musty-smelling space, pulled a sheet of chipboard over my head and looked to see what was inside the tissue. Joy of joys! A sherbet lemon! I slipped the sweet inside my mouth and began to roll it around. I felt my face flush. A knot of warm lemony pleasurable sensations spread around my palate. I felt little shivers in unexpected zones of my body. My toes begin to tingle. My penis decided to join in the carnival fun, wriggling awake and pressing for a better view. My salivary glands gushed and bubbled merrily. Folly! Sensual distractions! Blurring my – your – awareness of The Barrier. The Barrier trapping me there. There in The Dump. Not the conventional glass wall, not something you come up against like a dull-eyed dim-witted blackbird – SMACK! – hitting a lounge window, no, not like that at all. It was invisible but not tangible. It was a barrier but more like a force field than a wall. Like a rippling, billowing curtain, in fact. You couldn't touch it or stroke it or try to drill a hole in it or smash it with a hammer or blow it open with explosives. These had all been tried, had all failed. Nor did it stay in exactly the same place all the time, as he, The Historian, had proved with the aid of markers. There was no question that it surrounded The Dump, but it was like a sea, subject to tides. There were risings and fallings in its power. There was a theory, a foolish theory... But The Barrier was dangerous if too many people approached it at once. There had been fatalities, serious injuries. The Historian said that rushing it in groups was not advised. When I told Leo he shook his head. My voice made his head ache, he explained. "There is nothing like a good shake of your head to free it of pain and nonsense," he informed me. His clothes were enormous. Far too large for him. Those trousers! He turned a dreadful smile to me. "Insurrection grows irresistibly out of events! The masses make their own history! The art of revolutionary leadership in its most critical moments consists nine-tenths in knowing how to sense the mood of the masses!" Eh? Medium-sized was Leo, with a head-shaped head, upon which he wore a cap of the sort which Lenin used to be fond of. His nose was sharp and upon its bridge perched a pair of grimy granny glasses. A gift, he explained, from his grimy granny. Dot, she insisted on being called at the end, though until her ninety-fourth birthday it had always been

Dorothy. His webbed feet? Of no real importance to the tale I have to tell, simply a family quirk. The same can be said of his plump Uncle, Nat, who used to hang around outside the Corn Exchange in a kangaroo costume until a copper told him to hop off. Of utter irrelevance is his Aunt Martha, who in a thoughtful gesture had the gateway widened for the hearse which she knew would one day need to reverse up her modest suburban driveway. Of little consequence was his Grandmother's parrot, Jolly Boy, trained by a sailor named Baxter amid the stifling heat of Borneo to croak, fluently, "If Democritus were alive now, he should see strange alterations, a new company of counterfeit vizards, whifflers, Cumane asses, maskers, mummers, painted puppets, outsides, fantastic shadows, gulls, monsters, giddy-heads, butterflies!" – after which it would emit a long screech and sham sleep until roused to repeat itself with nuts. "Whifflers?" I enquired, upon first hearing the story of Jolly Boy. "People who whiffle," retorted Leo, flash as a quark. But all this was a long time ago, long before that cold February day when poor Biddle died. I say February and I am reasonably sure though I cannot be absolutely. "February!" ejaculated Leo. "On the 23rd – International Women's Day! – red banners appeared in different parts of the city! 90,000 workers went on strike! Demonstrations, meetings, skirmishes with the police, began in the Vyborg district and spread across the river to the Petersburg side!" Why February? Why so sure? Because of the weather. Intermittent leakages of sunshine lacking in any warmth. On some nights: frost. Most days grey and cold. Misery upon misery. Some days raining from dawn till dusk, others thick with the black promise of storms which never burst. A rum month, all told. But of course I cannot be entirely sure. To all the other insecurities of life in The Dump I must add the worrying loss of my Scenic Views of the West Country Calendar. I relied upon that to get me through the year in a sound state of mind. The satisfactions of ticking off the days and weeks. The one month turned over and the new one begun. The delightful photographs of trawlers at anchor in ports crammed with whitewashed houses and hedgerows brimming with yellow gorse and wild white roses, a robin perching on the nearest twig. The charm of sunlit Lostwithiel merging into The Purple Splendour of Land's End At Dusk. Bodmin Moor under snow. Wave-lashed Tintagel and Merlin's cave. "About one half of the industrial workers of Petrograd were on strike on the 24th of February!" (fragment of Leo's continuing chatter). The day Boodles died I scraped my teeth with a lolly stick and crawled from beneath my sheet of corrugated iron, full of urine and wind. How dimly I recollect the subtle textures of my mood that muggy morning when poor Bangle expired. Another day, indeed! How thickly, falteringly flickers the muddy fluid of my gutter's dribble of consciousness! Another day, another probably February day. Another fucking lousy day. "No, no!" cried Leo. "Not all. For that brave morning the workers made their way in processions to the city centre. More and more people drifted out in the streets. The slogan 'Bread!' had lost its oomph. Now there were cries of 'Down with autocracy!' or 'Down with the war!' Compact masses of workmen sang revolutionary songs!" Shut up. I'm trying to think. Trying to remember. That day. That at-first-sight-same-as-any-other-day. Slept badly, cold, peculiar dreams. A dream about a soup tureen, a dream about a cautious young girl from Penzance, a dream about a sea-green porpoise and a wrapper of scarlet flannel, a dream about Britt Ekland naked in the deserted Chateaux of Nymphenburg, saying (as she says on page one-hundred-and-twenty-one of *Sensual Beauty*), "Personally, I'm all for stretching and the point is to keep going further and further." A dream about a recently married man and his wife's powder-puff, a dream about Sharon Stone, a penis-butter sandwich, the Freudian slop. Bladder full as Loch Morar, rectum bloated as a zeppelin. A plum-sized pile plugging my anus like a champagne cork. A strained expression on my pasty face. Heroic effort involved paralleling attempts on the poles, the top three summits. The explosion rattling windows seventeen miles away. Fingers trembling. A minute or so afterwards the usual agonising dribble. Went back to sleep, if you can call it that. A sort of frozen stupor. "Leo," I said, when I got to know him better. "What exactly *is* whiffling?" He winked. "Knew you'd ask me that sooner or later. Whiffling is –". And then the explosion. "Ah," I said. "I see. Thanks." Then shuffled off in search of the next square meal. "Soldiers in the war hospitals waved from balconies and windows! But the Cossacks kept charging the crowds. Their horses frothed and sweated. People had lost their fear. Crowds surged from one part of the city to another. 'Down with the police!' they bellowed. The mounted police were pelted with stones and lumps of ice. The –". SHUT UP, LEO. Woke about five thirty I should imagine, then again at six. Heard seven chimes an hour or so later. Donggggg... Donggggg... Donggggg... Donggggg... Donggggg... Donggggg... Donggggg... Though "Donggggg" probably creates a misleadingly rich impression of that thin cheap tinny sound. Seven chimes. Without question seven. I counted them one by one. Quite possibly real. Discuss, with reference to omnipotent and impotent narration. Listen! I have heard that there is one place in The Dump from which you can see a church. Allegedly. I have never myself found that place, never seen the old vicarage clock or the alleged spire or the blue, peeling dolphin weathercock which inflamed witnesses have described, merrily adjusting itself to the spasmodic gusts of indecisive wind. "Just shuffling, Leo?" "Shuffling in the archaic sense, Jack. An evasion. A trick. To change the relative positions of. To shift ground. To evade fair questions. Shuffling as whiffling. To wit: prevarication. One who frequently changes his opinion or course to another. The use of evasions. To be fickle or unsteady. From whiffle, a fife or small flute." Sweet Dump! Once, I remember, I excavated a well and sought to escape – bim-bom! – by tunnelling. A deep, deep well. My friends lowered me in a bucket. When I saw it was coming to a finish I shouted at them to stop and they brought the bucket up near level with the end of it. I knew my depth, and I was out of it. Bim-bom. I began to look round, knowing not all the while what I looked for. A warm tunnel enclosing a distant disc of golden light, I suppose. A hole in the wall? Perhaps a chink opening into a mighty cavern. But I could perceive nothing. What made it more difficult was the walls were lined completely with ideology and looked identical. I examined the common sense as closely as

I might and took it course by course, til I was afraid of getting giddy. But to little purpose. I called for the working classes but they would not come. My masters could see me and knew no doubt what I was at. "What are you doing?" they cried. "Have you found nothing? Can you see no sunlight?" "No," I called back. "I can see nothing." I feel giddy, feverish. I'm not the man I was. My limbs have turned to jelly. I think I may be a fish. Some sort of eel? "Are you sure you have measured the plummet true?" called a sweet female voice. I heard other voices, harsh and masculine. They talked together. I could not make out what they said for the bim-bom and echo. Then one shouted, "They say you are too high, you must try lower." The bucket began to move lower, slowly. I crouched down in it again, not wishing to look into the dark below. And all the while there rose groanings and moanings from Peruvians, from Paraguayans, as if yammering together that the revolution should be so near. Clear above them I heard the voice of the television, forbidding me to think of such things, telling me of fast women and cars, of empty sandy beaches and capitalism's shine. Such gloss! But I had set foot on this way now and must go through with it. Bim-bom. If you get my drift. Hours later I crawled back to the surface to find everyone gone. I never saw them again. A strange place, The Dump. The stupendous torrs, praecipices and casmas bring amazement, yet courted by delight, that for a time you may seem to have arrested time with admiration; these crested rocks and proud brows of her hills are fann'd with a delicious air: and the delicate breezes that pass through the valleys are a sweet vernal zephyr to refocillate and animate the pasturage; and in winter she hath snow in plenty like a coverlid to keep her herbiage warm. Etcetera. Seven in the morning. Wednesday? So what? The whole fucking cosmos is a load of rubbish, right? A big BANG, right? Next thing there's just leftovers, right? Matter. Who needs it? What does it do? If you ask me: nothing. Bugger antimatter, what I need is a nice cup of tea. Twining's Irish Breakfast, you can't beat it. Almost impossible to get hold of. Have to make a special trip to their shop on the Strand. Afterwards a pint or two at The Edgar Wallace. Dipping my crumpled copy of *Time Regained* into the head. Giving it suck. Sipping and dipping, sipping and dipping. The translation it now turns out was a lot of balls. Went out of print before I'd completed the set. Bastards! Give me a break, play me "Where Are You Tonight?" How I abhor daylight! Hurts my wrinkled eyes. Also I abhor chit-chat. I desire the offspring not of daylight and casual talk. Ah what a blessed relief it is to do without haircuts. That regular ordeal. A blotched creature from twenty-thousand fathoms glaring at me from the bright mirror. The oily attendant with his razors. The stench of spray. The bottles of rose and gold and purple lotions. "Got the day off today, sir? Going out tonight, sir? Going somewhere nice on holiday, sir? See the Arsenal match on Saturday, sir? A shame about the poor Princess, wasn't it sir? Shocking about that bomb, wasn't it, sir?" Cretins. Out there, such garbage! Much better off here. Heard the revised Clause Four? Reminds me of the Treaty of New Echota. Not to mention the Dawes Allotment Act. A dynamic economy! In which the rabid enterprise of the market and the slippery rigour of competition are joined with the fluff of partnership and co-operation to produce profit and yet more profit for the running dogs of capitalism. Casual labour and shit wages! Eh? Where those undertakers, sorry, undertakings essential to the public good are accountable, in a cosmetic sort of way. Bubble bubble bubble. Squeak. Much better off here. No need for grooming here. Grooming, ha! My face a frowzy dirty-coloured red. Give me scruffiness any day. Sloth and dirt. Lolling around. Like today. My day for a lie-in? Or Monday? Or Saturday. The hell with it. Another day. Another fucking lousy day. Turned over, watched the lice shower off me and begin their sport anew on adjacent flesh. Caught a glimpse of myself in a silver hubcap that happened to be nearby. Observed myself phlegmatically. My raw, red, out-of-doors complexion. Hair longer than Lear's. Next moment hair half gone, stinking old age. A clutter of greasy greying strands and decaying shrubs. Teeth no better than the gravestones in the Quaker graveyard by the Nothe fort. Unshaven. Puffy beneath the eyes. A wreck. Fifty? Thirty? Sixty? Hard to say in The Dump. Everyone ages fast. And the smoke and grime and general absence of washing facilities don't help. Today's worldly belongings: a satchel containing a notebook, three apples, a tin of condensed milk, a soiled rag and a lolly stick. A light morning mist spreading across the wastes of The Dump. Lousy meaning mean. Meaning low. Meaning contemptible. Low! You couldn't get much lower. Talk about the Trail of Tears! Sleeping rough in The Dump. A torn rusty camping mattress underneath my body, my body covered in scabs and sores and feasting creatures with disgusting suction extensions. My body covered by nothing more than a pair of dirty tartan blankets. White trousers brown with dirt, pullover in rags, all the air gone out of my Doc Martens. Anorak mucky. Another day! Time for that first invigorating scratch! Kill one or two of the little blighters. Hopefully. Impossible to make much impression of course. Cripes! Entire battalions of lice burrowing among the shrubs and scabs. Dug in for the winter. No real hope of ever coming across a bottle of toxic lice shampoo, its smell curiously similar to sloe gin. Used to make my hair tingle. In the days when. Another fucking day, yes. But needless to say in spite of that tired expletive no serious hopes of fucking anyone today. Fucking is very rare in The Dump. Because. Because of the smoke and dirt and filth. Because of the wasps, lice, worms. The diseases. The off-putting stench. The lack of romantic situations. The unavailability of sweet, relaxing music. Everyone in the same putrefying, malodorous state. Many of course arrive fresh from Out There. Some in party frocks or even bridal dresses. Some in crisp, nicely ironed cavalry twill. Some in spotless Levis. These new arrivals are inevitably in a condition of shock, anxiety, agitation, fear, melancholy, anguish and perturbation. Copulation is far from their minds. Orgasm is not a pressing need. Those hungriest for sex are those in their first year. They still remember the organised orgasms on Saturday nights and Valentine's Day's desires and slimy embraces under the dripping hairy pier at nightfall and fornication's abandonments in the abandoned fortifications near the pulsing erect lighthouse not to mention fellatio in St. Anton and frenzies amid the Frensham ferns and the pungent moist pines and Acnahannet lust amidst buttock-tickling thistles and sweating tittle-tattle in Seattle and getting the hots at at the Hôtel de Paris and among the loose dunes at drenched Dieppe. The new arrivals naturally do not wish for sexual congress with smeared stinking ragged wretches of indeterminate shape and gender. After the first year, desire ebbs. Something to drink, something to eat, somewhere warm to sleep, those are the three essentials. To keep one's stench down to a reasonable minimum. An absence of toothache. In The Dump, surrounded by detritus and filth, these are the things that really count. Nails, nuts, bolts, trace chains, bits, collars. Sex is just a foolish spasm, a brief sticky inconvenience resulting at worst in diseases and foul-smelling babies. The brown slime. The stunted lives. The consumption, the discarding. A sense of waste amid the vile wastes. Those gripped in the vice of lust invariably resort to fruit and vegetables. The women engage in a brisk trade in carrots and parsnips, the men direct their attentions to marrows. Or pumpkins. There is nothing quite like a fat-bottomed pumpkin to put lead in your pencil. But this lusty phase soon passes. Soon they are as apathetic and listless as the rest of us. Balchin, Lister. Rotting Celia. The others. Too tired, now. Too old. The impulse gone. Total lack of lust in a lacklustre locale. Lacklustre? Not after a fresh shower of aerostat piss. On those days The Dump was as glistening and brown as Mozart's last dying vomit. Repeat myself? Of course I bloody well do! Guzzle and dribble. Whizzpoppers. Reminds me of the day I encountered the sign to Clinton. Thanks. I have it! By that day I had long since given up any wish to plug my discoloured but still precious penis into a slimy dangerous socket located inside a complete stranger who harboured unknown thoughts. It did not take long to get there. Inside Clinton was an odour of human faeces, pungent and raw, very reminiscent of the open drains of St. Anton-am-Arlberg. There was a strange echoing, as if Clinton was a soot-black railway arch and I was huddled underneath, hearing a dull and empty echo leadenly bouncing to and fro on the dirty brickwork. It was on the evening of the second day that I encountered an unidentifiable piece of brown fruit coated in a shimmer of off-white maggots. Beyond it lay the yellow-green pools of urine, rainbow-shimmery pools of enticing toxicity, and on the shore a heap of rags, a silver hypodermic. Feverish and fretful I floundered around Clinton, teetering and grimacing as I staggered past the wall of crazy mirrors. I began to run my fingers over the keyboard. Soon it was Tuesday. I had spotted a piano earlier in the day. I can't remember exactly what I played. Fragments here and there mixed in with a lot of improvisation. The transitions as abrupt as Washington State's, in your remembered days there. Clinton's smile is a strange, desolate region, dung-brown, with a painful glare. The insincerity reminded me of an egg yolk cultured with salmonella, both homely and poisonous. I was reminded of the folk who ring your doorbell and say, "Hi!" and tell you their first name, which is always Mike ("Hi! I'm Mike!"), and then ask if you are the houseowner ("Hi! I'm Mike! Are you the houseowner?") and then when you say "No" the expectant eyes grow dull, the smile ebbs, the shoes retreat back to the street. In time, as ever, I left that region of terrible echoes. The first thing to be done was to see to my pistol. You will perhaps notice that I had lied, earlier. I was born in a short street that opened off a square. Inside the rectangle (for how many squares are square?) there stood a public urinal, a statue of a famous man named Alexandre-Auguste Ledru-Rollin, two sandstone benches, and twenty-four lime trees. As a boy I would cross the square dizzy and nauseous at the thought of Clinton's vast vistas of emptiness. Such hollowness. Bim-bom! When I at last emerged my face mask was coated in shining amber filth. Daylight washed over me. I bellowed with a strange ardour, with an avidity rarely seen in these days of wind and drivel. "Long live the glorious October revolution!" is one interpetation, highly plausible if you ask me. It was then that I became aware that someone had entered the room. A nurse? The Prime Minister? "I hope you don't mind me making these sounds. There didn't seem to be anybody about." "Not in the least," said the Prime Minister. "It's a relief to hear something different from this appalling situation we're in." "It is true then? About Europe I mean?" I ask you! Requesting the truth from that clammy pobble! That glossy mucilaginous pillar of blab and slither! Expecting an honest answer from that truckling, bobbing, pliant, unctuous, windy, creeping Jesus! A man whose fixed smirk showed him to be oblivious to Hegel's contention that only one body of mutually coherent propositions is possible. Ignorant equally was he of Dewey's argument that empiricists use propositions as the means of inquiring into things and events which are the materials and objects of inquiry, not to mention the consonance between Reichenbach's probability theory and the argument that things are a metaphysical delusion and that the truth of basic propositions depends upon their relation to some occurrence, and that the truth of other propositions depends upon their syntactical relations to basic propositions. As a boy I would cross the square to get fresh bread from the baker's and when I had glanced at the sky and all twenty-four trees, to make sure that they had neither multiplied nor disappeared, I would study the surface of the square. Extraordinary, the things that I found through that habit. A woman's handkerchief; a button-hook; a box of mysterious medicine in the shape of globular, transparent pills; a bill with an excessive discount for cash payment made out by my own father; and, once, an illegal incitement to revolution, which cried through the medium of smudged printing: "Citizens Unite!" The next day I took my first, faltering steps in the direction of the vanished republic. For lack of even the most essential data, I am able to say little about the People's Socialist Republic of Nambuangongo, other than that it was established around February 1961 in the Dembos forests in north-western Nambuangongo (between the rivers Loge and Lang) in the immediate wake of the 1961 rising in Luanda. Changing direction, I came across a sack of old telegrams. BAFFLED AND HURT BY YOUR SILENCE STOP PLEASE GET IN TOUCH STOP EELS STOP TELL ERICA NOT TO WORRY STOP CHARLES STOP PLEASE PHONE REGARDING DORCAS STOP URGENT STOP VICKY STOP WHATEVER HAPPENED TO DORCAS STOP GEORGE STOP AM GOING TO ALEPPO STOP DO NOT TRY AND CONTACT ME STOP ALICE STOP

Eels? Dorcas? Sounds like a bloody sitcom. Sitcom? So far I have said nothing about the light entertainment side of things here in The Dump. Sometimes it is possible to watch situation comedies. Sometimes even the news. Frequently alas reception is only achieved in time for the pathos of the final item, after which, all too frequently, the image dissolves into a moment's abstract expressionist masterpiece, all barbs and colliding coils, white incandescent sparklings, after which, invariably, the screen goes dead. The final item! Designed to cheer up the viewer up after those gabbling ministers and agitated witnesses and survivors and the fires and crashes and murders and shoot-outs and assaults and the dense dark smoke the colour of mushroom soup billowing prettily upward amid the villages of a sunlit landscape faraway. How, in time, they blur together. Stranded whales and royal tours and oily sea-birds and dogs and princes, the courtiers wagging their tails, the prune-faced sour-eyed monarch – Ickpling Gloffthrobb Squutserumm blhiop Mlashnalt Zwin tnodbalkguffh Slhiophad Gurdlubb Asht! – resting her tons of blubber upon her massive stomach and vast, elongated arse. The anchor-man coated in deference, everything bright and sleek and shining with a rainbow-hued slime, the putrefaction barely visible, the stench not to be nosed. And not just news! In The Dump the opportunity does not often arise to go to the movies for there are no cinemas. In my wanderings I have never encountered a projectionist (which does not mean to say that they don't exist). I have never come across discarded screens or rusting projectors. Nevertheless it is occasionally possible to take in a good film. This is all thanks to the unstinting endeavours of one or two film-crazed individuals and technological whizzkids who have made it their business to forage for old video recorders, lengths of flex and abandoned batteries. Once in a blue moon the batteries function and the elaborate wiring works and you get the chance to watch a good film – always provided you have the price of admission. Prices vary. Sometimes a ticket of admission to a video-show ditch costs (say) a Valium tablet, two cans of beer, twenty bars of soap, two tins of talcum powder, four toilet rolls (soft tissue) or something which the admissions man regards as being of equivalent value. Complete sets of the works of Scott or Dickens are not welcome, but deals can often be thrashed out involving bars of chocolate, boiled sweets or grotesque sexual favours. The choice of films on offer is very limited, and usually involves those which people have thrown out as being either boring or completely unwatchable. But oddly enough these are just the kinds of film which people in The Dump seem to enjoy. Firm favourites are *The War Game*, *Les Jeux Interdits* and *Stalker*. Living off the thin of the land has its compensations, eh? Sossing in an easy chair, mildewed and blotched. As for the chair! But things could be worse, eh? Better off am I than the six million child workers of Pakistan who work in carpet factories, brick-making plants, on farms and as servants. I'm better off than Iqbal Masih who was sold into slavery aged four and who spent the next six years chained to a carpet-weaving loom tying tiny knots between 4 am and 4 pm each day and who was shot dead at the age of twelve in the village of Muritke twenty miles from Lahore on Sunday 23 April 1995. I'm better off than the young women workers in New Vietnam's Export Processing Zones who work a twelve-hour day at a basic rate of £12 a month. Not to mention the workers in the garment and micro-electronics factories of Shenzhen who work twelve to fifteen-hour shifts, live in damp dormitories and have one of the highest rates of industrial accidents anywhere in the world. I'm better off than factory workers contaminated by toxic dioxins as a consequence of exposure to chlorine-based products burned in incinerators who suffer from weakened immune systems and reduced testosterone levels. I may be covered in scabs and infested with lice and worms but at least I'm alive! No nine to five grind for yours truly, no sir! If I want a lie in, I have a lie in, no matter what I'm lying in. Shit! Things could be a lot worse, eh? I might, after all, have been part of the population of Tokyo's shitamachi a little after midnight on the morning of 10 March 1945 when 334 B-29 Superfortresses began dropping 1,539 tons of incendiary bombs during a three-hour bombardment in which 270,000 buildings and 15.8 square miles were razed and people burned bubbling and popping and hissing alive in their homes, or choking coughing hysterical gasping were overcome by fumes, or were boiled bubblingly alive as they leaped into seething bubbling boiling canals. Better off (much better off) than people in Somalia and Egypt etc. (Long list here, eh?) Makes yer proud, considering. Da da da da da da da, da da da da da da, da da da da da da da da dumb dumb dumb dumb dumb dumb. Yush! Thoil-oil-ways-bin-un-un-gland-woil-thuz-a-cunt-tree-loin, wireover-thuz-a-cut-age-smell, beshite-a-toxic-foiled. Da da. February 27. Slept badly in the afternoon. Everything is changed. O I ha'e Silence left, yes. Farewel. At present all I can write would be but the history of my miserable feelings. Thus I was tossed and so perplexed, especially at some times, that I could not tell what to do. I saw myself in a forlorn and sad condition; and would also often, with lifting up of heart, sing that of the fifty-first Psalm, O Lord, consider my distress; for as yet I knew not where I was. Possibly in Komsomolsky, shovel in hand. Banished. Learning how to eke out my miserable days. A good word, eke. Ee as in knee. Eke as in creak. And me on my knees, creaking in every joint. Tormented by arthritis, red hot needles stabbing into my phalanges and ginglymoids. A glowing poker thrust up my tight, squirming arse. My head beginning to crack with aches. As if some preposterous metaphysical entity was zooming in. Taking the mick out of the Kalmyks. Making me sweat for a lifetime of unspeakable pleasures. Punishing me for my dreams. Mocking my mockery of a life. Pissing colourfully on the tattered sallow descendants of the Golden Horde. Demoralising yours truly as he tends as best he can his squalid vegetable plot beside a ramshackle hut. Withered, curling cabbages going brown. Shrivelled carrots. Oozing sour sweetcorn looking like a nose covered in scabs. Sand getting everywhere. Into my eyes, my mouth, my dripping nostrils. Into my curdled carrot soup. Into my rickety hut. My hut? A labour of love. Old rotting fenceposts with knuckles of wire deftly intertwined with corrugated sheeting, enticingly rustpatched with blotches oddly reminiscent of the crumbling stacks east of Ballard Downs. The wind blew it down. The structure sank into the sand. Perhaps it never existed. Just one of those ditch-dreams you sometimes get. A hut! A nice cosy hut! Instead of this open-air filth, this ditch half full of plastic containers and rat droppings and scraps of oily blairspeeches. For several days, remembering my bright ditch-dream, I was greatly assaulted and perplexed, and was often ready to sink where I went, with faintness in my mind. But one day, after I had been so many weeks cast down therewith, as I was now quite giving up the ghost of all my hopes of ever attaining life, this sentence fell with weight upon my spirit, *All that is solid melts into air, all that is holy is profaned.* "Chin up," I said to myself. "Things could be worse. At least you were never a motorist." Motorists find life in The Dump particularly hard. It is difficult to say which is worst – separation from their car or the loss of mobility. Poor wretches. Some sit for days in solitary, broken front passenger seats, reprising commercials. They reach through the gaps in their shredded shell suits, listlessly scratching the leaking sores around their genitals while their rotting minds project sun-drenched Z-bends where dark-haired sun-glassed women loiter by the flanks of gleaming saloons, moist with desire, skirts pushed up against their strong bronzed thighs, waiting to be pleasured by a vacuum unit fixing screw as white foam explodes against those backdrop Mediterranean rocks beyond the glowing band of pure untarnished sand. Some hum old Clapton tunes redolent of speed and throbbing stereo systems, the gusts of empty motorways at dawn, the harsh manly screech of rubber marking heroic getaways on the tarmac. Some devote their remaining days to reconstructing their heart's delight, often starving to death before completion. They trade wizened but serviceable carrots for crankshaft sprockets, swop reasonable potatoes for pistons and big-end bearing caps. I remember one, a mechanic, a greasy, gruesome, blair-eyed, overalled, nixonish sort of man, of average torso, who constructed a car from scratch, obtaining engine support bolts, camshaft retainer plate and clutch driveshaft screw by dint of theft and buggery. Luminous with stupid delight was his dripping rodent's face as he twisted the pipe-cleaner and got it going. So happy was this wretch that he drank an entire bottle of meths to celebrate. Roaring off at speed, he collided seconds later with a traffic island (which, as he pointed out, dying, hadn't been there the day before). The vehicle erupted like a car-bomb and he was, I'm delighted to say, hideously burned. He died, surrounded by an excited crowd, in agony. Sheets of white, dripping skin hung from him like champagne-splashed flags. But most never get that far. Most sit alone, clutching rootless steering wheels, blubbering. For a week or so they find consolation with other sufferers and exchange long stories of hold-ups on the M5 and short-cuts through Surrey and which lane to get into when entering the Hanger Lane gyratory system and the time they had to wait two hours for the AA and how they slithered on Snake Pass in the snow and the time they had to wait three hours on the A606 because of the cones and the road menders weren't even working, just drinking tea, and how best to avoid the jams in Brent. And then they die, holding their ignition keys with personalized key ring. Key rings portraying their initials in upper-case gold, or miniatures of their favourite Porsche, or of their blonde girlfriends. The lower-middle classes die with a puzzled frown, clutching hub caps or number plates which contain their initials or their date of birth. In The Dump there is simply nowhere to drive a car, and this, in their eyes, is a nightmare greater than death, which is everywhere. You might manage to accelerate ten metres past the heap of sacks on your left but beyond that, you can be certain, lies rough, impenetrable ground, broken glass, a patch of burning rubbish gushing fierce flames and thick dense black choking smoke, a ditch, a pool of oil, a toxic residue, a bubble of explosive gas just waiting for some prick to pierce its flimsy membrane. Death is everywhere in The Dump, which is why there is nothing like coming across a good obituaries page to perk you up. The younger or more famous the better. Serve the bastards right. The unexpected death of Labour MP John McSmug has come as a great shock to our galaxy. Three purple-skinned paranoid humanoids on Jupiter were seen openly weeping, and as a mark of respect McSmug's favourite piece of music – Karlheinz Krzcecebit's

Obtuse Variations in F Minor for Whistle and Anus – are to be broadcast unceasingly for the next seventeen years in all telephone booths on the asteroid belt. John McSmug died yesterday while attempting simultaneously to devour a mushroom omelette, a buttered croissant, two slices of toast and marmalade, a bacon butty, a crumpet topped with greengage jam and a bowl of peaches and cream while drinking a half pint of whisky. McSmug was heard to say to his cleaning woman, "I feel I'm getting bigger," when, without warning, he exploded. All the windows in his luxury penthouse apartment were blown out as lumps of McSmug showered down on passers-by. McSmug came from a humble bourgeois Scottish background. After several years at Edinburgh University, where he is still vividly remembered as "even in those days an unctuous, oily, ambitious little creep", he became a barrister, specialising in defending companies from charges of negligence made against them by limbless or poisoned workers. His retort to one claimant – "You say you were poisoned by toxic dust and malodorous chemicals, but I say to you it is your mind that is poisoned – poisoned by left-wing troublemakers and a lot of silly speculation about pollution put about by lunatic environmentalists" – is fondly remembered even today by the legal establishment. And. And the death has been announced of Gavin Blore, General Secretary of the Union of Boltmakers and Flex-worglers. Widely tipped as a future TUC leader, Mr Blore had been ill for some time from regressive softening of the spine. Gavin Blore joined the U.B.F.W. when he was fourteen, as a tea-boy. His ingratiating manner, mental vacuum, hatred of strikes and enthusiasm for laying out the papers at committee meetings soon brought him to the attention of his superiors, and by the age of eighteen he was a full-time official, with special responsibility for demoralising members engaged in local disputes. His attitude to filing-cabinet systems earned him widespread respect in the Labour movement. And. And the death has been announced of Sir Nicholas Swill. Swill will always be remembered as of one the most colourful personalities the House of Commons has yet thrown up – a glistening mass of turd browns dappled with streaks of chocolate and attractive bright splashes of red, redolent of the bowel cancer which finally killed this turbid fascist. He will be fondly remembered by his many friends in journalism, television and politics. Yup, there's nothing like an obituary to cheer up yours truly. And quite frankly those of us who inhabit The Dump need all the cheering up we can get. Newspapers are a real boon in such circumstances. Once, I remember, I encountered a newcomer, a tattooed man in rags. He was holding up a home-made placard that read ANUS. At first I admired his flexible attitude to market realities. Having nothing to sell other than his body he was prepared to rent out any orifice that might earn him a few pennies from a passing sodomite. Having long since given up orgasms I naturally had no interest in responding to his enterprise. To my surprise and dismay he no sooner saw me than he bounded towards me across the waste. "I'm not gay," I snapped irritably as he grunted and pawed at me. It took some time to discover that he was in fact a vigorous young working-class masturbator in a state of considerable nervous agitation at having been separated from his favourite daily newspaper. Only semi-literate, he was also prone to dyslexia, hence his misleading placard. I reversed the sign and wrote on the back what it was he was seeking: A SUN. This is The Barbarians' favourite newspaper, named after a sphere of hydrogen and helium gas. I told the youth that I had never yet come across a copy in The Dump. Besides, I cautioned him, looking at it for long periods can seriously damage your eyesight. "You may even go blind!" He shook his head, as if to say: "What rot!" Thanking me for correcting his placard, he scurried away, saying he had an appointment to keep. The Dump, The Dump. A queer place. Eight hundred square miles of garbage. At the very least. A tip, literally. Prone to sudden subsidence. Heap upon heap of piled rubbish. Place of sludge and stains, landscape of dregs and draff and sweepings. Ah, the gleam of feculence and mildew! One day Jesus tapped me on the shoulder, said, "John, why are you resisting me?" I said, "I'm not called John. What's more, to be brutally honest, do you know how bad you smell? You smell about two thousand years old.

And the stuff that's clinging to your sandals. As for that prayer of yours. I always had this image of God as a fat, red-faced landowner who put up PRIVATE KEEP OUT notices all round his estate, and who hated trespassers." Jesus shook his head. "The meek shall inherit the earth," he said. I said: "Yeah, but only if they grasp their power as workers within the capitalist system, and benefit from the presence of a revolutionary socialist party with substantial roots in the class able to help them understand the reformism of the trades-union leadership and to see that the structures of the capitalist system – parliament, the police, the army, the judiciary – cannot be reformed but must be smashed and replaced by a workers' state based upon councils of workers' delegates and a workers' militia." Jesus looked a bit perplexed. He was silent for a while. Then he brightened. From under his dirty robe he produced a folding table, some Sainsbury's croissants, a packet of rainbow trout and some cups of water. He proceeded to perform some very impressive conjuring tricks. "Hey, not bad," I said, munching a grilled trout sandwich and sipping a very agreeable glass of full-bodied red wine which I could have sworn was made from Fer Servadou grapes. Afterwards I clubbed him over the head with the empty, rigged up a rough cross and crucified the bastard. It was at this point that I discovered Jesus had no sense of humour. The things he said to me! A couple of days later someone made off with the corpse, almost certainly to recycle it for kebabs and burgers. Time passed, passes. Night, sleep, piss. Another day! I have some unfinished business in Tepl, too bad. The emerald mould, the billowing fungus. The cesspools stinking under a rancid sun! A plain tangled with remnants, remainders, rumps and stumps, scrag-ends and dog-ends, stubs and bones. Wreckage! Débris! Place of ruins. Learn to make shift with the leftovers. One morning I encountered a tall, thin-faced leather-jacketed male biped identical, almost, to M in *L'Année dernière à Marienbad*. He was hand in hand with a denim-jacketed female who greatly resembled the silent-movie star Marie Prevost (who, after dying, was eaten by her dachshund). We passed in silence. Ah, what a touching sight is love and friendship! I am on my way to the Dianahof, to think about her while staring at my butter dish. Drink up that cracked cup of watery sediment, whore! Bathe amid scum, old friend. Feast on peelings, comrades! This is the zone for those whose services have not been retained by the company! Dump of the expired, the unconsumed, the depleted. Ravel out weaved-up follies. The Dump, The Dump. A good three Glonglungs in length if you ask me. Here you are truly useless, truly superfluous, truly inadequate and unemployable. Place of muck and dross! I fall upon the thorns of life. I seep! I ooze and drip. I vent stenches. What's more I've had a dicky ankle for weeks. But don't you worry about me. You go on enjoying yourself, out there beyond The Great Barrier. After all, there's heaps of vitamins in orange peel and potato peel and carrot peel and turnip peel. I can pretend I'm at the Schloss Balmoral & Osborne. I can suck wood when times get tough. And what's wrong with rags? I dress like everyone else, in scraps. Old clothes, cast-offs. Bits of carpet. A nice pair of trousers with the name Len-something daubed at the back with a marker pen. Dump of functionless folk, purposeless people, pointless ambitions, unworkable dreams, effort-wasting aspiration. That Russian I once met. Alexander. Toiling on his own to raise a cathedral. A structure made out of rubbish, including dark red plastic trays from a bakery. The spire reminiscent of a witch's hat. Seven days he toiled, and in the evening of the seventh the entire structure collapsed. A fascinating figure was Alexander, with his paunch and his Nietzsche moustache. One morning he just wasn't there. This often happens. Come and go. Erasures and deletions. Thin spectral figures. An Irishman clutching a lengthy, much-annotated recipe for Mulligan Stew. Dump of cast-offs and time-yellowed offprints. A torn package with half a dozen bright Italian stamps addressed to Professor Binns. Wasn't he in *Loch Ness*? Starring Lemuel Gulliver and Constance Chatterley? It's a small world, eh? Dump of poor Joe Beaumont, of whom more later, perhaps. Perhaps not. Dump of broken videos and chucked-out paperbacks and nonreturnable bottles and all that is superfluous, expendable, unneeded, unwanted. Things and people once fit as a fiddle, now fit for nothing. Built-in obsolescence, the very marrow of every gleaming product. And people. You give the best years of your life for the company, for the economy, for England – and then? Dumped. Just like that. Made redundant. Globalism. Can't be helped, say those fuckers rolling in dosh. Barristers, politicians, media creeps. Glossy and sleek. Whereas we here are shabby and blotched. Broken down, outmoded, bootless. Prone to giddiness, given to tottering. No cheap cracks s'il vous plait. Here we are not worth the paper we're written on, eh? Worthless as Argentinian bonds, polluted as an English river, filthy as a saddle of British beef. Here there is nothing to write home about. Here, at best, all you can hope for is an epic of bits and pieces, of odds and ends, of ended odds and odd ends. But mustn't grumble, eh? No matter how bad things are in The Dump at least I'm better off than the six million child workers of Pakistan, eh? Mustn't grumble. Some mornings Lady Luck smiles. You step past a fly-encrusted rib-cage, jump a puddle of rainbow-hued oil and spot, lying on a pink scrap of *The Financial Times*, not yet pierced by wasps or worms, an apple. An honest English apple! A September's Bramley, April-fresh thanks to a stiff dose of carbon dioxide and nitrogen gas in the silo in which it has been stored, a homely metallic structure with a bracing whiff of this and of that. Glory be to God for modified atmosphere storage! Glory be to God for waxed cucumbers! Glory be to God for Tecnazene to spray upon potatoes inhibiting sprouting! Glory be to God for fungicides W230-233 to make our citrus fruits and bananas wholesome as the creator intended! Glory be to God for salmon dye and gas-flushed fish! Glory be to God for gas-ripened apricots! Glory be to God for the market, for Lo! did not the first bourgeois economist Adam Smith say e'en in the glorious eighteenth century, "It is in the nature of every man to trick, fart and get laid." Let us spray, let us spray, let us ask no questions. Sleep now, your maggoty narrator insists upon it. For every word hath its marrow in the English tongue for order and for delight. Tea anyone? Tea and sleep and sweet dreams and another night gone by. Next another day, another fucking day. Correction. Another fuckless day. Those were the days, eh? The good old days. When I was still interested. When I'd think: fucking on a day like today? Fat chance! Haven't met a soul for weeks, let alone a woman, a nice ripe amenable juicy woman with a sense of humour and an easy-going fuck-me attitude to life. The women I've met in The Dump aren't interested in sex. Gone off it. Or never went in for it in the first place. Won't do it for fear of disease. Pregnancy. Worms. Loyalty To Another. Crabs. Lice. Piddling objections like that. Makes a man sick. "More interested in other things", as one of them said to me. Forget her name. Trish? Other things! I ask you! More interested in giving gentle suck to a banana, sipping the last drops of yellow-brown mulch. Twisted. Pathetic. Totally uninterested in eight inches of throbbing penis. (Well alright, five and a half inches.) (Oh very well, four inches, and not a centimetre less.) Unbelievable. What's gone wrong with the world? I've still got my looks, haven't I? I'm still young, aren't I? I still stiffen, don't I? It's not as if they are anything to write home about. Mucky Mary. Louse-encrusted Lil. Dirty Diana. Filthy Felicity. Said what made me attractive was my habit of incessantly cleaning the nails of one hand with the nails of the other. And, when seated, rubbing the sole of my long right foot up my left shin, disseminating a grave-like odour. As for Sarah. Safe sex with her was nothing to write home about. She rigged up a tape of "Moonlight Becomes You" and sucked on a beet to get me going. A parsnip up the rectum, I ask you! Fucking confabulators, all of them. Prefer versification to the real thing. A perverted enthusiasm for prosody. Rub your crotch and think of Walthamstow. Walking up the High Street, two carrier bags of groceries in each hand. The signs of the stallholders. CHEDDER CHEESE. ANTI-FREZZ. Each stall blaring the same song on the transistor radios. The longest street market in Europe, fucking feels like it, how many times have I trudged it, hundreds, thousands, know every fucking inch of it, in rain, in snow, in sleet, in hail, in tropical heat, most of them on grey dull featureless days. *Watch me fucking jogglies!* screamed the stallholder obscurely as I brushed his bottoms with my bike. Ah, memory! The old days, the days before The Dump. You get back there to that littered street via an electrical impulse. Cool. Propagated is it down the axon conveying a message to the next cell. One nerve cell excites, another inhibits. Different cells releasing different chemical substances. That's neurostransmitters to you, mate. Affecting the next cell. The miry message is transmitted across the synapse by about forty different neurostransmitters. Did you know that different cells release different neurostransmitters? Of course you bleedin' didn't. And different neurotransmitters predominate in different parts of the brain. How can I put it? A black hole leading straight to an old April. Neil Young singing "Heart of Gold". The years, the changes, all before The Dump. Oh shut it, SHUT IT! When I doe think back I doe know how verrie luckie I bee ande wythe soe muche toe bee thankful for how toe rite and figger. Eh? Your words no more clear, can hardly swim. I alternate between spells of fatigue and indifference. Eh? Once, I remember, I took a cabbage into town to buy some cloisters. Once I dreamed of putting on a double-breasted reefer jacket, white nankeen sailors' trousers and black leather boots and setting sail for Lerici. The years passed. I favoured the exercises of Professor Müller. I starved, dreaming of spicy sausages the size of an elephant's prick. I craved a pint of iced lager in Alexandria – or the Rose & Crown. The TV was babbling. "War is not a humane activity," said General Johnson. "The United States was in the war to win." Deranged. You know I'd give anything to get out of this place, even if it was only for a few days. Just to do the ordinary things again – use a telephone, walk in a dogshit-smeared park, puke on a carpet, fall downstairs, piss in a phone box, spend money, and have to make a decision. Excreting, accreting. Accreting memories, experiences. Accretion amid the castoffs, paradox, bah! Where are they, the great hostesses of the ilk of Sibyl Colefax and Emerald Cunard? Beautiful things. The blue teapot. The gold eggcup. The fish knives. And all of them royal. The royal insignia. The regimental drums. Cretinous. Having lost all their faculties they sat motionless in their various chairs, some looked at television with their eyes closed. Me too.

My eyes, my ears are going, everything is going. My legs are going. My arms are going. Quick! A brisk narrative transition. She had broken her hip but was still full of sparkle. Ah, the old days. We never stopped dancing. I doted on her, you know. Eh? Wanted: more Personality and Decision Making. Give me my boots, I say! Eh? Wanted: more analysis of the structure of words (morphology), more sounds of a given language (phonology), more systems of versification (prosody). Cup of tea? What's this? A headline? Bliss! *TUBERCULOSIS THREATENS THIRD OF WORLD'S PEOPLE, W.H.O. WARNS. Tuberculosis, once considered a vanquished Victorian disease, is spreading rapidly throughout the world because of failure to use low-cost drugs which can cure it, the World Health Organisation said yesterday. The disease will kill at least 30 million people over the next decade, and could infect more than a third of the world's population – some 2 billion people – the WHO warns in a report published in New York.* I cheered vigorously. In my imagination. In real life (joke!) I emitted one or two croaks, like a punctured frog. The newspaper was old and sodden. When I tugged at the page it ripped silently away. The light was bad. I screwed up my eyes, tried to make out a day, a month, a year. Nineteen-ninety-five already! Jesus, three years out at least! I'd been convinced it was still nineteen-ninety-two. But now I knew it was nineteen-ninety-five or maybe even later. Nineteen-ninety-six, or even seven. Had we reached the new millennium yet? I did not think so. I had seen no fireworks. I was reasonably convinced it was not yet the next century. Stretched out on a sodden roll of carpeting I idly fingered the encompassing muck. A worm. An empty two litre plastic lemonade bottle. A few tabloid newspapers from the early eighties. Some recent broadsheets. I sprang to my feet and ran across to Bodge. "Marvellous news, Bodge! Israeli planes have bombed the village of Nabatiyet, killing a mother, her seven children (one a four-day old girl) and two teenage relatives! That will teach 'em to go on soaking up the Lebanese sun and ignoring our plight here in The Dump, eh? And listen to this! Four gunmen screaming 'God is great' machine-gunned a coachload of elderly Greek tourists, killing seventeen! They are dead and we are alive! How sweet the scent of death is. How delightful to know that The Barbarians are keeping up the good work, zapping fellow Barbarians without cease! Hurrah! More wars please! More terrorist atrocities! And *do* keep driving that car as much as possible, eh? Last year's road casualty statistics were phenomenal! This year's promise to be even better. So keep that accelerator pedal pressed down hard, my friend. More air bags, more recklessness! Things are distinctly getting amusing out there! Thirty million to die in the next ten years!" Bodge beamed. He was draining a few inky drops from the stagnant base of a dirty Martini bottle. "Good ol' Henri Paul!" he slurred. "Give us something to talk about, eh? October the First is Too Late!" He burbled and burped. I could see I'd cheered Bodge up no end. He was a tall good-natured youth, his father born in Penge. "A third of the world's population infected, did you say?" He grinned. Molatuendalaas! "That's what this report says, yes. Here, see for yourself." "Bloody marvellous," grinned Bodge. "Bloody, bloody marvellous." He departed in high spirits, vaulting over a nearby oil drum in a manner which reminded me of scenes from *The Wooden Horse*. Alas, dietary deficiencies and high-altitude pulmonary edema had sapped poor Bodge's strength. His scrotum slammed into the rim of the drum and he screamed in agony. Picking up an adjacent pomegranate, spitting out pips and patches of musty-tasting mildew, I watched with interest as Bodge fell to the ground in slow motion and made writhing motions. "Fuck! Shit! Buggabuggabuggabuggabugga!" he said, sounding like a fashionable Scottish novelist when at last able to emit language. I made the most of the situation. Kicking Bodge in the face, I ran off with his radio. Christ! Hear that! Thought For The Day! Remnants of the old life. Everyone had a Thought For The Day. Mostly it was: Survive At All Costs! Or: Must Get More Food Today! Or: It's bram an gathe. Or: Christ I'd Give Anything For A Cool Glass Of Lager! Or: I Wonder If Christine Would Let Me Fuck Her For This Tin Of Peaches? Moi, j'y pense tous les soirs. Alors, attention Emily! Regarde-moi dans les yeux. Allez! Little crotchets and curves of her own (and what curves!). Fucked and lost, squeezed out and lost. Lost for words. The sadness, the waste. The shame. Precious time spilled on idle conversation. Consuming alcohol. Sweaty satisfying sex. Time which might have been better spent – spent! – discussing or at any rate accumulating information about Ionian Speculation or Descartes' Epistemology or Spinoza's Ethics or Locke's Theory of Knowledge or Berkeley's Idealism or Hegel's Philosophy of History or Marx's Historical Materialism or Kierkegaard's Christian Existentialism or what to do if you tear your thoracic cartilage or Weber's Historical Sociology or the ins and outs of Nietzsche's Perspectivism or James's Pragmatism or Habermas' Critical Theory or coded references to masturbation in the diaries of Matthew Arnold or Kuhn's Paradigm or Quine's Ontological Relativism or Byron's letter to John Cam Hobhouse of October 12, 1821, or Rorty's Neo-Pragmatism, enough to drive anyone to drink. Or even something practical and likely to be of use in the late capitalist era. The psychology of selling. Telephone power. The secrets of closing the sale. How to win customers and keep them for life. How to power-pack your days. Time and stress management. How to unleash your imagination and clear away those pesky idea traps that hold other people back. How to win the game when you are playing in someone else's ballpark. Discover the secrets of leadership. Reverse the ageing process with special herbs and a top-secret recipe handed down by monks. Put pep into middle-age with melatonin supplements. Obtain Australian citizenship and stay on top when your world turns upside down. Use the latest techniques to overcome your fear of alien abduction. Lose weight at Dachau. Experts help you to apply the latest communication techniques in dealing with young goats. World famous thinker V. I. Lenin reveals the secrets of building up a successful organisation and how to cope with difficult people. Let image expert Ronald Reagan help YOU to communicate confidently and clearly. *In Tough Times Tough People Stick It Out*: Nobel Prize Winning Author Slim Y. Bucker shows how to cope with setbacks, identify threats and create new opportunities. What's that? Give you more data? More of that monstrous mass that accrues from the moment-by-moment of a life? Friends and oneself by now somewhat tired and elderly. Elderly and forgetful. Forgetful and irritable. Ha – ha! Keep time! Prone, alas, to exaggerate. To suppress. Full of gorgeous inventions and fib. Anything to sharpen the story. Lewdness, even. Filth! Living here amid cardboard boxes, treasures. A film of dust over everything. Old snapshots. Faded Polaroid snaps of cunt and cock. Of rumps and squelch. My eyesight, my digestion, my joie de vivre, all quite gone. Jack-of-the-clock. The end is in sight. Ho there! Fetch me my binoculars! My binoculars? One day I came across a pair of in The Dump. It was a crisp February day and I'd spent a not very rewarding morning rummaging through a heap of commercial refuse – rusting filing cabinets, faded swivel chairs, rolls of tatty mildewed carpet. So far the best thing I'd come across was a Mickey Mouse pencil sharpener and a miniature bottle of gin which had fallen down the back of somebody's filing cabinet drawer. I spent a long time sniffing the gin before I drank it. I even splashed a drop on my skin to see if it was really acid. You can never be too careful in The Dump. There's nothing The Malevolents like more than finding empty bottles and filling them up with unpleasant or even downright dangerous liquids. I've known newcomers to The Dump whoop with joy at the sight of a golden bottle of fifteen-year-old Laphroaig, unscrew the cap, take a deep gulp and – "Aaaaaaaaaaaaaagh! Yuuuuuuuuuugh!" Puke! You guessed. Not whisky at all but malt urine. Once I came across a smartly dressed city type with a briefcase and a recent copy of *The Times* at his side. He was slumped in a ditch, his back against the muddy side, his pinstriped legs splayed out, stiff as corrugated iron. Dead. About twelve hours dead, at a rough guess (you can learn a lot about rigor mortis in The Dump if you make the effort, and believe me it sets in a lot quicker than most people realise). City Type was holding in his right hand a bottle of gin. The label showed a beefeater and the Tower of London, but whatever was in that bottle wasn't the genuine article at all. A Malevolent had filled the bottle with hydrochloric acid or similar. Whatever it was had snuffed out City Type on the spot. His lips were drawn back in a terrible snarl, his teeth bared like a tetanus sufferer. His eyes were screwed up and glaring. Dead as a door-knocker. So when I saw the gin miniature I didn't allow my emotions to run away with me. First of all I checked for booby traps (sometimes The Malevolents attach trip wires to interesting-looking things such as booze, objets d'art, tempting packing-cases). I've seen people snatch at something like a bottle of port, next thing it blows up in their face, or a precariously poised car chassis comes crashing down on them. *USEFUL TIPS 1. Never allow your emotions to run away with you. You never know where they may lead you. 2. Before picking up an interesting object, whether it is a book, a bottle of booze or an unmildewed cushion, examine it carefully for wires, string and black cotton. 3. Avoid rummaging for food or souvenirs in comfy-looking ditches which have old cardboard boxes, agricultural machinery or wrecked cars piled at the edges. It may be a trap.* As it happens, I was in luck. There were no wires or other suspicious attachments in evidence. The seal of the bottle was unbroken. The contents smelled of gin. A drop splashed on my skin didn't hurt at all. I took a little sip, and the gin ran thrillingly down my gullet and into my seedy innards. With greedy excitement I tipped the little bottle upside down and felt the liquid rush through me, its fire warming my guts. I suddenly felt it was one of those rare good-to-be-alive days, when everything goes right. I scrambled to the top of a nearby rubbish heap, feeling on top of the world. Lustily I vented a cubic metre of wind, whistled a few bars of "Jumping Jack Flash" and admired the view. Weather-wise it wasn't a bad day at all, only about eighty per cent toxic cloud, with inspiring glimpses of blue sky and occasional shafts of smoggy sunbeams. A family of rats emerged from inside a dead baby which someone had abandoned on a nearby mattress and I cheerily threw the empty bottle at them. The bottle missed and smashed with a merry tinkle on the burned-out skeleton of a pram. The rats glanced at me with weary indifference, then slouched off in the direction of Westminster. I scrambled back down the tangled mound of cold ashes, rotting vegetables and heaped black sacks. I'd almost reached the ground when I slipped on some cabbage leaves and went crashing sideways against some sacks. The weight of my body caused one to split open with a sudden bang, as if it contained something putrefying and gassy. Out from the split came a a slow ooze of cold chicken curry. And not just curry: borne on the sludge-coloured tide was a hard unidentifiable object. The curry was what you might call a bit high, and dappled with patches of green mould here and there, but you soon learn not to be fastidious in The Dump. I squatted excitedly on some back numbers of *The Economist* and began scooping the curry into my mouth. "There," I said to myself, "I just *knew* it was going to be a good day." The gin had given me quite an appetite and I tucked in heartily with both hands. As I ate I gradually worked my way towards the mysterious curry-covered object. Finally I pulled it out and began to lick off the curry to see what lay underneath. As soon as I'd lifted it free from the curry I had a pretty good idea from the double-barrelled shape what I was going to find and I was right. It was a pair of binoculars! Not just any binoculars either but Zeiss binoculars, with a X7 magnification. "How on earth does a pair of binoculars end up in a rubbish sack coated in chicken curry?" you might wonder. No use asking me. Let me just say that that one of the intriguing and interesting things about life on The Dump is the strange things that get thrown away for no apparent reason, not to mention the strange juxtaposition of things which don't belong together at all. You get a real sense of life's rich variety and mystery, living in The Dump. In fact you probably end up knowing more about life among The Barbarians than The Barbarians do themselves. Sometimes I must admit I've been quite shocked at the things I've discovered – pornographic magazines wrapped inside Church Diocesan Newsletters, used condoms concealed inside jam jars, obscene photographs hidden away in abandoned handbags and (once) a discarded Scout Master's uniform. Not to mention intimate letters containing graphic and astonishing descriptions and remarks which might have shamed the Marquis de Sade, all jostling together with mountains of empty gin bottles, empty whisky bottles, empty beer bottles, empty bottles of port and Martini Bianco and cider and Cointreau and sherry and brandy and vodka. You name it, The Dump will have it. Somewhere. Sometimes you get the feeling that all The Barbarians are interested in is sex and alcohol. Sometimes I think the only other place where you must learn about the truth of things is down in the city sewers, in among the shit and the gin bottles and the thousand-and-one things that guilty shamefaced folk flush down the lav when no one else is about. People make me puke but I don't have the sort of temperament ever to become an Apathetic. Admittedly I sometimes feel bilious, admittedly sometimes I nearly lose my head. Once I burst into tears over a cistern of goldfishes. But the thing I like about The Dump is that just when you start to get the glooms something turns up out of the blue to make it seem worth going on. Like that long-desired pair of binoculars. I licked the binos clean and was impressed by their appearance. They were a heavy, handsome black pair. Holding them I felt a real sense of power. I had a hunch they were probably German and had once been used in vitally important espionage work. I reached into my pocket for a tissue, gave the lenses a final polish and raised them to my eyes. Amazing, truly amazing. I could see the carcase of a rotting dog in vivid detail, even though it must have been three-hundred yards away. I could even make out the feverish activity of scores of grey-white maggots as they burrowed and frolicked in the bloodied blue-brown gash of the creature's burst stomach. I could see the whirr of tiny wings and the shimmer of sunlight on the bead-like bodies of bluebottles circling and spiralling amid the rising fumes of putrefaction. I was thrilled. I gave a little whoop of delight. The gin still jigged in my veins, bringing out the impulsive side of my nature. I decided then and there to set out at once in search of visual adventures. It is always a little hard to know in which direction to go in The Dump. One way is much the same as another – an endless uneven vista of rubbish heaps, sprawled garbage and broken machines illumined by spurts of emerging subterranean fire and shadowed by dark familiar toxic clouds. I stood there for some minutes, my heart thumping with expectation. Should I head South, in the direction of the Isle of Dogs? West, towards Tottenham and Finsbury Park? To the East the M11 beckoned, highway to the cloisters of Cambridge, the Fens, the rush of traffic going up and down the Great North Road. Northward lay reservoirs, bird sanctuaries, lonely islands, the call of the wild... Or how about South West, to Penge? Perhaps it was spring, perhaps I should try – Nique ta Mère! – Paris. Pop across on le smouldering Shuttle and commit verbal outrage against public authority. Or piss in the Panthéon. Or instead head for Carthage. It would be nice to head for Carthage to see if it still exists. There's a rumour, a suburb of Tumour. Eh? Or perhaps Lacedaemon. Or Zug. Zug sounds like the sort of place someone like me would enjoy. So many choices, so many miles of unending, fresh rubbish to explore. My appetite for travel was often whetted by the travel brochures I'd come across in The Dump. There's nothing quite so pleasurable as squatting in a warm ditch gazing at pictures of tanned young women stretched out invitingly in skimpy bikinis on deserted sandy beaches. I have spent many happy hours turning the pages of glossy brochures, absent-mindedly pinching my fleas, or pleasurably picking the crispy limestone-like formations inside my nostrils, or using the narrow end of a biro's cap to scrape the sportive threadworm from their cavortings and convulsions around the plump crater's lip of my hot, reeking anus, all the while excitedly comparing the merits of Poros and Zakynthos, of Agistri and Skopelos, of Rhodes or Kos. To head for Corfu or Crete? – an agonising choice. Would the climate damage my parasites? – the cretinous blonde girl in the travel agent's would be, I felt certain, quite unable to tell me. She would press a concealed button and the manager, a sleek bryclreemed thug named Den, would escort me out of the complex. Pity. I used to love going in and helping myself to a clutch of luminous brochures (no thanks, just browsing). I suppose it's because a travel brochure brings out the existentialist in all of us. A travel brochure makes you face up to iron choices and the randomness of destiny. I have spent months pouring over the relative merits of large Greek villages offering friendly hospitality and close to bustling Rhodes Town while still retaining their character, apartments in the centre of Ixia ideally located just 345 metres from the beach and 250 metres from the nearest disco, comfortable two-bedroom apartments with kitchenette (cooking rings and fridge), bathroom with shower and that all-important w.c., and rooms on the main road about 470 metres from the main street of Falikaris with a disco just across the road and a nearby supermarket. My idea of hell, if you must. Vomiting youths, stinking traffic, girls shrieking, the moronic electronic all-night throb of idiot music. Sometimes I used to scoop up half a dozen fleas and bring them into my agonizing decision-making. I'd line them up and watch them hop across the grids in the brochure's table of preferences. For some reason Lively After Dark almost always came out the winner, closely followed by Good Food. Local History, Great for Families, Good Beaches and Variety of Watersports never did very well. But many's the day when I wasn't in the mood for Greece, no matter how louring the sky. Stuff Lindos, a lovely magical place which everyone should see at least once, with the formidable walls of a castle looming over the town halfway up a steep rocky hill, with sand beach and harbour below and the remains of a temple to Athena on top of the rock and a quite breathtaking view over the village to the turd-dotted sea. As often occurred at the end of a dizzying perusal of brochures, I closed my eyes, spun on my heel – and fell flat in the mud (my heel had fallen off). So many choices in life! Once I took a cabbage into town to buy some cloisters but today I decided to head in the direction of my nose. Always a good idea if the existential grandeur of available choices threatens to overwhelm. My nose, half-immersed in a sort of grey sludge I instantly recognised as wet ash, was pointing approximately south-west. Right, I thought. Penge it is. I staggered to my feet, snorting a few times to get the muck out of my nostrils. I made half-hearted efforts to scrape some of the slime off my blazer and trousers just in case I bumped into someone I might need to impress. Then, slinging the binocular straps over my right shoulder I set off across a grey ocean of waste paper and smouldering ashes. I walked all day without meeting a soul. All day I sang to myself, or whistled, or hummed. "Hallelujah, I'm a Bum!" "Though cowards flinch and traitors sneer..." "A great while ago the world began..." Etcetera. The sun was blotted out by cloud and it became a typical Dump day, grey and empty. Periodically I stopped by small mountains of garbage and scrambled to the top. Raising the binoculars to my eyes I scanned the smoky distances for signs of life or interesting rubbish. Apart from crowds of lively rats and the occasional distant emaciated dog nothing moved. As the afternoon waned I found shelter beneath a mahogany table. Like Madame de Clèves I was not in a state to sleep. I say mahogany, for all I know it was oak. The only wood I have ever been able to identify is balsa wood, from my childhood glider days. Let me simply say that it was everything I imagined mahogany to be. The table was dark brown, knotty and still had an inspiring shine, as if refusing to be bowed down by adversity. It was a table that had seen better days. It had probably spent many happy years in Buckinghamshire, weighed down by fine food and wine and sprayed with Lord Jenkins' spittle and his fat-bottomed, plump-bellied, florid-faced very agreeable political wisdom, not to mention a splatter of freshly lisped anecdotes concerning the contemporary press. Then its owners had decided to replace it, and now here it was, all alone in a waste land of ash and rain and smoke. Somewhere along the line it had lost a leg, and as I crouched beneath it I watched it sway a little in the breeze and heard the rattle of its leaves. Some black rubbish sacks were conveniently to hand, and I split them open with my knife. There is nothing like a good rummage through someone's rubbish just before nightfall. The tease of enigmatic scraps. *Whatever happened to Dorcas?* scrawled in an agonised hand. What can we say? The pressure in the script is erratic. The t bar crossing is wavy. The westward swing of the p and the shrivelled d give the game away. I see lurches of mood, a powerful mother, instability, a yearning for islands, stamp collecting, a fondness for Tolstoy. As for *Buses back every hour, quarter past the hour at Dollarton. Transfer to 910 at 2nd Narrows Bridge.* Note the phallus-shaped upper loops. This is the work of a man of deranged politics and abnormal sexual appetites. Ripped pages, scraps. Sheer bliss. *This is the story of a man, one who was never at a loss.* Once, I remember, I actually found a tin of condensed milk which some sweet, mischievous child must have tossed into Mummy's swing-bin, doubtless in revenge for some harsh parental admonition. But this time there were no treats in store, merely cold chips, used tissues, empty baked-bean cans and the torn-up remains of someone's insurance policy which stated in a quaint copperplate font – don't ask me which one, fonts were never one of my strong points – that the policy did not cover loss or damage directly or indirectly occasioned by or happening through or in consequence of war, invasion, acts of foreign enemies, hostilities (whether war be declared or not), civil war, rebellion, insurrection, terrorism or military or usurped power, riot or civil commotion nor legal liability of whatsoever nature directly or indirectly caused by or contributed to, by, or arising from ionising radiations or contamination by radioactivity from any irradiated nuclear fuel or from any nuclear waste from the combustion of nuclear fuel or the radioactive toxic explosive or other hazardous properties of any explosive nuclear assembly or nuclear component thereof, or abduction by intergalactic aliens whether miniscule, gigantic, slimy, fanged, winged or of leathery appearance, from any zone of the universe whatsoever, not excluding parallel universes, worm holes, black holes, yellow supergiants, double stars, white dwarfs, orange giants, Cepheid-type variables, large globular clusters of all classes of stellar luminosity, planets and moons, including The Moon, whether or not at gibbous phase. All of which perked me up no end as I reflected upon what The Barbarians had coming to them. It would be no use them coming to me for sympathy, no way. And on this happy thought I gulped down the cold chips, used two of the rubbish sacks as a pillow and fell asleep under the possibly mahogany table, its leaves still rattling gently in the evening breeze. A trail of cartoon zeds emanated from my lice-infested scalp. Inane rhymes rattled away. *Little Peter Rabbit had a prickle in his prick, so he pulled it and pulled it and – ooh!* And Thanatos. Thanatos in the darks outside, Thanatos gathering in the hollow boring afternoons, Thanatos in the empty mornings, the empty bed. Inanition! The old noble endeavour to be heard above – pardon – the wind. Pope John Paul II crawled across the floor. I expected him to look a faded yellow, like old yolk on a tie. The spectacle of a large hairless humanoid came as a considerable shock. He was kneeling, naked, in front of a crumpled picture of Jayne Mansfield, vigorously massaging his inguinal region. Beyond his wizened buttocks I caught a glimpse of the crosses that run from Tata Mai Lau down to Lake Tacitolu, near where the stinking old man said Mass in 1989. I turned away in disgust and decided to go trampolining in Australia. Somebody said something about Aztecs. The educational system ensured that my child learned the dates of wars, the surnames of portly statesmen. Australia? Australia is formed of a layer of honey and dead Aborigines. These rest on sheets of cardboard several miles thick. For understandable reasons the study of geology is restricted to an élite. Question. For ten points. Is Australia the shape of (i) a stain (ii) the damaged remains of the fossilised skull of a hitherto undiscovered dinosaur (iii) the mildewed pear we discovered in Jane's kitchen, after her death? Bigger and better trampolines are being invented all the time. On the best you can bounce more than six miles into the air. The blue skies are filled with young, healthy, streamlined figures passing hither and thither. Sarah sniffed her scrapings. "These are the droppings of a postmodernist," she said, with an air of knowledgeable authority. Mandeville broke in. "Have you had" – he paused. He looked at me keenly. "Have you had any strange experiences?" I told him about the earlier episode when someone tried to shoot me. "But of course," I explained, "it was just an hallucination. Probably a chemical reaction in that tin of condensed milk I ate." "No," he said. "Not an hallucination." "Not an hallucination?" "By no means. You were experiencing that most dreadful of all forces. Worse than a raging storm. Worse than tempest or typhoon. Worse than an elephant's fart. Worse than a Japanese earthquake. Worse than the blast of a bomb." I waited expectantly. He did not disappoint me. "Revision!" he said. "The creative process. Deletions, tinkerings, rewritings. 'Silver Blaze,' say. An old story. "'We are going well," he remarked, looking out of the train window and glancing at his watch. "Our rate at present is fifty-three and a half miles an hour." I sighed, realising the seriousness of my poor friend's condition. "Yes, yes of course we are," I said, soothingly. "The telegraph posts upon this line are sixty yards apart!" "Yes, yes. Sixty yards apart. Of course. Clever of you to have had the foresight to measure them." My poor friend's descent into madness had been evident for some months and was a source of continual concern to everyone who knew him. Earlier in the year he had emerged from a polling booth, grinning like a monkey and shouting that he had just voted Conservative in order to get the economy moving again. On another occasion he had been distinctly heard to say that the royal family were a credit to the nation. As a doctor I was unhappily aware that there had recently been some severe outbreaks of Delusion in the south, and my friend's case was the worst I had come across. "I am afraid that I shall have to go," he had remarked that morning at breakfast. "Go! Where to?" "To Dartmoor – to King's Pyland." A furtive glance at a gazetteer of Britain revealed that there was no such place, but I decided to play along with my friend's little fantasy. "I should be most happy to accompany you," I replied, reaching for my bag of sedatives and tranquillizers. "Good. Your time will not be misspent. There are points about this case which promise to make it an absolutely unique one. No one should be surprised that this is the one topic of conversation throughout the length and breadth of England!" "No one," I echoed blandly, disturbed to hear my friend talking like a journalist on one of the cheaper newspapers.' And so on," Mandeville gasped, as I hurriedly erased him. Night fell like all the other nights. Like the night we drove up Bredon Hill. The night I saw movement on the step at the back of that Cotswold pub. Cockroaches, gleaming like creatures from Mare

Acidalium. The night at Brindisi. The Athens night. The night in Seattle. The night at Claremont Road. The night you were caught in the draught from an unfinished draft. So to speak. Between drafts, yes. That bullet was real. I am in terrible pain. I bleed. I need a nurse. A nurse? Nurse Molly Ffunntt. A sexy little thing. Black hair, cheeky eyes. Fishnet stockings. Breasts like melons. Her eyes conspired with her armpits to give her away. Asking for it, she was. Begging for it. Dripping. Reeking. Juicy seaweed slopping on a brimming tide. Wanting it, over and over again. Acrobatic. Broad-minded. Interested in experiment. Christ. What? I've got an erection! My first for seventeen years! It will drive me mad, I know it will. I haven't even seen a woman all year. I mopped my face. I stared anxiously at the tumour welling up in my lower midriff. Grotesque. "Wake up for Sharp's sake!" a voice screeched. "You haven't listened to a word I've been saying, have you? I can see you've repaired to a brown study. I thought I'd made it crystal clear. The bullet was from the first draft. It was real. Then he spared you. For something altogether worse, I wouldn't mind betting. And by the way, you didn't drink any condensed milk." "I swear I did! I remember it vividly. It had a white label. I searched for days before I found a suitable tin-opener." "You don't know your own mind. You're talking nonsense." "Oh really?" "You'll see. You'll find out. Until this bloody thing is published we are all at risk. Anything can happen at any time. Death. Mutilation. An operation performed by a bungling amateur." He shuddered. "An operation?" "He bought a second-hand book about surgery when he was on holiday in Dorset. A terrifying thing." "Who did? What holiday in Dorset? What on earth are you talking about?" "For God's sake keep your voice down! He might hear us!" "Who?" "Shut up. I'm going. I never saw you before. I hate you. If you suddenly find yourself requiring a Hodgen's splint don't say I didn't bloody warn you. And even when the book's out you won't be safe!" "What do you mean?" "Remember Henry James! Not satisfied with the published version, oh no. A right one for the scissors and ink, he was. And remember what happened to the end of *Great Expectations*. Not to mention *The Magus*. Some of these bloody writers are no better than Hollywood producers. They'll do anything. Sometimes to suit themselves, sometimes to please the punters. For example, John Barth's first book, can't remember the title. Not to mention what might have happened to *Under the Volcano*. Lowry was quite prepared to countenance cuts for a paperback edition. Cuts! I ask you! Admittedly by 1952 the poor sod was getting desperate. So don't say I haven't warned you. Don't think your genitals are your own, they're not. You're never safe in this game." My hands dropped downward, forming a protective cup around my crotch. He was raving. All the same, best not to take chances. I watched him run out of sight, skipping along as if in extreme discomfort from spermatorrhoea. About twenty minutes later I heard a scream of pain followed by a soft of PHUT! A greyish pillar of muck erupted into the sky from beyond the horizon. Whether this event had anything to do with the previous sentences remains uncertain. I hurried away, extracted a shiny brochure from my rags and relaxed beside a malodorous mound of putrefying pilchards. Four-score dead eyes gazed listlessly at me. *What could be better than a weekend in Amsterdam? Don't miss De Pijp. The perfect spot to observe Amsterdammers going about their business.* What a disgusting suggestion. Why should I nourish a desire to observe zipped bilinguals going about their malodorous business? The notion sickens me. I shall go nowhere near the Low Countries. A filthy, depraved, drug-ridden brackish place, by all accounts. The sickly reek of tulips would make me puke. I would end up in swordfights with belligerent windmills. The same goes for everywhere else. Three nights in New York? Hell. I do not wish to Discover Turkey or anywhere else. To mooch around fountains and piazzas is a loathsome prospect. The faintest thought of shopping sprees or lazy canal trips brings on a severe migraine. I have a vampire's attitude to sunlight. Stuff the glorious views of the Palatine or the Castelo de Sao Jorge. Who wants to waste a second of their lives gawking at Sainte Chapelle and the Palais de Justice? I wish to avoid places Where Art Meets Architecture. Balls to the Museum of Classical Art (a load of Bosch). Balls to the places where PoMo style meets gothic elegance. Faced by La Casa Pedrera I would only yawn. Force me on to the Laederstraede and I would flee, propelled by explosive farts, bored and unwell. I can do without The Liberties or the Alfama. I shudder to think of the ideal weather conditions which can be experienced at Aqaba. The very word resort makes me resort to the little room. As mother always called it. I detest scheduled seat configurations. The very idea of an itinerary makes me sick. I can do without a walk through the siq. Bugger Belém. Bugger the monumental arch and the royal tombs. Bugger the Mosteiro dos Jerónimos with its marvellously elaborate cloister. Sod the turn-of-the-century stucco and impressive wooden panelling. Sod the Schönbrunn palace, summer residence of the imperial family. Air-conditioning, yech. Gentle spring sunshine brings me out in a cold sweat. Fresh air, exercise, horror. Company? Horror. As for the food! Defecate the lot, the Viennese patisseries, the roast pork and sauerkraut, the grilled prawns, the vanilla ice with brandy-soaked raisins resembling a blend of grout and rabbit shit. The very thought of the glamour of the Côte d'Azur chills me to the marrow. I can manage at best a spark of interest in Les Lanternes des Morts but I shall never visit them, no. I do not wish to get on, let alone get off, the beaten track. Just leave me alone, will you! In my warm ditch. My most memorable ditch contained an intriguing excavation about the shape of a large ham. In it I read in its entirety *Hamlet*, which I had only once seen performed, by a hambone. Its widest space at the innermost end. The hole through which you entered was the narrowest part, the knuckle of the ham. I masked the hole with an armful of oxidised paper. The size of the hole itself I reduced with rectangular blocks of language. Scraps of Tolstoy, Turgenev, whatever came to hand. Dostoyevsky was never much help. Each block was faced with dirt, rubbish and leftovers. The small remaining aperture allowed foul air to pass both ways. Compressed alongside gigantic Molly, whom I had lured into my hidey-hole with the promise of jelly, I found myself kneaded into the swelling thigh of the ham. I had expected to suffer from cold but the earth was dry and surprisingly warm. Molly's huge body exuded heat, moisture and bursts of succulent, bubbling gas. The atmosphere quickly became more than tropical. Her coarse pubic hair grated against my stomach like sandpaper. She munched her jelly contentedly, smiling tenderly at my pitiful wrinkled drooping organ. Despite our best efforts it refused to budge. "Not since–" I began, but she pressed a finger to her lips and winked. Incidentally, my mind is going. It may just be age. When I was tested I had the top score of anyone on the Holmes and Rahe social readjustment rating scale. I was advised I would never, ever readjust. "Interested in brass rubbings?" I asked the shrink. I know the type, sneaking up beside girls on the tube, muttering "Dost want ter walk wi' me?" and "I could die for the touch of a woman like thee" and "Eh! Tha'rt lovely to touch!" and "Why it's suicide for a man to go in there!" and "Sibelius's Fourth Symphony is a veritable White Dwarf in the musical firmament!" and "'Appen as yer'd come ter th' cottage one time" and similar drivel. I am sick of women. Of bipeds in general. Give me solitude and a nice warm ditch any day. Are you, like me, nervously aware of the fallibility of engines? You can guess how carefully I chewed over what I was to tell mother. What's that? Good news! Bubonic plague has returned to New York! Cholera has also made a comeback! Word spread. Across The Dump a cheer went up. Schadenfreude is a delicious emotion. We savoured the thought. The big apple – rotten to the core! Next morning after breakfast I scrutinised the climate. Breakfast? A rind, the creature unidentifiable. I sucked it, dreaming of three martinis and a bowl of nembutal. It was a windy day. One of those days when tired butterflies depart for California. One of those days when a filthy old man crouches behind the hut in the park, humming the Agitato from Schnittke's third string quartet. One of those days when you are liable to encounter degenerate centrist fragments of the Fourth International. One of those days when it seems more important than ever to touch your toes. Tone up those muscles! Avoid lapsing back into a form of Second Internationalism! One of those days when you encounter the abbreviation CUN'T. As in *I won't say it to you 'cause you cun't understand it.* As disgusting a piece of innuendo as you could possibly hope to come across in a book about pubescent boys. And by Richmal Crompton too! I shall write and protest. At least, I would if I could ever breach The Great Barrier and get back to the land of the Barbarians. Ah, The Dump, The Dump. Shut off from the outside world as if at the request of a Chief Constable and granted by the Home Secretary both equally concerned that a trespassory assembly might occur without the consent of a member of the ruling class, resulting in serious disruption to the concerns of bigots, capitalists and/or Conservatives under Section 14(2) of the Public Order Act (1986). At times like a battlefield, like Passchendaele, or the broken temples, the wastes, after the Tet offensive. Eh? Eh? Easy now, Robinson. Calm down. Your face bright red. Your hair, what's left of it, lets drop a few more grey tufts. You need a break, sport. A brisk stroll in an imaginary park. An invigorating circumnavigation of the spectral lake. Pause amid the Siberian breeze to admire the defecating ducks, the howling sobbing children, the screaming mother, the hatchet-faced warden, the cretinous bourgeoises towing their shit-bloated quadrupeds past the NO DOGS notice. Easy, easy. Time for your tumbler of Bénédictine. The bouts of deafness get worse. Sleep, it is a blessed thing. Until woken by the traffic, the mental hammering, the tilt and spin of the planet. A terrifying thing to be whirled around all the time at 70,000 mph on a lump of rock! Pinned down as I am by gravity. Given a risible breathing space. Time for a fizzing mugful of health salts specially formulated to ease upset stomachs, *Angst*, indigestion, biliousness, constipation and acute dehydration. Just the thing at one thirty in the morning to flush away the mouthslime, that parched middle-of-the-desert sensation, that you've-done-it-again-you-fool feeling. Drink before effervescence subsides. No sweat. What's that? For heartburn. Heartburn! It will take more than two spoonfuls and half a glass of water to put out that inferno, I can tell you. I feel awful. Sick and ill. Cramps in my chest. Too ghastly for. Words. But I'll. Try. I'll do my. Miserable best. It horrifies me to think that the duty of the peritoneum is to anchor the intestines to the front of the backbone and to convey blood-vessels and nerves to the walls of the intestine. It disgusts me to discover that the muscular coat has fibres of muscle arranged lengthwise on the outer surface and round and round on the inside. I don't think I can bear to hear any more about that loose tissue between the muscle and the mucous coat or details relating to that inner mucous layer which contains the various digestive glands. It is nauseating to contemplate the folds of the mucuous membrane of the small intestine. Or the various types of glands opening on the inner surface of the intestine. Speak to me not of succus entericus. Eh? The yellow alkaline fluid, you oaf! It blends the juices of these glands. Whisper not of the multitude of very small projections which cover the surface of the inner side of the small intestine. Never mention digestion, never tell of how lumps of ingested matter (food, if you must) pass from the stomach into the duodenum. A hideous fate, to be swamped by bile and pancreatic juice. Screen me from knowledge of how the dissolved portions are rapidly absorbed by the mucous membrane while the unabsorbed parts pass onwards to the large bowel, of how these savaged lumps from the small intestine enter the large intestine through the ileo-caecal valve and are then subjected (poor things!) to brutal peristaltic movements, not to mention rhythmic segmentation, until for some (vile thought!) putrefaction occurs. Tell no one that the contents of the large intestine are bacteria, bile, mucus, unabsorbed food and excess of digestive juices. That the bacteria form nearly half of the solids excreted. That the colour of shit is mostly due to the bile. That the presence of food in the stomach has a marked reflex action in making the rectum contract. That this tendency is most marked when food is placed into a stomach which is completely empty. That the most suitable time to void the bowels and send a cosmic stench surging through the household is directly after that buttered, pockmarked crumpet. "The bowel is a creature of habits and to make it work with maximum efficiency it should be made to contract and expel its contents at precisely the same time every day," said Stevenson. "Experts believe 8.37 a.m. (Greenwich Mean Time) produces the best results. The rectum can also be important when dealing with very ill people. There is some evidence to show that such persons can be kept alive by pumping a glucose solution up their arse. This treatment is very popular with passive homosexuals." Some mornings, when he walked, Stevenson felt that one leg was shorter than the other. His thin lips incessantly twisted into a malevolent smile. He was an expert on runes. He could talk for hours about R F S H F + (a rough, crude, inappropriate transcription) the earliest runic carving in England. Sixteen hundred years old! Apparently. Found in the cremation cemetery at Caistor, just outside Norwich. Carved on the ankle-bone of a roe deer. Its text, says Professor Page, reads *raïhan*. Which means "roe deer". Apparently. Far away, on the shore at Selsey, two strips of gold were washed ashore. The rune on one reads *brnrn*. This, says Professor Page, "does not look as if it ever meant anything". Seventeen million dead last year, not bad, not bad at all, eh? As for me, you. Be patient. The game will soon be up. Half an hour at best. I stir my dregs. Call me a whirl-brain that talks whatever comes uppermost. Observe my alternating layers of muck. Muck? A paste comprised of mud, soot, cement dust and chicken blood. Encrusted upon my skin from brow to chin. Only natural in my condition you might think. Owing to the perpetual clouds of thick black smoke. A richly toxic smoke emanating from burning tyres, incinerated plastic, foam-filled furniture, you name it. Apart from hygiene nuts and a handful of new arrivals, everyone in The Dump is black as sin (as mother used to say). Indeed, members of the ethnic community are often surprised to discover that they feel quite at home in The Dump. Racial discrimination is unknown. The only white people you see in The Dump are the new arrivals and The Soapers. No matter how trim and fragrant they might be when they first arrive, by the end of their first day the new arrivals are as grimy and foul-smelling as the next person. Unless, of course, they arrive clutching a tablet of soap. Soap is especially prized by members of deranged religious cults, who scrub themselves like lunatics. Often they foam at the mouth. They dream of a new home in one of eight available styles (Classical, Tudor, Georgian,

Neo-Colonial, Imperial, Chic French, Enchanted Greek or Machiavellian), the nice sun shining down from a nice clear sky. A blue sky. A winnowing wind, small gnats engaged in hybridized discourse among the river sallows, drowsy tinklings, blushing roses, a stern Lawrentian rainbow in the russell sky. It was on such a day that I met the old man with an inexhaustible fund of stories. The story of the bucket and the beautiful woman. The story of the old man and the missing comb. The story of the princess and the cod. The story of the long queues at the local supermarket. The story of Sibelius's silence. The story of G's forty winks. The story of the traffic warden. The story of the Great Trigonometrical Survey of India. The story of the de Sade study aid with excellent illustrations drawing attention to difficult passages, common areas of difficulty and areas which carry most marks in any examination. The story of the important letter that disappeared. The story of Louise Bryant's six months. The story of the trader who lived on Konkumba island. The story of the young man who flew to a strange city and had many remarkable adventures there. The story of Dobson. Dobson was a moody fellow who did not much like people, other than loose women, whom he loved to shake and jangle, cocking his ear and grinning. Sometimes he brooded about the silent compulsion of economic relations, sometimes about commodity fetishism. Sometimes he'd shriek: "Storm the Reality Studios!" And so the years go by. This is a keyboard, that is a window. This is not a mountain, it is my thumb. Over there is the fireplace and the red train. This is my llama. This is my biscuit. These are my piglets. I have seven. I am not. You are not. He is not. She is not. It is not. Berwald is not. He died on April 3. Kjerulf died on August 11. Lalo died on April 22. Chabrier died on September 13. Lekeu died on January 21. Fibich died on October 15. "The sea is hungrier than death," asserted Swinburne, East Anglia. We are not. You are not. They are not, especially Plomer. Who are you? How are you? All is tickle with me. Eh? What are you all? *In the background – behind the affably grinning old gentlemen, the fashionable dandies, the elegantly infirm old widows and the perfumed beauties in their cashmeres, ostrich feathers, and garlands of flowers and diamonds – stood the constable with his waterproof coat, greasy oilskin hat and truncheon – the reverse side of the coin.* Is that right? How many books are in my head? How many windows are there in your mind? Please leave at once. I at once cried out. He knew at once what had happened. Anyone suffering from diarrhoea alternating with constipation should consult a doctor at once. Coat lightly with flour and laugh. Avoid Cairo. "And?" said Dobson. "And that was that." "Ah, well. You know what they say." "What do they say?" "Man is born unto trouble, as the sparks fly upward." "Being old and full of gas." "Fancy! I hadn't heard." Flauerbouiller! They yearned for the legible. Night fell. A mist came down. And behold, there came a great wind from the wilderness, and smote the four corners of the structure, collapsing it. They are all gone now. Little more than ghosts. Bare bones. As for little me. I look like a human porpoise. Or did, once. In my heyday. All gone. I only am escaped alone to tell thee. Then there were other times, times I'd be feeling rather gloomy and downcast when a sudden streak of cheerfulness would break in and off I'd go, over the sludge and the mass graves, humming some such tune as "Jerusalem" or "Land of Hope and Glory" or perhaps chirpily whistling "Roses Are Blooming in Picardy". Or perhaps I'd overhear the tunes of others, a robust ex-postman greatly resembling Dirk Bogarde crooning "I'm Laughing On The Outside But Crying On The Inside", a nuclear physicist with a blooming complexion bellowing something soulful by Norma Egstrom. A waif humming "The Tennessee Waltz". "Cold, Cold Heart". Next I tried to cry but could only raise a squeak like a bat. Beneath me the powdery crackle of broken glass, quite distinct from the faint distant throb of amplified sounds predominantly characterised by the emission – the emission! – of a succession of repetitive beats. Sorry, didn't I mention the mass graves before? I've got so much to tell you I can't possibly hope to remember everything, can I? Be fair. The Dump is such a stimulating environment there are bound to be things I've forgotten to tell you about and which just slip out by accident. The mass graves. Her smile. My poor old dick, for example, as the woman says in Peckinpah's last. Peckinpah's thirteenth I wrote in the first draft, quite overlooking, as you should, *The Deadly Companions*. Hollywood! Conversation was somewhat spasmodic for the next half hour. "We'll get the data hot off the line. Art's coming with us." "We can always leave early if we get bored." "You never know where you'll end up." "I've seen her somewhere I'm sure. Who is she?" "Do you mean you don't know?" "Fragmentary in the extreme. Nobody can fit the facts together." Hollywood, yes. I work there, you know. Really? Yeah. In animation. Mostly. I sketch chipmunks. But sometimes I work on screenplays. The doctor turned. "Why don't you go home. You can, you know." "I'm waiting for my hat." Her smile, her smile. In that long fresh light of waning April days which affects us often with a sadness sharper than the greyest days of autumn. As for the mass graves. The mass graves represent quite an interesting conundrum (a word Dobson taught me). You do not come across them very often, and always by accident, but nevertheless they are there (although I have often met Wanderers who indignantly deny their existence just because they have wandered for years and never come across one). They are usually discovered when half a dozen people get together and decide to have an organized excavation. A description? Pull the other one. If I don't get this manuscript off soon it may go up in smoke. Or be found in fragments. Worse, in multiple drafts. Next thing you'll have P zealously promoting the Z version, while Q defends the A-text and R holds fast to his B-edition and S prefers the C version. Or worse, reduced to a solitary scorched sheet. Like the blackened certificate I found one day. A very nice, very pretty certificate, with some lovely gold scroll around the margins. *THIS CERTIFICATE DOES NOT* it began *DOES NOT* it repeated *cover any consequence whether direct or indirect of foreign enemy hostilities (whether war be declared or not) civil war civil commotion rebellion revolution insurrection nationalised industry or military or usurped power or any consequence of aviation including defecation or urination royal or ordinary or mental illness or wilfully self-inflicted injury or illness or desperate headaches or cycling, motor-cycling, walking, hopping, swimming, pot-holing, nose-picking, fishing, hang-gliding, the breaking of wind, belching, parachuting, winter sports, summer sports, copulation, onanism, cunnilingus, buggery, bestiality, skin-diving, fetishism, transvestism, leather garments, thongs, intoxicating liquor, drugs or drug-addiction, and especially NOT drugs prescribed and directed by a qualified registered medical practitioner for the treatment of venereal disease.* One day, holding my valuable certificate, I shall drop down a hole without warning, a sixty-foot hole with barbed metal at the bottom, treacherously concealed by cardboard, perhaps a loose scattering of ash. Perhaps I will wake up in the Joy House shelter, Milwaukee. "All of a sudden, you think everything's okay, and then boom!" said Cynthia Geiger, who blames herself for believing she would get a warning notice before her welfare payments were docked. State and county officials vigorously deny that Wisconsin's aggressive welfare reform programme is responsible for the city's rise in homelessness. Or perhaps Indonesia. The Foreign Office minister said, "If water cannon is used to try to stop peaceful demonstrators, that is of course totally unacceptable; if it is used to stop rioters, that may be acceptable." Or perhaps I will be caught in one of the blow-outs, incinerated, or (more probably), just horribly burned, causing me to run here and there, soaked in fire, before collapsing on an old sofa, my skin hanging from me like seaweed. Unseen. In a flash. Goodbye! Night... Sweet dreams. A wheel started to turn round in my head and when I looked at the moon I saw that it was rotating in time. Goodbye. Hello, what's this? Scrap of old newspaper. Mrs Gillian Shephard, the Agriculture Minister, said she saw no problem in dealing with neo-fascists. "They are democratically elected," she said. Ah, the press! Ennui. Fatigue. Boredom. These are the dangers of life on The Dump. If it wasn't for the newspapers we would probably all succumb. It is the newspapers that alert us to the outside world, that give meaning to our poor miserable days. It is not a good thing to have a parochial attitude. Ennui must be fought, vigorously. Baudelaire must be blotted out. Dolour of mind and discomfort of flesh must be resisted. There must be no asking after Mr Campbell or George Hardt or the Snow Bird. One must never say, "By the way, what's become of Claude Fessenden?" What becomes of anyone? Older, wrinklier, more fragile, patches of dry white flaking skin breaking out at the tips of your elbows, across your kneecaps, in patches on your back. Wind, and worse. The broken sheds, the heartbreak, the dews at even. Thickest dark. The slow clock ticking. And then... The gray-eyed morn. One morning, a morning when I might otherwise have decided to stay in my ditch, dozing (or worse), I came across an old newspaper which alerted me to the fact that I was not merely an inhabitant of The Dump. I was also A YEW-ROPE-EEEANN. As fit as an international flea, I ran along a foul-smelling ridge of imported vegetable refuse. Someone had scattered old German tyres there like stepping-stones and I hopped athletically from one to the next. Then, suddenly, all the enthusiasm seemed to go out of me. I stopped, got off the tyre upon which I was trembling and clambered down a slope of rotting apples to a shady dell where mushrooms were growing. I muttered to myself, a most satisfying mutter, then paused a moment for reflection. I considered the career of Courbet. Tick! tick! tick! Incidentally, I wish to deny absolutely the rumours about the disease in the temporal lobe of my brain. Total rot! As for those concerning my anus. The misrepresentation is fundamental. Tick! tick! tick! Autoscopic hallucination? Nonsense! Pass me that telescopic sight at once! Nightmare on Elm Street? Hold on, I won't be a tick. A quick scratch of my burning scalp, then time to take aim! Time to take stock. Of everything. Especially the. Not forgetting that. And above all. Tick! tick! tick! A pair of jackdaws dressed in trim, clean lounge suits were pecking at a garden tub. I lay down beside a heap of fractured plastic flowerpots and felt a great sense of ANXIETY surge through me. To what extent, I wondered, should the direction of improvements in the welfare state be halted or changed in the interests of controlling public spending and improving competitiveness by reducing business costs? Is it possible to engineer a switch of taxation which would prove beneficial to the environment? Can the European Union keep pace with the next industrial revolution of information technology? Can new forms of remuneration be found to encourage the unemployed to rescue the environment? Can layabouts be put to work caring for the increasing numbers of elderly people at less than the cost of a traditional public sector wage? Or would it be better to adopt an individualistic approach, involving oneself (say) in a multi-million dollar swindle to sell counterfeit money? Fortunately I was diverted from these weighty conundrums by a piece of good news. Cholera in Somalia had killed 675 people between February and June 1994, the United Nations reported. I quietly chuckled at my good fortune. So old yet so alive! Better still, very much better still, the year's toll of infectious diseases. Perks us up no end. Here, in The Dump. Here in this despised recess. Feeding on the scraps of others. Devouring their leavings. Ho! What's this? *A well-regulated militia* comma. *Being necessary to the security of a free state* comma. *The right of the people to keep and bear arms* comma. *Shall not* – CRACK! – *be infringed* – CRACK! Full stop. Tuning in, full stop. To sweet Dolores, full stop. Singing "I Just Shot John Lennon", full stop. To maugre winter's cold and the summer's worst excess. With an anacreontic swagger, no less. More cheering news! The British Housebuilder of the Year Awards were presented during an awards luncheon at the Hilton. Buyers were asked to judge their housebuilder on eleven key areas of customer service. God bless! Ah, the pleasure of porches. How do YOU shelter from the sun? Australians use verandahs and Greeks attach shutters to windows to keep their homes cool. In Britain we have the humble porch. The word porch (from the Latin word porticus) is the entrance area to a home. It not only acts as a shelter from the weather but is a convenient place to store umbrellas, overcoats, shopping bags. The porch is often lit, providing extra security for the householder when he returns home in the evening. Most importantly of all, it provides visitors with their first impression of a home and is a perfect place to hang plants. Or why not enliven your home with a reproduction? Incidentally, did I mention how erratic the news is? Drifts of old newspapers form in The Dump like dirty snow. Like dirty sand dunes. Dirtier even than the dogshitdotted dunes at Hunstanton, proud England's cleanest filthy beach. A story no sooner appears than it vanishes under the drift of a new story. Like the ancient WW2 anti-tank blocks at Hayling, submerged by fresh formations of sand. Elections, for example. Local elections, county council elections, general elections. Immense excitement. No one, of course, votes, but the results are always awaited with keen excitement. The electoral status of the inhabitants of The Dump is something of a puzzle. In theory everyone still has a vote in their old abode, but in practice since no one is able to get back there it is impossible to vote. This does not stop the parties occasionally drifting overhead in hot air balloons. The Conservatives warn ominously of the nightmarish future under a Labour Government. Taxes and prices would rocket. Hordes of discoloured immigrants and glistening aliens would pour in from all quarters of the planet, copulating like rabbits and defecating on posters of Constable's immortal "Haywain". The Labour candidates gaze down from a vast height with a shiny look of immense sympathy for our plight. They assure us that if they ever get elected they will certainly do something about the disgraceful housing to be found in The Dump. Under Labour things will certainly get better, though it is a question of waiting to see how this will happen, it would be unwise to make rash spending commitments. New cardboard roofing is certainly a possibility, though it will not be possible to be sure of this within the lifetime of a single Labour Government. Leo said bitterly that pink balloons had been drifting over The Dump throughout the whole of the twentieth century and nothing had changed. He was hushed to silence by Leopold, who was pointing excitedly at a yellow aerostat. "Look!" he cried excitedly. "Hot Air Liberal Democrats!" Words plummeted down upon us. "Liberals believe in the three ems: in middles, in moderation, in mildness." It began to rain. Someone enquired about the history of The Dump. Traces remain. Bones, possibly of mammoths. Buckets. Old pipe stems. Bits of red brick. Mysterious black pipes. Old signs. LUNATICS ONLY BEYOND THIS POINT and BEWARE. Rusty vats. Bars. Dirty straitjackets. Megaphones. Lengths of flex. Cracked lenses the size of dinnerplates. Coils of bleached film with torn sprockets. It was not far from the mysterious black pipes that I first encountered the literary critic one autumn afternoon. He was sitting on a Michelin tyre, with a disconsolate expression upon his face. Greying, going bald on top, he was a little bearded man in his forties. From the absence of soot and stains on his jacket and trousers I deduced he was a new arrival. Also, his teeth were white and in excellent condition. Good teeth are a dead giveaway. Anyone who has been in The Dump for any length of time inevitably displays a mouthful of rotten teeth, the result of poor diet and a complete absence of dental practitioners. When he saw me he gave a nervous start, and yelped, "How squalid, commonplace and unliterary this whole place is." Then he burst into tears. I allowed him to lean on my shoulder and gave him an encouraging pat on the head. Sobbing, he muttered a peculiar jargon, asking for the direction of the nearest seminar group. He didn't care what period. Normally he was an Eighteenth-Century man (although he did sometimes teach a course on Hemingway), but in the circumstances he was prepared to partake in a discussion of absolutely anything – Silver Poets of the Sixteenth Century, the novels of George Eliot, imagery in Woolf. He was so desperate that he was even prepared to talk about critical theory, something which, as a traditional English empiricist, he abhorred. I shook my head and broke the news that critical seminars did not exist in The Dump. Not wishing to encourage false illusions I also bluntly told him about The Great Barrier. He snorted and gave a rasping laugh. "Your Barrier doesn't bother me," he said. "Critical penetration, that's all that's needed." He set off at once in search of an abandoned copy of *The Principles of Literary Criticism*. I did not see him again until several days later, when I strolled over to The Great Barrier to see how he was getting on. I must admit I was not at all surprised to find him sitting, motionless, on a broken sofa. He was trembling and seemed wet. And his face! A dirty, unwashed, unshaven face. Red-eyed, in fact. In utter misery. All around him lay torn pages of literary criticism. His clothes were filthy and torn. Dirt smeared his elbows, which protruded through the rags. "On Margate Sands," he muttered. Over and over again. "Oh en em ess." Months later was observed waving a cutting. "Where, in Trollope," he screamed, "are the millions who filled the factories worked the mines fought the wars and so created but never shared in the wealth that enabled his characters to rub along so comfortably?" *Michael Hutton, SE5.* A very good question. But such little dramas are rare. Most days nothing happens at all. The occasional blackened banana skin is discovered, is greedily joobled and slanked. Sometimes a brittle crust, perhaps even encrusted with flaked wheat and sesame seeds. An original, unforgettable taste from a far-off land, a remote region of Russia. A loaf made from an original fifth-century recipe, including emulsifiers (E471, E472e), Flour Treatment Agent, Ascorbic Acid and genetically engineered soya beans. But most days neither skin nor crust. Most days you have to get by with a munched mouthful of empty matchbox, or a box of grass cuttings. Most days it just rains ceaselessly and you have to huddle somewhere dry and cosy, as best you can, and starve. And when I say it rains I do not mean a dramatic rain, clattering like pistol shots on old sheets of corrugated iron, backed up by incandescent twigs of lightning, flashes, stupefying thunderclaps, nonsense like that. No. I mean a soft enfeebled rain, barely more than drizzle, the most boring rain imaginable. The sort of rain that makes you want to scoop a shallow grave in the sludge and lie down forever. The sort of rain that makes you think of Berryman, of the Orwell Bridge outside Ipswich. A passing barque. The road to Pin Mill. The cobbled concrete islands upon which the legs of the bridge rest. Some days it doesn't even rain, there's just cloud, grey unending cloud, and nothing happens, not even the rats are out. Some days you have to invent yourself anew. Spent and frail as you are. Do not think I am unaware of the comparison which has been made between myself and Mr Muddle, that popular children's cartoon character who goes through life walking backwards and is forever banging into things, all the while grinning stupidly. Some days you have to make do with licking the rust-coloured sauce left in someone's discarded tin of baked beans. Some days you're so starved and wet and depressed you think you can't face another day, and you start looking at the knife-sharp edge of the tin lid with unspeakable longing. Most days are like this in The Dump. Don't be fooled into thinking life on The Dump is one long round of picaresque adventure. It isn't. My real adventures finished long ago, before I got here. Most days in The Dump are wet and dirty and boring and at best dangerous. But mustn't grumble. Far away in Thailand the 200,000 child prostitutes are going about their business with American sailors and tourists from Japan, France, Germany, the Netherlands and Britain. Far off in Mesopotamia, thousands of slightly under-nourished children not-yet-five are quenching their thirst with brown water. On Smokey Mountain, in Manila, the feverish children scavenge and cough and spit in the ashen rain. After six hours of sorting through garbage for pieces of glass, tin and plastic you can make fifty pesos. What's that? The light's bad over here. My voice is going. Why don't we just trade stories? As Richard Gere says in *Intersection*. Half-senseless sense of an ending. *Dear Sir, I am in a Mad house and quite forget your Name or who you are you must excuse me for I have nothing to communicate or tell of and why I am shut up I don't know I have nothing to say so I conclude.* Once full of youth, radiance, enthusiasms! We shall weather these dreary times yet & drink our bottle together of an evening. Then back to abandonment and rain. Back to the old beginnings. Slime, blood, cord, scissors, scream. Weighing scales. Breast, nipple, slurp. The first howlings. Welcome to the rain. Many of the graves contained personnel items. Welcome to the lands of things that don't work anymore. The rejected, the worthless. The unwanted pages, the unwanted words. Place of desolation. The breakage and the waste. All that's used-up, finished with, gone. Rubbish everywhere. Talk about the environs of Fort Dimanche! A faint amber blotch on the smoky horizon indicating where the dawn sun is beginning its slow, wounded crawl across the grey polluted sky. Of course, it might not have been the sun at all. It might just have been the glow of flames from burning underground tyres. But on that particular morning I was in a good mood. As far as I was concerned it *was* the sun. It seemed to cast a warm, friendly glow over The Dump, turning the rust-powdered burned-out shell of a distant Volkswagen Beetle to burnished gold. It transformed puddles of oil to shimmering rainbow-coloured windows into a world of infinite mystery and beauty. My humble dribble of urine became a noble, bronze arc of the sort triumphant centurions might once have marched beneath. I gazed in delight and wonder as it dropped to mother earth, a triumph of liquid engineering. It splattered loudly across a colourless, rather washed-out portrait of John Major. For some reason – who was he? (the name was obviously bogus) – pictures of this man littered a patch of The Dump, like the object of a personality cult the morning after a people's revolution. The patch was not much of a patch. I remember I was trapped there for a while, as in a mire, my ankles immersed in a foul, sucking ooze. I used to call him the man with the frozen smile. From his phoney "Mr Average" appearance I assumed he was an actor who had fronted an advertising campaign for a major building society, a campaign designed to persuade investors to put their money into an exciting five-star ten-year saving scheme which would allow them to buy that long-longed-for dream house/dream car/world cruise for two but which had flopped miserably, resulting in a mass discarding of publicity material. "Busy old fool, unruly sun, why dost thou thus, through windows, and through curtains call on us?" I playfully bellowed as I zipped up my fly, causing a nearby family of five black mice feasting on the head of an old woman to scamper away in fear. I picked up my binoculars and set off once more across The Dump. I hadn't been walking for much more than an hour when something caught my eye in the distance. The black outline of a human figure, performing a strange ritual by a sack of rubbish. The sack of rubbish was vertical. It was a little like one of those strange packages you see in the warehouse in *Reservoir Dogs*, but darker. Except (tee hee!) it's not a warehouse. I trudged closer. The figure was

Welsh, or perhaps Afro-Caribbean. I realised at once what was happening. The man was a fiery socialist who had slithered almost to the top of New Labour. He'd been made a Privy Councillor and hadn't broken the habit. The bloated, foul-smelling sack was obviously intended to be the sovereign. The fiery socialist bowed, and approached the sack. He lowered his right kneecap on to a bucket. He then moved to a second bucket. The buckets were blue and smeared with a brown substance. A limp, rolled, rain-sodden copy of *The Financial Times* protruded from a split in the gross, noxious, gassy sack. The fiery socialist took hold of the pink paper and inserted it into his mouth, chewing on it with anxious, agitated eyes. The sack seemed to shudder, and the newspaper exuded a kind of snotty slime, which the fiery socialist swallowed. Then, without wiping his lips, he stood up and backed away from the sack, his gait spavined, his demeanour fawning, his whole manner something between that of a groggy crab and a kind of sly, bloodshot cockroach. Prescott was his name, sometimes Boateng. Still backing away, he tripped over the second bucket and fell rump-first into an emerald pool, which exploded with a massive, screeching fart. Grinning, Prescott bowed solemnly at the erect sack and returned to repeat the ritual. I passed hurriedly on. I hadn't been walking for much more than an hour when something caught my eye in the distance. Whatever it was was irregular and low on the horizon. In The Dump I had intermittently encountered the outline of things new and strange, but never quite like this. I at once dropped to the ground like a well-trained infantryman and lay flat on my stomach among a pile of dying forsythia branches (you are not supposed to leave out garden refuse for the dustmen, but people do). I raised the binoculars to my eyes and brought the mysterious structure closer. Horrors! The lumps were people's heads. At first glance it looked like a bad case of decapitation, but then to my relief I saw that the heads were moving. There were seventeen of them (twelve men and five women) and they were sitting astride a fence, in a line, as if on an extended version of one of those iron horses you sometimes see in park playgrounds. Their bodies were absolutely motionless, apart from their heads, which were in constant motion, swivelling first one way, then another. I sharpened the focus and examined them carefully. The fence was a stout wooden affair, very reminiscent of the famous picket fence in Dallas, Texas. The fenceposts narrowed at the top to an arrow point and why anyone should want to sit on them seemed baffling. The fence looked very uncomfortable, an impression reinforced by the rather agonized expression on the faces of the sitters. What was particularly striking was the apparent paralysis of the bodies of these people. Their right legs tightly gripped the side of the fence, their right arms were stretched out rigidly and their hands clutched the fencepost immediately ahead of them. Beneath each of them a wooden arrow point embedded itself between the curves of their buttocks. They were facing right, north westward, in the direction of Stratford-upon-Avon and the Isle of Man. But in sharp contrast to the total immobility of their bodies the heads of these people continued to move from side to side in an oddly predictable, mechanical way. They were alive, but what they were up to was anyone's guess. I decided they must be members of some outlandish religious sect, one of the sort that believed in harrowing the flesh and in lengthy periods of meditation. I had never come across a religious cult in The Dump before, but I had heard vague and sinister rumours, and I decided to steer well clear of the folk up ahead of me. They seemed to be quite smartly dressed (through the binoculars I could make out uncrumpled jackets and blue-striped Marks and Spencer shirts) but it was best to be on the safe side. I changed direction ninety degrees and began crawling towards Ypres. I must have crawled for about two miles before I felt it was safe to stand up again. As crawls go it was not a particularly memorable one. I crawled across patches of broken plaster, I crawled through a swathe of soot (messy, nasty stuff), I crawled past blackened, shattered chandeliers, enigmatic amongst empty cement sacks. I crawled past charred remnants of mosaic tiles and a Campbell's soup tin. I came across what might have been a chemical warfare suit, cut to ribbons, useless. I encountered dried excreta, pieces of bone (possibly human), stained Mills & Boon romances with nurses on the cover. At one point I came across an almost empty jar of strawberry jam and paused to lick it clean. I also found the remains of a child's birthday party, and eagerly packed into a brown paper bag a nice collection of broken biscuits, half-eaten cake and nibbled cheese. It was going to be a treat for later. Unfortunately this reeking bag of treasures simply attracted a cloud of flies which absolutely refused to be shooed away. There was nothing for it but to eat it all up there and then. Munching my way through jigsaw-shaped pieces of wheatmeal digestive and lumps of angel cake evoked a familiar feeling in me. I felt like – eh? – the ghost at the banquet. Or an empty echo. Or a sort of dull oozing afterbirth, grey as dripping sperm, reminiscent of the wallpaper paste at the Earle. Sleek, florid, wealthy men in dinner jackets sat with tanned hollow curvaceous elegant women around dinner tables in Knightsbridge and Kensington, not knowing that their little celebration would find an echo a week later in The Dump as a pair of Swillers squatted around the Cordon Bleu scraps on an upturned banana box, passing the greasy leftovers to their ragged, filthy, blistered, companionable whores. Businessmen pushed aside their plate of mousse of sole garnished with salmon, not seeing the filthy trembling hands waiting in the shadows to scoop up the uneaten debris of their greed. Small paper-hatted children spilt crumbs, knocked over fizzy drinks, farted and shrieked and sobbed with birthday fury, oblivious of the wretches lying on a patch of far-off sludge who would greedily devour the tasty morsels of marzipan, the crumpled lump of sponge cake topped with a curl of snot. I sometimes wonder if it isn't the case that every mealtime among the Barbarians gives birth to a repeat performance in The Dump. I remembered what somebody had once said about history repeating itself the first time as drudgery, the second time as farts. Overwhelmed by emotion (and stuffed full of angel cake) I rolled over on to my back and went to sleep. I awoke, aching in every bone. Merde! Les deux fesses dans l'eau, et gelées. Plus each delicate pore of my dappled skin plugged with dirt and icy slime. With trembling fingers I made use once more of the binos. The people on the fence were still there. Plus in exactly the same positions. Their heads continued to swivel from side to side, as if manipulated by an unseen puppeteer. I stood up. I began to cough. The Dump's effluvium was no worse, no better. My throat hurt. I sneezed, once, twice. A shudder ran through my body but soon became tired and started to limp. I farted four brief bursts. Trumpet-like, it was said. Orchestral. Possibly reminiscent of Mozart. It was cold, very cold. I groped about in my shreds and eventually located my wrinkled, petite member. Pointing the barrel at the parliamentary page of a prone broadsheet I waited, grim-faced. After seventeen minutes thirty-seven seconds my pitiful penis finally expelled a pitter-patter of greenish drips. They missed the newspaper and splattered my socks. Brushing drifts of yellow and pink crumbs from my lapels, humming "Kozmic Blues", I continued on towards Ypres. With luck, and assuming I could find a gap in The Great Barrier, and provided I had the strength to swim the English Channel, I estimated I should be in Belgium in ten days' time, knowing full well, of course, that the likelihood of this happening was precisely zero. I walked on. Ahead of me was a low rise of waste paper. I could see bundles of old newspapers and brown sacks split at the sides, spilling documents, important-looking sheets of A4, discarded envelopes, carbon paper, computer listings paper with the perforated strips still attached. The philatelist in me wanted to linger and collect the stamps, but time was getting on and I wanted to see what lay the other side of that papery ridge so reminiscent of Senlac. When I reached the top and saw what was in front of me I gave a low whistle of surprise. No, I tell a lie. I didn't give any sort of whistle, even though it was one of those situations where in the better sort of narrative a low whistle of surprise would not only be called for but would be vigorously indulged in. I am afraid I merely gave a sort of arthritic gasp, at best, and perhaps not even that, never having been a very expressive person. Hearty backslapping, loud whoops and eager embraces are frankly not my cup of tea. Though almost certainly mute, and blank of expression, I was nevertheless amazed at what was there, about six-hundred metres away, on a fairly typical dump plateau of waste. It was enormous and I recognised it at once. It was an American B52 bomber. Its shape, size, grandeur, engine cowlings and enormous wing-span were unmistakeable. I had once made one with an Airfix kit, and I'd sometimes seen the real thing on the telly, so I was quite certain it was a B52. For a moment I thought it had only just crashed, and I felt an immense surge of excitement. All I had to do was run across to the bomber, provide what help I could to the crew, perhaps even try out a spot of first aid, and be airlifted back with them when the Barrier-breaching U.S. army helicopters came to the rescue. The crew would be friendly, gum-chewing blue-eyed young men with crew cuts, named Hank, Chuck, Ron, Johnny, Cary, Jack, Tom and Bob. They would be forever in my debt for having extinguished the flames which threatened the fuel tanks. I would marry Cary's sister Lola, spending my later years in California running a successful pest-extermination agency. The side of the B52 had been torn away and I could see frenzied movement inside. I was about to charge down the far side of the low hill, ankle deep in white ash, a sour, urgent look on my face, when something made me pause. Something was not quite right. For a start, if the bomber had just crashed, why hadn't I seen or heard it come down? I sank down to the ground and concealed myself behind a large cardboard box. I adjusted the binoculars and scanned the aircraft. There were people inside the fuselage of the aircraft, and the aircraft looked as if it had crashed (why? when?). But it had obviously crashed a long time ago. It was an adapted B52 I was looking at. The vast interior of the aircraft had been divided up into what were unmistakably committee rooms, each of which contained a committee table and some committee members. In each committee room there were six people vigorously nodding their heads, and another six people emphatically shaking theirs. The committee members were dressed in light casual clothes and were strikingly reminiscent of the strange people astride the picket fence. At the front of the B52 an area had been set aside for worship. An enormous stars

335

and stripes hung from the ceiling to the floor, and a group of worshippers could be seen before it, prostrate on a deep-pile carpet. I scanned the area around the bomber, and observed that there were a number of other fences dotted around, each of which had its quota of familiar sitters. Everywhere I looked heads were turning from side to side as if propelled by little wind machines. Although the total population of The Dump probably runs into hundreds (even thousands) (even, some would say, tens of thousands) I had never encountered so many people together in the same place. I felt a little glow in my heart. I had, at long last, come across a community! It was like being present at the beginnings of a society. One day there would be houses here, car parks and a church, a litle shop on the corner selling milk, yogurt and laxatives. One day there would be a school, an ambulance station, a police station, a barracks, an art gallery, a bookshop, a biological weapons research centre. It was too exciting for words – so I said nothing. Baffled by the strange activities in and around the B52, I shifted my attention to the far side of the great aircraft. Beyond the smooth navy-blue nosecone could be seen one of the B52's immense, slug-shaped 500lb bombs. It rested on the ground, wedged firm by two of its tail fins. A young man was lying on his stomach on the bomb, and a line of other young men were queueing patiently, awaiting their turn. At first I thought the man on the bomb was doing press-ups, and it was only when the to and fro motions of his upper thighs and rear reached a sudden frenzy that I at last understood. There were some other unpleasant surprises. Scanning the area at the back of the B52, I encountered a vast cratered wasteland dotted with overlapping circles of stagnant water. The ground was churned-up and slushy and littered with splintered, unidentifiable metallic wreckage. There were also scatterings of bone and several broken black sacks which were not black sacks at all. There was a stench of chicken soup and diarrhoea. Bits of bone were everywhere – leg bones, arm bones, lumbar vertebrae, innumerable rib-cages, smashed skulls, sphenoids, broken bits of pelvis, lengths of clavicle. I moved back to re-examine the bomber. As I did so I spotted something

I'd missed. Something that was going on towards the rear of the aircraft. A solid iron hook had been attached to the underside of the fuselage and a primitive pulley system had been set up. Another of the 500lb bombs had been winched up on a chain by its tail fins, and hung in the air, nose downward. The chain was moved by a small steering wheel, evidently cannibalised from an abandoned car. The nose of the bomb was of a dark purple colour, edged by splashes of bright red. Why this was became evident a moment or so later. I suddenly saw that at the back of the plane, underneath the tail, was a cage. It was made out of wood and held half a dozen small, dark figures I recognised as Underdogs. The Underdogs were squealing and sobbing, and even at that distance I could hear their little shrieks of anxiety. I was not surprised, since Underdogs have such a strong aversion to daylight. Even as I watched, some young men in strawberry pink blazers clambered up on top of the cage, opened a hatchway, reached in, and dragged out an Underdog. The Underdog kicked and bit, until subdued with truncheons. Then they dragged him (I think it was a him) to what appeared to be a purple slab. Here they forced the Underdog on his back on to the slab and attached chains to his arms and legs. The slab was directly underneath the winched bomb. One of the pink-blazered men began to turn the wheel. The nosecone of the bomb trembled, swung a little from side to side, then steadied and began slowly to descend. The Underdog, eyes swelling like plums, began to writhe. And then it happened. As if from nowhere Underdogs emerged from all sides and swarmed towards the inhabitants of the B52. They came from behind rubbish sacks, out of cardboard boxes, from behind burned-out cars. They emerged like the dead from the bowels of the earth. There were scores of them, hundreds of them. I was astonished by their vigour and unity. In the past I had only ever seen them cowering in ditches, or peeking out from barrels. Underdogs are passive, shy, subservient, cowed, feeble, ingratiating, humble, cowardly, grateful-for-small-mercies and above all solitary and isolated. Yet here they were, on the attack, like an army! I swung the binoculars from side to side, astonished by what I was witnessing. The young men in pink blazers seemed stupefied by what was happening. They stood statuesque and motionless, as if dipped in liquid helium, mouths gaping open. A crowd of Underdogs swarmed over them, chopping them down. The man with his hand on the wheel fell forwards, both hands pressed against his stomach. From between his fingers protruded a black arrow. Someone torched the bomber. Flames began to lap the cockpit. The stars and stripes erupted in fire, showering the worshippers in sparks. Shrieks and screams carried in the still air. Now the tail was also spewing smoke. The Underdogs backed away as the fire took hold. Almost as quickly as they had appeared they were gone, swarming back into holes in the earth, disappearing into the elaborate network of subterranean tunnels and bunkers where they live and work. Suddenly there was an immense, shattering explosion. It was followed almost immediately by a second thunderclap of noise. A pillar of white light surged into the sky, sending out boiling black clouds in every direction. The force of the explosion catapulted me backwards down the slope, where by great good fortune my fall was cushioned by a mattress. I lay there, winded. Then a more powerful force threw me into reverse. I flew back up the slope, landing on my feet. The billowing smoke shrank and was sucked away, the fragments of bomber miraculously collided and formed a seamless whole. The cast of my preposterous drama ran jerkily backwards, hither and thither, like scalded ants. I myself moved backwards, gasping like a fish, nausea slopping around in my guts, a dark streak flashing across my vision as it yielded a glimpse of the hands of my wristwatch performing dizzy backward rolls. In next to no time I found myself back on top of that papery ridge, observing instead of a B52 a vast wilderness of rubbish, into the portals of which I vomited, colourfully. It started to rain. Rain always makes me think of the time I wasn't crushed and drowned by the great mill wheel. I dived to the bottom of the racing stream and swiftly located a length of rusted tubing. I used it to breathe through until the stupid police had gone. The chance discovery of the mangled cadaver of a tramp satiated their turgid desire for D following on from C. I was present at my own funeral, chuckling delightedly as I peeked through the shrubbery. I have visited my banal, unmarked grave on many subsequent occasions, marvelling at the spring in my gait. Walter Grannage, a murderer! The very idea. I may be a little demented. I may have turned my living room into a shrine to M. I may have been over-fond of kisses from little Judy. I may have many quirks (rubbing my hands, waltzing, babbling on about the past). But the idea that I slipped away from *Tristan und Isolde* in order to waggle the ladder on which my poor wife stood, toppling her into the greenhouse and severing her jugular! Who, then? Who slipped arsenic into that bedtime milk? I should have thought that was obvious. Scrutiny of Doctor Boswell's medical qualifications might be a starting point. The name is surely bogus, eh, Inspector Johnson? An interview with the pregnant girl he abandoned in that boarding house in Bournemouth might yield insights into his devious character, his propensity to violence, his interest in poisons and his bizarre sexual appetites. Or how about putting Nurse Marlow into a cold, unfurnished cell for forty-eight hours and breaking that fiery spirit of hers. A slippery, lying slut if ever I saw one. Talk about Lady Macbeth! Perhaps she put them both up to it. Evenbridge reeks. Yes, reeks. Behind those long drives and lace curtains. Your mind would boggle if you knew. Pornography, silver needles, strange and unnatural practices. Complete editions of the Marquis de Sade and Winston Churchill. Framed signed photographs of Margaret Thatcher. Whips. Pickles. And do not overlook Judy. A snickering little Lolita if ever there was one. Seriously disturbed. The things she knew. Eggs. Parsnips. The tricks she got up to with the grown-ups. Your mind would boggle if you knew. They were all in it. Just like *The Stepford Wives*. All except poor M. That was why they had to get rid of her. Once she found out. The strain of trying to keep up appearances. Wondering who to turn to. Telling the police. A big mistake, that. She didn't know the leader of the coven was Chief Superintendent Blair. A weasel-eyed bi-sexual goat-worshipping pederast if ever there was one. You only had to be in the same room as him to sense the evil in him. Poor M. She told me everything. About Judy. About Welling. About her desperate quest for an orgasm (clitoral or vaginal, she really didn't mind). "Come with me," I said. "My love, my dearest. My little alligator." And she came. And came. And came again. And they found out. And that is why I languish here, in the old, derelict mill, my house empty, unsold. I am old and bald and confused. My bones ache. Soon I will have no alternative but to gather up my scraps, my darling darling's scraps and knick-knacks and the knickers with the exciting stains. I'll slip them into my old battered suitcase. And slip away. Away down the slippery road to the railway station. I think I may slither to Vienna and waltz, waltz, waltz away the icy night. Sorry. The gears in my mind are slipping. My mind is wandering. Oh my railway spine! The rain came harder, faster. My thoughts turned briefly to the Newport rising. The thought of my impotence was bitter. Angrily I reached for my poor old turkey-necked pecker. I tugged back the foreskin, knocked away a crust of purple fungus and squashed a handful of the tiny crunchy creatures which thrived in the hot mildew of my raw flesh. At once I felt better. I buttoned up my bonnet, tightened my scarf. From my tucker bag I removed my pocket atlas and stared at the pages. Ust Labinsk! Vatomandry! Vijayadurg! Yaapeet. Xau and Zell and Zvonce. So many places I would never get to, not now. Trapped as I am in The Dump. But mustn't grumble. Such is life. An endless passage between a snore and a fart. No hope now of ever exploring the environs of Whitby, say, or Irbid. But mustn't grumble. Goodbye, Tongue. No chance of going with Callinicos up the Caicos Passage. No use now for that toy compass, its little palsied silver needle throbbing with uncertainty. No risk of being tempted by fraud on Crooked Island. Staring at the precipitation graph for Ilfracombe I began to wonder where my old friend Bones might be. On the Rue du Jour, peut-être? Claremont Road? He might be anywhere. I closed the book, re-opened it at random and saw that my forefinger was resting on Peru. "Merde," said the clocharde, beginning the complicated task of getting up. I therefore set off in that direction. I thought to myself, self number eighteen, I thought: be in good heart! Goodheart? Lionheart? My baffled heart. My paper heart. Arthur Cravan! My cold, cold heart. Cheer up! This bright day is different to all the others! Polly unpopped her pillbox packed with pink powder, patted it upon her parrot. The parrot let out a satisfied, wicked laugh. "Eh?" screeched self nineteen. "You wanna watch *Track 29.*" "Reality or nothing!" "Friends, comrades, countrymen!" interjected a voice, stronger and louder than all the others. A fruity voice, almost certainly going by the name William, although the case has been put for John, Joan and Wolfgang. "This sweet day," cried the voice, "is the day I let go of my tale." As the mad dog said to the actress. Tale? Aha! A goodly narrative. An accurate rendering of the noises that human beings currently make in their daily simple needs of communication. I have written it all down, yes. I, furious Ronald, cycling furiously – no! recycling furfuraceously – I have done my very best. Half-deranged? You bastard! Why not a quarter? Why not three-quarters? Eighty-five per cent. Eh? No matter. Get lost, you beast! Hope you wind up in The Dump. A real jungle. Plenty of time here to speculate about a possible echo of Hawthorne's garden of death, eh? To consider the cruellest month. To fill in your wilderness days with a wild memoir. But no foulness; no phonological couplings. No homophones, thank you very much! The compositors bugger it up for you in the end, of course. Printing prose as verse and verse as prose, anything to stretch that prick and swell that void. F into Q2? Don't fucking make me laugh! A paraphrase will contribute to everyone's understanding. Sick Malc, say. In the dark tavern. Which is bitter. Zip Koade. Cromer Switchman. Henri Looney. Bucky Binns. Tiny O'Toole, swollen with lust. Hear that? "Read me selections from the Bodleian MS. Laud Misc. 581!" The voice sounded tired, shaky. Hungarian. American, almost. It began to croon a Steve Earle number, "Billy Austin" by the sound of it. Broke off, and in a Wenatchee accent whispered, movingly, "Mais où sont les neiges d'antan?" Bloody shut up harping on about the past! cried Aeolian, breaking wind. The voice ceased on the midnight hour, began yanking out a memory. "Gook tries to put the fire out while you're trying to burn his hootch, he fucks with you, you fuck with him, right? You push him away, or kick his ass, or you do what we usually did which was to shoot him. You can't see anything because of the smoke. Awful smell. All kinds of shit burning. Bodies all over the place. Near me was a dead old woman holding a spattered copy of *The Ambassadors*. And a young girl. She'd lost one leg and was going round in a circle on the ground, crying out 'Why? Why is that in Jane Austen we sit quite resigned in an arrested spring?' A marine flipped her over, pummelled her walnut, stuck it in, grunted, shot his load. Erect above all for her was the sharp-edged fact of the relation of the whole group, individually and collectively, to herself – herself so speciously eliminated. Yes, took out he afterwards the marine a handgun and shot dripping her in the head. I was completely pissed by the fucking thing, all of it. All I wanted to do was trash people and that's what I did." A marbled, iridescent text. With many recognitions. Bleak solo cello, a woodwind's cry. That Finn again! Suppose that instead of a biped upon a stage concealing and betraying his thought we watch the thought itself, the hidden thing, as it twists to and fro, fro and two and three. Ah, how sweet it is to grasp the shadowy and phantasmal form of a book, to stroke its spine and kiss its delicate chapters. To turn it over and plunge in and frown and grunt and sweat. This whole world is a copy of some of the bits from another, the more normal world! The deviations open to Flaubert are innumerable! Doesn't have to be a book of course. Something shorter would do. Pamphlets seditious, profane, scandalous rebellious, Atheisticall, and Blasphemous (besides nonsensicall the most grievous of all). And afterwards? How sweet it would be to win The Governor General's Award! Or The Inspector General's. Or a General Inspection. Or to provoke a stormy General Synopsis. To assist the mentally impaired with useful questions enabling them to master any exam, for example: *Hardy was always interested in music. What evidence is there in Hardy's poetry that he preferred Fleetwood Mac to Nico?* To be applauded for my compulsive readability, my style and verve. To become useful to the State. To campaign for the reinstatement and extension of decree number 02030 (1968) of the Central Committee of the Communist Party of the Soviet Union. Be rewarded with truffles, cars, pianos, etc. To be able to drop a line to Celia Kirwan of the Information Research Department. *Dear Celia, I haven't written earlier because I have really been rather poorly. I could, if it is of any value, give you a list of journalists and writers who in my opinion are crypto-communists, fellow-travellers or inclined that way.* Ah, to be a writer! To fondle and tickle and chew and wiggle and ejaculate words! To risk the wrath of the New York Court of Special Sessions! To have relations with publishers! To drop a note (May 28, 1859) to Franz Duncker in Berlin or – more recently – to S. Assersohn in London. To submit and wait. And wait. And wait. *I am sending you today under separate cover a manuscript entitled "Orpheus and Other Poems." Enclosed find postage for its return if the manuscript be not accepted.* To foam, to be rabid! To triumph, alone. To tear it, language, with teeth and paws, ravenously! Savagely! Synapses uncoordinated, connectives misdirected, linkages lost in excesses of verbiage! Gorgeous! Devastating rather than creating! Ah, for the sansculottism of eloquence! The oratory of a Silenus drunk with anger only! To be ragged and rapid, strong and rough, yet neologistic, expressionistic, often incantatory and hypnotic! *The Beneficent Spider* would be a good title I have always thought. To be a writer, yes! Jones and the other man carried the coffin up the stairs. To knock together something full of political animus, sensual liveliness, English and popular instincts! Coarse, elementary, swarming with ignoble vermin, like that which appears in a great decomposing body! Learning how to gasp and convulse amid a surge of the shorter early Saxon verbs! To note *Last year I wrote 282,100 words, exclusive of rewriting. I made no particular advance commercially. I had several grave disappointments.* Un pisseur de copie! Exulting in exquisite moments of syntactical uncertainty! To be not afraid to speak out, no. *There is a need for a firm even implacable theoretical and political fight against the petty-bourgeois tendencies of the*

343

opposition, an implacable ideological fight which should go parallel with very cautious and wise organisational tactics. Be extremely firm but don't lose your nerve! P.S. The evils come from (i) bad composition (ii) lack of experience. I shall show every respect for the proprieties, naturally. Grammar, syntax. Besides endeavouring to curb my fondness for conditional clauses. Only trimming polysyllables where absolutely necessary. Cutting verbs and participles only where superfluous. Chapters. The chapter of landscapes. Hills, sir, and the sundown, and a pink, patched inflatable doll. The chapter of the white cottage. The chapter of false, malicious and factious libel. The chapter beginning: *It is not worth telling, this story of mine – at least, not worth writing.* The chapter of the blister. The chapter of erotic reminiscences. The chapter of the wedding with the adventure of the lost key. The chapter of mountains. The chapter of Shakespeare's missing years. The chapter beginning: *"You are a lovely man, Gussy, but I wish you were a woman," big Alois said facetiously when he had squeezed me into the hole.* The chapter ending: *I put two biscuits by his bed in case he woke and turned the light out.* The chapter beginning: *It was after they had gone that he truly felt the difference, which was most to be felt moreover in his faded old rooms.* The chapter ending: *We walked along together all going fast against time.* The chapter of motels. The chapter of London. The chapter of St. Anton. Of Seattle. And Dachau. Of the nervous collapse. Of the melancholy return. Two hundred chapters of madness. The chapter of plagiarisms. The chapter of striking metaphors. (*I had noticed her shudder when the front-door bell pierced the silence as sharply as a serpent's fang breaks the skin. That warm London afternoon saw him jangling like some battered piano in an Alma-Tadema house, the lid open and mad rats gnawing and scraping at the wires. Giant brown cockroaches, the feet zigzagged until they came to a solid stop. A prostitute hailed us, a sound with the sweetness of poisoned orchids in the forest of the sleeping town.*) The chapter of long walks. The chapter of answers. I shall pile them, one on top of the other, until the manuscript is eight metres high and hailed as. As a towering achievement. Reading down through its dense vastness. All the way through to. Its ephemeral "end" hailed. As a truly rewarding task though. Here's a professorial tip for impatient readers who may have bogged down on that. That difficult second page namely go. Straight to page fifty-seven where. Things really begin. To. Crackle or if that still leaves. Too many pages to tackle skip. The chapter of long walks and jump. Straight to the final section, especially the. The last couple of. Pages. The chapter of inexplicable phenomena. And jokes! Elephants, telephone boxes, cogs, turnips, f-stops, beards, actresses, precision screws. Fascinating facts. The Bible contains 3,566,480 letters, 773,746 words and 31,102 verses. DESUDATION: This term is applied when any unusually violent sweating takes place. Are you, perhaps, too warmly clad? Dust your skin at once with a powder consisting of zinc oxide and starch. (See also SWEAT, DISAGREEABLE.) And other useful tips. Out of sorts? Have you tried effleurage? This is a stroking movement which may be done with either one hand, both hands, or the palmar surface of the fingers and thumb. The hand should be moulded to fit the contour of the part being massaged and the movements should be carried out slowly, smoothly, and rhythmically, if a soothing effect is sought. For stimulating effects brisk and firm strokes are recommended. The LOFTIEST ACTIVE VOLCANO is Popocatapetl – "smoking mountain" – thirty-five miles south-west of Puebla, Mexico. Challenging assertions! "The earth goes round the sun?" said Swayne incredulously. His mind was clear and though he looked tired his expression was serene, almost happy, and there was a cheerful, warm glow in his eyes. The proof that this earth moves around the sun lies in the parallax of the stars? Stuff and nonsense! In the last two-thousand years the earth has travelled 819,936,000,000 miles, agreed? Now this distance is four-thousand five-hundred times the distance that is the base line for orbital parallax, right? In that case displacement of the stars by solar-motion parallax in two-thousand years should be four-and-a-half thousand times the displacement by orbital parallax in one year! Give to orbital parallax as minute a quantity as is consistent with the claims made for it and the Great Dipper would be twisted, the Sickle of Leo nicked! But not a star in the heavens has changed more than doubtfully since the stars were catalogued by Hipparchus two thousand years ago! If, then, there ARE minute displacements of stars that are attributed to orbital parallax, THEY WILL HAVE TO BE EXPLAINED IN SOME OTHER WAY. Unless, of course, you wish to subscribe to the DELUSION that the Sun is moving from Sirius towards Vega. In short, contrary to what a foul conspiracy of SCIENTISTS wishes us to believe, the earth is MOTIONLESS. As common sense ought to tell you. Do you REALLY believe you are travelling at 70,000mph on some sort of gigantic, spinning football floating magically in space? I mean, COME OFF IT. Scattered twos put together. Fours stored up in mind to give a good papery yield. The life and adventures of Scriblerus! I was always a putter-inner rather than a taker-outer. The occasional autobiographical tit-bit to whet the appetite of my future biographers. The fag-end of that summer with Monika, with whom I still keep in – sic – touch. Her legs had the specialized tension common to aerial workers. But she went away – and the dash should be as long as the earth's orbit. My darling, I have been with Zumps. I have got you a hammer and a pair of pliers to twist your wire with. May every one, my dear, vibrate sweet comfort to my hopes! I had reasons for my behaviour which, if they could not be approved, could yet be discussed. Ton souvenir en moi luit comme un ostensoir! That Saturday afternoon, we lay in bed in one another's arms. After a tumultuous fuck we watched Star Trek. The episode in which the starship begins – horrors – to dissolve. Sweating, Scotty wielded his tool. He fingered it deftly, brought the surge of liquefaction to an end. I turned you over. Madam, there's a bite! John called out to me from the hallway. I answered him stiffly. I was afraid he would open the door and come into the room. Moments later (blessed relief) I heard the front door slam. Monika, Monika. To me you will always be as you were then, your dark hair almost down to your waist. You loaned me your precious copy of Sahaeijueoi Nodongja. You did not mind that I was in the grip of annotations. Your grasp of the General Law of Capitalist Accumulation was firm, your lips slender and voracious. To me faire friend you never can be old. I shall always remember your muddy complexion and foul vocabulary, your bleary eyes, your dripping nose and oozing gash. The loose slack feel of your skin, your corseted hips, the way you drove down the dew with a pair of heels as broad as two wheels! 'Tis impossible to describe what I have suffered since I saw you last, I am sure I could have bore the rack much better than those killing, killing words of yours. I want you to be aware that I know you have treated me infernally – infernally! There is a great gulph between us. My dear, my darling, do you hear me where you sleep? I live in a bye corner of the kingdom in a vast unfurnished house; my family consists of nowt but a steward, a groom, a helper in the stable, a footman, a diseased Nietzschean and an old maid. I am prone to fits of depression, no getting away from it. Your true friend and Injun Cowboy. PS Section 3 of the 1983 Mental Health Act is naked fascism! All's ill with me now. I live in a constant endeavour to fence against the infirmities of ill health. Deaf, giddy, helpless. My sufferings alleviated by but a daily half pint of wine and some new great tasting corn chips made from fresh flame-grilled corn with twenty-five per cent less fat than potato crisps, in three irresistible flavours: tangy cheese, savoury beef and spicy chicken. It rains every day. People understand me so little that they do not even understand when I complain of being misunderstood. As Kierkegaard remarked. Thank Christ for easy to use, non-leak, non-drip caps. Man that is born of a woman, is of few days, and full of trouble. But nothing revives body and mind like a herbal hair and body gel with a secret blend of 13 herbs and minerals and a revitalising fresh herby fragrance. Even with this gel my life admittedly has not been without its ups and downs. The coughing. The coffin poem. The day I was fitted with my set of false teeth, only the upper okay. The time I bought a hot water bottle. It was made of rubber. In time, it perished. The time I borrowed two shillings and sixpence. A Thursday, it was raining. The fits of coughing were so severe that I had to double up when

I coughed. I greeted trains with a howl. The fever tired me a great deal. Sweat broke out on my forehead. My whole body trembled. Round about me only boredom and despair! I could not do without auxiliary constructions, powerful deflections, substitutive satisfactions, intoxicating substances! Oh! W! X! Y! Z! In complete helplessness barely wrote two pages. My career in aroma management never took off. I make ends meet. In fits and starts. I presume the printer has brought you the offspring of my *poetic mania*. Four is good being square! May Jupiter Feretrius grant that I languish not by the Eurotas. *Audi Samuelem*. I occupy myself, eh? Carving figures of birds and beasts out of the turnip parings in my lap. I demand a hearing before the North Thames region mental health review tribunal! I want to get out of here! I want to go shopping! Go shopping, yes. Shopping? I should cocoa! I have bought you ten handsome brass screws, to hang your necessaries upon. I purchased twelve but stole a couple from you to put up in my own cabin. I shall never hang or take my hat off one of them but I shall think of you. And drink of you. And stink of you. Adieu, brat. Feverish? Just a little. Le dérèglement de tous les sens, eh? I am a sick man, I am an angry man. I am an unattractive man. And you? You'll shine more bright in these contents. Ah, language! A voluptuous release. It took – primate brain circuits working overtime – five million years to get here. So, damn you, you might at least pay attention. Thanks. As I was saying. A book. In the agglomerative style. As soon as my work comes out, it will be published in French. A worthy follow-up to *Dictes and Sayinges of the Philosophers* and *Tyranipocrit Discovered* and *Telephone Selling Techniques That Really Work*. And whatnot. To be deposited in all the proper places. Aberystwyth, even. Cydnabyddir yn ddioichgar dderbyn yr eitem hon/eitemau hyn, a anfonwyd yma yn unol â gofynion Deddf Hawlfraint, 1 & 2 Siôr V, pen. 46.15 a SI 1987 No. 918. No sweat! No go. No go. Land of abandonment and rain. Place of bottles and cast-offs. "Compulsively readable" – *Sunday Express*. "A dazzling postmodernist voyage to the foul, stinking underside of late capitalism" – *Mail on Sunday*. "Anyone who likes a good story will love *The Dump*, which is a wonderful, surprising novel all about friendships and daily life in East London. It is hilarious and moving with a magically happy ending which cheers you up for days afterwards" – *Socialist Review*. "When I first read the book I found the opening movement rather slow and dragging and I believed the final section to be superfluous. I am now convinced that every word is essential, both dramatically and musically" – Jake Berlitz, *The Sun*. *The Dump*, yes. A glorious title. Producers falling over themselves for the movie rights. Starring Mel as Jack and Meryl as Mary. A film of truly epic proportions. Original score by Jarré Junior. *Set out with Mel on an adventure that is both a visual extravaganza and a wry comedy of East End life. Laugh along with Mel at the wonderfully observed scenes of domestic life.* "Can you make the tea, Mary?" "Yes of course I can, Jack. Is there any water in this kettle?" "See for yourself, Mary." "Ah, yes. I can see it now. But where are the teacups?" "The teacups are in the cupboard. Can you find them?" "Yes. Here they are." "Hurry up, Mary! The kettle's boiling." "Piss off Jack and make it yourself, you lazy bugger." "But why, Mary?" "Because I am busy with other things, Jack." "What things, Mary?" "I am pondering the stars, Jack. A hundred thousand million stars, Jack, turning in the circle of the Milky Way. I can never look at them without wondering from which of them the emissaries are coming. A brisk mental interlude from this absorbing account of Dirac's efforts to relate the theory of relativity to the quantum theory." "Well, bugger me." "That's not my cup of tea, Jack. Not even with this handsomely proportioned courgette." "I can't see any courgette, Mary. I can see some spoons, but I can't see any courgette. I can see some hammers, but I can't see any courgette. I can see some cups, but I can't see any courgette. I can see some coffee, but I can't see any courgette." "You need your glasses, Jack." "I suppose so, Mary. Why are you frowning, Mary?" "Because I am concentrating, Jack." "Quantum theory, did you say, Mary?" "I did, Jack, yes. You see the quantum theory's dung to blauds the classic picture o' the world. You see, Jack, relativity theory can be understood within the framework of classical physics. Events that occur in space and time. But quantum theory challenges the very epistemological foundations of science." "I see, Mary. I think. Mary, what are you doing with that vase?" "I am going to put it on the radio, Jack." "Don't do that. Give it to me." "What are you going to do with it, Jack?" "I am going to put it here in front of the window." "Be careful! Don't drop it! Don't put it there, Jack. Put it here, on this shelf. There we are! It's a lovely vase. It goes nicely with the courgette." "And with the dustjacket of your book on elementary particles, Mary!" "So it does, Jack." "Those flowers are lovely too." "Yes, they are. Yes." "Oh look! It is another fine day today. Mr Jones is with his family." "All his family are diseased, did you know?" "Yes, I did know that, Frank." "They are walking over the bridge, Mary." "The bridge that is about to explode?" Yes, that bridge." "Oh, look. There are some boats on the river. Some horribly burned people are jumping off the boats." "Sally is crouched by the wall. She is doing a big shit. The shit drops into the river. The shit is going under the bridge. The bridge explodes." "Tim is watching the bridge explode." "Tim is diseased, too." "Yes, I know." A lump of débris hits Tim. Tim drops into the burning river. An aeroplane flies over the river. The aeroplane is from the United States of America. It carries an atomic bomb. The aeroplane drops the bomb. The bomb falls. Look at the city! What has happened to it? Where is everyone? "I don't know," said Jack. "Can you make the tea, now, Jane? "Yes, of course I can, Jack. Is there any water in this kettle?" "See for yourself, you bitch." "Where's that tea, dipshit?" "It's over there, you cunt. Behind that fucking teapot. Can't you fucking see it?" "I can see the fucking teapot but I can't see the tea." "There it is! It's there in front of you!" "Ah, yes. I can see it now. But where are the teacups?" Discomfort guides my tongue. Worn out. Blistered. "An elenctic masterpiece; like electro-shock; electrovalent in structure; the ellipses are terrific" – *The Echo*. Thunderous orchestral score, melancholy tortured violins. Don't miss it. *The Dump* has it all: comedy, romance, suspense. With dazzling special effects. No expense has been spared. The odour of human excrement will be pumped into every auditorium to create that extra touch of authenticity. All-star cast. *The Dump* – a spectacular film created from a fascinating story. Admittedly at present nothing much more than a few soiled pages, a scrawl here and there. But one day... I can dream, can't I? Counterfeit an hundred dogged fables, eh? My scraps held in an air-conditioned vault at the Sterling Memorial Library, Yale. My lust for... Sorry, must dash. My blanks and ellipses a matter of continuing scholarly hatreds. One day I shall come to something, eh? You mark my words. One day more than scrawls, much more. A thick wadge of words. Words! Springing from line to line like so many monkeys, pointing, grinning, chattering, howling, biting. Pastiche, parody. The sweetest of allusions. Taking care to avoid gross hanging participles. Vibrant, vigorous vignettes. Venereal texts voided verbatim! A novella, say. Almost a book, perhaps one day to be a real book. A real book! Bliss! Perhaps one day to be translated into Dutch, Peruvian, Martian. Perhaps a Translator's Note at the start. That droll one prefacing *The Sweet Cheat Gone*, for example. A real book, with a spine. A handsome jacket to beat off the dust. Printed on one hundred per cent recycled paper, friendly to whales, using no artifical colours, edible (a boon in a siege). Not merely recycled. Paper which in every way meets the guidelines for permanence and durability of the Committee on Production Guidelines for Book Longevity of the Council on Library Resources. A book with a countdown on the verso, indicating its absolute unpopularity across the lengthening years. 10 9 8 7 6 5 4 3 2 1. A book not afraid to exhibit tributes from impartial admirers. THE BISHOP OF SODOR AND MANN: "What a lot of work you have put into it!" MRS L. COHEN, O.B.E., J.P., Leeds: "I have been arrested and thrilled by the perusal of your book." CHARLES W. HOPPER: "I do not claim to know anything about literature but I read your book with the keenest interest. Congratulations on piloting your Saucy Little Bark into Fame's Eternal Harbour." Herr FITZ J. STARKE, Ph.D., Berlin: "I am writing this from the Bay of Biscay. Your book is nothing less than a joy to me in my seventy-sixth year. It is quite a straight story. It gripped me and instructed me." Thanks. And thanks to the Keeper of Printed Books. Thanks to to the thin, frail, stooped, malnourished figures whose names I could never be bothered to learn, whose risible role in life is to wander, draped in cobwebs, along shadowy aisles, servicing the stacks in the Bodleian. Miss E. C. Lay helped to minimize the difficulties which beset a scholar working away from his home base. My old friend Alison Rump helped me with a number of difficult passages. Thanks to Canada Dry for a much needed tonic. Thanks to everyone involved. Thanks to my nameless typists, whose hysterical female whingeing about Repetitive Strain Injury obliged me to contact the agency, which sacked them on the spot. Ingratiating thanks to my well-heeled in-laws, bearded Rear-Admiral and whiskery Mrs Buttle, who have regularly ruined pleasant Sunday afternoons with their repeated descriptions of how blows from a spring driven electro-magnetically controlled hammer on a steel diaphragm which is in contact with water in a tank secured to the hull produces a sound impulse which is transmitted through the water to the hull of the ship, which acts as a diaphragm, and re-transmits the impulse to the vast fin-filled waters beyond the hull, impulse upon throbbing impulse which, like a continuous rhythmical fart, echoes back from the ocean's arse, three every second, to be received in a hydrophone which is secured to a tank in the same manner as the transmitter, and who have never failed to warn me of the danger of false echoes, Mrs Buttle crooking her finger waggishly, the Rear-Admiral flushed and intense as he bellows that muddy bottoms do not give such good echoes as hard, sandy or rocky bottoms. Thanks to the University of Penge for appointing me as Sesquicentennial Fellow of the Institute for Leisure Studies and Latin American Dancing, without which your amorphous mass of disreputable energies would never have been able to comprehend that foot changes in the Samba are not difficult and are achieved by stepping forward or backward with or without turn, using right or left foot. For gross lack of encouragement I should like to thank my addled Head of Department, Professor Humpbum, for whom Lenin's favourite adjective, cretinous, might well have been exclusively invented.

(Hambone, whose remaindered books I have encountered heaped and dust-coated from Southwold to rainy Goodge Street.) A tale, yes. Destined for publication, no doubt. A worthy successor to my previous international best-sellers *The Albugineous Bouillon* and *Lengthening Trousseaus*. Not to mention my smash-hit self-help collaboration with Mick Dooly, *Engild Viduage*. I have written it all down, yes. I have done my very best. Admittedly much left unsaid, so much undescribed, or quite forgotten, or returning in too late flashes, or rotted away into vaguenesses and mists. The free market ideologues, reduced to eating their own flesh. Not forgetting the aerostat-hater, Hitler. Looked like him, anyway. Same sort of moustache. I met him on a Saturday. He was hunched over a pile of dirty paper, trying to set light to it. Hearing the crunch of footsteps he whirled round, eyes bulging. "Burn them!" he shrieked. "My personal papers! The Bolsheviks must not see them!" The stench was that of excrement and rotting apples. His hair was as lank and floppy as in the photographs. Not so his face, all puffy and discoloured, chin and brow blue with lack of oxygen. His right arm began to tremble violently. He seized it with his left arm and unsuccessfully tried to quieten it down. "Burn them!" Hitler frothed. The froth reminded me of the yellowish scum blown ashore by the strong winds at Brancaster beach. His left leg (God had not failed to observe or forget a single furtive spurt) began to twitch uncontrollably. "Shoot them all, shoot them all!" he frothed afresh. His eyes were Margaret Thatcher's at the retaking of South Georgia. From the pile of unlit paper he snatched a map and bit into it. It was an out-of-date street map of Berlin. The ground shuddered as sudden explosions encircled us. I could hear the crackle of small arms fire. The Russians were only two blocks away. With his left index finger Hitler jabbed at the map, tearing shreds out of it. He called for Panzers but none came. He put on a grotesque rubber Thatcher mask. "Everyone has betrayed me!" he screamed. Distinctly uffish, you might say. I realised with a shock he was addressing yours truly. It was all too much for me. I ran off over a low grassy knoll, brushing aside two C.I.A. men. Such pretty mugwort! But the hill tried to throw me off balance with its wobbles and squirts of foul gas. Buried animal cadavers, I guessed. Herds of diseased cattle and radioactive sheep fled in panic across my mind, pursued by officials and men in protective suits. The minister came on TV. "No cause for concern, none whatsoever," he beamed. The beam was later shown to be radioactive. I continued running until I came to this quiet sunlit valley of tranquillity. The bees hum, the butterflies flit. Here I have built, in conditions of strictest secrecy, my balloon. A balloon! Circular, like God. Or so Trismegistus sayd, bless him. A balloon? A modest affair, not much bigger than a football. Not in the first draft, anyway. Then I got more ambitious. Now it's altogether more impressive, measuring five metres by five, with a volume of eighty cubic metres. In the absence of easily obtainable helium gas I have been eating prodigious quantities of beans and farting into the sack on a daily basis using an old football valve. Now my device is as inflated as it ever will be. Now I am close to the last page. Now the rain abruptly ends, a gust whirls away the dark clouds. The sun, bless its incandescent heart, is coming out! Blue skies – yip! yip! – are here again. Now – swell of an orchestra, boom of a chorus – now I am about to seal my manuscript up in the finest cellophane (please forgive water stains, tea stains, piss stains, pale suspicious splashes, malodorous smears, spelling mistakes, any errors or lapses of good taste). Oozing like the ooze of sadness from J.T.'s mute mouth. In a tight squeeze, he was. Enough of that earthbound throbbing brute. Now I am aiming at the stars. Now I am about to strap my delicate package to the carefully constructed lightweight harness beneath the balloon. A work of genuine craftsmanship, hewn from six supermarket plastic carrier bags. Eyesight dimmer than ever, I see it all. Singing "Faithful Forever" I let go of the string. Wheeeeee! Yaaaaa-whooooo! My dainty craft shoots up into the empyrean, two hundred metres, three hundred metres, a mere speck. If this was a movie "Humidity Built The Snowman" would now blast out. It isn't, it doesn't. At last I found what I wanted, the three posthumous sonatas. I started on the F sharp Minor. Almost gone, now. A dot. Less than a dot. A thermal catches it, whirls it westward! You require assistance. Time to cock your gigantic telescope, you brute! And still my delicate craft grows smaller, smaller. Heading for somewhere nice by the look of it. Enfield Chase! The M25. The Bug River. Potters Bar! How far I know not. Could be anywhere. Bridport. Dores. Shoreham-by-sea. Dunwich. Dragged down by leaks and gravity in the end. I know that tomorrow I shall not pass the Gemmi and get to Thun. I shall not linger at the Hotel Bellevue and then proceed by slow stages down the Rhine to Cologne. Gravity, gravity, it is a grave and heavy matter. My frail craft discovered lying in a grassy meadow where mares graze. Or skulking in *Duck-Lane*, pitifully totter'd and torn. Or wrapped around someone's satellite dish, spoiling the reception. Or falling slap into someone's blazing garden waste, consumed in a trice. Or landing in quicksand, of no interest for a million years until finally, gloriously located by a pretty, cautious, trowel-thrusting linguistically gifted paleopedologist. No, not that, please. No. Saved! Found by you. You, a Barbarian. I have a mind to be very angry. You are a set of people drawn almost to the dregs. You must try another game, this is at an end. *I now walk into the wild. Alex.* No, please! I take it all back. You. One morning. On the way to work. A quick glance. Hmm, this looks interesting. Haven't yomped through a good yarn for yonks. Oh! Heaps of exhaustion! Thinking like Q that the getting to it is taking a long time. Upon a once. Textual/ontological unity well and truly taken to the cleaners. You chuckle and screech, I see it, hear it. Boy, I'd sure like to get my hands on a rope again. Derevaun Seraun! Keep your pecker up. Let's be off to Flint Castle, eh? Good-bye Kansas! Good-bye Wisconsin! Good-bye Utah! Good-bye Uranus! Atishoo! Atishoo! And so on. All good gifts, eh? Taken home later. Cellophane removed and the damp pages given a brisk going-over with the hair drier. You begin, begin, begin. Or fade. A low frustrated mutter. What is all this story about? I was five glass spheres without foliage! Eyes somewhat dimmish grown. Eye am sore eye. Fade sound and vision. Eh, Orrery? Poor Tom. Dr Presto? Madox perhaps. No. No way. It's over. Don't ever leave me, Dolly! No, wait! A late insertion! More good news! The UNICEF annual report has just come out. Last year thirty-seven thousand children under five died every day from malnutrition and easily treatable diseases like measles and diarrhoea, not an easy word to spell. Shit. Is. Hell, I don't like stories with people dying in the end. Said Goldwyn, supposedly. And so that ghostly closing shot, Merle and Olivier's double. Better a riveting climax on a lonely beach, eh? A digitally enhanced pterodactyl's flapped wings. Or some broken-hearted loner walking away down a street while louder gets the last track of *Zooropa*, throbbing as the credits roll. Settled instead for common-as-muck words, the glories of glossolalia. Inspired by *The Replycacion*, a disorderly jumble of skeltonics and eccentric prose, heavy with alliteration, euphistic, *avant la lettre*, accompanied throughout with lengthy marginal glosses. How are you? Fine, fine. To clear away from off the very threshold of despair. All the old. Which we call memory. For information about the Free Presbyterian Church in England and Wales contact BURRYPORT (01554) 833221 or OULTON BROAD (01502) 573641. Eh? Wuzzmoor? Wossmurr in South Asia alone no less than eighty-six million children under five are malnourished! So mustn't grumble, eh? Life here in The Dump not so bad after all. The occasional spurt of melody. Cool blow of a pair of clarinets in the chalumeau register. Art's *Live Across America* album, say. Embedded in treacle, like dinosaur droppings. Or a Fool's Song with accompaniment of strings and harp. And good, very good, to know those foreigners are being kept in their places. Might have a little cerebration later. Ah, the sweet throb of cogitations! With some mastication for afters. A piece of cheese I've been saving. A little carton of flat lemonade. Some Kendal mint cake. Pass the zimmerframe! Forward to the Hillary Step! Must go. Now! Want to see *The Night of the Hunter* again. I've finished here. *In principio erat verbum*. It, this is, truly. All wrapped up. Jacketed in dust. Forlorn. My little capsule of words, sent to drift through space and time, the words growing old and flaky and weird. Talk about the Geystes of Skoggon! How sweet must it be to hang-glide above th'*Aonian* Mount! Klaatu barada nikto!

Pipperoo, pippera, pipperum! Hurrah for thermophiles! Adieu bright wit and radiant eyes! Adieu those midnight wranglings over iamb and spondee, anacoluthon and the open vowel. Voice almost gone. *Okay, I won't.* As Ellis said. I mean Elvis. What news? A bit wonky in my left flipper. Invalided out. To this place. The Dump. Invalid. Past my sell-by date. What can I say? With each new draft the number of visitors increased sharply. Such characters! Though demonstrably wrong on such facts as time and place, much of what he recorded has gained currency, albeit no corroboration from any other source. If the cap fits... For the last two decades we've been drifting here in Britain in a thoroughly aimless fashion! *Ubi nunc?* Nowhere. Let's talk. Worms, epitaphs. With rainy eyes. Eh? Be off with you! A skulking, miserable *scholasticus*. Eh? Okay. Thank you for the information. A mere driveller. Become lumber, probably. Cheer up, eh? It is 6.20 pm. We both came to a halt. Ron was muttering imprecations. "Please don't worry too much." I need a change. Bottled oxygen is for wimps. Onward to that abandoned cylinder and survey pole! Though emaciated and indecisive, Alexander is jubilant again. Deaf as the sea, hasty as fire. Eh? Speak up! My brain I'll prove the female to my soul. Since I left you, *I had a most eventful time*. Eh? Naught else but tricks. I feel sore, everywhere. I need a Tyrozet, a splash of after-sun lotion, a kilo of courgettes, a sack of potatoes, a pint of milk. Alas, the *épicier* has cancelled my credit for the last three weeks. The last thing the millennium's crepitant skies require is floccinaucinihilipilification! Ek sal'n plan maak! De secourir ma lâcheté! Et nunc progressi alibi observamus. And Solomon awoke: and, behold, he was hypoxic. It was a dream, yawn. So drowsily I conclude. The doctor made the movements common to a dumbfounder, making the back and elbows move in a series of honesties, dusting his chin with a puff, thinking himself unobserved. All withered, all discoloured. With a smile did then his words repeat. Oh worthless world, oh transitory things! Ah, shaddup, Sol! Shucks. If I could only see the sun just one more time. Brimstony, blue and fiery. Eh? Not true! Stuff univocal order! Double cheers for constructivist epistemology! Don't be so stiff and ill-at-ease. Some have seen (or rather felt) nautical motions and implications. *Mi contra fa diabolus in musica est.* Please, please, plunge and plunge again! Make notes – wheu – - u – – – - u – – – – – – – - if you must. Sit on your rump and scream in Erse! Reinstate the third trumpet! Start, perhaps, by giving up crunching lumps of sugar! What news from Oxford? It's not true what they say about annotation, eh? Plunge into the wastes of all that's used-up, finished with, gone. The distance separating Halifax from Helsingfors has been appreciably diminished. After so many deaths... I think the world's asleep. Flimpf! Resurrect the teachings of Sorbo Soboleff! Or sit quietly. Sit quietly, trap shut. Pretend to be buried in a book. The dew, the rain. As if awake in the midst of sleep. Bah! Boo! Analphabetism? Who? Doctor, Doctor! I think I'm a strawberry! Oh dear. Said the narrator, from whom I wish vigorously to dissociate myself. Eh? A Mardi Gras whim. Was Harlan Potter in on all this? By dint of putting various sixes and sevens together get the whole story bent. Discharged to the last drop and dreg. Eh? A lunatic, lean-witted fool? Not by a long chalk! At last, you think. At long last. The end. Bliss. All together now. In the altogether. At last. Eh? Mar a curious tale. Well, let this pass. One morning... Eh? After all. Eh? When all's said and done. The antic sits. Grinning. Eh? I shall waste no more words, but tell you simply how it all happened. I do not regret this journey, which has shown that Englishmen endure hardships. Oh! A painless piss. Bliss! Eh? Have you noticed that everyone on TV has teeth? Snowed in. Disaster. Yo Ho Ho! I remember there was a clucking of hens from somewhere. Twenty moonshines ago. Once, in a kloof not far from the Letaba... In summertime... All hopes collapse! Now I come to the worst *Pech*. They tolled the one bell only. There is the book, Inspector. I leave it with you, and you cannot doubt that it contains a full explanation of the tragedy. We still don't know why it was done but at least we know *how*. Different worlds remembered and then all put together to form a strange new world. Like perspectives which, rightly gazed upon, show nothing but confusion; eyed awry, distinguish form. Switch them off! Eh?

Mais je divague. Parot is my owne dere harte. The train is waiting. Going where? Ah, to Pitchipoi. Crosses, cares and grief. Say hello to Frieda for me, will you? I think I can do better elsewhere. I need at least eleven theses on Feuerbach. Fetch me a Higgs particle! For Pete's sake let's give a party, I feel swell! Take me to Ellis County! I'll see you in the banyuls café at eleven. Deal me a yarborough! The game will soon be up. "Can you keep a secret?" asked Booth. "Yes, yes," said eagerly Robertson. "I can, yes." "So can I," replied Booth. Adwe good nyght. *Crescent in immensum me vivo Psittacus iste.* Give me your hand! Determined still to do our best... I have agreed to go to Zante for a change of air. Fetch me esculents and a bottle of Waters of Moses. Secure me the *mollia temporara fandi*! Dethe dynges one my dore, I dare no lengare byde. Benatewgana! Fut! The sooner we get finished, the sooner we get started. To deal plainly, the fact of the matter is